C0-DYB-442

ONE DELIBERATE ACT

ALSO BY LM REYNOLDS

Spies in our Midst

Spies We Know

ONE DELIBERATE ACT

A NOVEL

LM REYNOLDS

ONE DELIBERATE ACT
Copyright © 2021 LM Reynolds
All rights reserved.

No part of this book may be reproduced, scanned, or distributed in any printed or electronic form without the prior consent of the author.

This book is a work of fiction. Names, characters, business organizations, places, and incidents either are the product of the author's imagination or are used fictitiously. The author's use of names of historical or public persons, actual places, events, and characters is incidental to the plot and is not intended to change the entirely fictional character of the work. Any resemblance to other actual persons, living or dead, or actual events is purely coincidental.

Published in the United States of America by Mirage Books

ISBN 979-8-9851692-1-8

Cover design by Nancy Blanton
Cover photograph by Catuncia: Baščaršija Square, Sarajevo
Map of Kurdistan by Peter Hermes Furian
Map of Bosnia and Herzegovina by Peter Hermes Furian
Map of Sarajevo Valley adapted from map produced by U.S. Central Intelligence Agency

For my son, Brian,
who has been the light in my journey.

*The purpose of terrorism lies not just in the violent act itself.
It is in producing terror. It sets out to inflame, to divide,
to produce consequences which they then use to justify further terror.*

—Tony Blair,
Speaking before the
House of Commons
2003

*If you want to control someone,
all you have to do is make them feel afraid.*

—Paulo Coelho,
The Devil and Miss Prym

PROLOGUE

Khalid

April 1991

KURDISTAN, CIRCA 1991

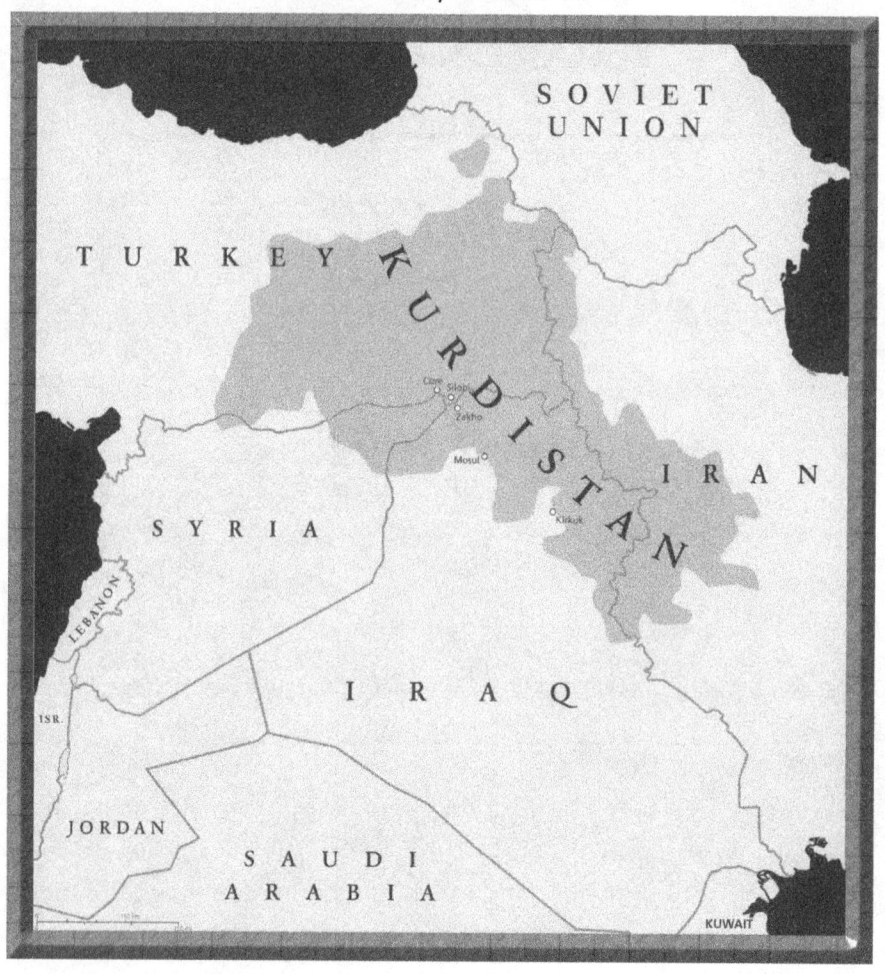

Prologue

April 1991
Kurdistan Region
Eastern Turkey and Northern Iraq, Near the Syrian Border

Khalid stood apart from the group, his eyes darting from man to man, assessing, attentive to clues about the identity of the men they had come to meet. He shifted his weight and propped himself against the truck, seemingly relaxed. But beneath the calm demeanor, all his senses were screaming that the exchange could easily devolve into a shitstorm.

They had driven out of the Silopi camp, in Turkey, at fifteen minutes before ten that morning. They were ostensibly destined for Zakho, a city twenty miles to the southeast. Zakho was across the border, in Iraq, in the region known as Iraqi Kurdistan. Instead, the driver had remained in Turkey. He had turned in the opposite direction, west, toward Cizre, a town hugging the Syrian border. Khalid had raised a mental eyebrow but kept his expression neutral, seemingly unaware of anything out of the ordinary. But the change in plan had sent a shiver down his spine. *Keep cool*, he told himself. *At least find out what's going on before you get yourself killed.*

The base at Silopi was barely two weeks old, having been hastily constructed as a staging area to provide humanitarian relief for Iraqi Kurds. Before the war, the Kurds had been victims of a massive genocide campaign conducted by the Iraqis. Thus, they had no reason to support Saddam Hussein and the Iraqi army when war broke out. Instead, the Kurds had chosen to align themselves with the US-led coalition. While the Americans had emerged victorious and had exacted a terrible toll on Iraq, they had no wish to become an occupying army. Instead, US troops had begun their withdrawal shortly after the peace accord was signed.

Only a few weeks later, the Iraqis had unleashed their vengeance on the Kurds, slaughtering tens of thousands before the United States could effectively react. Now, having declared northern Iraq to be a no-fly zone for Iraqi aircraft, the Americans were trying to save and protect those who had escaped the massacre.

Five days ago, Khalid had joined the two thousand troops at the base, carrying documents that identified him as a communications specialist from Kuwait who happened to speak some Kurdish.

Since arriving at the base, he had studiously avoided becoming friendly with the soldiers, an approach that would have garnered attention and suspicion. Instead, he exchanged simple pleasantries but remained largely aloof, keeping to himself and facilitating conversation between the American soldiers and Kurds. He had accompanied convoys to Zakho for the past four days, dropping off supplies, then traveling into the mountains and urging bands of displaced refugees to seek shelter in the camps that the troops had set up. He had hoisted people into trucks—men and women on the brink of starvation who had no strength to walk—and comforted children whose parents could not be found. He helped distribute food and water, directing refugees to the medical tents for treatment when needed. And through it all, he kept his eyes and ears open.

The two men he accompanied today had drawn his attention right away. Both were blue-eyed, of average height—five-ten or eleven—stocky, muscled, and with scruffy facial hair. From a distance, it was easy to mistake one for the other. The only noticeable difference was the color of their hair: Donnie's was red, while Joe's was light brown. Unlike most of the soldiers, who pitched in and approached the task with compassion, these two had kicked back and let others do the work. They were openly contemptuous of the locals, continually referring to them as *ragheads*. Quite a few of their fellow soldiers had shaken their heads and thrown them withering looks, but others just shrugged it off and moved on. Khalid wondered what the two men called him when he was out of hearing range. While he was not afraid of them—in the sense of being terrified—he was uneasy in their presence, wary of what they might try to do if given the chance. He knew, all too well, that such men often had short fuses.

Khalid had been surprised when the two soldiers had approached him just after daybreak, saying the colonel had assigned them a mission to deliver a truckload of special supplies to the Kurds. They might need a translator. Something about the story had felt off, made the hair stand up on his neck. He had waited until they left, then pulled his vest open. He had tucked a camera underneath his gear and rigged a remote shutter trigger, cutting a small hole in his shirt and two others inside the waistband of his pants, then threading the wire through to the camera. To take a picture, all he had to do was face the subject, rest his hands on his waist, loop his thumb over his belt, and gently press the trigger.

Thirty minutes later, he had encountered the colonel at the mess tent, scooping eggs and toast onto a plate. The colonel eyed him carefully.

"I heard you're doing a good job out there, that you're good with the Kurds. Makes our job much easier. Makes them more comfortable, too."

"Yes, sir," Khalid had answered, the words laced with a slight accent of indecipherable origin.

"And, son, I know you're new here, so I want to impress on you the importance of what you do," the colonel had said. "You never know when the situation might slide right into a cesspool. Watch out for my men. We don't need any kind of incident involving my troops."

"Yes, sir," Khalid had replied.

He had tried to find some hidden meaning behind the colonel's words, some inference that could be applied to the mission he would be undertaking that morning. But the colonel had spoken only in general terms—a pep talk that he probably used with any new person acting as a liaison with the locals. It was as if he were completely unaware of the mission that the two soldiers had mentioned. Khalid had felt his skin prickle. An hour later, he had climbed into the front of the Deuce and a Half—the workhorse cargo truck of the U.S. Army—sandwiched between the two sweat-soured men, Joe driving and Donnie by the passenger window.

What the colonel and his soldiers did not know was that Khalid was not his real name and that he was not new to the area. Nor was he Kuwaiti. His US passport was currently stashed, along with his other identifying documents, in a safe in Virginia. Genetics had endowed him with dark hair, dark eyes, and a Mediterranean complexion, allowing him to circulate unnoticed in many of the world's most volatile locations. And he did not just speak "some" of the local language; he was fluent in Kurmanji, the Kurdish language of northern Iraq, along with Arabic, Farsi, French, and English.

As the threat of war had been building, his bosses had decided it could be beneficial to have reliable human intel on the ground in Kurdistan. It was a prescient idea that had given them critical, real-time knowledge of the events taking place in the area before and during the war—and critical human intel when the Iraqi army had swarmed back into the area after the US pullout. He had been active in the area since September, living among the locals, months before the launch of Operation Desert Storm. He had been warned of the risks.

"It won't be just the Kurds and Iraqis you'll have to worry about," his boss had said. "There's going to be all kinds of chicanery going on over there. The place is a veritable smorgasbord of bad actors—just watch your back."

The load in the back of the truck was concealed by the camouflage tarp tethered to the vehicle's framework, but Khalid would have bet a year's salary about the nature of the "supplies" they were carrying. *Not food. Not water. Not clothing. Weapons, almost certainly.* The cargo raised a host of questions: *What kind of weapons? How many? Who is the buyer? How deeply involved is the colonel?* And the last uncertainty, the one that had gnawed at him since leaving Silopi, *Why are they allowing me to witness this?*

With the war in the Gulf and the war in the former Yugoslavia, the entire region had become a magnet for illegal arms traders. There were stockpiles of weapons to be had, myriad prospective buyers, and a host of shadowy merchants willing to broker the deal. Most of the weapons had their origins in the old Soviet Union and its satellite nations, like Bulgaria and Romania. The market was booming, not only in Eastern Europe, but also in places like Lebanon, where—until the peace agreement in 1990—the Palestine Liberation Organization and the Christian militias had spent fifteen years slaughtering each other. It was a lucrative trade, made even more so when the weapons for sale were American.

During the drive, they had encountered two convoys of supply trucks—both traveling in the opposite direction—likely coming overland from Incirlik, the big air base near Ankara. Nobody had given them a second glance, none questioning the circumstances of an unescorted, fully loaded truck moving away from the border with Iraq instead of toward it.

The town of Cizre sat on the Tigris River, about twenty miles northwest of Silopi and within spitting distance of the border with Syria. The sky was overcast, threatening rain, the temperature hovering just above seventy. It was nearing the end of the wet season, and the fields on the outskirts of town were plump with wheat, barley, grapes, and pomegranates—a patchwork of gold and green. By June, the amount of precipitation would plummet and the temperature would soar. Any land not irrigated by the river would revert to parched desert.

Ten miles out of Cizre, they had turned off the pitted highway onto a dirt road running north toward the mountains, then plunging into the fields on a narrow dirt track that had probably never seen such a large vehicle. They had turned around in a wide spot devoid of vegetation, blackened from a recent burning, with the smell of smoke still hanging faintly in the air. The skies had cleared and they had remained in the truck, protected from the blistering rays of the sun. Thirty minutes later, a convoy of eight small trucks had pulled into the clearing.

Their leader had stepped out of his truck and exchanged a handshake with the two American soldiers. The others had initially remained in their trucks, until some invisible signal had directed them to step out. The doors had opened with almost simultaneous precision, and the men had stood stiffly near their vehicles. The newcomers were dressed like Kurds but, except for their leader, did not utter a word. Khalid had noticed their clothing immediately—a haphazard mix of traditional and modern garb—all new, straight off a store's shelf. These men, supposedly from the rural villages of Kurdistan, had not a single stain or smudge.

Weird, he thought. *They look like a bunch of guys who were rounded up by a casting director and costumed by an inexperienced wardrobe specialist.*

Khalid faced the group and pressed the trigger on the remote shutter release. *Click. Click.* He turned toward the man who was acting as their leader, the only one talking. The man was tall for the region, six-one or two. His dark hair was buzz-cut short, but his skin was noticeably fairer than his men's. Surprisingly, his English was quite good. *Click. Click. Click.* Khalid imagined the *ka-chick* sound of the shutter opening and closing. With a big SLR camera, one grew accustomed to the noise, depending on it to affirm that the shot had been taken. But the Minox was exceptionally quiet, the frame counter on top of the body the only indication that the film had advanced. Unable to see the counter, he was working on faith.

Khalid was no fool—he knew the risks. If they caught him, he would be a dead man. He took more photos as the truck was unloaded, capturing the markings on the cargo as it was transferred to the other vehicles. The leader ignored the crates of mortars and pried open one of the long, narrow, green metal boxes. A satisfied smile spread across his face.

Dragons, Khalid realized, recoiling involuntarily. Deadly and highly transportable, the shoulder-fired antitank missile could destroy bunkers and other hardened targets. *Who are these people?* As he shifted position to better capture the transaction, he caught the profile of a man he had not noticed before—a man who was not standing outside his truck but who had remained seated inside.

This man, too, was light-skinned, but older—with high, prominent cheekbones, a hawklike nose, and a dusting of gray in his tightly cropped ash-brown hair. *Head held high. Arrogant. Not a peasant*, thought Khalid. The man was staring intently at the weapons, his eyes crinkled and his lips turned up ever so slightly at the corners. The smirk was unmistakable, and Khalid felt a moment of nausea, a sixth sense telling him that this was a man who enjoyed killing. He snapped several photos before realizing that the man, no longer focused on the weapons, was staring straight at him. His skin prickled.

He was turning back toward the Deuce when he heard the tall man bark an order to his men. *What was that? Not Kurdish, not Arabic, either. Something Eastern European? Or Slavic?* The realization hit him like a hammer. *Slavic.* He had heard rumors of illegal weapons being shipped via the Black Sea and then transported overland to the Balkans, where the states of the former Yugoslavia were embroiled in a deadly conflict. Even with an international arms embargo in place—an effort to stem the bloodshed and ethnic cleansing that was going on there—the traders of death respected no laws. *But where exactly are these weapons destined? Serbia? Bosnia? Croatia?* He had no knowledge of the language, no sense of how to identify the men's ethnicity. He kicked himself for not having taped a recorder to his chest.

Joe hurried over when the tall man gestured toward one of the small trucks. He yelled at Donnie, calling him over, and yanked a big black bag across the truck's bed. He unzipped the bag and opened it wide. The money was clearly visible. *Click, click, click.*

Joe's head jerked up and he roared, "What is this? D-marks? You promised American dollars. You never said anything about Kraut money!"

Khalid processed the information. *D-marks?* So, the buyer was either European or someone who otherwise had easy access to deutsche marks—the currency of Germany.

The tall man murmured something to Joe, took three long strides toward the occupied truck, propped himself against the door, and canted his ear toward the older man, listening intently. His body language was deferential, and Khalid instinctively understood that the man inside the truck was the boss—the actual buyer. The tall man was merely a stand-in. Suddenly, the man straightened, turned his head, and slid his eyes toward Khalid.

Khalid kept his expression neutral and maintained a nonthreatening posture, just a soldier guarding his own leader's flank, but felt a chill as the two men assessed him. After a few seconds, he let his gaze shift away toward the other men, who were now clustered near the weapons. He allowed his hand to drift toward his sidearm. Joe and Donnie, their M16s slung over their shoulders, were so focused on the money that any sense of situational awareness was forgotten. But the men from the trucks were all alert, hands on their weapons, eyeing both their leader and the Americans. Unnoticed, Khalid withdrew his Glock and stepped back, behind the Deuce's massive engine.

Khalid called out, "Joe! Everything okay over there?"

Joe looked up, finally recognizing the danger. "Whoa," he shouted, looking over to the leader for confirmation. "Just a little misunderstanding. We're good!"

Wordlessly, the leader waved off his band of men, but Khalid could see the residual tension in their posture and the narrow squint of their eyes. And Joe was visibly angry, a deep frown on his face and his movements choppy. Khalid gripped his own weapon tighter, attentive to every move as Donnie and Joe hefted the bags into the back of the Deuce and strapped them down.

Khalid kept his eyes tight on the group of men as the two soldiers secured the money. Joe, dripping with perspiration, climbed into the cab. Khalid slid in beside him, followed by Donnie. Joe started the engine and threw the truck into gear. Khalid stiffened, his heart pounding, half expecting a hail of bullets or a well-aimed mortar. Nothing happened.

"Hoo-yah! That was a rush," shouted Donnie, bouncing up and down in his seat as he came off the adrenaline rush.

Joe gripped the steering wheel hard, attempting to stop the trembling in his hands. Khalid took several deep breaths, trying to normalize his heart rate.

"The guy spoke good English, for a Kurd," Joe said. "Guess we didn't need you to translate after all. And ... uh ... thanks for the heads-up back there." He squinted and looked sideways at Khalid. "You're okay, man."

Khalid nodded and said, "Yes, his English was very good." For a fleeting moment, he wondered if the soldiers actually believed they were dealing with Iraqi Kurds. He dismissed the thought quickly. Cash had been exchanged. That was not how the US military conducted business. The transaction had been a for-profit deal. Then he realized that he had just passed some sort of test by warning them of the danger. *I might actually get out of this alive.*

On the drive back to Silopi, their conversation centered primarily on the region's frequently inhospitable weather and how it was still an improvement over the blistering sun and choking dust of southern Iraq. It was as if the transaction in the field had never happened, as if they did not have five large bags of money in the back of the truck.

Donnie jabbed Khalid in the ribs. "Bet you boys were glad to get your oil fields back, huh? I wonder how long it will take to put out the fires. All that money, up in smoke." He was referring to the actions the Iraqis had taken as they fled Kuwait, setting fire to many of the country's oil fields.

"I've heard it could be months before all the fires are under control," Khalid offered. "It's a catastrophe for my country."

"Maybe the US should just step in and take over the entire region," Joe taunted. "Save everyone a lot of trouble."

Khalid stayed silent, controlling his temper. The soldiers backed off, remaining quiet for the remainder of the trip. They dropped him at the edge of camp, near the housing tents, then drove away from the base. He wondered where they were taking the money—and how many were in on the scheme.

He slipped into his tent. Finding himself alone, he stripped off the camera and removed the film cassette. Gripping the heel of his boot, he rotated it to the side and pushed the cassette into the hollow, then repositioned the heel. He wrote a report about the encounter, folded the paper into a small rectangle, and stuffed it into the heel of his other boot.

Tomorrow, he would hand the film and the notes over to his contact, a colleague posing as a photojournalist for a major news-gathering organization.

Ninety minutes later, he made his way to the mess tent, ravenous after spending most of the day without food. He piled his tray high with slabs of beef, mashed potatoes, and soggy green beans. As he was pulling out a chair at an empty table, he noticed a major waving him over. He took a seat across from the major, who was then joined by a captain. The two officers talked intelligently about the challenges facing the region, both revealing that they had decided to remain in the military for the long haul. They seemed to be interested in his perspective, particularly as a native of a Gulf state.

It was eight o'clock when the three exited the mess tent, the sun having slipped below the horizon and daylight fading fast. The major extended his hand.

"Thanks for the cultural lesson," the major said. "I appreciate the insight. Maybe you could teach us a few words of the language, if you have time."

Khalid nodded, inwardly questioning the wisdom of such an arrangement. It was hard enough working undercover around different groups of soldiers every day, more difficult when they got to know you.

"It would be my pleasure," he said, knowing he would never follow through with the idea.

He turned into the night, toward his tent. He was half a step from the major when the crack of a rifle shot ripped through the still air. He never heard the sound, never saw the muzzle flash, never felt the bullet strike him. Khalid collapsed into the dirt, his blood draining into the Turkish soil.

The tall man tore down the concrete stairs, his elbows ricocheting off the walls, until reaching the doorway. Seeing no one in the street, he sprinted through the darkness and ran full speed until reaching the market. Finding the spice stall, he shoved the security gates apart, slipped into the shop, then pulled the barrier back together and secured it with a lock. He squeezed himself under the counter and, pushing the curtain aside, stepped into the small, dimly lit room at the back.

The older man was seated on a brass-studded leather cassock in the corner, sipping a cup of tea. He sat erect, the bearing of a military man. He asked quietly, "Is it done?"

"Yes," the tall man replied. "I am waiting for confirmation."

At precisely ten o'clock, the phone rang. When he answered, a voice asked, "Will it rain tomorrow?"

He responded, "Yes. But only in the morning."

With the code phrases exchanged, the voice on the other end gave a brief report about the shooting's aftermath.

After issuing instructions to be notified if there was any additional news, the tall man ended the call and propped himself against a freestanding wooden cabinet stacked with spice tins. "They loaded him onto a helicopter and evacuated him to Incirlik—the American air base," he said.

"So, you failed."

The tall man seethed inwardly at the insult but kept his anger in check. In an unperturbed voice he said, "I did not fail. Our asset tells me that he was very badly injured and will probably not survive. We will learn more soon."

"*Probably* is not the answer I am looking for. That man was more than just a translator, I guarantee it. He was studying me in the same way I was studying him. We cannot allow him to identify either of us or reveal that we were present at the exchange. It would compromise our plans. When we deliver these weapons to the Serbians, they will use them against the Bosnians. The blame will then fall to the Americans. They will lose their credibility. The Bosnians will think America has turned its back on them and any hope for a peaceful outcome will be dashed. The Serbians will win control of the region."

He put his hands on the tall man's shoulders and fixed him with a hypnotic stare. "This is just the beginning, one of many tactics we will use to sow distrust and division. We will eventually bring the Americans down, but not through a massive military strike, which would only serve to unite them. Instead, we will inflict death by a thousand cuts."

"Yes, sir, I understand," the tall man said, although he was not sure that he truly grasped what the older man was saying.

Six hours later, the phone rang. "I have word from Incirlik," the voice announced. "The man is dead."

PART ONE

Cat

August, Present Day

Chapter 1

August 14
Georgetown, Washington, DC

Lindsey Carlisle set the shopping bags on the bed and flipped on the light in the walk-in closet. Although Christmas was still months away, she had passed several inviting shops while out on her daily run. Naturally, she had felt inclined to stop and browse. Naturally, she had made a few purchases. Naturally, the run had been forgotten. Now all she needed was a sturdy tote to carry them home to Boston.

She rooted around in the closet and spotted a possible solution in the back corner: a patch of blue vinyl buried under a pile of shoes—women's shoes, Maggie's shoes. She was surprised, although she should not have been—it had once been Maggie's closet. While Maggie's clothes were gone, the shoes remained. Lindsey suddenly felt like an intruder.

Pushing the thought aside, she moved the shoes out of the way, gently, as if she were disturbing something that she had no right to touch. She pulled the bag free and held it up, judging that the size was about right. Switching off the light, she turned back into the guest room. She tossed the bag on the bed and proceeded to stuff it with all the goodies she had found. Lindsey believed that gifts should mean something, and she had chosen the items carefully.

She stroked the beautiful, hand-painted silk cover of a journal she had purchased. She imagined the pleasure that it would give her friend, an intrepid traveler who kept a colorful record of her adventures in far-flung destinations. She wrapped the journal in candy apple-red tissue paper, perfect for the season, and pushed it into the inner pocket of the bag. It should have slipped in easily, a little snug, but the dimensions were right.

Instead, it caught, refusing to go all the way down into the pocket. She thrust her hand into the pocket, at first not finding the source of the problem, and then her fingers touched a bump, something wedged vertically into the bottom seam. She wriggled her fingers around, finally withdrawing a small plastic square with metal contacts. An SD card, she realized—the kind you find in a camera.

Setting the tiny rectangle of plastic aside, she packed the rest of her treasures and changed into something more suitable for dinner. Maggie's husband, Paul, had made reservations for dinner at one of the newer chichi restaurants in Georgetown—table for three—where Adrian would meet them. Lindsey had hoped that her sister, Cat, and her husband would join them, but Cat was still in Europe—*Paris*, Lindsey thought. But Lindsey was never truly certain where Cat was, or even who she was.

Adrian was flying back from meetings in Chicago, and Lindsey had been bunking at Paul's house—Paul and Maggie's house—while their team tried to trace the source of yet another attempted cyberattack on the government. The team's first inclination had been to blame one of the three big bad wolves: the Russians, the Chinese, or the North Koreans. Like most people, the men and women on the team had their own biases. But more than that, the three countries seemed the most likely culprits. But then they had found an unusual snippet of code—like the signature of some graffiti artist, only much more harmful. They had contended with attacks before, but this particular innovation had a unique twist that had left her feeling a bit edgy. A relaxing night on the town seemed just the ticket for giving her a fresh outlook.

Paul Marshfield was waiting in the den, sipping a Scotch and looking every bit the high-powered DC-insider that he was. He was a close friend of her sister and considerably older, but he was still fit and handsome, even with the white hair. He was charming, as befitting a diplomat, and smart as a whip. But Lindsey thought that he had lost some of his spark without Maggie by his side. Now he seemed to be devoted solely to his work. Lindsey declined his offer of a drink, eager to get to the restaurant, eager to see Adrian.

With a twinkle in his eye, Paul asked, "Ready? The Uber will be here shortly."

Lindsey felt her cheeks flush. "Is it that obvious?"

He laughed. "About as subtle as a neon sign."

They arrived a little before seven, with time for a drink before the seven-fifteen reservation. They took seats at the bar, where Paul ordered a single malt Scotch for himself and a luscious pinot noir for Lindsey. She let the delicious, silky wine linger in her mouth for a moment. Raising her glass for a second sip, she caught a glimpse of Adrian conversing with the maître d'. She put the glass down and watched.

Tall, ruggedly handsome, and with a confident stride, Adrian turned a number of female heads as he moved through the crowd. Lindsey took a deep breath as he approached. Despite a rocky start, her relationship with this FBI special agent had morphed into something much more. He was gentle and caring, and she had fallen head over heels in love with him.

"How was Chicago?" she asked.

"Windy, and still striving to become number one," he said, in a snarky reference to the city's homicide rate. "Makes DC look like child's play."

She shrugged in feigned nonchalance. "You could always ask for a transfer."

"When Mrs. O'Leary's cow apologizes for the Great Fire," he shot back as he kissed her on the cheek and signaled the bartender for a ditto to Paul's Scotch. "How's the cyber hunt going?"

Lindsey shook her head. "I'll bring you up to date tomorrow. We're working on a couple of things that have just come up."

"That's soon enough, Lindsey. I need a good night's sleep and full light of day before I can listen to a lot of geek-speak."

"Speaking of light of day," she said, turning to Paul, "I was in Maggie's closet, looking for a small bag to borrow, and found an SD card, like from a camera. You might want to take a look and see if there is anything interesting on there."

The color drained from Paul's face, and his expression morphed from enjoyment to alarm. In a fierce whisper, he asked, "Which bag?"

He spoke with such intensity that Lindsey's first thought was that she had done something wrong. "Paul, I'm sorry. I didn't think you would mind."

"No, it's fine," he said quickly, but his voice was still tense. "Tell me which bag."

She tried to picture it. "Um ... rectangular, maybe fifteen by eighteen, navy blue, vinyl, older, zipper on the top, smaller pocket on the front. It's been used quite a bit."

"Oh, my God," he said, looking first at Adrian, then at Lindsey. "Where did you put the card?"

"On the dresser, next to the lamp," she said, still confused, not understanding the urgency.

Paul stood, tossing back his drink as he waved a credit card at the bartender. "My apologies, but I have to bow out of dinner."

Concern clouded Adrian's face, but he followed suit without hesitation, downing his drink. "I'll order an Uber," he said.

Lindsey took one last sip of the wine before Adrian ushered her out the door. Something about the memory card had obviously touched a nerve.

As they waited for the ride, Paul paced the sidewalk and tried to explain. "That bag was Maggie's carry-on—she had it with her on her trip to Sarajevo and Istanbul. The thing is, she sent an email to Cat, mentioning that she'd taken a picture of a man and that she wanted to discuss it with Cat. Was the picture important? Did it have anything to do with what happened to Maggie? We had no way of knowing because Cat never received a photo, and we never found the image file. It has nagged at us all this time."

Ten minutes later, they were back at Paul's house. Lindsey turned on her laptop and raced up the stairs to retrieve the memory card. When the computer finished booting, she slid the card into the slot and pulled up the file manager.

Paul said, "The email was sent from Sarajevo. Look for those photos."

She clicked through the images of scenery, mosques, and monuments, finally reaching the last file. What emerged was the face and torso of a man, sinewy and sunburned and windblown, topped with a tangle of white hair that brushed his shoulders. Lindsey imagined him on a boat, reeling in the day's catch. But he was standing in front of a shop, holding a tray. *A waiter?* she wondered.

Paul leaned in and stared at the image, burning the man's face into his memory. "I'm not sure what I expected, but I don't recognize him." He put his hand on Lindsey's shoulder. "Send it to Cat. Maybe it will have some meaning to her." He started to walk away and, instead, turned back. "And Lindsey? Let's go dark."

Lindsey looked up at him and flicked a glance at Adrian, who nodded his agreement. *Dark.* Their entire team used high-end, government-level encryption and other security measures that made her head spin. But if they were going dark with this, Paul was worried about their email being monitored by the very providers of the technology they generally used—or perhaps someone with in-depth knowledge of that technology. She nodded, now sure that whatever this picture was about, it was damn serious.

Lindsey pulled out her other laptop, the one that Gabe, the team's resident ace hacker, had set up. After the machine booted, she clicked the Tor icon and accessed the email that Gabe had assigned to her. She wrote a short message, shoved the SD card into the slot, attached the photo, and clicked the *Send* button. The email was on its way to Cat—via the dark web.

She unlocked her phone and sent a text to Cat:

767

767 could have been many things: an airplane, the beginning of a phone number, or the corresponding letters on a phone's keypad, such as POP or PMS. But in their little corner of the world, it meant SOS. They used it when they smelled trouble, when they wanted to fly below the radar. It was their code for *check your inbox on Tor.*

Chapter 2

August 15
Zagreb, Croatia

Swinging her legs out of the rental car, Cat Powell tapped the band on her arm and checked the time: nearly eleven-thirty in the morning. She planted her feet on the pavement and cautiously pulled herself erect. Three and a half hours in the low-end Renault had taken a toll on her back and butt. *Getting creaky,* she mumbled. Stretching her neck and spine, she worked out the kinks and bounced on her toes to start the blood flowing again.

She had left early from Pjescana Uvala—a seaside village on the Adriatic—allowing plenty of time for the drive, car return, and security formalities before the Air France flight, scheduled to depart Zagreb for Paris at 3:00 p.m. Her stomach growled, a reminder that she had not eaten since a predawn coffee and slice of toast. Once through the inspection checkpoint, a primary order of business would be to find a café.

Cat pulled her bag from the car, wheeled it the hundred yards to the terminal, collected a receipt from the car rental counter in the terminal, and proceeded to the check-in area. Retrieving the passport from her purse as she turned toward the check-in counters, she lifted her eyes to the Departures board. She easily located the Paris flight—showing on time thus far. From long-held habit, her eyes scanned the list of flights departing just prior and just following Paris. One never knew when circumstances might require a fast rearrangement of one's travel plans. *Rome, Frankfurt, Sarajevo, Dubrovnik* before the Paris flight, *Brussels, Split, Vienna, Zurich* after.

After receiving her boarding pass from the agent, Cat passed through the immigration and security lines and found a small coffee shop. The place was cozy, with thickly padded wooden chairs that seemed more like benches with backs. The coffee looked dark and rich, and she sniffed the aroma with appreciation. As she waited for the brew, she pulled her phone from her tote, popped in the battery and SIM card, powered it on, and connected to Wi-Fi. Having pulled the battery a week ago, she expected to be bombarded with pings and beeps and was not disappointed. Dozens of emails waited in her work and personal emails but she started instead with the texts, believing that it's always better to start the day with lighthearted words from friends.

She was surprised to see the 767 text from her sister, Lindsey, sent at 1:45 a.m. With the time difference, it would have been 7:45 yesterday evening in Washington. Lindsey should have been at dinner.

Cat opened the small tablet computer that she used specifically for accessing the dark web. She clicked the icon for Tor, a piece of software that enables anonymous, encrypted communication.

In the intelligence community, staying in the shadows is paramount to survival. Browsers that track your site visits and monitor your location can prove perilous, and systems through which adversaries could eavesdrop on communications were even more dangerous. Tor addressed many of these challenges and, indeed, the US government had sponsored much of its original development to protect the intelligence gathered by its operatives. On recommendation from several tech hotshots at the Agency, she had installed the Tor software about fifteen years ago. She opened TorBox, an email program that would only receive messages from providers it certified, further ensuring anonymity.

The attached image drew her attention first—a grizzled man with wild white hair. She squinted, puzzled by the eerie sense that he was somehow familiar, and read the message:

> Paul wanted me to send this picture from an SD card that I found in one of Maggie's old bags. He doesn't know the man and thinks the photo might register with you.

Recognition hit her like a hammer. She had seen this man before. Without warning, her heart began to race, and the air seemed to whoosh from her lungs, as if someone had landed a blow to her solar plexus. She staggered, her legs buckling. She made a feeble attempt to steady herself by squeezing the wheelie's handle, only to discover that her fingers were numb. *What is happening?*

She was aware of people crowding around her, of advice uttered with urgency, whispers of concern, hands supporting her elbows, and one deep voice boring through the fog. "Madame? Madame? Pouvez vous parler?"

Cat's brain registered her own uncertainty as she found herself looking up into a set of concerned hazel eyes. The man's question had been in French, asking if she was able to speak. *Does he think I am choking?* She performed a rapid self-evaluation and waved away the other onlookers. *Okay, it's not a stroke, not a cardiac event. Just lost it for a minute.* She opened her mouth to respond, the words forming on her lips, the neurons simultaneously firing off the warning—*French. God, Cat! You are using a French passport, your luggage IDs are in French, and today your name is Marie-Françoise Bourget. Pull yourself together!* "Je suis bien," she managed, telling him that she was fine.

Gathering her wits, she invented a tale of low blood sugar and failing to eat properly before arriving at the airport—a story not terribly far from the truth. The stranger escorted her to a seat, handed her a container of orange juice that seemed to materialize from nowhere, and shoved a croissant sandwich into her hand. She fished a few euros out of her bag, offering them as payment, but he refused. He glanced toward the departure gates, and she could sense that he was concerned about making his flight. She gave him a grateful nod.

"C'est bon. Tu devrais y aller," she breathed, letting him know that she was okay and encouraging him to go. He left reluctantly, making his way toward the departure area and glancing back over his shoulder, as if to reassure himself that he was not abandoning a dying woman.

She had witnessed similar meltdowns over the course of her career, with operatives unexpectedly falling apart under seemingly mundane circumstances. Post traumatic stress disorder—PTSD—had found its way into the vernacular in the early eighties, an unwelcome legacy from the Vietnam War. Although the psychological effects of combat and other violence had been known for as long as humans had been doing monstrous things to one another, the condition had finally been assigned an official name. To the gung-ho, macho culture of the military and clandestine intelligence services, *PTSD* was sometimes derided as just another politically correct term for *bonkers*. Until, of course, it finally became accepted as a viable medical condition.

Cat Powell, candidate for mental disorder? Her nostrils flared at the thought, as if an unpleasant odor had wafted by. *Well, girl, if exposure to life-threatening situations is the measuring stick, you would certainly qualify.* She had killed, others had tried to kill her, and the bullet she had taken in Afghanistan had given her a taste of her own mortality. Yet, after last month's physical and psychological evaluations, the doctors had pronounced her to be in better shape than most women half her age. She certainly would do nothing to dispel the notion, having no intention of reporting this little episode. *Alive and still kicking butt. This is an isolated incident, an unexpected shock, all because of a picture.*

She had seen him, four years ago, in Istanbul. *Did I ever get his name? No.*

Four years ago, Maggie Marshfield—her best friend, maid of honor, comrade in adventure, and closest confidant—had spent several days in Istanbul after visiting Sarajevo. They had planned to take the trip together— a girls' getaway—until a crisis at work had derailed Cat's participation. Maggie had gone alone.

All this time, Cat had kept her feelings tightly corralled, had not relaxed her vigilance for even an instant. Now, the mere mention of the city threatened to release an avalanche of emotional debris. She closed her eyes, wanting to forget ... forcing herself to remember. If she had gone with Maggie, if Maggie had chosen not to go at all ... *if, if, if.*

She had never been entirely satisfied with the results of the investigation. Sure, the FBI and other agencies had done their jobs. They had been thorough and, ultimately, ruled it an accident. Cat herself had scoured Maggie's activities in Istanbul. There was nothing out of the ordinary, nothing that would lead to any conclusion other than an accident. Still, she could not escape the feeling that they—and she—had missed something.

Studying the picture carefully, she searched for a hint about the location. The name of the shop was obscured by the door's overhang. Sliver of a cobblestone street, Mediterranean-style tile on the roof. It could have been nearly any town in southern Europe. *How long would it take the NSA to figure out where this shop is? Less than a day? An hour? Five minutes?* Her finger was poised to dial when she noticed the giveaway. In the top-right corner of the background was a wedge of land, a peak, its hue blending almost perfectly with the blue-gray of the sky. *Mountains*. Maggie had made two stops during that trip, and only one had mountains like this.

Cat thought about the flights listed on the Departures board and glanced at her watch, wondering if she could possibly make it in time. In one fluid motion she swung her tote over her shoulder, grabbed the handle of the roll-aboard, and sped to the gate. As she ran, she typed a message.

> Possible photo taken prior Maggie Marshfield accident. Sarajevo? Need pic location, info on subject. ASAP. Advise when sent.

She pressed the *Send* button just as she reached the gate, explaining to the agents that she needed to cancel her flight to Paris. An emergency, she told them, careful to speak in French-accented English. "Could you please get me on the next flight to Sarajevo?"

An internal whisper told her that she should stick with the plan of flying back to Paris and immediately thereafter vaporizing the identity of Marie-Françoise Bourget. It would be the smart, safe thing to do. But the photo had rattled her, thrown her off balance. For four years, she had waited for the break that would explain Maggie's haunting last email:

> When I get back, let's talk about this guy.

There had been no photo in the email, no guy to talk about, no hint about what Maggie had wanted to discuss.

Cat boarded the airplane to Sarajevo.

Chapter 3

August 15
Sarajevo, Bosnia and Herzegovina

The plane touched down forty-five minutes after leaving Zagreb. When she had last visited Sarajevo, it had been a city in Yugoslavia. Now it was the capital of Bosnia. Or, to be exactly correct, it was the capital of Bosnia and Herzegovina. *There's a mouthful*, she thought. *No wonder everyone just calls it Bosnia.*

Grabbing her tablet, Cat powered it on and waited for the signal to sync, hoping that her message had yielded results. *Come on, come on,* she whispered to herself.

Finally, the phone vibrated. She clicked the incoming message.

24646

Melodie's code! BINGO! Cat enabled the hotspot on her phone and connected the tablet.

> Shop is Sretna Kafa, map attached. Photo is owner, Goran Terzić. Subject of station investigation in 2010. Dossier attached. Get DNA sample.

Surprised, Cat read the message again. *DNA?* She was tempted to ask why, but Melodie was the best sleuth she had ever come across. In the years that had passed since their first meeting, she had proven her value over and over. It was easy to understand why Melodie had earned a reputation as one of the top intelligence and threat analysts in the United States. If she was holding her cards close to her chest, she had a good reason.

Cat gathered her belongings and stepped off the airplane into a terminal that was surprisingly busy. Stopping at an information kiosk, she tried to reserve a room at the same hotel where Maggie had stayed, but was told it was fully occupied. It was only after several unsuccessful attempts at booking a room that she learned about the film festival taking place over the next few days. She gave up and fired off a message to Melodie.

Pls find me a room

Twenty minutes later, the response came back.

Done. 3 bdrm, old town $89

Thank God for geeks, she thought. *Price is right, location perfect, and much better than having to camp in the woods*. The good fortune did not, however, extend to the rental car. There were none available for the next four days.

Looking through the taxi's back-seat window during the drive into town, she could not help but notice that, while many modern buildings dotted the cityscape, Sarajevo still bore the scars of the war that had besieged the city twenty-five years before. *This is a place*, she thought, *that will always be a symbol of man's inhumanity to man*.

Cat settled into the apartment and pulled off the wig. After wearing the thing constantly for nearly a week, she squealed with delight as she raked her fingernails over her itchy scalp. The wig was a medium-length, shimmery auburn with an asymmetrical cut, chosen to attract attention—particularly from the opposite sex—and to confuse facial recognition software. It had worked like a charm for her recent covert mission in Croatia, but she had intended to ditch it immediately after arrival back in Paris. Now, she had been through an additional passport control and would have to pass through yet another when she left Bosnia. It added up to more time and more opportunity for her real identity to be uncovered. *I should have boarded the flight to Paris*, she thought. *There would have been nothing to trip me up, and Marie-Françoise Bourget would no longer exist*.

Cat stuffed the wig into the mesh bag with her underwear and threw it into the suitcase, where it would remain until her departure. In the interim, her natural brunette hair would allow her to blend in more easily with the local population. There was no going back. She was here, in Bosnia, and her mission was to find the man in the photo.

Caution would be prudent, but fretting about the consequences of her hasty decision was a waste of time. She briefly considered contacting the station chief—a woman she had met several times, the last occasion at a colleague's retirement party in Virginia a few months earlier—but the circumstances gave her pause. She liked and respected the woman immensely, but this entire operation was off-the-books. The Agency believed that she was still in Paris. They could not be involved. Not yet.

Chapter 4

The film festival had attracted her attention immediately, not from the entertainment being offered, but because of the possibilities it offered for a few hours of borrowing someone's identity. The Bosnian Cultural Center and the National Theater, the hub areas of the festival, were within easy walking distance of the apartment. The coffee shop from the photo was also close by. But she had no intention of entering the shop as a Westerner, alone, at least until she knew more about the shop's owner. What she needed was another identity, someone who would not arouse suspicion and with whom the patrons—and the man in the photo—would relax and lapse into easy conversation.

She set off, on foot, a red-striped tote looped over her arm and a black ball cap on her head. She owned several similar bags, in varying sizes and colors, but all had one thing in common: with just a couple of quick zips and unzips, they were completely reversible. The interior fabric was always a dull tan or gray, the exterior an eye-catching pattern of bright colors. Within the tote were several lightweight articles that she might require in everyday life: a sweater, scarf, spare eyeglasses, sunglasses, flat shoes, another ball cap in beige. The other item she carried was a hijab, the headscarf worn by many Muslim women. But it was not for comfort that she hauled the wardrobe around. Her job was just much easier when she could—within the space of half a minute—change her appearance so completely that anyone following would think they had lost her.

Cat walked several blocks and turned into the well-appointed hotel where, before Cat was forced to cancel, she and Maggie had originally planned to stay on their vacation. Maggie had, on her own, sought and found a smaller, more authentic accommodation. Cat passed by the reception desk, nodded familiarly to the staff, and kept moving. "Always look as if you know exactly what you are doing, as if you belong," her mentor had cautioned long ago. "The slightest uncertainty can spell disaster."

She followed another guest who, key in hand, appeared to be headed to the elevator. She waited for him to select his floor, and then pressed the button for the fifth floor, two below him. She wished him a good day as she got off, then looked down the hall. Not finding what she wanted, she returned to the elevator. On the sixth floor, she spotted the housekeeping cart. The maid was nowhere in sight. Cat quickly grabbed two notepads and a handful of pens, each bearing the hotel logo. She dropped them into the tote and returned to the lobby. Five minutes after entering the hotel, she was back on the street.

Approaching the National Theater, Cat found an elevated perch from which to observe. She stifled an urge to laugh as she took stock of the hordes of film professionals, Hollywood wannabes, paparazzi, and gawkers milling about. Vendors in makeshift stalls hawked all manner of things cinematic— from T-shirts, to mugs, to posters, to promises of instant fame. Urgent whispers floated through the crowd, hinting that this or that celebrity had been spotted, but few onlookers scored even a glimpse.

Cat ignored the hubbub and focused on the roped-off press area, using her phone's camera to zoom in on the people assigned there. She was intimately familiar with the profession, having maintained a covert identity over the years as a renowned photographer known as Adele Rutledge.

In that perfectly designed role, she had traveled to some of the most dangerous cities on earth, creating portraits of some of the world's most dangerous and violent men. Her work seemed to look into the souls of these men, capturing their brutality, their disdain for compassion, their cruel darkness. During that time, her circle of colleagues had been primarily comprised of hardened photojournalists who made their bones documenting the atrocities committed by the men whose portraits she created, not those who fawned over celebrities.

Now scanning the faces of the dozens of photographers present, she recognized only one: a woman who had received training at the Rutledge School of Photography, a CIA front bearing Cat's nom de guerre.

She zeroed in on the scowling countenance of Toni Swanson, a lanky brunette who had proven to be as adept at bedding her subjects as she was with a lens. Her dalliances had become public fodder a decade ago, after an unsuspecting spouse, scheduled for her own portrait session, spotted a full-color photo of her husband's tattooed derriere on the wall of Toni's studio. To make matters worse, the aggrieved woman was subsequently offered a position on a network morning show, giving her a national forum. Toni's budding career took an instant downturn from which she had never recovered. Thus, instead of elite assignments from big-name newspapers and periodicals, she was behind the ropes in Sarajevo, covering a film festival.

Toni had little use for wardrobe variety, and today was no exception. She was outfitted head to toe in her color of choice: black shirt, black pants, black shoes. She stood behind her tripod, one hand bunched into a fist on her cocked hip and the other on the positioning handle, panning the camera and searching the crush of people. The eye of Toni's camera passed over Cat and kept going, without the slightest pause or hint of recognition. She and Cat were similar in appearance: hair color and length, height, and build. Even their facial structures bore similarities. Looking down at herself, Cat almost laughed. Black pants, black shirt, black shoes. She had no doubt that it would be easy to mistake one for the other. That was all she needed.

Thirty feet beyond Toni, an expensively groomed young man with gelled hair stood observing the teeming mass of bodies. He preened more than he worked, tilting his chin just so and flashing white teeth at anyone he perceived to be important. Cat rolled her eyes involuntarily. She judged him to be one of the I-am-rich-and-good-looking-and-entitled set, someone who believed money and looks held an equal value with talent. Mounted on his top-of-the-line tripod was a new Hasselblad, with a retail cost somewhere north of the price of a new Audi. Lenses were extra. At his feet lay a large black backpack that would hold enough kit for a photo shoot anywhere on the planet.

She turned her attention to the scene in front of her—the ebb and flow of the crowd, the positions and situational awareness of Toni and the young man, the security personnel and cameras—and gauged the difficulty of walking out with what she needed. While most of the press gaggle wore their badges dangling from a neck lanyard, Toni, never one to abide by the rules, had draped her lanyard over a knob on the tripod. On top of the young man's pack was a small day pouch with a Nikon nosing out. Cat smiled to herself. *Easy pickings.*

Cat threaded her way through the throng. As she drew abreast of Toni, she jostled a heavy male passerby, causing him to stumble. Toni's eyes widened as the man careened toward her, and she thrust out her arms to shield herself from being crushed. Quick as a snake strike, Cat's hand shot out and snatched the badge.

Moving quickly away from Toni, Cat neared the gelled-hair young man and shouted excitedly, "Oh wow! There's Jennifer Lawrence!"

While heads craned for a look at the Hollywood megastar, Cat stooped, snagging the day pack and dropping it into her tote. Fifty feet along, she ducked down and, pretending to tie her shoe, switched caps and donned the sweater and the eyeglasses. As she stood, she zipped the top of the tote, unzipped the bottom, and in a well-practiced move, reversed the bag before fading into the sea of bobbing heads. The entire dance had lasted fewer than thirty seconds.

Cat took a detour to the same hotel she had visited an hour earlier. This time, instead of taking the elevator, she strode toward the restrooms behind the lobby. She tucked into a stall and opened the tote.

Professional-grade photography gear was expensive, with costly camera bodies and outrageously pricey lenses. Many photogs now used electronic trackers, with chips tucked into bag pockets or affixed to the equipment itself. She found the small plastic square almost immediately, carelessly dropped into the day bag. Shaking her head in disbelief at the young man's naivete, she pocketed the device and strolled out of the hotel at a leisurely pace. She followed the sidewalk until she spotted a convertible moving toward her and, as the car passed, casually flipped the tracker into its rear seat.

She took a roundabout route back to the apartment, watching for faces she had noticed before, clothes she had seen along the way, shoes that had caught her attention fifteen or thirty minutes earlier, and the giveaway gait of a person's walk. Cat's success as an operative was due, in no small part, to her skills as an observer. There was little that escaped her. As she opened the door to the condo, she was confident that she had completed her task unobserved.

From behind her, a voice asked, "Enjoyin' the film festival? You should have let me know you were coming."

Startled, Cat's body jerked. It took a moment to register her familiarity with the Texas drawl—the *g* dropped from *enjoying* and sounding more like *en-jaw-yin*—and the person who went with it. She turned around and came face-to-face with Pat Desmond, the CIA's Chief of Station in Bosnia.

"How's the apartment?" Pat asked.

As the realization washed over her, Cat was stunned. Melodie had found a place for Cat not by conducting a skillful search of available accommodations in Sarajevo, but by contacting Pat. She was astounded that she had not accounted for that possibility. *Slipping*, she thought.

"Oh, don't go feeling sorry for yourself, honey," Pat said. "I've been at this game a long time. Not as long as you, but maybe you're just getting a little long in the tooth." She laughed heartily and stuck out her hand. "Welcome to my part of the world. Let's go have us a drink. I think there's a bottle of Grey Goose in the cabinet."

Cat groaned. She had not only been spotted, she had been led around by the nose. "This is *your* place," she said.

"Well, technically the building belongs to the American taxpayers. Heard you might be needing a place to stay. Thought I might accommodate. Quite clever, I thought. So, what do you think? Sweet, isn't it?"

Aggravated at herself, Cat was hardly in the mood for polite chatter. "Yeah, sweet. Really great," she snarled.

Pat was a tall, lean woman, pushing six feet and seeming to confirm the adage that everything is bigger in Texas. She had the easy grace of an athlete, and wide, alert brown eyes that missed little. Her once-long blonde hair was now veined with white, and had been shorn into a spiky, low-maintenance style that had not seen a blow dryer in months.

Cat smiled inwardly, thinking that if she gave Pat a cap, a clipboard, and a whistle, she would look more like a women's basketball coach than a spy. *But then,* she thought, *that is exactly the point.*

Pat poured two glasses of vodka, handed one to Cat, grabbed the bottle, and led Cat into a large, windowless office off the downstairs living area. Half of the room was occupied by a freestanding tentlike structure—an enclosure designed to shield against audio interceptions.

"I duck in here for any secure conversation. There is new technology every day that we can't begin to keep up with. I'm told this is state-of-the-art, but what would I know?"

Cat stepped inside. The space was tight, with a small table, four chairs, a phone, a computer, and a video monitor. She thought that perhaps four or five more could be crammed in, standing room only.

"Who's listening?" she asked.

"Everybody. The Bosnians, the Serbs, the Russians, the Iranians, maybe even our own people ... shall I go on? It's tight, but it beats the hell out of having to go into the office for every sensitive call."

Pat gestured at one of the chairs, inviting Cat to sit. She shed her jacket, revealing long, ropy muscles—the result of weekends spent rowing the rivers of Bosnia. There were few rowing clubs in the country, and fewer female members. But as a two-time Olympian, Pat had transcended the scorn of gender.

The two cradled their glasses of vodka, Pat's stern, angular face bearing no traces of her earlier joviality, as Cat explained why she was in Sarajevo.

"I met Maggie once," Pat finally said. "There was a ceremony at Langley, and her husband was one of the honorees. She was lovely and, as I recall, hilariously funny. I'm willing to help in any way I can, up to a point. I'm assuming you are here just as a tourist, and not on official business?"

Cat nodded. "For now, just a tourist exploring the city. Where that leads, I cannot predict."

After refilling both glasses, Pat said, "Then we will go with that for now. I think it might be helpful for you to meet with one of our assets tomorrow. We used him a few years back, when we looked into the man in your photo. Maybe it's time to revisit that discussion. What are you using as your nom de plume today?"

"Ellie," Cat said, snatching a name out of thin air. "Ellie Lamberton."

Pointing at the press badge dangling on Cat's chest, Pat tilted her head in a question and let out a loud guffaw when Cat told her about the visit to the film festival.

"You *stole* the guy's camera?"

"Borrowed. I'll get it back to him after I'm done. I do feel bad about Toni Swanson, though. It's a lot of aggravation when you lose a badge."

"Yeah, I've heard her story. Bad break. But you're going to make it up to her, aren't you?" Pat said with a knowing smile. "You're not half as coldhearted as your reputation would have us believe."

Cat shrugged. "Yeah, I'm just all warm and fuzzy," she said, rolling her eyes. "But she got a raw deal. I just made her miserable life even more so."

"Next thing is, you're going to expect us to honor you with a halo," Pat said with a laugh. "So, what's your plan?"

"Go over to the coffee shop, Sretna Kafa."

Pat nodded. "I know the place well. Great coffee."

"I'll down some caffeine, take as many pictures as I can, snoop around, and see what makes my nose tingle," Cat said. "Oh, and try to gather some of the owner's DNA."

"DNA? Well, the owner is personable enough, but I'm not sure he'll let you just swab his cheek. That said, I've always thought there was something going on, I felt it in my bones. Without some evidence of dirty dealing, though, there's not much we can do. Not enough money, not enough people, not enough time. All the crazies out there are keeping us busy."

"Yeah, I face that every day. I keep thinking I should find another job, one with a little less stress."

"What, and be bored for the rest of your life?"

"There is that," Cat agreed.

"Since you're just out seeing the sights, I'll go with you. Maybe while you go into Sretna Kafa, I'll check out another café just a few buildings down, one with outside seating. I'll just hang out while you go about your touristy business."

"Whoa," Cat said. "I can't drag you into this. If something goes wrong and the proverbial shit hits the fan, you don't want to be within a thousand miles of the blowback."

Pat spread her arms in a so-what gesture. "What can I tell you? You're a tourist, right? Aside from shaking hands with De Niro at a fancy luncheon earlier, I've had an otherwise deadly boring day. If you say no, I'll just have to turn you over to the police. I'll bet that camera has a serial number."

Cat laughed and said, "Ah, yes. But payback is hell. Don't come crying to me afterward."

Pat's eyes widened. "Should I be worried?"

Cat gave her a wink. "Always," she said.

Chapter 5

Several streets away from their destination, Cat climbed out of Pat's car, tucking her hair under the black ball cap and perching the black-framed glasses on her nose. Pat drove away to park, then fast-walked to the café and found a seat outside. Cat adopted a slow pace and reached the coffee shop shortly thereafter. She spotted Pat a few doors down and took a position across from Sretna Kafa.

The coffee shop was warmly lit, cozy, inviting, and for nine o'clock at night, unexpectedly crowded—the place was teeming with twenty-somethings. Having said goodbye to her twenties years ago, Cat knew she would stand out from the shop's patrons. It was an unaccustomed and uncomfortable role, and she was glad to have the press badge and the Nikon slung over her chest to explain her presence.

She put her eye to the viewfinder, capturing the scene with her lens. Assorted languages drifted on the night air, and Cat caught snatches of conversations ricocheting from Myanmar, to South Sudan, to Syria, to Yemen, to Venezuela. *This is a worldly group*, she thought. Another surprise: few were talking about the United States, seemingly resigned to ignore the current state of affairs there.

Zooming in with the telephoto, she peered into the shop, where she could see that a young woman was having a heated argument with an older man. Recognizing him from Maggie's photo and from their encounter in Istanbul, the hairs on her arms stood up, the breath left her lungs, and every sinew in her body tightened. *Goran Terzić*. She studied him as he angrily shoved a canister back onto a shelf, then turned and pulled a tissue from a box on the counter. He coughed spasmodically into the tissue, wadded it up, and tossed it in a nearby waste bin. She snapped dozens of frames in rapid succession, capturing every gesture, every nuance of expression on the man's face, before he turned and stormed to the back of the shop. *Fingerprints and DNA*, she thought, before recognizing the absurdity of trying to abscond with the canister. *Get the DNA. That's what Melodie asked for.*

Keeping her eye on the waste bin, Cat snapped several more photos of the exterior and then crossed the street. Her press badge garnered some attention—there were always people who wanted their picture in the newspaper—and the clientele smiled cooperatively. Some of them asked questions about her work, to which she gave a vague answer about being on assignment for a major publication. Given what she had overheard, she expected them to probe further. Instead, *Cool!* and *Awesome!* seemed to be the responses of choice.

The young woman looked up as Cat approached. Her coloring was fair, her eyes an arresting gray, and her smile genuine when Cat asked if she could take a few pictures. Her gaze zeroed in on the badge, and she nodded excitedly. Like most small shops, this one welcomed free publicity. They chatted for a few minutes, and Cat pulled out the small notepad and pen she had taken from the hotel. She noticed that the woman's eyes drifted to the hotel logo. Cat knew she had scored a point. She was staying in a fancy hotel and she had a press badge, therefore she must be reputable.

"Your shop is quite charming," Cat said. "Is it a family business? Have you owned it for a long time?"

"My father's family came from Goražde," the woman said. "It's a small city about a hundred kilometers east of here. My uncle had lived in Sarajevo for quite a few years and, after the war, he urged my father to come here. There was nothing left for him in Goražde—our family home was destroyed, much of the town was in ruins—so we came. Sarajevo was in ruins, too, but he felt there was hope here. In Sarajevo, for the entire course of the war, people lived in basements, trying to avoid getting shot or bombed. They never saw their friends, never sat outside to enjoy the fresh air. My uncle and my father wanted to recapture Sarajevo's energy and goodwill, like it was when the Olympics were here. They wanted a place where people of all nations and faiths could gather and talk and be happy. Thus, *Sretna Kafa*. It means *Happy Coffee* in English."

Cat nodded, appreciating the thought behind the name. "It's completely charming and welcoming. And I want to compliment you on your English. It's very good. I'm afraid my Bosnian is nonexistent."

The woman laughed. "My grandmother was a teacher. She made my father learn English, then he forced me to learn it, too. I remember resenting the way he insisted on perfect pronunciation. Now, of course, I appreciate what he did. And it helps that I am able to practice every day," she said, gesturing at her customers.

"Are you the owner now? Are your father and uncle retired?"

The woman almost choked with laughter. "Oh no! This is still my father's business. He is here every day. And," she said, rolling her eyes, "every night."

Cat chuckled. "The kids think they know how to do everything, and the parents think the kids don't do anything well enough. It's a story as old as the ages. But your uncle must come by to help out?"

"Oh, at the beginning, he was here all the time. But now he travels a lot. He is not often here."

As they talked, Cat edged closer to the counter and the waste bin beneath. She glanced down and saw the tissue, a mound of rubbish beneath it. But what caught her eye was the splatter of blood. *He's sick,* she realized. A new customer entered the shop, diverting the woman's attention. Cat turned slightly, pretended to trip, and dropped the notepad onto the top of the trash. She bent over and reached into the bin, scooping up the tissue as she retrieved the notepad. With the tissue sticking out from between the pages, she hurriedly stuffed the pad into her kit.

The woman returned to the counter and set about filling an order.

"What is that?" Cat asked, pointing to the cup in the woman's hand.

"Salep. It's made from wild orchids," she said, swirling the mixture. "They say it has healing properties."

"And what do you say?"

The woman smiled sadly. "Some things can never be healed."

No, they can't, Cat thought. She looked up as the older man reemerged from a room at the rear of the shop. She forced a smile and lifted her camera. "Good evening! Are you the owner of this wonderful shop? Would you mind if I took your picture?"

It is said that time dulls all memories, but to Cat, seeing this man brought back all the pain of Maggie's death. He did not, however, appear to recognize her. Instead, his expression suggested that he was horrified at the idea of a photo. He waved his hands wildly and shouted, "No pictures! No pictures!" He turned on his heel and disappeared into the back of the shop.

The woman spread her hands in resignation. "My father," she said. "I am sorry, but he is not feeling well today. Perhaps another time."

Cat wondered about the man's illness, if he was being treated, if he was terminal, how much time he had. But she had his DNA and the photos she had snapped even as he was denying permission. What she did not have were answers. Yet. And if the DNA and photos did not hold the key, she would be back. *If he survives that long,* she thought, coming full circle in the conundrum. She swallowed her curiosity and forced herself to exit the situation gracefully.

"I would enjoy another visit. I apologize if I upset him. That was not my intention. I hope he recovers soon," Cat said. She shook the woman's hand and left the shop.

Cat ambled the quiet streets for three blocks, as she and Pat had agreed, then turned the corner. At the next block, she turned again and kept walking. She had no reason to suspect that anyone might follow her, but would be forever a captive of her training-induced paranoia. She slowed as she passed a few shops, pretending to browse the window displays, but detected no one. Two minutes later, Pat's car pulled up beside her.

"Get in!" Pat commanded.

Cat threw herself into the car, and Pat gunned the motor, taking an immediate left, followed by another left.

"I have a tail?"

"It's a possibility. A man. It might have been random, but he stood shortly after you left and headed in your direction. That coffee shop is a place where friends congregate. They arrive at about the same time and leave together. He was already there when you showed up, but he was alone. I found it unusual."

Cat frowned. "I didn't notice him at all. What are you thinking? Professional?"

"That's my guess. There was just *something* about him. If he is a professional, then the question becomes, who is he working for?"

"Who, indeed? But I did take photos of every nook and cranny of that place. What did he look like?"

"Close to your age. Tall, six-one, maybe. Salt-and-pepper hair—mostly salt—trimmed enough that his ears showed, but not a buzz cut. Dark pullover sweater, with a reddish tint. Totally ordinary, except that he was left-handed. I wasn't close enough for much else."

Cat swiped through the photos. *There.* Enlarging the image, she centered it on the man fitting Pat's description. "This guy?" she asked, holding up the camera.

"That's him."

As she studied and memorized the face in the photo, Cat said, "I'll send it in as soon as we get to the apartment. We should know who he is soon enough. But what's the angle? He wouldn't have been there because of me—no one knew I was going there."

"Except your friend Melodie. She seems pretty adept at anticipating your moves."

Cat nodded, but the crease in her brow deepened. "Yep, she's incredibly intuitive. But that's not it. No, he was there for some other reason."

"Something to do with the owner? Or those shady deals we were talking about?"

Cat thought for a moment. "Maybe. Let's yank the thread and see what unravels."

"Yank it tomorrow," said Pat. "I need sleep."

Chapter 6

Toni Swanson slipped clumsily off the stool, hefting her kit onto her shoulder as she stumbled to the door. A knot of photogs had urged her to come along for the evening, and she had not put up much of a fight. After the day she'd had, she had needed a drink. Or three. While she could admit to herself that she actually liked Sarajevo, she resented the circumstances that had led her here. *Film festival. Blech,* she thought. All afternoon and into the evening she had snapped photos of people who were pretending to be important, pretending to matter. All this glitz, while the world was going to hell. It paid the rent, paid well, actually, but this was not what she had planned.

She knew she had talent, worked harder than anyone, was ambitious, and welcomed every opportunity to learn. Her mom had worked three jobs, scraping for every penny, to provide her with an education. She had been so proud when Toni was accepted to study at the Rutledge School of Photography, and almost burst with excitement when Toni landed the job at the most important newspaper on the planet. Toni wanted, no, *deserved*, to be working on big news stories, to be capturing moments that had an impact on the world. She should be on the path to a Pulitzer. Yet here she was, all because of that bitch of a wife.

The latest disaster had come when she was denied entry to the big ceremony tonight—the one where De Niro was being honored and awards were being presented—and she could not find her badge. She had hung the lanyard from her tripod because it would sometimes get in the way as she was angling the lens. When a microsecond could make a difference between a great shot and a dud, the lanyard had to go. But somehow, somewhere, she had lost the damn thing, and no amount of cajoling had worked to overcome the bureaucracy. No badge, no admittance. Thus, she had joined the party of "toddlers," as she disparagingly called the young people who were new to the profession. They, too, had been excluded from the main event, but not because they had lost their badges. They were simply too inexperienced, with only a limited body of work, to have earned a place at the table.

They plowed through the crush of people to a small nightspot across from the National Theater. It was a quirky place, with its cozy-meets-industrial decor, but the bar was well-stocked. And Toni appreciated the view. The bartender was tall, muscular, and wow, so damn good-looking. He was, unfortunately, gay, as she figured out within two minutes of taking a seat. But his smile was radiant and the scent of him intoxicating, and when he suggested she try a rakija, she accepted gladly.

"Plum brandy," he had said. "Everyone visiting Bosnia should try it." He poured with a heavy hand and, two drinks later, she did not even notice the burn as the clear liquor slipped down her throat. She stopped counting after three.

The toddlers had long since departed, proving—yet again, she had thought—that the younger generation simply did not have the sinew for this business. Now, as she stepped outside and took a staggering step in the direction of her hotel, she decided that perhaps they were just smarter. *Five-minute walk*, she said to herself. *No prob.*

The streets were eerily quiet, and the hotel was straight down the road with no turns. She was within sight of the building when a man wearing a hoodie approached, walking swiftly toward her. She shifted to her right, giving him room to pass, but he mirrored her movement. Her senses dulled by the alcohol, her brain flashed the warning a second too late. She saw the long blade swing up and felt the punch as it plunged into her lower abdomen and ripped upward, slicing into her intestines and stomach. She let out a groan and her knees began to collapse, the searing pain coursing through her body. He grabbed her around the torso, holding her tight as he drove the knife into her side, twisting it to collapse the lung and rupture the aorta. She slipped to the ground, her eyes open and confused and her brain function dimming as the man tore the camera satchel from her shoulder and fled.

Lying on the walkway, the blood pooling beneath her, Toni's last thought was that she wanted her mom.

Chapter 7

August 16
Sarajevo, Bosnia and Herzegovina

The courier was scheduled to pick up the classified diplomatic pouch at the embassy at 6:00 a.m., in time to make the flight to Vienna at 7:40. Agreeing that the pouch was the quickest and most secure method of sending the DNA sample back to the States, Cat and Pat rose early.

"We'll take a walk when I get back," Pat told Cat. "Your meeting with the asset is set for eight o'clock."

Cat picked up the tissue with a pair of tweezers and dropped it into a small, brown paper bag. Pat drove to the embassy, carefully boxed the paper bag, addressed the box to Paul Marshfield, stamped it as classified, and delivered it to the pouch room. The young man on duty dutifully recorded the receipt and added it to the canvas bag. The bag would be closed and sealed before leaving the embassy, with the courier accompanying it on the flight to Vienna and on to Washington.

Cat tapped out a message to Melodie and Paul.

> Sending sample today via Dip pouch.

She sent a second email to Melodie, attaching the photo of the man from the coffee shop.

> Who is this?

Closing out of the mail program, she realized she had missed an opportunity and reopened the mail. She composed another message to Melodie, attaching several photos taken at Sretna Kafa.

On second thought, run all of the faces in these photos.

Waiting for Pat's return, Cat felt a moment of unease about the upcoming meeting with the asset and the possibility that she had been followed the previous evening. Years of working in the shadows had taught her to pay attention to those feelings. She grabbed a bright blue scarf from her bag and wound it around her neck, then checked the contents of her tote to verify she had everything needed to alter her appearance.

When Pat returned an hour later, they left the apartment and set off through the old part of the city, on their way to At Mejdan Park. After a few blocks, Pat paused at a large open space, Baščaršija Square, and pointed out the magnificent wooden fountain in the center. "We have time," she said. "Take a look around."

Designed in the 1700s, the structure's octagonal kiosk was mounted atop several layers of stone. The stone formed steps leading up to two fountains, with their adjoining basins jutting from the base of the kiosk. Cat had seen such fountains before in her travels through the Middle East, in public squares and in front of mosques. Historically, travelers had found them at crossroads, and Muslims often used them to wash before prayer. Cat speculated that some still did, as this fountain sat only steps away from the Baščaršija mosque.

As they left the square, Cat turned toward Pat and said quietly, "I read the file you sent me on the guy we're meeting, this Mirko Stefanović," Cat said slowly. The name refused to roll off her tongue. She pronounced it twice more, trying for the correct sound. Satisfied, she looked at Pat. "Now, give me your take on him."

Pat took a deep breath, composing her thoughts. "As you've learned, he's Croatian, but has lived in Sarajevo since the mid-1980s. He is well-connected and has friends on both sides of the ethnic divide. He's provided valuable intel over the years and even sent an alert that a local ISIS cell was planning a suicide attack at the embassy. His warning saved a lot of lives."

"Yeah, got that. But tell me what's not in the file. How did we land this fish? Discover he had two wives? Find out that he has stolen millions from the Bosnian government?"

"None of the above," Pat said, looking squarely at Cat. "He came to us."

Cat stopped in her tracks. "He what?"

"Hey, it was before my time. I inherited him."

The revelation stunned Cat. Certainly, there were occasions when people volunteered to supply information to the CIA. Their reasons were generally political, driven by some wrongdoing—real or perceived—within the country's government or industrial complex. Such people genuinely wanted to help right the wrong. But more often, operatives from the Agency set their sights on specific targets: people whose information could be bought or traded, or people who had secrets they did not want exposed. It could be a dirty, ugly business, but it yielded results.

"You won't mind if I make my own assessment, will you?" Cat asked.

Pat arched an eyebrow. "Ha!" she scoffed. "As if my answer would make any difference."

Her face pinched in thought, Cat asked, "What have you told him about me?"

"Only that something has come up in one of our investigations, something that we're hoping he can shed some light on. I made it sound like you're a desk jockey bureaucrat."

"Perfect," Cat said.

They crossed the river via the Latin Bridge, an old, arched stone bridge from the Ottoman era, to the park on the other side. Mejdan Park was lush, densely shaded, and tranquil. Birds chirped, the leaves rustled, and she could barely detect the whoosh of cars passing on the other side of the river. Cat remarked on the beauty of the setting and its calming effect.

"Once upon a time, not so calm," Pat said, pointing in the direction of the bridge they had just crossed. "Archduke Ferdinand was assassinated just over there, just beyond the end of the bridge."

Cat's eyes widened. "As in the assassination that triggered World War I?"

"The very same. This entire region has a long and tortured past. I sometimes wonder if they will ever manage to bury it. Don't get me wrong, I love it here. The people are wonderful, and I love their spirit. But even today, I can sometimes feel a current running through the place, like it's just waiting for someone to flip the switch." Pat shivered and rubbed her arms.

Cat nodded, knowing that emotions and memories ran deep in this region of the world. "Yep. We Americans only have a couple hundred years of feuds between political parties to worry about. These people carry grudges for centuries."

"Tell me about it," Pat said, shaking her head in frustration. "It will never end." She sighed and pointed her chin toward the meticulously restored music pavilion. "Unless you need me here, I'll just leave you to it. Go sit in the back, at one of the umbrella tables. Keep your hat on and order two Bosnian coffees. He'll come to you. You know where to reach me if something comes up."

Cat grinned and said, "Okay, Mom."

Chapter 8

Mirko Stefanović was tall, about six-two, with deep brown eyes, a two-day stubble on his chin, and shaggy hair that had probably once been light brown but was now the color of weathered concrete. For a man in his early fifties, he was also very fit—his pale blue, skintight knit shirt revealed a modest six-pack and bulging biceps. As he approached, Cat noticed a slight catch in his gait, as if he had an arthritic knee. His smile was warm and handshake firm. Cat thought he seemed composed and relaxed, with no outward sign of nervousness. *A good start*, she thought, *but let's see if it lasts.*

"Ellie Lamberton," she said, introducing herself.

The formalities complete, Mirko pulled a chair from under the table. As he sat, the leg of his pants hitched up and Cat realized that he was wearing a prosthesis. He met her eyes for an instant, then ordered a beer from the passing waiter.

Turning to face her, he said, "I lost leg in war." He gestured toward the trees, and said, "Meet in park not so good. Embassy office better."

His English was ragged. Cat could piece it together but would have to be careful. Like most Slavic speakers, he dropped the leading article before the noun. *I lost leg. Meet in park.* It would be easy to misinterpret what he was trying to say. But more striking was the irregularity of the conversation. From an American, his words would be taken as criticism. But with the language gap, it was not as cut and dried. Still, the warning bells were clanging in her brain, *This is a man who likes to be in charge. He wants to lead this conversation. Why? Because he thinks I am just an underling? Cultural differences? Gender issues? Or something to hide? Well, let's just see where this goes.*

She kept her face composed and decided to play the subordinate as she replied, "My boss suggested that we meet in a public place, away from the embassy, for your protection."

He seemed to mull this over before replying, "It is good."

She smiled. "This is such a lovely city. I understand you have lived here for a long time."

"Yes," he replied. "Is complicated place, but beautiful. Sarajevo have much history."

"What brought you here?" she asked.

"My friend come here after university, for job. He like very much. I decided come here, like him."

"You are Croatian, correct? Was your friend Croatian?"

"He Bosnian, but we were much brothers."

"Were?" Cat asked.

"Killed. During war."

Cat lowered her head respectfully.

"I'm sorry. It is incredibly painful to lose a good friend."

Mirko flicked his hand, as if brushing the thought away. "Long ago. Why you bring me here? Ask about my friend?"

Cat caught a hint of annoyance in his voice. *Why such a short fuse?* "Not unless there is something that I should know," she said.

"No. But I give same answers, many times, to other Americans. I do not know what you want."

She decided to play into his sense of superiority. "A few questions have come up. I have to be able to answer them to my boss's satisfaction, so I'm hoping for your insight."

The tension seemed to dissipate as he mentally built a case that Ellie was an underling, just checking off the boxes on a form. Begrudgingly, he replied, "Humph. Is okay. Ask."

"Several years ago, we looked into reports that a coffee shop in the old town was actually a front for an illegal operation. You helped us. Do you remember it?"

He showed no reaction. "Yes, Sretna Kafa," he said.

"Did you actually know the owner?"

"He was, what is word ... um ... acquaintance."

Cat noticed that he did not actually answer the question.

"I've read the file, but could you just give me your personal thoughts on the business? What might have caused someone to report illegal activity?"

"Ah," he said, relaxing his shoulders. "You see, they have coffee shop. And also bakery. They send pastries to many hotels and restaurants here. They have jealousy, I think, from other businesses."

The mention of a bakery took her by surprise. There was something, but she could not put her finger on it. "So you think that competitors were jealous, and so they spread the rumor? Why?"

"They losing money, so wanted to end Sretna Kafa."

"So other bakeries were losing business to them. Can you give me their names?"

He frowned, then looked up toward the sky, as if seeking an answer. "Not here now."

"Not here? They went out of business?"

Nodding, he said, "Yes. Out of business. Kaput."

Cat smiled at Mirko, wanting to put him at ease. But her antennae were bristling. The man had answered questions with only the barest of details. Walk-in assets were generally eager to provide more information. She trusted her instincts, and her instincts were telling her that something was not right.

She had a sudden inspiration. "Perhaps I could talk to the bakery manager? Perhaps ask him a few questions?"

He straightened, suddenly attentive. "Is just bakery with many baking pans and ovens. Maybe not possible. They busy, and English not good."

"You could always translate for me," she said.

He said slowly, "I will discover if possible."

She smiled brightly and said, "No pressure, but it would help remove the cloud over Sretna Kafa and put these rumors to rest. Don't you agree?"

Cat kept the smile plastered to her face until Mirko disappeared behind the pavilion, then dropped the pretense. She put on her glasses, stood slowly, picked up her tote, left the table, and walked at a leisurely pace for about fifty yards. The glasses were custom-designed by a friend in Paris. They had cost a small fortune but were worth every penny. The lenses themselves, when removed from their frame, looked as if someone had taken a bite out of the outer bottom corner and replaced the voids with two gold-colored, sparkle-crusted embellishments. Any person facing Cat would see only bling. But on the inside, there was a mirror coating that allowed her to see what was happening behind her.

The reflections in the mirrors could be a dizzying distraction, initially making her nauseous whenever she wore them. With time, her brain had adjusted to the unaccustomed input. Now she let her peripheral vision track movement at her rear. She picked up her pace and, as she walked, pulled off the blue scarf, slipped on the jacket, and tied the charcoal-colored hijab over her head to cover her hair.

Crossing the bridge, she spotted Mirko at the other end, moving fast. She picked up her step, determined not to let him out of sight. He headed into Baščaršija, where she had just walked with Pat, but headed into the bazaar itself. The bazaar's maze of streets was lined with tiny cafés and shops. The stalls were brimming with traditional copper pots and spices, as well as all manner of modern goods. For the most part, Cat found the stalls indistinguishable from one another. The walkways were bustling with shoppers and tourists, but it was not as choked as the Grand Bazaar in Istanbul or the souks in Marrakesh, where visitors jostled one another as they tried to navigate through the crowd.

Cat varied her speed, sometimes farther back and sometimes closer, working to keep a wall of people between them. At one point, he turned around suddenly and eyed the street behind him. Knowing that a sudden turn or movement disturbed the visual flow and captured attention, Cat kept moving. She was only fifty feet away when, at last, he resumed his walk. It was impossible to know if he had recognized her. She abandoned the immediate surveillance and turned down a side street, deciding to run a roughly parallel course to his direction of travel. She would have bet her paycheck that he was headed to Sretna Kafa,

As she walked, she slipped off the jacket, reversed it, put it back on, and traded the hijab for the beige cap. Seven minutes later, she found herself just north of the coffee shop. She took a street-side seat at a small outdoor café and pulled the camera out of the tote. She tucked it into her lap, not wanting to draw attention to herself, and pretended to be absorbed in her phone. Without actually facing Sretna Kafa, she kept the entrance in her field of vision. She ordered a coffee and pastry and was beginning to think that she had misjudged Mirko's destination when he stepped out of the shop, the sick proprietor on his heels. She dropped a few coins on the table, stood slowly, stretched her back, and made a slow turn in their direction, camera at her hip. *Click, click, click.*

The men were hustling down the street, talking heatedly, with arms waving and heads shaking. At that moment, Cat would have given anything to hear what was being said. She watched as they turned right, out of sight. Cat took off and, passing the narrow side street, glimpsed the doors closing on a dusty gray sedan. Moments later, the car sped by.

Spinning around, she waved frantically at a nearby taxi, while trying to keep an eye on the gray car.

"English?" she asked the driver when he pulled up beside her.

He nodded. "Da." He wiggled his hand back and forth in the universal gesture. *Some.*

Not wanting to worry the driver, she willed herself to be calm. Then she opened the door and climbed into the taxi. She pointed at the sedan, held up in traffic at the next corner. "Please follow that car," she said.

He turned and looked at her, wide-eyed. Then he broke into a grin and stepped on the gas. *Everyone wants to play spy,* she thought.

Following the sedan, they headed east, out of the city, but not on the main highway. Instead, they turned north, looping and climbing around the hills and then speeding south, then north again, until Cat's sense of direction was scrambled. All she could say for certain was that they were going steadily upward. They had lost sight of the gray car, but there were few turnoffs and no evidence that their quarry had taken one.

Hoping for a swatch of gray paint through the foliage, she swiveled her head from right to left and found nothing. The phone in her pocket vibrated and she ignored it, concentrating on the search. They crested the hill and found themselves in a clearing, with the mountain dropping off to the right. The road was visible below, snaking in and out of the trees. She expected to catch a glimpse of the sedan, but the road was empty. In a flat, treeless landscape she might have seen a dust trail, but here, they could stumble around for hours and find nothing. The driver looked in the rearview mirror and raised his eyebrows in question.

She cursed silently, aggravated at having lost her quarry and frustrated that she had no understanding of what secrets they were hiding at Sretna Kafa. "They are gone," she sighed to the driver. "Please take me back."

The phone vibrated again and, annoyed, she almost let it go. Relenting, she picked it up. And gasped.

Toni Swanson killed. Come to office.

"Scratch that," she ordered. "Take me to the American Embassy." As an afterthought, she added, "Please."

Mirko had spotted the taxi behind him—trailing him since leaving the coffee shop—and had taken a more circuitous route. After looking once again in the rearview mirror and, satisfied that he had lost the tail, he glanced over at Goran. "You are sick. You should not even be at the shop. Your daughter should handle the business. We agreed, after Istanbul, that you would keep a low profile, yet you continue to disregard our wishes. Now the Americans are focused on you again! I do not know what caused this latest surge of interest, but you must stay out of sight."

Goran turned toward him, his face a mask of pain and sorrow. "When I am gone, there will be no one to manage Daris. He is an angry man. I worry about what he might do. But now I am tired, and I can do no more. It is time."

They drove up into the mountains, the narrow road twisting painfully between the trees, until reaching the clearing. The tan-colored building ahead was plain, minimalist, unwelcoming, a small sign its only concession to the outside world. *Mountain Kafa*, it read in faded red lettering, with the word *Pekara*—bakery in Bosnian—beneath.

The entire scene would have had no appeal, had it not been for the drool-inducing aroma of baking bread, roasted nuts, and simmering fruit. The scents wafted through the air, mingling in a delicious tease of the senses.

Mirko parked on the side opposite the entrance. He hustled Goran in the back door that led directly to the office suite, where Goran had an office and they would not be seen. He eased the frail man onto a small sofa in the office and laid a shawl over his lap, then stepped into the hallway. He looked back at the gaunt man, a shell of his former self, pale and out of breath after a distance of only twenty meters. The stage-four lung cancer was relentlessly consuming Goran's life. *He is right,* Mirko thought. *It is time to end it.*

Chapter 9

In the sanctum of Pat's office, Cat asked, "How? When?"

Pat sat behind her desk and rubbed her forehead. "Stabbed, last night. The police are calling it a mugging. Thing is, they only took her camera bag. She had a Breitling watch on her wrist and a wallet, stuffed with cash, in her jacket pocket." She looked steadily at Cat. "Sound like a mugging to you?"

"What are you saying?"

"You were wearing her badge. You went to Sretna Kafa with that badge and took pictures. You bear a close resemblance to her. Need I say more?"

"You think they were after me." Cat said it as a statement, rather than a question. She slumped into the chair across from Pat's desk, absorbing the news. *Not good. Is it possible that I'm responsible for Toni's death? Yes. Not only possible, but probable.* Her stomach roiled. She reached into the tote and retrieved the badge. "This needs to be destroyed."

Pat stood and poured a glass of water from the side table, handing it to Cat in exchange for the badge. Turning it over and staring at Toni's photo, she said, "I'll take care of it. God, talk about a great cover gone wrong."

Cat closed her eyes and shook her head slowly. "Yeah. I never saw it coming. The question is, what triggered it?" She took a deep breath and frowned. "It has to be the pictures I took last night at Sretna Kafa. What else could it be?"

Pat tapped her pen on the desk. "Don't be too hard on yourself. That's only one answer, that there is something, or someone, in one of the photos you took. But she could have been working on some story that got her into trouble. Or maybe she unknowingly snapped something she was not supposed to see."

"Maybe. But there was also the guy you thought was following me. I sent all those images to Melodie this morning. I haven't heard back, but Toni's murder puts a different light on it. I'd like to run those pictures by some of your people here."

"Good idea. I'll set it up for later today. How was the meeting with Mirko?"

Pressing the heels of her hands into her temples, Cat said quietly, "When I suggested a visit to the bakery, it rattled him. He went straight to the coffee shop after our meeting. Next thing I know, he and Goran jumped into a car. I managed to snag a taxi and follow them into the hills, but lost them. All I know is that they went somewhere northeast of the city."

Pat knitted her eyebrows. "The bakery is up there. Let's take a look." She turned to her computer and pulled up the satellite imagery of the area.

The images were only two months old, taken during the summer when the trees provided a canopy for many of the structures in the hills. The bakery, however, was situated in a clearing, fronted by a parking lot and abutting a cluster of smaller buildings. Cat was surprised by the size of the facility. "Big place," she said. "What are these small buildings?"

"Housing. Most of the staff live on the grounds."

Staring at the images, Cat noticed an anomaly, hard to detect, but a shape in which the edges were just a little too sharp. She squinted at the screen. *Man-made.* Pointing to a group of trees near the complex, she instructed Pat to zoom in. "What is that?"

From a distance, the object blended in almost perfectly with its surroundings. The close-up view gave an entirely different perspective. Pat's eyes opened wide. "Is that a camouflaged satellite dish?"

"Yep. And portable. You can just make out the edges of a trailer," Cat said.

Pat toyed with the image and said, "And not just one." She pointed out two more dishes.

Cat studied the screen and asked, "Nobody caught this?"

"Obviously not."

"How big is their operation?"

"They supply a couple of major hotels in the city, and some of the upscale restaurants. Their pastries are quite good, actually."

"How many employees?"

"About thirty, mostly immigrants."

"Immigrants? Huh. From where?"

"Refugees. From Syria."

Cat froze, stunned, the words striking a chord. Bosnia, the bakery, Syrian refugees: all these elements had been present in the original investigation into Maggie's accident.

"I need a secure line," she said. "Now."

Minutes later, she was in a secure communications room, in a videoconference with Melodie and Paul. "There is definitely a connection to Maggie," she said, explaining about the bakery and its ties to Syria. "I heard about this bakery and Syrian refugees when we were interviewing people in Istanbul. That cannot be coincidence. At the moment, I haven't a clue what they are hiding. Whatever it is, someone is going to great lengths to protect the secret."

Paul held his composure, but the pain was etched in his face. Cat quickly moved on.

"There's more. A woman was murdered last night, a woman who looked enough like me to be my sister. I don't want to go into the whys and wherefores right now, but I am convinced that whoever murdered her was after me. They have probably figured out the mistake by now."

"Are you in danger?" Paul asked.

Cat licked her lips. "Maybe. I'm not sure. I came here, spur of the moment, because of the picture that Lindsey found. Now I have tripped some invisible wire—probably like Maggie did—and triggered a domino effect. I just don't have a clear understanding of how the pieces line up."

"What do you need?" Paul asked.

"A team, official. There are too many unknowns, and we could get caught with our pants down. If something goes haywire, I don't want the team to suffer the consequences. Frame it in the context of national security—that we have discovered a potential ISIS cell here, and evidence points to its involvement in Maggie's death."

"Sign-offs should not be a problem. No one is going to look me in the eyes and refuse," he said. "Who do you want over there? Adrian? Arnie? Gabe? Jones? Jazz?"

Adrian and Jazz were special agents with the FBI, Jones was FBI counterintelligence, Arnie was an electronics and surveillance expert contracted to the CIA, and Gabe was one of the world's most skilled software hackers. They were all part of a clandestine, compact, multiagency team led by Cat and Paul. The team's primary mission was to prevent, deter, and disrupt terrorist activity targeting the interests of the United States and its citizens. The parameters of their mandate, however, had been known to be flexible.

Paul is correct, Cat thought. *They would never refuse him on this. Maggie was family.*

Cat thought for a minute before replying. "Let's start with Adrian and Arnie. My initial thinking was to keep Gabe stateside. The Bosnians are no fools. When we announce ourselves, they will be on the lookout for our cyber sleuth. Gabe has a reputation that would put him squarely in their crosshairs. With that said, we may need his talents here. If we are official, the most they can do is deport him. So yeah, let's bring him along. Talk to Arnie about equipment. At a minimum, we will want to surveil the bakery. It's remote, so we will need a drone. Audio and thermal imaging would be helpful."

Paul responded immediately. "I'll set up the plane and arrange a diplomatic container for the drone. We do not need complications with getting equipment into the country. You'll need a place to stay; Melodie will work on that."

A tiny crease flared on Cat's forehead, a tic that meant she was going to refuse Paul's suggestion.

She let out a long breath. "That's already been taken care of," she said. "But there might be an issue with the name I used to enter the country."

"Should I ask?" Paul asked.

"No," Cat replied.

They were on the verge of disconnecting when Melodie held up her hand. "Wait."

They watched as she typed on the keyboard at her right side. "Bingo," she said. "Hang on a minute."

Melodie's expression was inscrutable as she studied another monitor on her desk. Suddenly, her eyebrows shot up.

"Whoa! Holy moly!" she exclaimed. "Last night, Cat sent me a picture of a man at the coffee shop. I just got a hit. The guy is GRU."

The GRU, Russia's military intelligence agency, was known for its aggressive tactics—including sabotage and assassination.

Trying to absorb this new information, Cat's forehead creased in puzzlement. *Was the encounter random? Or did he somehow recognize me and decide to follow? Worse, did he know I was coming? Was Toni killed because of me?*

"What's his name?" she asked.

"Grigory Kornilov, according to his profile. But this is about the thinnest file I've seen. He's not a young man, so we should have more on him—a lot more. I'll send you what we have and keep digging."

"Grigory Kornilov," Cat repeated, rolling the name around on her tongue. "Not familiar, but Russia is not really in my wheelhouse."

"There's more," Melodie said. "There were several other people in the picture, so I ran those as well." She shared the photo on her screen and zoomed in to a table at the rear of the shop. "See the woman in the yellow blazer? And the man at the next table, opposite the woman?"

Cat leaned forward, memorizing their features. The woman was pretty. Striking, actually. Cat had seen them in the shop, but only in profile. The man, at first glance, might have appeared handsome—probably because of his strong chin and wavy black hair. But on closer observation, Cat could see that his eyes were too close together and his face pinched. He evoked an image of someone who spent too much time in front of a computer.

"The woman is a Russian socialite named Antoniya Davydova," Melodie added. "But the guy is DIA. It could be that the Russians were following him and he's just a naive tourist, but that seems unlikely. It feels like a meet."

Cat's eyes narrowed, and she pressed her lips together, digesting this piece of news. An employee of the US Defense Intelligence Agency meeting with a Russian socialite? In Sarajevo? She folded her hands and tried to put the pieces together. *Why had the older man, Kornilov, been there? Is the woman his protégé? His mistress? Or had he been surveilling her? What have I stepped into?*

"Before we put anyone on an airplane, I need a few hours to go over all this," Cat said. "I want a clearer picture of what we might be getting into. Give the team a heads-up and tell them to be ready."

Chapter 10

August 16–17
Sarajevo, Bosnia and Herzegovina

Mirko shut the door to Goran's office and stepped across the hall. Daris Terzić was sitting at his desk, wearing a T-shirt that exposed an ugly scar on his neck. Daris looked up, annoyed at the disturbance.

"What is it?" Daris asked.

"Goran is in his office. I am sorry, but we need to shut down the operation. There are questions being raised. A journalist was nosing around the shop last night. Today an embassy official wanted to know more about the previous investigation. We need to execute our escape protocol."

Daris grimaced, then nodded. "When can you leave?"

"In the morning. I have some unfinished business to take care of," Mirko replied.

Daris's eyes narrowed, expressing his displeasure. "Is it the girl? You should never have become involved with her."

"She arrived yesterday, without telling me that she was coming. What was I supposed to do?"

"She's bad news, Mirko. She's Russian."

"I'm in love with her."

Her name was Antoniya. Mirko had met her eight months earlier on an unseasonably warm evening at Sretna Kafa. He had been sitting outside, alone, cradling a coffee and reading a two-day-old copy of the *New York Times*. She had taken a seat at the next table, leaned his way, and asked, "Vaat do you recomment?"

He had been charmed by the accent, with the *wh* in *what* becoming a *v* and the *d* in *recommend* becoming a *t*. He had decided that she must have assumed he was American, because of the newspaper. He had been charmed even more when he raised his eyes. Antoniya was take-your-breath-away beautiful, with a head of long, wavy hair and ample breasts that a man could lose himself in. His pulse had quickened.

"Their house blend is very good, but strong," he had replied with a smile.

Antoniya had stood and walked to the counter to place her order. Mirko had noticed that she was fashionably—and expensively—dressed. When she returned, he had asked her if this was her first time in Sarajevo. She had giggled, asked him if he would like to be her tour guide, and his heart had melted.

Daris groaned. "You know how this is going to end? It's going to end with you begging her to marry you and her laughing as she goes to bed with someone else. I've known women like her. She will never be content with just you."

His face reddening, Mirko hissed, "Let me worry about that. You just make the call."

Daris sighed and pulled the burner phone from his pocket and dialed his brother Zlatan. He waited for the call to be picked up, then said in Bosnian, "You're on speaker. I'm here with Mirko. We need to push up the timetable. How close are you?"

Zlatan replied, "Our last test was more successful than we could have imagined. We need to insert additional security protocols and run one more test before we deploy. Two weeks, at the outside. What is the urgency?"

"We can't wait that long. Time is short. You have twenty-four hours at the most. Twelve is better."

After a long pause, the response came. "It is foolish to rush this." The anger in the voice was palpable.

Daris would have none of the argument. "If we delay, we run the risk of having the project uncovered prematurely or, worse, having to abandon it completely. We have to move quickly. Wrap it up!"

The response was chilly. "Is there anything else?"

Daris thought for a moment and made a decision. "Our brother is failing," he said softly. "He is in constant pain."

After a pause, the voice said, "He has suffered enough. Do what you must."

Mirko nodded to himself. Goran was a liability, that much was certain. As his illness had progressed, he had grown confused and increasingly short-tempered. And he had said that he no longer wanted to live.

The man on the other end of the line, however, was of even greater concern, having become more volatile with each passing day. Hiding from his past and carrying a heavy burden of guilt and remorse, the man had lived a lie for most of his adult life. He had not seen Goran for years. Despite what had been said, Mirko worried that Zlatan might completely unravel when Goran died. *Hang on, my friend,* Mirko thought. *I will be there soon.*

After Daris disconnected the call, Mirko said softly, "I have the cyanide for Goran. Do you want to be there?"

Daris hung his head for a moment before answering. "No. I would be compelled to stop you. Just make sure he does not suffer."

Mirko retrieved Goran's coffee mug, filled it halfway with water, and walked back to the reception area. He opened the middle drawer of the desk—a desk that had never been occupied. The amber-colored bottle was still there, just where he had placed it weeks ago. He opened the bottle and sprinkled some of the white, sugary-looking powder into the mug, wiped his prints from the bottle, and returned it to the drawer.

He slipped quietly into Goran's office and spent a few moments gazing at the man, who was now fully reclined and drifting into sleep. He sat on the edge of the sofa and cradled Goran's head in his right arm, then placed Goran's hand around the mug and tilted it to his lips. "This will take away the pain," he said softly. Goran's eyelids fluttered, then closed again. He watched the liquid stream into Goran's mouth, and held him tight when the convulsions started.

After Goran stilled, Mirko draped a shawl over his body, closed the door, and went back into Daris's office. "He is gone," he said. "Now we must proceed."

The two men stared at each other for a drawn-out minute, knowing that their long and troubled partnership had reached an end. Finally, Daris nodded. Mirko would handle the technical aspects of the shutdown; Daris would manage the human assets by adding a strong sedative to their dinner. They stepped into the hall and went in opposite directions. They would be out of the country within hours.

Daris walked briskly into the reception area and opened the drawer where Mirko had stored the cyanide. He looked over his shoulder to ensure that Mirko was out of sight, then grabbed the bottle. He unbarred the heavy door that led into the bakery. The women who worked in the bakery were never allowed into the offices—not under any circumstances—and the bar across the door did an admirable job of keeping them out. The door popped open and he breathed deeply, the aroma filling his nostrils. *I will miss this,* he thought.

He turned into the large kitchen, where three women were preparing dinner: two large kettles of stew known locally as Bosnian Pot. "Good afternoon!" he said jovially. "We have decided that you should all take the afternoon off. Gather the women. Tell them to fill their lunch buckets. Goran and I will take care of the ovens."

He shooed them out of the kitchen and leaned over the pot. "Mmmm! Delicious!" he called out, waving the steam toward his nose with his left hand. And with his right, he poured half of the amber bottle's contents into one pot and half into the other.

The women began lining up to fill their dinner buckets. When everyone had taken their share, he ushered them out of the building, where they waited on the lawn for the men.

After leaving Daris, Mirko walked down the hall and punched a code into the door in the coatroom. He heard the *thunk* as the lock released.

The long room in front of him was full of men, all hunched over their keyboards. The only reaction to his entrance came from the two people who sat in the middle of the room, in an elevated, soundproofed glass box separating them from the workers. A red light had illuminated inside the enclosed space when Mirko opened the door, and both occupants turned their heads toward him. Mirko waved and stepped onto the thickly padded, sound-absorbing floor. As he made his way forward, the soft whir of computer cooling fans was barely discernible. None of the workers looked up. They knew better.

A glass partition slid open, and he stepped up and into the "Treasure Chest," as they called it. The entire operation was managed, and tightly supervised, from this room.

The partition closed behind him and he said, "Shut it down. Send the data and then shred everything. No trace."

Despite months of trying, Daris and Mirko had been unsuccessful in learning the true identities of the man and woman in the box. Like most hackers, they protected their identities with ferocity. They were known only by their online monikers of "Khartoum" and "Blue Vanguard."

If Khartoum and Blue—as Mirko called her—were surprised by his announcement, they gave no sign. Mirko wondered if they were accustomed to such abrupt changes because volatility in the workplace was the norm in the software business, or if they simply did not care.

He looked at Blue. "How long will it take?"

She replied, "Uploading recent files will be quick. Shredding the data on all the internal and external drives? Maybe two hours."

Her hair was as black as the night, board-straight, and hit just above the collarbone. The style accentuated the severity of her face. She was a striking woman—not beautiful, but someone who caught one's attention. When she had first arrived in Sarajevo, he had asked her out to dinner. She had rebuffed him without an excuse or hint of remorse. The woman's command of English was excellent, but not native, and Mirko had often puzzled over her unfamiliar accent.

Khartoum was unequivocally American and an admitted chocoholic. He had a mop of curly brown hair that brushed his chin and bounced with every movement. A sloppy dresser who was consistently late with a shave, his appearance made a statement about his disdain for convention. He was exactly what everyone imagined a geek to be: quiet, socially awkward, and brilliant. Most of the architecture of the bakery's computer network was his doing.

The two had been thoroughly researched, not only for their coding skills, but also for their willingness to thwart the law. There had been five original candidates, all of whom had been anonymously recruited for the job. Two had declined without any discussion. A third had accepted, then backed out a day later after learning more about the project. He was killed two days later by a hit-and-run driver. The money had won over the remaining two.

Mirko said, "Signal me as soon as you are finished here. You will need to leave the country, tonight. Activate your emergency communications protocol. Your final payment will be processed tonight."

He did not reveal that all of them could easily be on an Interpol Red Notice within the next forty-eight hours. The risks had been evident from the start. Now they would simply have to manage. Mirko could not help but wonder if they, too, awaited a hit-and-run. He shook their hands and exited the box. Blue followed and began snatching devices from desks.

Khartoum, having planned for this eventuality, remained at his computer. He had, over the last few months, grown increasingly uneasy about the nature of their work—activities that were far from what had been described when he took the job. But by the time he fully understood their plan, he was trapped. Fleeing the country or alerting the authorities were not options. He knew that he was being watched and was certain that his apartment in town was bugged. He had heard rumblings about what happened to those who tried to escape. And he had already committed enough cybersecurity sins that would never be forgiven in a court of law.

Nevertheless, he was determined to make amends. He had spent his spare time over the last two months secretly working on a special software package. He had finished it ten days ago. He was fully prepared. All he could do now was hope that someone smart would find it.

Mirko stepped out of the Treasure Chest and announced to the men that there was some maintenance work to be done and that he was giving them the remainder of the day off. Their wives were meeting them outside with the dinner buckets. The outside grounds, however, were off-limits, as a crew would be laying out poison for rats. Everyone would be confined to their quarters until morning. The men, cheered by the unexpected gift of a few hours free, followed him out of the room and through the outside door to the lawn.

Daris and Mirko carefully watched the men and women as they trudged into their tiny apartments, then began barring the doors. As they did every night, the two of them worked from the ends of the building toward the middle, so that anyone trying to escape would be caught between them. They were three doors away from completing the job when two couples bolted, running at full speed toward the rear of the complex. Mirko shouted at Daris, who sprinted back to the office. He emerged seconds later, bearing an AK-74M assault rifle, and opened fire.

Mirko shouted, "No! No!" But he was too late. Killing the staff had never been part of the plan they had agreed upon. But Daris was a hard man with a short fuse, and his anger ran deep. He had never been easy to control, particularly with regard to the bakery's vile business and the part he had been forced to play. Horrified, Mirko felt the sweat break out on his brow. With the sound of gunfire and four bodies to manage, their situation had just become infinitely more precarious.

He secured the three remaining doors and was turning back when he spotted movement: a woman peeking around the corner of the shed. He shouted at the woman, coaxing her back. But Daris, alerted, sped after her. The woman, carrying her child, stumbled and fell. Daris was on her in an instant. He grabbed the little girl and shoved her into the shed, the woman pleading frantically. He held the door open, waiting for the woman to make the decision: save herself or protect her child. Tears streaming down her face, she hung her head and walked into the shed, where she scooped the child into her arms. She looked up at Daris and begged him to let them go. He slammed the door, dropped the barricade to lock them in the shed, and strode back to the bakery. When he returned, he was carrying two shovels.

Mirko and Daris completed the gruesome task of burying the two couples, returned to the office, stripped, and took turns in the small shower by the toilet. After washing off, Mirko changed into a spare shirt and pants that he kept in Goran's office. Daris scrubbed his clothing, hung it in his office, and wrapped himself in a towel.

One hour and forty minutes after issuing instructions to dismantle the operation, Mirko got a terse message from Blue.

Task completed. Goodbye.

He responded quickly.

Leave now. Use the front door.

Mirko stood and faced Daris. "Safe journey," he said. "Perhaps we will see one another again." He paused, then said, "I am deeply sorry—for everything."

Daris waved his hand dismissively. "Get going. You do not have much time. Let me know when you are safe." He watched the dust swirl as Mirko's car crunched over the gravel. He hung his head for a moment, then went back into the building. Pausing at the door to his brother's office, he took a deep breath, and then turned the knob.

Over the last few months, Goran had appeared to always be in pain, his face a complex pattern of wrinkles and grimaces. Even now, he seemed to find no relief. The only blessing was that his death had been quick. He kissed his brother lightly on the forehead and smoothed the blanket over his body, then turned and left the room. He gathered his few belongings, turned off the power, locked and barred the front entry, walked to his car, and drove to the gas station at the foot of the mountain. After filling the car, he got on the highway.

Mirko sped down the mountain and was home in twenty minutes. He threw open the door to his apartment and called for Antoniya, who ran to his arms and lavished him with kisses.

"We have to talk," he told her. "I have to leave the city, and I can never come back." He noticed her look of shock and said, "I have done some bad things, things that I am ashamed of, but that is over now. I only have some business to take care of and then I want you to come with me."

Antoniya's eyes widened. "Where are we going?"

"Vietnam," he replied. "We can live in Ho Chi Minh City or on the beach. Daris has contacts to help us, and we would be protected from extradition."

Antoniya tried to hide her dismay. *Vietnam?* She knitted her eyebrows and adopted what she hoped was an expression of concern. "Will it be safe? What about money?"

He waved his hand in a dismissive gesture. "That is part of the business I have to take care of. Do not worry," he said.

She trailed him to the bedroom and, following his lead, packed her suitcase. She waited for him to tell her more about the business he was taking care of, but learned only that he was flying to Toronto in the early morning.

"I could go to Toronto with you," she suggested. "Then we would be together, and I would feel safer."

He shook his head and pulled an envelope from his jacket pocket. "No. It will be better if we travel separately. Here is a paper copy of your e-ticket. The flight leaves midafternoon. It is not an easy place to get to, and it is a very long trip. But you will be comfortable with a seat in first class. And I got you a credit card for any expenses."

She looked at the platinum card in his hand. "Are you sure that we should do this? Is there no other solution?"

He reached for her and cradled her head against his shoulder. "There is no choice," he said.

Early the next morning, Antoniya woke as Mirko was dressing to leave for the airport. He leaned over her, ran his fingers through her hair, and whispered that all would be fine. He explained that the man in Toronto had something that was worth a lot of money. Mirko would convince him to sell it, and they would both make a fortune. Antoniya held him tightly, wished him luck, kissed him goodbye, and promised to be on the plane that afternoon.

After Mirko left, she showered and dressed, then waited for the shops to open. At nine-thirty, she grabbed her passport, two credit cards, and her phone—leaving her other documents and belongings behind—and walked to a nearby clothing store. She found two outfits, two scarves, and a drawstring tote bag. After changing into one outfit, she put the other in the tote, along with her own clothes. She used her own card for the purchase, then found a shoe store nearby. Selecting one pair of shoes to wear, she dropped the second in her tote, along with her old shoes. As the salesgirl turned away, Antoniya shoved her phone under the cushion on the bench. Then she found a rubbish bin and dumped her old clothes and shoes.

Antoniya had done enough work for the Americans to know that their capabilities for tracking people should never be underestimated. She had, on occasion, slipped microscopic devices into pockets, shoes, purses, and wallets and had never been detected. She reasoned that someone could be tracking her, too. She was not going to take any chances.

She visited the local bank from which Mirko had obtained her new credit card and took a substantial cash advance. The bored teller did not give her a second glance. She found an ATM, withdrew the maximum from her own account, flagged a taxi, paid cash for a ride to the airport, and found an accommodating airline agent who changed her Vietnam ticket for a routing to Moscow. Then she strolled to the Turkish Airlines counter and paid cash for a second ticket. She bought bottled water, along with several packages of snacks, and boarded a flight to Istanbul.

Daris drove all night, traveling southeast thorough the mountains and hills of Bosnia and Serbia, and over the plateaus and plains of Bulgaria. The sun peeked over the horizon just as he crossed the border into Turkey. On the opposite side of the highway, the inspection point at the border had created a logjam of trucks going west. The backup stretched for miles, and he was glad he was not going in that direction.

He waited until early afternoon to make the call. His voice was soft as he gave the news to his brother. "Goran no longer feels pain," he said. "He is resting peacefully in eternal sleep."

Zlatan bowed his head, silently mouthing a prayer. A few moments later, he asked, "Where are you?"

"Turkey. I drove all night and want to get through Istanbul before I stop. The more distance I can put between me and Sarajevo, the better. I still have a few days of travel. I will contact you when I can."

Zlatan Terzić laid the phone gently on his desk, smothering his urge to throw the device against the wall. *I should have been by Goran's side, not here,* he thought, cursing at the situation he was in and hating Mirko and Daris for their part in it. He bunched his hands into fists and pressed them hard against the desktop, his knuckles turning white at the effort.

It had not always been like this—the distrust, the hatred, the violence. There had been a time, a lifetime ago, when he had known joy. He had endured hardship, to be sure, but he had lived an existence in which people had cared about one another, in which people of differing beliefs had managed to coexist and find compromise in the face of disagreement. Or maybe he had just been—as some of his associates put it—naive about what had been in front of his face all along.

How have I come to this? Once, I could have walked away. How did I not have the courage to end it? Because, he told himself, *I was young and hurting and angry. And naive and foolish. And now it is too late.*

He sat heavily in the plush leather chair, trying to remember exactly when, and why, he had sold his soul.

PART TWO

Zlatan

1980 – 1993

FORMER YUGOSLAVIA, CIRCA 1980

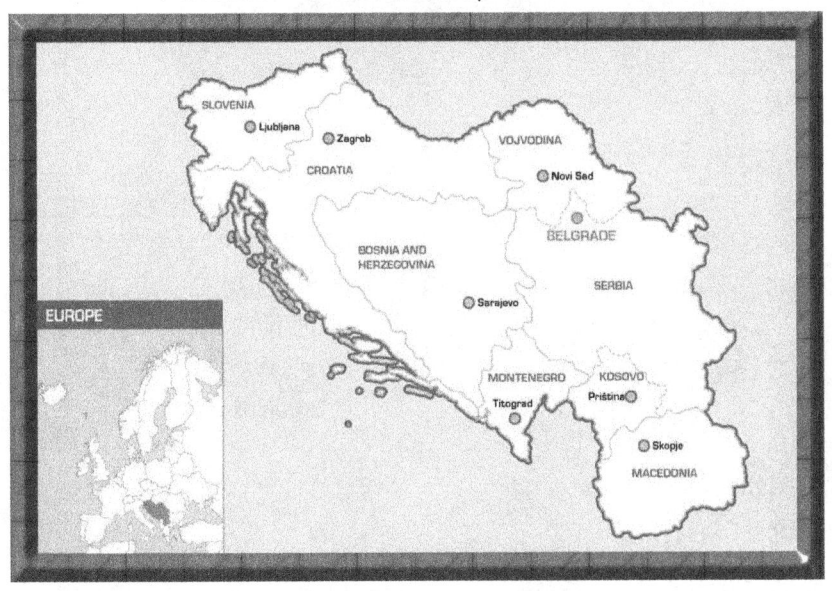

BOSNIA AND HERZEGOVINA, 2020

SARAJEVO VALLEY, JANUARY 1994

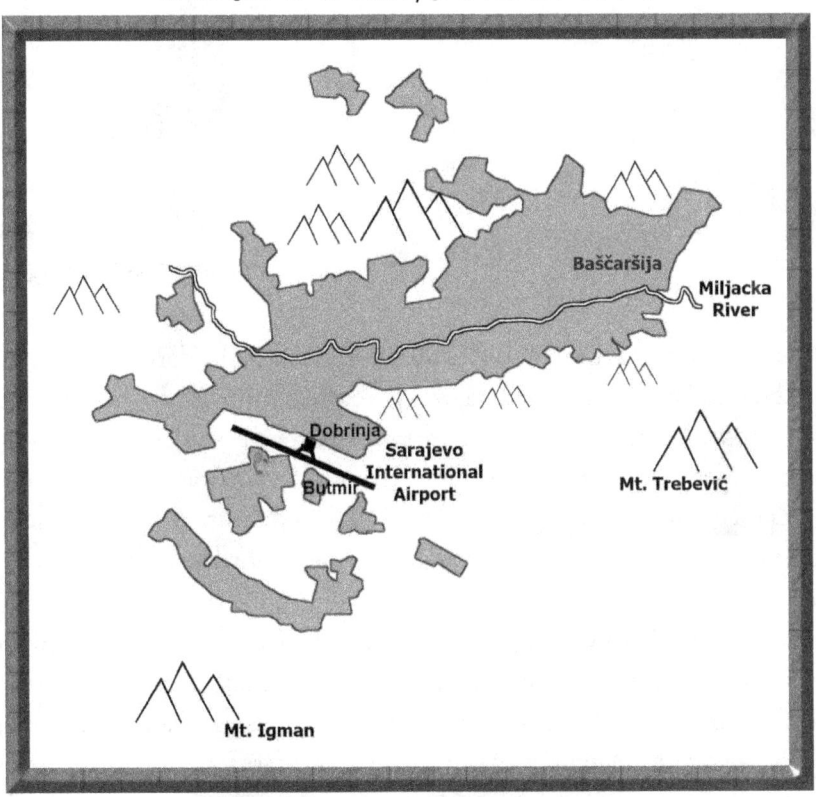

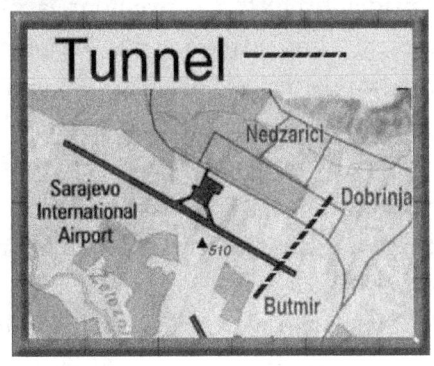

Chapter 11

1980–1981
Newport News, Virginia

In the summer of 1980, Zlatan Terzić checked a large suitcase and boarded an airplane in Sarajevo. Like the hundreds of other teenagers across the globe selected as foreign exchange students, Zlatan was wildly excited about the adventure. His destination was Newport News, Virginia, a town in America. He had read all the literature, yet still felt he was stepping into the unknown. *America.* How much of what he had heard was true?

Sarajevo was hardly a major airline destination. Even less so was Newport News. As a result, the routing between the two cities required several stops. The first and second legs—from Sarajevo to Belgrade and then on to London—were on Yugoslav Airlines. An hour later, he was on a British Airways flight to Philadelphia. After a five-hour layover, spent clearing Immigration and Customs and exploring the terminal in a land quite different from his own, he boarded an Allegheny Commuter plane.

At 11:20 p.m., after almost twenty-two hours of travel, he stepped off the tiny commuter aircraft and onto the tarmac in front of the rundown terminal at Patrick Henry airport. To his surprise, he was greeted by a crowd of enthusiastic students and their parents. In that moment, he knew he would enjoy his time in America.

Zlatan marveled at life in the United States. He was initially bewildered by the Americans and their overt familiarity. He was astounded by their ignorance of international affairs, as if there was no world outside of Newport News, Virginia. But he also saw displays of the quality that had, for years, made them so admired. They had a strong sense of fair play. They stood up for what they believed to be right and were not afraid to voice their opinions.

He attended Homer L. Ferguson High School, experiencing what most of his fellow countrymen could only dream of. His sponsors, Dr. and Mrs. Jonathan Meade and their only son Chip, showed him moneyed America: the stately columned house overlooking the James River, sailing the local waters, dinners at the country club, expensive cars. Dr. Meade, a trauma surgeon, worked in Portsmouth and suffered the long daily commute through the tunnel beneath the waters of Hampton Roads. For a long time, Zlatan entertained the idea of studying medicine, believing that all doctors in America must be very rich. Only later did he learn that Dr. Meade's wealth came from family money.

At first, he found his new life to be overwhelming. Americans were so open, so direct. There seemed to be no question that could not be asked, no part of his personal life that could not be probed. They were curious about everything, and incredibly outspoken. No topic was off-limits—not religion, not politics, not one's personal viewpoint. And they had an appetite for fun. It seemed that there was a party every weekend—if not at the Meades', then at the home of one of Chip's well-heeled friends.

He quickly learned that America was truly the land of opportunity. The American girls swooned at the sight of him: light ash-brown hair, tall, athletic, handsome, and a smile that melted hearts. They were entranced by his polite manners and his uncertainty with the nuances of the English language. They loved his sexy accent and swooned at his frosty-gray eyes that were reminiscent of waves breaking on a stormy sea. They smothered him with attention.

Zlatan eventually fell into the company of Suzie Thomas, a cheerleader and the most popular girl in school. A witty and gregarious redhead, she zeroed in on him within weeks of his arrival, tidily dismissing other hapless pursuers and claiming him for herself. He marveled at his luck.

A virgin when he set foot in the United States, Zlatan was stripped of his innocence in short order. He succumbed to Suzie's considerable charms and his own aroused sexual appetite on a chilly October night, while the elder Meades were spending a weekend in New York. After gulping two Heinekens from his father's stock, Chip quietly led his girl of the moment to his room and locked the door. Zlatan remained frozen on the couch, uncertain of the next step. Suzie solved the dilemma for him, taking him firmly by the hand and leading him back to his bedroom.

He was shy, blushing furiously as she first stripped him, and then herself. The blush turned to rapture shortly thereafter as he let Suzie guide his hands and his heart. He would forever remember that first time: the taste of her mouth and the fire of her flesh against his.

Zlatan and Suzie remained an item through the winter and into the spring, until the day of his departure back to his homeland. Sitting in the passenger lounge at the airport, tears streamed down Suzie's face as she whispered her goodbyes.

"An ocean cannot come between us," she whispered.

"I love you," he murmured. "I will come back, and we will be together forever."

"I will write you every day!"

"Every day, I will also write," he vowed. "But I will also save money and find a way to call you every week!"

He climbed the steps to the aircraft and looked back at her beautiful face just before crossing the threshold. He choked back tears, found his seat, and pressed his forehead against the window for one last look. But she was already gone.

Chapter 12

1981–1990
Sarajevo, Socialist Federal Republic of Yugoslavia

Within days after his return to Yugoslavia, Zlatan received the first letter. A steady stream of mail appeared for the next two weeks. But when he made the first call, Suzie seemed distant, as if a wall had come between them. He wrote her, as promised, every day. The return flow, however, dwindled steadily, before ceasing altogether a month later.

His next two calls to the States were answered by her mother, who claimed that Suzie was studying at a girlfriend's house. Zlatan knew it was a lie. Suzie rarely studied, and never with another girl. He later learned, from Chip, that Suzie had moved on to another, more geographically suited, conquest. Initially, he was devastated, then bitter, about the failed relationship and vowed to never allow another woman to steal his heart. He accepted a spot at the University of Zagreb and threw himself into his studies, concentrating on mathematics and simultaneously earning a reputation as a bright star in the emerging study of computer engineering.

Zlatan's friendship with the Meades, by contrast, flourished over the next few years. They exchanged letters frequently, and the family flew into Yugoslavia on three occasions. Their first visit came in 1984, for the Winter Olympic Games. On the day of the Olympics' closing ceremony, Dr. Meade pulled Zlatan aside and gave him two bulging envelopes.

"German deutsche marks and Swiss Francs," the doctor said. "Keep some for emergencies and use the rest to fund your studies."

Wide-eyed, Zlatan stared at him. "This is crazy! I cannot take this money!"

"Yes, you can. You have become part of our family."

Zlatan was quiet for several moments, his dreams for the future battling against his pride. His parents were not wealthy. The money would allow him to finish his education. "I will find a way to repay you," he said.

The doctor shook his head and gripped Zlatan's shoulder. "No, this is our gift to you," he insisted.

Zlatan swallowed hard, blinking back tears. "Thank you."

Dropping his hand, the doctor said, "I will try to get more to you, but the situation is, well ... let's just say it is challenging."

Zlatan nodded. Yugoslavia had laws about transferring money in and out of the country. The doctor had taken a risk to carry so much cash. "This is very generous, Dr. Meade."

The Meades' second visit came in 1986, to celebrate Zlatan receiving his advanced degree from the university; and the third, in 1990, following Dr. Meade's attendance at a symposium at the World Health Organization in Geneva.

On each visit, Chip brought news of former friends. He also brought a bag full of VHS tapes—the latest movies available. Zlatan was obsessed with all things Hollywood and reveled in the magic of movies. American movies also helped improve his English. His grasp of the language was nearly complete, his pronunciation almost flawless—he could even mimic an American accent. But he never told Chip that the United States and Europe used different recording and transmission systems. The US tapes were useless, except as currency on the black market. Zlatan sold them. He needed the income.

True to his word, the doctor brought additional cash on each trip. On the final visit, he pulled Zlatan aside, where others could not hear their conversation, and passed an additional envelope to Zlatan.

"A Swiss account, with enough money to get you clear and settled elsewhere," Dr. Meade said quietly.

Dumbfounded, Zlatan gaped at the account booklet and the amount of money shown in the deposits column—to him, a staggering sum. "But what is this? I have never been to Switzerland."

The doctor looked at him steadily for a few seconds. "There is something else I want to discuss with you. The chance for a new life, should it become necessary."

"What do you mean?"

Dr. Meade pursed his lips. "Let's just say I have informed friends who are expressing concern about Yugoslavia's future stability. With the region's history, I can see their point. We would hate to see a major conflict start here. I have told them about you. They admire what you have done with your studies in computers, that you have worked so diligently. And they, like me, are concerned about your future. They think that, if the situation here deteriorates, you could help each other. They will send someone to talk with you, to explain more. They would give you a passport—an American passport. This is a big deal, Zlatan. It's yours if you will talk with them."

Zlatan frowned, wondering how the doctor's friends could make such an assessment. His own experience with Americans had taught him that few would be able to pinpoint Yugoslavia on a map, much less have any understanding of its underlying issues.

His first reaction was to rebuff the offer, to say he could not imagine any circumstance that would lead him to abandon his homeland. But he had to admit that Yugoslavia was changing and that no one knew what tomorrow would bring. Each of the six socialist republics that made up the federation came with its own ethnic and religious makeup. Along with those divisions came biases and hostilities that had persisted for centuries. The unlikely union had led a largely peaceful coexistence for thirty years, all under the leadership of Marshal Tito.

Tito had run the country with a firm hand and was intolerant of dissent. Those who opposed his policies frequently suffered severe consequences, even death. It was a philosophy fully supported by Yugoslavia's next-door neighbor, the Soviet Union. There had always been a looming threat to the survival of the Yugoslav federation: that the Soviets would find reason to invade the country, as they had done to Czechoslovakia in 1968. But Tito had managed to keep the oppressive Soviet regime at bay—and had even acted in ways that infuriated its leaders. Contrary to Moscow's urgings, Tito allowed Yugoslavian citizens to travel freely, encouraged tourism, and maintained a neutral posture with regard to the Cold War.

Since Tito's death in 1980, however, cracks had been appearing in the country's veneer, and its citizens had been growing increasingly restless. When the communist bloc began to unravel in 1989, so did the Soviet

Union's hold on the Yugoslav states. With the threat of Soviet aggression effectively nullified, some Yugoslavs began calling on their fellow citizens to support separatism, declaring they would be better represented if they withdrew from the federation and could forge their own ethnically shaped nations. Tensions were high, and while Zlatan was hopeful that the various factions would find some compromise, he had his doubts. Still, he was proud of his country.

"I'm sure I will not need the passport," Zlatan said with as much emphasis as he could muster. "The people of Sarajevo are not so engaged in all this talk of ethnic nationalism."

Dr. Meade gave him a long, probing look. "It's good to be optimistic; hope is what keeps us going. But when someone comes to talk with you, hear them out. And if you receive a passport, keep it in a safe place and never tell anyone that you have it."

Chapter 13

1990
CIA Headquarters
Langley, Virginia

While Cat's territory encompassed primarily the Middle East and South Asia, the complicated makeup of the Balkan states and their proximity to Turkey made them a frequent topic in her circle at the Agency. There were few assets in Yugoslavia, and a number of very smart analysts were saying that the place was a powder keg. All that was needed was someone to light the fuse. Everyone agreed that a major conflict in the Balkans would be disastrous and that more local assets would be helpful in assessing the situation. There were, however, simply not enough volunteers.

When Clyde Banks—an experienced forty-something officer operating under official cover out of the consulate in Sarajevo—contacted her about a potential asset in Bosnia, she was elated. Then he dropped the bomb.

"I need a US passport for him," he said.

Cat's voice rose an octave. "You *what?*"

"Look," he said. "I got a tip about this kid, that maybe he would be receptive, but that a passport was needed to seal the deal."

"You got a call? From whom?"

"It was anonymous ..." He hesitated as he heard Cat clear her throat. He explained quickly, "Hey, I pegged him as a colleague who didn't want his name in the paper trail."

Cat frowned. Spies did not usually come into the fold via anonymous recommendations. But Clyde had always possessed good instincts. "Go on," she said.

"I figured he might be JSOC, probably out of Virginia Beach," he said, referring to the US military's Joint Special Operations Command. "Whoever he was, he knew things. And I got the feeling that he knew me, that maybe we'd worked together in the past. But I don't know who it actually was."

"Why the passport?"

"I detected an emotional attachment there, like there might be some personal relationship—not sexual, more like father-son."

"You know the drill—we don't hand those out like cookies at a picnic. You said he's a kid. What makes him valuable?"

"He works at the Assembly building in Sarajevo. He's some sort of computer whiz."

That drew Cat's attention. "For the government? Someone on the inside? Someone with access? Hmm. You've met with the kid? What else do you know?" Cat prodded.

"I followed him a few times; he definitely works there. And I've seen where he lives, but I didn't want to get too close. I believe he's a straight shooter. And he speaks English like a native."

"Now that's interesting. How did he learn?"

"Unknown. Like I said, I have the sense there is some relationship between this kid and the guy who called me."

Cat wrinkled her nose. *Personal attachments have a way of going bad,* she mused. "It's a big ask."

"It is. But we could use a set of eyes and ears on the inside. With all the talk of separatism, a lot of our old channels are drying up. They're running scared. I think we should take a chance. I went ahead and sent a photo in the pouch. You should have it tomorrow." he said.

Cat took a day to weigh the merit of the request. Clyde Banks had a maverick streak—his file was peppered with observations that made that clear enough—and he made no secret of his intolerance of bureaucratic bullshit. But in all other matters he was the consummate professional: well-respected, smart, intuitive, and he had brought in a wealth of intelligence. He had also successfully recruited several valuable assets during his tenure.

Still, Cat could not shake her feeling of unease. The kid had no training. His skills with computers notwithstanding, he might not be equally adept at covering his tracks. And if he were caught, the connection to Clyde could be trouble.

Clyde had been less worried. "He's a computer genius," he had told her during one of their calls. "The number of people who would have even a clue what he's doing is next to zilch. And he's one of those guys that people are naturally drawn to. They like him, so they talk to him. And yeah, he has seen my face. But he also thinks my name is Larry, that I have frizzy salt-and-pepper hair, wear glasses, speak with a drawl, and have a gold front tooth."

Cat laughed. Clyde had a way about him that encouraged people to support his ideas. Ultimately, on Clyde's recommendation and on the premise that the subject's position—inside the Yugoslavian government—had the potential to yield valuable intel, she made her pitch to someone with approval authority. She walked away with a signature.

Chapter 14

1990
Sarajevo, Socialist Federal Republic of Yugoslavia

Two weeks after Dr. Meade departed, a man snaked through the crowd and nudged into a space at the bar, elbow-to-elbow with Zlatan. He was middle-aged, average height, with a slight beer belly, and had mousy brown hair and red-rimmed brown eyes that spoke of too much alcohol. Zlatan ignored him until, beer in hand, the man turned to him and said, in English, "This is a great place! Reminds me of a hangout near where I live, in Newport News. That's in the United States, in Virginia."

Startled, Zlatan whirled toward the man. "What did you say?"

"Newport News. It's a great town. Been there most of my life," he said. "Ever been there? Oh, my name's Larry." He held out his hand.

Zlatan stared at him, then shook the proffered hand. "I'm Zlatan. You're American," he observed.

"Darn straight! How did you know? I'll bet it's my accent. Well, never mind."

The man was friendly, loud, and enthusiastic, all the things that had shocked, amused, and endeared Americans to Zlatan during his time there. He could not help but smile.

"Zlatan! Helluva name," the man continued. "Hard for us Americans to get a name like that right."

Zlatan laughed and shook his head at the memory—his classmates had rarely pronounced his name correctly. "I was in Newport News for a while, as an exchange student. Most of them called me *Zit*."

"*Zit*? Really? Kids are terrible. How long ago? How did you like it? A lot different than here, right?"

The man continued to babble, all the while gently guiding Zlatan away from the crowd and to a quiet table in an adjacent room.

The man asked about Zlatan's time in Newport News, probed his thoughts about the United States, asked questions about Zlatan's opinion of how Yugoslavia was faring, and nodded thoughtfully at the answers. "I think some tough times are coming," he said. "I hope I'm wrong, but the signs are there. You know, I care about this place. My grandparents were born here, in the middle of the country, near Tuzla. They immigrated to America when they were in their early twenties, along with their parents. I've visited their old home, met some of my cousins. I was touched, but there's a lot of difference between our worlds."

Zlatan thought that the man did not look particularly Yugoslavian, but then realized that his mother or father could have been from anywhere. Americans married for love and did not care so much about where you came from.

The man asked, "What kind of work are you in?"

"Computers. I work in the Assembly Building," he replied.

"That's a big building. Must be a big job."

"I like it. It keeps me busy."

The man's demeanor turned more serious. "I hear a lot of rumors. The people I talk to are worried. You must know more about what's going on. Are you worried? What are they saying behind all those doors?"

And just like that, Zlatan made the choice to step onto the CIA's dance floor. "What do you want from me?" he asked.

Chapter 15

July 1992
Sarajevo, Bosnia and Herzegovina

Dr. Meade and his friends had been right, of course. Within two years, Yugoslavia had devolved into chaos, and the entire country had become a war zone. The shelling of Sarajevo, a thriving stew of religions and ethnicities, had been at fever pitch for five long months, blasting people and buildings in wanton savagery. Upper-level apartments now sat deserted. Owners and tenants throughout the city lived together in the confines of basements lined with stacks of sandbags, which helped deflect the shrapnel and absorbed some of the shock from the shelling.

Other dangers lurked in the high hills around Sarajevo and the tall, modern buildings in the central part of the city. From their elevated positions, men with long-range rifles targeted the innocent, killing anyone unlucky enough to become the focus of a sniper's scope—men, women, children. Still, the citizens braved the streets, bolting from one sheltered area to another, and died for the simple act of trying.

By the time Zlatan realized the gravity of his situation, he was trapped. Telephone service had been disrupted for months, there was no electricity, and walking anywhere in the city could be terrifying. Driving was equally hazardous, assuming one could even find fuel. He knew of people who, paralyzed by fear, refused to leave their homes. Some had been killed by bullets and artillery that penetrated the walls of their bedrooms. There was no safe place in the city and no safe path out of the city. Each and every resident simply concentrated on trying to stay alive.

On a dreary morning in July, he pressed his back to the wall of sandbags and mattresses in the basement and listened to the dull thud of mortars striking buildings nearby, waiting for the screams that would inevitably follow. Mirko Stefanović, his best friend, huddled beside him.

"This is no way to live," Mirko said. "We have not had one moment of enjoyment in months. We should throw a party."

Astonished, Zlatan merely gaped at him. Mirko's imagination knew no bounds. He seemed to be always brimming with outrageous ideas, his extroverted personality at full throttle. They were similar in appearance—slender but muscled, fair-skinned, light brown hair, and taller than most of their countrymen. From a distance one might be mistaken for another. Close-up, however, their eyes told the difference. Mirko's matched his hair color, while Zlatan's eyes were a frosty gray.

They had met during the Olympic Games, Zlatan assisting with credential verification and Mirko lending his considerable local knowledge to the information center. Late one evening, after Zlatan resolved a dispute about Mirko's access, Mirko had invited Zlatan to join him at a local pub. Over several rounds, they had discovered a number of mutual interests. Both worked in government jobs—Mirko as some sort of clerk in the Ministry of Justice—and they shared a few hearty laughs over their misguided attempts to capture the attention of attractive women. They had formed a lasting and close friendship.

"It will be good for all of us," Mirko pressed. "We must do something, even this little thing, to remind us of who we are, what we had, and what we will have once again. I know of a place where we could go."

Mirko reminded Zlatan about an old, crumbling building in the center of town. It was rumored to have a large vault in the basement.

"Are you crazy? It's too dangerous! No one will come," Zlatan argued.

"Oh, sure, there is always a risk. But we would use the basement. I've heard of others doing it—they say it's bombproof. Come on, Zlatan! Why not?"

"Because someone might shoot us in the street? Or launch a mortar and demolish the part of the building that's still standing?"

Mirko shook his head. "We need to do this. For our sanity, if nothing else."

Zlatan reluctantly agreed to explore the idea, wondering if perhaps Mirko was right. The past five months had taken a terrible toll on the city's population, both physically and mentally.

The following day, they set out to examine the ruined building, working quickly through the streets, sprinting through the open spaces where snipers in the hills practiced their killing. They ran the final fifteen yards of the gauntlet at full throttle, gasping for air as they reached the collapsed entry. Exuberant at having survived, they picked their way through what remained of the old building.

Hit by mortars first, to weaken the walls, and then incendiary artillery to burn whatever was left, the structure had suffered extensive damage and had been abandoned months ago. But the huge vault in the basement had survived mostly intact. The underground space appeared to be sound, and it had obviously been used before. The stairway was clear, and there were a number of tables and chairs, damaged but still functional.

At Mirko's urging, and against Zlatan's own better judgment, they set the date for the following Saturday. They spent the next few days spreading the word.

And now, for the first time in months, he heard the sound of merriment, of people enjoying themselves. He descended into the basement, weaving through the crowd until reaching a table on the far side of the room. He slid into a seat next to Mirko and gawked at the commotion around them.

On this otherwise dismal afternoon, forty friends and relatives were laughing, hugging, and slapping each other on the back, glad to still be alive. They swapped horror stories about their recent experiences, exchanged condolences for those lost, and reminisced about life before the siege—all the while reveling in the opportunity to escape the reality of life in Sarajevo, even if just for an hour or two.

"Well," Mirko asked, "don't you agree this was a great idea?"

Zlatan smiled. "It would be much better if we had beer or wine, but yes, it is good to get together."

He leaned his arm on the table, cupping his chin in his hand. He watched the crowd, catching snippets of conversation, and let his mind drift. He had not had this feeling of connection, of camaraderie, for years. *I haven't seen a crowd having fun like this since my going-away party in Newport News,* he thought. His head jerked involuntarily. He had not thought about that gathering in more than a decade.

"Ah, you must be thinking about your wild times in America," Mirko said.

"Why would you say that?"

"Because you have that faraway, glazed look in your eyes."

Zlatan raised an eyebrow. "Really?" He drew a deep breath. "Sometimes it does seem like a dream. It was long ago and, now, so hard to remember."

"But it was good, yes?"

"Yeah, it was good," he said, "but now is even better."

"I think that love has addled your brain," growled a familiar voice.

Zlatan swung around, a huge grin on his face, and bear-hugged the speaker. "Daris!" he shouted. "You are here!"

Chapter 16

The middle child of the five Terzić siblings, Daris was widely accepted as the smartest of the bunch. His parents had scrimped for years to support his dream of studying abroad. They had been rewarded when he was granted a coveted scholarship to the University of Michigan. Proud of Daris's accomplishments, they believed that, of their five children, he held the greatest promise for the future. But Daris was also an outspoken supporter of Bosnian independence and, despite knowing that it would be a great disappointment to his parents, had recently joined the Bosnian Army.

Zlatan admired and envied his brother, who was everything he was not: committed in his beliefs, fearless, and full of lust for a fight. Nevertheless, he admitted to himself that he had no interest in following those footsteps. He found stimulation and challenge in his work, where he wrote computer programs to solve real-world challenges. And at night, he found comfort and pleasure in spending time with the love of his life.

He spent several minutes catching up with his brother, learning that Daris had moved into the field of intelligence gathering.

Mirko exchanged a glance with Zlatan, then studied Daris. Curious to know more, he asked, "Are you a spy?"

Quietly, Daris said, "I cannot reveal too much, even to you. Someday, I hope I can tell you all about it."

Mirko looked away, his disappointment obvious. Suddenly, he brightened and elbowed Zlatan, grinning wickedly. Inclining his head toward the door, he said, "The source of your consternation has arrived."

Zlatan turned in his seat and scanned the crowd. *There. Short, pale yellow dress. Brilliantly flowered knee-length jacket.* The woman tossed her head in glee at some remark from one of the revelers, and the long blonde hair fell back, exposing the perfect neck gracefully curving into the perfect face. Zlatan smiled and watched intently as he waited for the subject of his attention to notice him.

She chatted briefly with two other acquaintances before turning her head in his direction. She found him staring and flashed a broad smile. Zlatan grinned stupidly. She was the reason he had tabled any thought about trying to leave the city. He no longer thought only of himself. Imela Ganje was beautiful and the love of his life.

"Zlatan! I'm so sorry to be late," she said in a rush. "I stopped to buy flowers for Mother and started talking with Ejup. Well, you know how it is."

Ejup was a flower vendor. Zlatan had never known anyone who could talk so much on such a variety of subjects. The man was a walking encyclopedia. Unfortunately, his gift of gab deterred many people from buying his bouquets, and his profits from the business were thus negligible. No one was quite sure, in this city of destruction and deprivation, where he got the flowers to sell. Nor did they care. His stall was one of the few bright spots in an otherwise bleak landscape, and he remained a good friend to Imela.

Zlatan reached for her hand and pulled her close, inhaling the sweetness of her hair as he drew her face to his own. The party, memories of young love, and Imela's warmth washed together in his desire. He pressed his lips to her ear.

"I want you. Now. Let's get out of here."

"Zlatan! You are so naughty!" Imela giggled and pulled away. "I've only just arrived. Besides, I must talk with Hanka; her mother is very ill. And, there is someone I want you to meet."

He groaned in exasperation. Imela picked up friends the way a dog picks up fleas.

She laid the bouquet on the table. "Just a few moments," she said. "I'll be right back."

"Ten minutes. If you are one second longer, I will take you by the hair and drag you to your apartment, tear off your clothes, and ravish you in front of the cook."

Imela's retort was swift and well aimed. "Try that, and the cook will have an unusual offering for her next menu." She glanced downward at his crotch, then winked. He grimaced at the thought, then laughed and kissed her cheek. He squeezed her hand and whispered, "Hurry back." His eyes followed the sway of her hips as she walked away, a smile crossing his face. The "cook" was a joke they shared. Her parents had let the cook go months ago. There was barely enough food to survive, never mind putting on an elaborate dinner.

A decade after his adventures in Newport News, Zlatan Terzić was no longer shy. In the years since Suzie had broken his heart, he had sampled the wares of many women, firm and fleshy, eager and slow, sexy and sensuous. He learned that most women were cautious but curious and susceptible, and each wanted to be the one to capture him. They had all failed. He recalled few of their faces, and fewer of their names. No matter. He had been satisfied with these short relationships, and they had served his needs well.

Friends had been amazed that he still had his manhood intact, having envisioned some jealous lover taking her revenge after a torrid, but badly ended, affair. Zlatan had shrugged off their concerns philosophically. "If it happens, it happens. In the meantime, carpe diem—seize the day. The Soviets could invade us tomorrow, but I will have enjoyed myself. What will you have to remember?"

Then he had met Imela.

On a gray and chilly Saturday in March, he had stopped at Ejup's stand to purchase a bouquet for his landlady. He had politely lingered longer than intended, enduring another of the old man's tales. He was listening distractedly, shifting his gaze from one side of the street to the other, when he heard Ejup squeal in delight.

"Imela! You have made my day complete!"

Glancing sideways, he could see little of Ejup's friend. She was wearing a drab, shapeless raincoat with a voluminous hood. He might have excused himself then, had not a gust of wind blown the hood from her head. Fate dealt him a winning hand that day, for beside him was the most beautiful woman he had ever seen.

Her voice, when she spoke, sounded like a melody from the gods. Zlatan was instantly smitten. He pursued her relentlessly for three months before she finally consented to accompany him to dinner. It was another three months before he was able to coerce her into his bed. In all that time, he never once flirted with another woman. Imela was all that he might have asked for, and more.

Educated, well-traveled, gregarious, compassionate, funny, and a natural storyteller, Imela often regaled him with anecdotes from her life. Particularly hilarious were the tales of her brief adventure with Pan Am, in the eighties, when the storied airline had decided to open a flight attendant base in Dubrovnik.

She regaled him with tales of the training process in Miami, of serving pretend food and pretend beverages to pretend passengers in pretend airplane seats. She told him of the crazy rules they had about weight and how her friend, a world-class swimmer and the most fit woman Imela had ever known, was required to lose fifteen pounds or be ousted from the program. She described the hilarity of learning—in the hotel's pool—how to haul people into a life raft should the aircraft ever need to ditch in the ocean. She had viewed the job as a chance to see the world and travel for free, and had taken full advantage of the opportunity.

The adventure had not lasted long. Pan Am had closed the base, and Imela had returned to her studies. A keen student of human behavior, she was now a practicing psychologist.

And today, on this rainy afternoon, Zlatan basked in the sunshine of love. For the first time in his life, he felt complete.

He laid his hands on the arms of his brother and Mirko. "I'm going to do it."

"Do what?" they asked in unison.

"I'm going to ask Imela to marry me. Today. Here. With all our friends present."

Mirko's eyes widened, a big grin spreading across his face as he watched his friend lean over to pick up the small shopping bag on the floor. "This is fantastic!" he exclaimed. "I can't wait to …" He never finished his thought.

The two explosions occurred in quick succession, tearing through the vault's ceiling and blasting apart walls, tables, chairs, and people with equal abandon.

Dazed by the blast, Zlatan was momentarily disoriented. For a few long, terrifying seconds, he thought he was blind, the dust and smoke so thick it was as if his eyes were being sandpapered. He blinked rapidly, working to clear his vision, and tried to push himself upright, only to collapse from the searing pain in his left arm.

Zlatan turned his head and found Daris a few inches away, his eyes impossibly wide and his mouth opening and closing, like a bird expecting to be fed. It was then that Zlatan realized that his brother was trying to gasp for breath. Mirko was badly injured as well, his leg a pulpy mess, bringing with it the odd memory of Mrs. Meade mixing raw meatloaf.

Leveraging his good arm, Zlatan forced himself to his knees, furiously pulling his belt from his pants and looping it around Mirko's thigh as best he could in a crude tourniquet. He spotted the bouquet at his feet, its colors impossibly cheery in the midst of the carnage. Ripping away the wrapping, he laid the plastic over the gaping wound in Daris's upper chest. He tore his own shirt into strips and fashioned a wrap to secure the plastic, preventing air from entering the chest cavity. He had learned the basics of emergency first aid from Dr. Meade, and more desperate measures from dealing with the relentless bombardment of the city. But it was impossible to tell if any of his efforts were helping—there was so much blood.

As his senses returned, he found the scene erupting into chaos, with the injured pleading for help and a swarm of passersby responding to the desperate cries. He frantically pulled himself to his feet, the extent of the damage hitting him with devastating force.

"Imela!" he howled, terror engulfing him. "Imela! Where are you?"

The only replies were the moaning and screaming of the injured. Imela's voice, so sweet and melodic, was not among them.

Staggering over the rubble, he moved toward the area where he had last seen her. The remains of the dead and wounded, bloodied and burned and shattered and shredded, lay splattered across his path in a horrific canvas of gore.

There ... over there ... what is that scrap of yellow? And with sudden certainty, he knew. It was as if he had taken a brutal blow to his sternum, such was pain across his chest, and he found himself on his knees once more, gasping for breath, struggling for sanity.

Imela.

Chapter 17

August 1992
CIA Headquarters
Langley, Virginia

Over a two-year period, Clyde Banks's new asset had supplied a veritable treasure trove of intelligence for the Agency. He sent copies of paperwork and recordings of official meetings and photos from private ones. His reports were impressive, his analysis insightful, and Cat frequently included the information in her briefings.

But on a hot day in late August, Clyde called her with disturbing news: the asset had suddenly gone silent. After two missed reports, Clyde had gone looking but had been unsuccessful. Shortly afterward, with living in Sarajevo becoming more dangerous by the hour, Clyde had evacuated to Istanbul.

"Half of Sarajevo is in ruins," he told her. "The kid's apartment is pretty much destroyed. I asked people in the neighborhood, but they just shrugged. You have to see it for yourself to comprehend it ... everyone is displaced. There are thousands of people sleeping side by side with their neighbors in basements. There's no electricity and no fuel. I can't imagine what another winter will bring, with no heat and no food. The entire city is looking for someplace to go, for a place to sleep, a place with a roof, anything to feel safe. But there's no such thing. I tried hospitals and clinics but didn't find him. There have been hundreds of casualties. He's probably dead, and eventually I would have been, too, if I hadn't evacuated. I hated to leave, but, honestly, it's a relief to be out of there. I'll be having nightmares about it for a year."

"I'm sorry, Clyde. I know how hard it is to lose an asset."

"Something happened to him, Cat. He would not have just walked away."

Chapter 18

July 1993
Sarajevo, Bosnia and Herzegovina

Zlatan threw off the coverlet and sat upright, his body drenched in the sweat of his nightmares. The dreams were always so real, as if he could simply reach out and touch her again. But they always ended here, in a real world of cold and dark and terror. The religious zealots had it wrong. Hell wasn't fire and brimstone; hell was Sarajevo.

He swung his legs to the side of the bed or, to be more accurate, to the only space on the basement floor not covered by mattresses and blankets. They had burned the hardwood furniture months ago, chopping it into short splintered boards to heat food and water and briefly warm their hands against the bitter chill of winter. Nearly all sources of fuel and heat had been depleted, save for the one meager container of oil reserved for the lantern.

The city of Sarajevo lay in a long, slender, generally east-west-oriented valley—with the airport at the southwestern corner acting as a bottleneck. Bosnian forces held the territory beyond the airport, while Serbian forces occupied the hills and mountains to the north, south, east, and northwest. Their positions, and the hilly terrain, allowed the Serbs to maintain a choke hold on the city, as well as the high ground from which to target the citizens below. The airport, having been overrun by the Serbs at the start of the war, had seen little use in months.

With a deepening humanitarian crisis at hand, the United Nations finally reached an agreement with Serbian forces to have the airport designated as a safe zone, through which the UN organized an airlift to bring tons of food and medicine into the besieged city. While the relief effort brought supplies, distribution presented a major problem. Convoys carrying the desperately needed goods came under frequent attack. On those occasions when the convoys made a successful run into the city, the residents waited in long lines. They, and the personnel trying to save them, then became targets for snipers positioned in the hills.

The "safe zone" was by no means safe. Ten months earlier, a plane carrying relief supplies had been shot down on final approach. In the months since, flights had been curtailed. On the occasions when an airplane landed, it was because the aircrew had simply rolled the dice and won.

For Sarajevans trying to flee the city, salvation lay in the Bosnian-held territory beyond the airport. But the path to freedom might as well have been a flight to the moon. The agreement between the United Nations and the Serbs specifically prohibited passage for Bosnians, whether civilian or military. The Serbs on the hillsides had an unimpeded view down the length of the tarmac, and they held target practice on anyone daring to cross the runways. Yet, every night, desperate people tried to run the gauntlet across the airport grounds, struggling against the tangles of barbed wire and gambling their lives—and the lives of their children—against the accuracy of scope-equipped snipers.

Having endured the nightmare for almost a year after Imela's death, Zlatan had come to accept his fate. He could see only two choices: risk his life as a target trying to sneak through enemy lines, or slowly starve in the besieged city. He had lost over thirty pounds and his clothes hung loosely from his already lean frame. Then, he had begun to hear whispers of a tunnel being constructed—an underground supply route for food, fuel, weaponry, and people. His hopes lifted.

The tunnel's location was secret; it had to be. But he worked his friends, certain that someone would know someone who would know someone. Someone did, eventually leading to the right connection. He could get out of the city through the newly opened tunnel—for a price. He had paid, gladly, while silently thanking Dr. Meade for the money. The arrangements had been made—he would leave tomorrow.

Zlatan dressed, slipping on his boots and jacket before leaving the building. The day was dreary, like his mood, made worse by the steady rain. He tromped down the street, preoccupied with what he would say to his friend. He had not seen Mirko in over a month and was looking forward to a visit, yet dreading it. Farewells were never easy. This one was made harder because he had wanted to take Mirko with him, but Mirko's physical condition made it impossible—not just for traversing the tunnel but also for travel through the mountains.

That Mirko and Daris had survived the attack on the vault was nothing short of a miracle. The surgeons had stitched up Daris's throat and attacked the chest wound with tubes and drains and sutures. He bore horrific scars from the attack and spoke with a permanent rasp, but he was alive and—as far as Zlatan knew—back working for Bosnian intelligence. They could not, however, save Mirko's leg, leaving him to hobble around on crutches. Obtaining a prosthesis or wheelchair in Bosnia was the stuff of dreams.

In Mirko's apartment, Zlatan took a seat and, fixing his gaze on his friend, explained that he was leaving.

Mirko was stunned at Zlatan's news. "But where will you go?" he asked.

"Home. It's been difficult for my mother since my father died, and there has been no news from my brother Daris."

"And what are you going to do? Try to get through the lines at night? Across the airport runway? Do you know how many have died trying?"

Zlatan wanted to tell him about the tunnel, but had been sworn to secrecy. Instead, he said, "It's risky, I know, but every day in Sarajevo brings risk. Which is worse?"

"This war has changed everything. It may not go well."

Zlatan grimaced, conceding the point. He had heard the stories of murder and rape, of mass graves and extermination in other areas of the country. He looked at Mirko's worried face and decided to put his friend at ease. He told Mirko about the passport that Dr. Meade had given him.

"I will not take any silly risks. And if it does not work out, I will leave the country. I will go to America."

Mirko looked shocked. "You would go there? Think about what you are saying," he said acidly. "The Americans boast of being on the right side of justice and of always choosing to do the right thing. Instead, they have betrayed us. They have the power to end this war but are sitting on the sidelines, like Romans enjoying the sport of gladiators fighting to the death. It was *their* weapons that wounded your brother, that took my leg, that killed Imela. They have been supplying those who fight against us! They are *not* good people!"

It was not the first time that Mirko had spoken with so much venom about the Americans, not the first time that Mirko had blamed them for the attack. Zlatan had seen the damning reports—documents and photographic evidence confirming that the weapons had been American antitank missiles called Dragons. But the Americans had been vehement in their denials, insisting that they did not have such weapons deployed in the region and had not fired on any of the belligerents involved in the conflict. *Black market*, they had claimed.

Mirko cocked his head. "You are being naive if you believe what the Americans say. They look out only for themselves—for whatever serves their interests. They make promises and six months later switch sides and join the opposition. They cannot be trusted."

Zlatan accepted that there was some truth to what Mirko was saying, but shook his head. "But you are not seeing the larger picture. The Americans have been steadfast in their refusal to get involved here. They are still wearing the shadow of Vietnam. The war damaged their psyche, has made them afraid of getting involved in another drawn-out conflict that kills their people. So why would they suddenly decide to bomb a building full of innocent civilians? It makes no sense."

"What makes no sense is that you are talking about going to America—of living there."

"I am not sure. Part of me wants to teach them, to help them learn that they should broaden their perspective. They need to understand our suffering."

Mirko's eyes narrowed, and he gave his friend a penetrating look. "Would it not be better to teach them a lesson? To see them suffer as we have suffered? In this, I would be happy to help."

Zlatan picked up his rucksack and the paper he had been given—a tunnel pass from the Bosnian Army—and gave Mirko a firm hug. "Take care, my friend. I am praying that this will all be over soon and that we can live once again."

Standing on the stoop of the building, Mirko studied Zlatan's back as he walked away. *Our lives will never be as they were,* he thought.

Mirko stepped back into the building and closed the door, then navigated toward his bookshelf, cursing as one of the crutches snagged the worn carpet. He angrily yanked the crutch away, tearing the carpet further, rocking the haphazard stacks of books and sending a cascade to the floor. He collapsed into the old upholstered chair and railed silently at the forces that had led to his misery. *It was never supposed to be like this.*

Retrieving one precious sheet from the desk, he jotted down details of his conversation with Zlatan. He revealed Zlatan's acquisition of an American passport, arranged by Dr. Meade of Newport News, and closed by stating that there was no news of Zlatan's brother, Daris. It was assumed that he was either dead or had resumed his intelligence work with the Bosnian Army.

After folding the note several times, he slipped it into a small plastic bag. He picked up the paperweight, which appeared to be just a chunk of limestone about the size of a child's fist. But when the top and bottom were twisted, the carefully crafted rock separated and revealed a cavity the size of a billiard ball. He slipped the note inside, then screwed the fabricated stone back together.

Mirko pulled himself upright and hobbled out of the apartment and over to the small garden at the side of the house. He glanced around and, comfortable that he was not being watched, dropped the rock. Using one of the crutches, he brushed some of the soil onto the stone, making it appear that it had been there for some time. He hopped back up the steps and, struggling to maintain his balance, moved the flowerpot to the other side of the stoop.

Having left the signal, Mirko toyed with the idea of hovering by a window in hopes of seeing the messenger. He dismissed the thought almost as soon as it popped into his head—he had watched many times and never spotted the pickup. He struggled back to his apartment and collapsed into his chair, suppressing a sob.

He had been sent to Sarajevo with instructions to become Zlatan's confidant—to learn everything he could about his work and personal life. At the onset, it had been easy to play the role. Over time, however, he had grown to care about his target, thinking of him as a brother. And by becoming emotionally attached, he had broken a cardinal rule of tradecraft. Now, with Zlatan gone, he felt an overwhelming sense of sadness, mixed with a sense of relief. He would never again have to betray his friend. And now he could go home.

Chapter 19

Zlatan set off for Dobrinja, a neighborhood in the southwest corner of the city, just to the north of the airport. With almost six miles to cover, he was allowing almost four hours to navigate around the most worrisome spots for sniper fire. As he stepped out into the night, he said a prayer—his only protection against the random shelling.

The electricity was out, a common occurrence since the beginning of the war, but the moon was full, glinting off shrapnel and shards of glass in the streets. He walked briskly, sprinting across open intersections. Between them, he staggered his pace, occasionally even stopping for a few minutes, hoping to disrupt any sniper who might be following his movements with a scope. In the larger intersections, people had stacked wrecked cars and empty cargo containers in giant heaps, like a junkyard, to help hide the hapless pedestrians from the shooters above. The barriers were not perfect; there were gravesites to prove it.

Bosnian forces had taken steps to protect Sarajevo's citizens by digging trenches throughout neighborhoods and open spaces in the city. While the trenches did provide a measure of shelter from the snipers, they were less effective against the mortars. He flinched reflexively at the sporadic explosions—some distant, others uncomfortably close. Ten yards shy of the foot of the trench, his luck ran out.

BLAM!

The explosion shook the walls of the trench, sent stones rocketing, pummeled him with dirt, and knocked him to the ground. He fell in a heap, fortunate to have avoided a direct hit. Badly shaken by the close call, he checked himself for injuries and finally noticed a sharp sting on his scalp. He put his hand to his skull and it came away smeared with blood. He crab-walked to the end of the trench and then ran for his life. The fear and shock threw his adrenal glands into overdrive, his legs alternating between bursts of speed and periods of uncontrollable shaking.

Close to the airport, tracer fire painted pink streaks across the sky and mortar shells drummed dull thuds as they hit the grounds near the runway. By the time he approached his destination, an apartment building ringed by trenches and guarded by Bosnian forces, Zlatan's nerves were shattered. He stumbled, nearly collapsing into one of the camouflaged soldiers, before steadying himself.

"Show me your papers," the guard commanded, thrusting out his hand.

Zlatan pulled the tunnel pass from his pocket and handed it over, asking, "How much farther?"

Ignoring the question, the man examined the paper carefully, finally raising his head and handing it back. He waved Zlatan onward, where other men hustled him into the building. They led him to a room already occupied by almost sixty other travelers and their meager belongings. Another guard took the pass and bellowed Zlatan's name into a walkie-talkie—some sort of pre-clearance, Zlatan supposed.

The room was dimly lit by two oil lamps, their greasy smoke mingling with the clouds of smoke from black market cigarettes. Men and women sat in chairs, smoking and talking quietly, or leaning against one another with eyes closed, trying to sleep. A handful of children were sprawled across the floor in innocent bliss. One of the women studied him and then fished in her bag, extracting a jar of water and a small square of clean cloth. She stood and walked over to Zlatan, offering to clean the shallow furrow above his ear.

Dabbing gently at the wound, she asked, "Mortar or sniper?"

"Mortar. Close."

"You were lucky. It is a good sign for our journey through the tunnel."

Zlatan blinked. *Almost getting killed was a good sign?* He thanked the woman for her kindness, found a vacant space by the wall, and sat for a moment on his rucksack before leaning his head back and drifting into a light slumber.

He awoke with a start nearly two hours later to the sound of loud footsteps and voices raised in greeting. A band of fellow travelers—these coming into Sarajevo rather than leaving—tromped by, some stopping to speak with those still waiting. Minutes later, the group was led down to the tunnel entrance. They lined up, single file, and the line snaked forward. Approaching the dark, tomblike hole in the ground, his heart skipped erratically. He looped his rucksack over his shoulder, turned on his flashlight, lowered his head, gritted his teeth, and stepped forward.

Zlatan had been warned, as they had all been warned, about the tunnel's confining dimensions. But nothing could have prepared him for the suffocating claustrophobia that, fifty feet in, threatened to drive him mad. The tunnel was a little over three feet wide, in some spots just over two and a half. The width would have been tolerable if it were not for the height, which maxed out at five feet, eleven inches, and dropped to a pretzel-bending five feet, three inches. At six feet, two inches, he was forced into an uncomfortable crouch.

His neck and shoulders began to cramp after only a few hundred feet. He was tempted to turn around. He could not, of course. The tunnel was only wide enough for a single person and there was a steady stream of people plodding along behind him. He smacked his head on an overhead support, swore under his breath, and trudged on. The flashlights ahead bobbed with each footstep, the light dancing across the walls. Dug by hand and reinforced with rough-hewn timber and overhead metal beams, the tunnel stretched for a half-mile.

The tunnel dipped deeper as it neared the airport asphalt, threading under the runway at more than five feet beneath the earth. The line of people slowed as a message from those in front was whispered from person to person: "Remove your shoes." The soaking rain from the previous day had streamed into the lower sections of the passage. Zlatan soon found himself slogging through muddy, calf-deep water.

The air to this point had been ripe and musty—there was no ventilation—but now turned completely foul. He heard the sounds of retching in front of him and tasted the bile in his throat. *How much farther?* He willed himself to move, feeling ashamed. After all, hundreds of people made this journey every day.

The tunnel terminated in the cellar of a private home in the Butmir neighborhood. Spilling out of the house and into the Bosnian free zone, the travelers stretched and hurried on their way. Relief washing over him, Zlatan straightened to his full height. He stood for a moment, relishing the taste of clean air, and looked around to orient himself. His eye caught a weatherworn placard that some intrepid traveler had posted: *PARIS 1665 km*. Even in war, one can find humor.

Nearly all those who had accompanied him in the tunnel turned southwest, toward Mt. Igman and Croatia. He set off in the opposite direction, through the mountains and the enemy lines and the hidden trip wires and land mines that would tear a man apart. It took him eleven days to make the fifty-mile trip to his family home.

Chapter 20

September 1993
Goražde, Bosnia and Herzegovina

Zlatan expected his mother and siblings to be pleased that he had returned, but their happiness was overshadowed by the lack of news from his brother Daris. He had not been heard from for months and the family believed that he must be dead.

Conditions in Goražde were markedly worse than Sarajevo. Goražde had been under siege until last April, when the United Nations had declared the area a safe zone. But just as in Sarajevo, the term held little meaning. The Serbs still attacked civilians and UN personnel alike, shelling the convoys that brought food and medicine. The city was smaller and more isolated than Sarajevo, more easily controlled. Foreign journalists did not come here, the UN presence was skimpy, food was scarce, fuel nonexistent, and most of the buildings along the river were bombed-out ruins. The river was dotted with makeshift paddle-wheel generators that produced measly dribbles of power for the trapped residents.

Zlatan was in the barn—in the loft, stacking bales of hay—when he heard the commotion. He froze.

"Ти! Дођи!" a male voice shouted. The language was Serbian, the voices commanding someone to come over.

Who are they shouting at? he wondered, a flood of fear coursing through him. His mother and oldest brother, Goran, along with his family, had gone into town earlier in the afternoon. He had not seen them return. His sister, Zora, and his youngest brother, Vedad, had been at the edge of the woods harvesting mushrooms. *Where are they now?* He hesitated only a moment before dropping to the floor and belly-crawling closer to the hay door overlooking the yard. The barn had once been a source of familial pride, its boards tightly fitted together and smooth enough to rub your fingers over without getting a splinter. Now, the entire structure was falling apart, the wood decaying and split and warped—the result of too few supplies and too little money in a land plagued by war.

Peeking through a ragged gap between the planks, he looked down to see Zora and Vedad encircled by a group of soldiers. The men were dressed in woodland camouflage, the mottled dark greens and browns concealing their presence as they crept through the forested lands of the Bosnian terrain. Zora fiercely clutched Vedad's forearm, her lips parted, her eyes wide with terror. Zlatan's own heart was pounding so loudly that he thought the men would surely hear him and look up. But the men's heads swiveled casually, never giving the loft a glance. They pointed their guns at the duo and began to herd them away from the house. Angrily refusing to move, Vedad staggered when the stock of a gun smashed against his temple, then crumpled when another soldier kicked him in the buttocks.

Zlatan stuffed his fist in his mouth, suffocating the anguished roar that threatened to erupt from his throat and reveal his presence. His sister snarled, a rush of anger momentarily overcoming her fear, and spat in the face of one of her captors. A vicious slap silenced her screams and left her on the ground, dazed. Two men took her by the arms and dragged her toward the forest, while the others kicked his brother into submission.

He watched as Vedad tried to stand and then, succumbing to a barrage of kicks and blows, fell and curled into a ball on the rain-soaked ground. One of the soldiers pulled a rope from his gear and looped it around Vedad's neck. Using their weapons as prods, the men forced his brother to crawl on all fours, like a dog, in the same direction the other soldiers had taken his sister.

Revulsed by what he had witnessed and swimming in self-loathing for his lack of intervention, Zlatan nonetheless knew that there was little he could do. The soldiers were armed and held little moral conviction. The best that he could hope for now was that his siblings would somehow survive. He would have to be strong, stay out of sight, and be there to care for them in the aftermath. *Only a fool tempts the devil,* he reminded himself.

He watched closely, pinpointing the spot where they disappeared into the woods. He waited, remaining motionless and listening for any interruption in the stillness that ensued. Had any of the men remained behind? Surely they knew that the boy and the girl would not live here alone. Or perhaps, he realized, in the fallout of war, decimated families were simply part of the everyday landscape. He willed himself to wait. The sun would set soon, and darkness would be his friend.

Chapter 21

Eva Johansson Terzić urged her son into the car. The sun would set within the hour, and she did not want to be on the road after dark. She hated what had become of her adopted country, hated the war, hated living in fear of receiving news that something had happened to one of her children. For two years, she had worried about her sons Daris and Zlatan, living elsewhere and, with communications disrupted, rarely heard from. And then, by some miracle, Zlatan had appeared at the door—thin, dirty, unkempt, and haunted by tragedy, but alive.

Over the last few months, she had begun to feel increasingly insecure. While their house was well away from the main road and thus not on the path of soldiers patrolling the area, there were bands of soldiers everywhere. And Zlatan had brought money, foreign money, allowing them to buy a few supplies. Whether stolen or illegally bartered, some goods had been finding their way into Bosnia's new model of commerce. She did not splurge, however. Word would have spread, and that would have brought trouble.

Glancing at her oldest son, she was filled with the dueling emotions of pride and sadness. She could see herself reflected in the features of her two oldest boys. Goran and Zlatan had inherited her tall stature, light ash-brown hair, and fair skin. Their arresting ice-gray eyes had come from their father. But while Zlatan was generally well-liked and sociable, Goran had inherited his father's fiery temperament. Three days ago, his two-year old daughter had suffered a gash to her arm while playing in the loft. She and the toddler's mother had insisted that medical attention was needed. He had chosen to ignore them, until the wound, then the arm, turned puffy and red. She had finally prevailed, but worried that his penchant for standing up to authority would someday be his downfall. And in the country where he lived, it could be deadly.

Eva had felt uneasy about taking the car. No one drove now; there was no fuel. But there were four people to transport, and she wanted to be home before nightfall. *Daylight is dangerous enough, thank you.* She had several canisters of gasoline stored at the back of the barn—remnants from when the farm was active. The decision was made.

The drive into Goražde was uneventful. Thanks to Zlatan, she had enough money to convince a doctor to treat the injury—and enough money to pay for expensive antibiotics from a known black marketer at the edge of town. Even before Zlatan had come back, her family had been getting by. She was thrifty—careful with money and supplies—and had been ever since marrying her husband and settling in the country that had been Yugoslavia. But the doctor was worried about the wound, about the possibility of sepsis, and had insisted that the baby stay overnight. The mother demanded to stay with her child. Goran, however, had work to do. He would ride back to the farm with his mother.

The road was nearly empty, with few humans in sight, the sun just beginning to drop behind the mountains. She rounded a curve, and the blood in her veins turned to ice. Several soldiers were blocking the road with their vehicle, their guns held at chest level, the threat implicit. She had heard the stories, of course, of rape and murder, but had tried to put them aside and go about her business. It was possible that they meant no harm. And she had her own gun.

She hesitated for a moment, trying to decide what to do. It was a moment too long. As she threw the car into reverse, the men raised their rifles and fired.

"Are you hit?" she shouted at Goran.

"No! Go! Go! Go!" he shouted back.

Stepping on the gas, the tires screaming, she drove almost a quarter of a mile, then misjudged a curve and slammed into a tree.

"Out! Out!" she yelled at her son. "Run!"

"No! I'm staying with you!"

"No! Go! I'm coming!" But her door was wedged against a branch and would not budge. She saw Goran sprint away as she threw herself toward the passenger door, trying to scramble out of the car. Her foot caught in the footwell, and she fell to the ground, striking her shoulder. She had never taken her eyes off her son; he had reached the downhill edge of the forest.

"Run, Goran!" she yelled. "Run!"

In slow motion, she saw the soldier raise his rifle, aiming into the trees behind her, aiming at Goran. As she turned, she heard the sharp crack of a gunshot and watched, helpless, as her son fell and tumbled down the hill and into the woods.

The men shoved her into the back seat and rolled her onto the floor. Two of the soldiers climbed into the seat, pinning her with their feet. Another took the driver's seat, and a fourth the passenger's seat. She felt the car rock backward, then forward, and heard the roar of another engine close behind. They traveled a short distance and then turned up the hill. She heard the ping of rocks hitting the undercarriage and knew immediately where they were—on a dirt road not far from her house. She knew what they intended to do; she had been there before, in a different place, with different men. But these men would punish her for trying to escape, for having tried to save her son. Afterward, they would kill her.

She slipped her hand under the driver's seat, wriggled her fingers around the butt of the gun, found the trigger, pointed it at her face and, saying a silent prayer for her children, pulled the trigger.

Chapter 22

Zlatan waited over twenty minutes, until the sun dropped behind the mountain, casting the land in shadow. He slowly worked his way down the ladder and peered through the barn door, running his eyes over the property and finding the area empty of soldiers. He raced to the house and into the small dwelling, breathing a sigh of relief on finding it empty. His mother had not yet returned from the village. Her health was failing, more the result of his father's recent death than of any physiological malady. She would never recover if she lost her children as well.

He sprinted toward the trees at the edge of the property and spotted the furrows made by Zora's feet as she was dragged away. He followed the trail of vegetation disturbed and trampled by the soldiers, until he finally heard voices carried on the chill wind. He slowed his pace and crept deeper into the woods, his skin prickling with tension. He knew from experience that the soldiers would be difficult to spot. Their camouflage made them at one with the forest.

Glimpsing a clump of bright blue, he clenched his fists in fury as recognition dawned. His sister had been wearing a blue dress. A low, anguished moan drew his attention to a muddy patch between the trees. He caught a flash of pale flesh as a man, his clothing stained from the black soil, rolled off his sister. Another soldier eagerly pulled down his pants and lowered himself to the ground. Two others stood nearby, laughing and urging their colleague to finish quickly.

The men spoke in Serbian, but in their frenzy, he heard another language emerge. *English. Serbs speaking English?* And then another language that he did not immediately recognize. *Polish? No, not Polish. Russian?* The curious mix of words confused him. Were they Serbs who had picked up the English language along the way? Or Americans? British? Russians? In a disturbing realization, he peered more carefully at their clothes. *Not soldiers. Mercenaries.*

Zlatan did not see his brother, nor could he spot the remaining men. He crawled noiselessly to the base of a tree and rubbed dirt onto his face and clothing to help conceal his presence, all the while attempting to control his anguish and wondering if survival could even be possible.

Having lived through the cruelty of the siege in Sarajevo and the death and devastation he had witnessed while making his way home, he could easily have become numb to the brutality. Instead, he lay still, letting a wave of emotion flood over him, aching to recapture life as it had once been. His tears flowed freely, leaving crusty trails on his dirt-streaked face. Feeling an overwhelming desire to scream aloud, he bit hard on his fist. He had escaped war to return to his family home, and now the war had come to his very doorstep.

He wondered now if he should have stayed in Sarajevo. Dying there would have been easier than the anguish of seeing his family savaged.

The distant sound of gunfire interrupted his reverie. He flinched involuntarily and for a moment wondered if he had been struck. But he felt no pain. He jammed his dirt-encrusted fist harder into his mouth and pressed his face into the soil, silencing the sounds of his sobs.

The men took their time. Zlatan could hear his sister whimpering as she was repeatedly violated. And with each cry of pain, his hatred of these men grew stronger. It might take the rest of his life, but he promised himself that they would pay for their sins.

It was fully dark by the time the men finished their sordid assault. Laughing and hooting, they gathered their gear and their clothing and stumbled down the hill toward their colleagues.

Zlatan realized that it had been some time since he had heard sounds from his sister. He lay still, fervently hoping that she had simply lapsed into compliance, until the noise of the soldiers faded. Finally, he crawled toward the spot where he had last seen her.

"Zora," he called softly. "Zora! I am here!"

He ran forward in the dark, his hands groping the air, until he stumbled over what might have been a fallen tree limb. He fell to his knees and, reaching out to steady himself, planted his hand on the leg of his sister.

"Zora! Zora," he whispered frantically. "Wake up!" He ran his hands up her body, locating her jaw and pressing his fingers against her throat in search of a pulse. Finding none, he lifted her chin and pushed against her forehead to open her airway. *Airway, Breathing, Circulation*, he chanted to himself, as he registered the vile smell of her vomit. He tried his best to clear her mouth quickly, then sealed his lips over hers and gave two deep breaths. *Come on, come on,* he said in an anguished whisper. *Come on!*

Ten minutes later, Zlatan gave up the fight. He rocked back on his heels, cursing the men who had done this and vowing retribution. As he gently placed his hand behind her head to lift her torso, he recoiled in horror. Her hair and the back of her head were wet and sticky, and he immediately recognized the coppery scent of blood. The realization left him thunderstruck. The soldiers had hammered her head against a rock, crushing the back of her skull.

He carried her back to the house, a cold finger of dread snaking up his back as he approached. There were no lights, no sign that his mother and brother had returned. He laid Zora on the floor and wrapped a blanket around her abused body, grabbed a flashlight, and set off to find his brother.

Zlatan reentered the forest, taking measured steps. The beam from the flashlight illuminated the way, but the ground was rough and unstable and he could not risk a fall. He headed in the direction of the shots he had heard, knowing that the echoing in the mountains played tricks on one's ability to hone in on the source. Thirty minutes later, he knew exactly where he was: at the head of a narrow dirt road that dropped steeply to the Drina River, just a hundred and fifty feet below.

He played his flashlight over the area, his heart in his throat as the light bounced off an old car, his mother's car, just a few yards away. It was peppered with bullet holes, its tires shot out.

There was no sign of his mother or his brother Goran, Goran's wife, or the child. The bullet holes, blood, and shell casings, however, told most of the story. The disturbed vegetation going down the hill told the rest. His family, intercepted in their car, had been brought to this spot. His sister-in-law had probably succumbed to the same horrific fate as Zora, perhaps his mother as well. Goran and the child would have been shot, their bodies dragged down to the river and dumped into the water. He was certain of it. During the months he had been home, he had hiked to the river on several occasions. Each time, he had seen corpses drifting by, victims of the mass extermination that that was decimating his country and that the West was choosing to ignore. Now his family, too, had become casualties of their indifference.

Consumed with grief, Zlatan trudged back to his mother's house—now his house—knowing what he had to do. His first task was to bury his sister, with as much respect and adherence to Islamic tradition as circumstances allowed. While those who adhered strictly to the tenets of Islamic law would have condemned his decisions, he trusted no one else to take care of his sister. Certainly, there would be no one to call in the middle of the night. He gently bathed her broken body and dried her skin carefully before wrapping her in the creamy white tablecloth that had once graced his mother's dinner table. He dug the grave a hundred yards from the house, laid her gently in the soil with her head facing Mecca, prayed, and said goodbye.

He trimmed his hair and shaved his mustache, working as quickly as he could to better match the picture in the passport. He dressed for a night outside, in warm, dark clothes, and stuffed his few belongings into his rucksack. He pulled some provisions from the panty, added an album filled with photographs of his family, and retrieved his money and passports from a bin hidden in the loft. Outside, he stood back and stared at what had once been his home—a home that his mother and father had built, a home where his sister and brothers had been born. He snapped a series of mental photos, scattered a few bundles of dry hay around the house and barn, and lit the fire.

Chapter 23

After a night in the woods, Zlatan woke—cold and hungry and confronted by the bleak reality of his situation. The Serbs might be looking for him, having realized that they had not exterminated all the brothers. If he did not get out of the area quickly, he would be dead within days. Survival depended on getting out of the country; the American passport was his ticket to freedom. He wondered, but only briefly, if the document was still valid. He had not written a report for the Americans in over a year ... not since Imela had been killed.

He would have to find his way to a place with an operational airport and somehow arrange to board an airplane. That meant traveling back to Sarajevo, or even farther—into Croatia. The thought of repeating that journey on foot made the hair stand up on the back of his neck. The other option was to try talking his way into the UN encampment in Goražde and begging for a ride in a convoy back to Sarajevo. While his family had been well-known in the area, he had been absent for some time and, with the passport, could now pose as an American. What were the chances that he could slip into the town and not be recognized? It was risky, but the better choice.

He set off across the hills, to the rear of the Serb positions, avoiding the clearings that were reported to be littered with mines. There were two schools of thought among the locals: the best chance was to walk on ground that was heavily trodden, or the best chance was to avoid ground that was heavily trodden. Carefully, so carefully, he threaded his way through the trees. The first trip wire, strung low between two tall spruces, was nearly invisible. He had been lucky, avoiding the trap only because a beam of sunlight had glinted off a few drops of moisture on the wire.

Stupid, stupid, he muttered to himself, realizing that he had not taken steps to check for the trip wires. He had been more concerned about stepping on a buried land mine. Digging in his pack, he found the skein of cord he always carried and cut off about three and a half feet. He found a sturdy branch, nearly arm's length, and tied the cord to one end. By holding out the branch in front of him as he walked, the cord dangling almost to the ground, he would see a bend in the cord if it encountered an obstruction like a wire.

As he worked his way closer to town, he constructed a plan—and the story to accompany it. US passport or not, he doubted that the UN soldiers would welcome him with open arms. He would have to win them over, and the story would have to match the history—the legend—that Dr. Meade had provided. *Can I carry it off? Is my English still good enough?* In the years since leaving the United States, he had spoken English at every opportunity—but he was still rusty.

It was midafternoon before he reached the closest hill overlooking the section of town where the UNPROFOR—the United Nations Protective Force—was quartered. The unit swelled when a convoy delivered supplies to the town, but even then, the troops and trucks were in and out in a hurry. With the Serbs occupying the land around the town, no one wanted to stay long in Goražde.

He stumbled down the steep hill and walked briskly toward the UNPROFOR compound, trying not to break into a full-out run. He was about fifty feet away when the tall, burly soldier stepped out of the shadows.

The man had only a rough handle on the language, but he had drawn his sidearm, and the message was clear. Zlatan slowed, then stopped and took the plunge. "I'm American," he called, holding up the passport. "Please help me!"

The man's eyes narrowed, his expression flickering from confrontational to curious as he studied the intruder. Uncertain, he kept his weapon pointed at Zlatan's chest.

Zlatan finally realized what he must look like after a night in the woods. He spread his hands. "I spent the night in the woods. It's a long story. Does someone speak English?"

The soldier finally found his voice. "You're an American?"

Zlatan's pulse quickened. Most of the UN personnel were from countries where English was a second language. He had counted on them not being fluent, of not recognizing that his own English was not native, of not being able to detect his accent. *Here we go,* he thought. *Suck it up and stick to the story.* "Yes, I'm American."

Waving Zlatan forward, the man took the passport and thumbed through it. "Are you daft? What are you doing here?"

He had considered that some acting might be required, but his nervousness was genuine, and the words tumbled out in a frantic stream. "I'm a journalist. I was just trying to get a story," he said. "I want Americans to understand what is going on here."

A second man appeared beside the soldier and took the passport, examining it carefully. "You have been in Bosnia for quite a long time," he said.

Zlatan shrugged, trying to appear casual despite the wild thumping in his chest. *What will they do when they discover I am not American?* "Nature of the job," he managed to say. "I was following a story—it started in Sarajevo and eventually led here."

The man's expression was skeptical. "So why did you spend the night in the forest?"

"Yesterday I was interviewing a family that lives near here." He waved vaguely at the hills behind him. "Soldiers took them away, and they didn't come back. I found one body last night and then ran for my life."

The soldier raised his eyebrows. "And the family was not with you?"

Zlatan's mouth went dry. *Stick to some version of the truth,* he cautioned himself. "They had some documents and pictures they wanted me to see. They were in a trunk, in the loft, in the barn. I was up there when the soldiers came."

"And you did nothing to interfere."

Zlatan bowed his head in shame, knowing the soldier had seen him for what he was. He fully expected the two men to spit on him for his cowardice. Instead, their posture relaxed and they lowered their weapons.

"It is a terrible thing to bear, to feel so helpless. This is something we live with every day. You were alone, and there is nothing you could have done. You are alive to tell the tale. The world needs to hear the story."

With that, they let him inside the barrier.

Chapter 24

September 1993
Between Goražde and Sarajevo, Bosnia and Herzegovina

The convoy arrived in Goražde two days later and dropped off its supplies, spending one night in the camp. The group's leader generously offered Zlatan a seat on the return drive to Sarajevo.

Seven miles into the journey, the convoy ground to a halt, and Zlatan heard men shouting outside their vehicle. Serbian forces frequently set up blockades on the roads and demanded payment for passage. The stops were nerve-racking, because the Serbs had been known to kidnap members of the UN force. He cowered inside the truck, both grateful for, and fearful of, the American passport in his possession. He could become a prize to be held for ransom, or executed as a warning against American intervention.

A moment later, the rear door swung open. An ugly man with a dirty uniform, ruddy cheeks, and rotting teeth demanded that the occupants produce identification. He eyed each man, then swung his rifle toward Zlatan, yelling in Serbian. "You! Papers!"

Zlatan's heart was thudding so loudly he was sure that the other men in the truck could hear it. He stood, fumbled in his jacket, and produced the passport.

The ugly man's eyes narrowed as he took the booklet. He looked carefully at the passport, then at Zlatan, then back at the passport, mumbling as he studied the photo. Zlatan was puzzled, because it seemed that the man was mouthing the name on the document. The man turned and hurried away, the passport in his hand.

As the men in the truck waited, they speculated about the meaning of the delay, asking if there were any unusual visas or other stamps in the passport that might have aroused curiosity. Zlatan shook his head. He was trembling now, his neck and forehead damp with sweat, wondering what his chances were for surviving the encounter. *Are they going to pull me off this truck? Should I jump out and run right now?*

Ten minutes later, the soldier returned with another man in tow. The newcomer studied Zlatan and then said, in perfect English, "Americans are not welcome here. We are capable of managing our own country. You would do well to leave on the next flight." He handed the passport back.

Without another word, the soldiers slammed the doors of the truck. The engine rumbled to life, and the vehicle lurched forward. A few hours later, they pulled to a stop at the airport in Sarajevo.

The two men met at the airport, shielded from view by an armored personnel carrier parked on the tarmac. The younger man saluted his taller superior and waited. The taller man was lean and sinewy, his age given away only by the gray streaking the hair at his temples. His erect posture, the cant of his chin, and his intelligent gray eyes conveyed authority. He spoke without preamble.

"He was in the convoy? This is verified?"

"Yes, sir. He was identified at the roadblock, sir. The patrol sent a fax," the second man replied. He handed the older man a sheet of paper.

The older man studied the fax of the American passport with Zlatan's photo. The name on the passport, however, was Michael—Michael Cantrell. He folded the paper carefully and slipped it into his pocket.

"This is good work. I believe he will be quite useful for our long-term goals. He has lived in America, has exceptional technical skills, is already in bed with the Americans, and has an American passport. Plus, he has suffered greatly. With a good narrative and the right push, I believe we can mold him to our needs. I see great possibilities for the future."

The younger man nodded enthusiastically. "An excellent long game," he said. "But perhaps we should allow for the possibility that he could be discovered. His American passport would then become useless. Shall I develop a contingency plan?" He looked around, eyeing the multinational UN force that occupied the airport and the Canadian armored reconnaissance vehicles that had arrived yesterday. "I might be able to arrange a second set of papers for him."

"That would be excellent."

"Perhaps additional incentive? He has siblings, yes?"

"He had a sister and three brothers, actually, one with a wife and daughter," the older man replied.

"Had?"

"Some of our men were a bit too enthusiastic in their mission. One of the brothers and the sister are dead. But the other two brothers, well, they could be useful because they will protect each other. It is, as the Americans say, a *win-win*."

"Where are they?"

"The younger brother is with the Bosnian Army, in intelligence. We are unsure of his location, but we will find him. The one with the family is still in Goražde."

"He left them in Goražde? Why?"

"He thinks they are dead."

The younger man smirked. "And if he does not comply, imagination will become reality."

The older man spoke sharply. "You will not touch any of them without my permission."

The subordinate's cheeks flamed. He took a step back, muttering, "Yes, sir."

The older man turned away, his hand patting his pocket. *Found you*, he whispered to himself.

Chapter 25

September 1993
Sarajevo, Bosnia and Herzegovina

Zlatan learned that the next relief flights into Sarajevo had been delayed due to skirmishes in the vicinity of the airport. They were tentatively scheduled to resume the next day, but there was no guarantee. Airplanes presented attractive targets for the Serbs occupying the ground surrounding the airport. Flying into Sarajevo was risky business.

On days when flights were arriving with supplies, the terminal and tarmac were abuzz with soldiers from the multinational UN force. On no-fly days, many of the soldiers remained indoors, with knots of troops patrolling the airport. Zlatan wanted to visit Mirko before leaving the country, to check on his well-being. His heart ached to spend a few private moments at Imela's grave. He thought of trying to secure a ride into the city on one of the UN's armored personnel carriers, but was paralyzed by the thought of being discovered or becoming another victim of the violence that still consumed the city.

He fashioned a sleeping space in a corner at the back of the building, away from the field of fire. Realizing that he had a role to play, he scrounged up a few pens and several pads of paper from abandoned workstations in the terminal. *If I'm supposed to be a journalist*, he reasoned, *I should act like one.*

He was scribbling on a pad early the next morning when a stranger approached and offered his hand. "Good morning! I'm Pete," he said.

American, Zlatan thought, alarmed. He thrust out his hand and shook. "Good morning," he responded, deliberately omitting his name.

The man was not tall, but he stood straight and erect, his legs apart. He crossed his arms across his chest, his posture and stance unmistakably military.

"We've missed you, Zlatan. It's been a while," the man said.

Zlatan could not hide his shock, blurting out, "I don't understand. Have we met?"

"Not exactly," the man said calmly. "But I know you. Your previous friend, Larry, was transferred to a new post. I've taken his place. He told me all about you and I've been hoping you would surface."

Zlatan felt the color rise in his face. *Caught,* he thought.

"We have an assignment for you. You'll enjoy it," Pete said. "It will give you the chance to travel, to enjoy life, to have fun!"

"What kind of assignment?"

"Book a flight to New York. Check in at the Marriott Marquis in Times Square. You'll love it. You'll love it even more when we pick up the tab. We even took the liberty of obtaining a credit card for you. Charge whatever you need, but don't overdo it, buddy. If you go overboard, the bean counters will make us cancel the card." He handed Zlatan an American Express Gold Card. The name on the card was Michael Cantrell.

Zlatan nodded in understanding. But he had also gained a vital piece of information: they did not know about the account that Dr. Meade had set up for him. He smiled inwardly, pleased that he had an ace up his sleeve if needed.

"But I must caution you," Pete continued, "to avoid contacting your friends in Virginia. Your new identity would be difficult to explain. It could even put Dr. Meade at risk for having helped you."

"But ..."

"No buts. We'll be in touch. Enjoy New York, Zlatan," Pete said. With a smirk he added, "Oh ... oops, it's Michael now, isn't it?"

Zlatan remained frozen in place, watching the man's back as he sauntered away. He was stunned that they had managed to find him—and chilled that Pete knew of his relationship with the Meades.

I never told anyone, he whispered to himself. *Except ... except Mirko.* The realization took his breath away. He leaned against the cold concrete wall and tried to put the pieces together. *Is it possible? No, it could not be.* He thought back to that initial meeting with Larry in the bar. The CIA probably had some record of Dr. Meade's visit. And it was Dr. Meade who had suggested the possibility of a meeting with someone from the US government. His body sagged in relief and a single tear leaked from his left eye. *So, not Mirko. Thank God.* Losing his best friend would have been the final blow.

In the shadows of the airport terminal, Pete and the tall man stood apart, each smoking a cigarette. It was their second face-to-face meeting and, if anything, more intimidating than the first. The colonel was one hard son of a bitch.

The colonel asked, "Is it done?"

"So far, so good," Pete replied. "He's a survivor. He knows he doesn't have much choice. Plus, I think he genuinely wants to go back to America."

"We have a loose end: the man who arranged for the American passport."

"I've warned him about staying clear of Dr. Meade and his family. He was not pleased."

"He cares about them. He will want to contact them, regardless of your instructions. We need a more permanent solution."

"Do you want me to take care of them?"

"No," replied the colonel. "You cannot be involved. I will make those arrangements. I am more concerned about his documents. He has been out of contact for some time. There will surely be a flag raised when he uses the passport to enter the US."

"Only someone with high administrative authority would be able to make that change"

The colonel eyed him coldly. "Everyone has a price. I am sure you can manage to take care of that."

Zlatan got a lift on one of the humanitarian aircraft that had dropped its load in Sarajevo—a US Air Force C-130 attached to Ramstein Air Base in Germany, but operating the airlift out of Ancona, Italy. The passport worked its magic, Dr. Meade's money added its own mojo, the train ride through Milan to Switzerland was comfortable and on time, and the bank in Zurich was exceedingly cooperative. He tried to cover his shock on learning the account balance and worked hard to appear nonchalant when the account manager handed him the complimentary Platinum Visa Card.

Zlatan located a Swissair office not far from the bank and booked a flight nonstop from Zurich to New York. He intended to pay cash, but the agent balked. Initially suspicious and curt, the agent eventually softened at his apparent innocence, explaining that airlines are suspicious of passengers who purchase tickets in cash, particularly last-minute and one-way.

He apologized for the misstep and gave a silent prayer of thanks for the two credit cards in his wallet. He fumbled for a moment, trying to decide whether to use the Gold Card from Pete or the Platinum from Dr. Meade's account. *Nobody knows about this account in Zurich. Better to keep it to myself,* his inner voice whispered. He handed the agent the Gold Card and pocketed the ticket.

Chapter 26

September 1993
Newport News, Virginia

With the engine off, Clay and Fredo let the black skiff drift through the shallows until it was about fifty yards upstream from the pier. Clay squinted into the night and spotted the streak of luminous yellow paint they had splashed on one of the pilings two days earlier. At two-thirty in the morning, the mansions along the river were shrouded in darkness, and the waxing crescent moon emitted only a sliver of light. The work was dangerous. Navigating at night on the James River without running lights could be a recipe for disaster, but they were hardened sailors and long-accustomed to challenging assignments.

Clay leveled the oars and gave his companion a nudge. Fredo slipped in the mouthpiece, lowered his mask, and tipped backward—over the side and into the water with barely a splash. With his wet suit and black tank, Fredo was invisible.

The two men had worked together for nearly twenty years, infiltrating places as remote as the South Indian Ocean and as bustling as New York Harbor. They knew each other well and sometimes seemed to read each other's thoughts, communicating with the barest twitch of a lip or lift of an eyebrow. Both were master divers, both experts in the handling and placement of underwater explosives. This assignment, however, called for a more delicate subterfuge—a skillful setup that would lead to the mishap being declared an accident.

Clay leaned back, pulling the oars hard against the current and struggling to keep the boat temporarily upstream of the pier, while Fredo pulled the nylon line as he swam toward shore. Reaching the pier, Fredo secured the line to the piling with a mooring hitch—a quick-release knot that, when yanked, would free the skiff. If things went according to plan, the skiff would then float freely downstream, towing Fredo with it.

Fredo heaved himself and the waterproof gear bag onto the covered dock and took a moment to admire the thirty-four-foot express cruiser. The owner had chosen his upgrades carefully to add beauty and value. Fredo ran his hand over the teak trim, felt a pang of regret, then set about his business.

The touchiest part of the operation would be opening the hatch to the engine compartment. Ordinarily, one simply inserted the key at the helm and turned on the ignition. But without the key, Fredo had been left to devise his own solution. He pulled the twelve-volt lawn mower battery out of the bag, connected an improvised cigarette lighter—similar to those found in automobiles—and plugged it into the twelve-volt port on the helm. He pressed the actuator switch and breathed a sigh of relief on hearing the motor's soft whir as the hatch rose. *Presto,* he thought.

Working quickly, he loosened the hose clamps and disconnected the fuel line from one of the two big engines. He replaced the line with the one in his gear bag, a line that had a small hole where a section of the nylon braiding had worn through. He used a wire brush to fray the insulation of one set of wires, then loosened the connection. He positioned a wad of chewing gum, wrapped in its crumpled foil wrapper, on top of the exposed wires.

He stuffed the equipment into the bag, primed the line, reclosed the hatch, repacked the battery and connector, toweled down the boat and dock, and eased back into the water.

He looked at his dive watch. *Seven minutes. Piece of cake.* After strapping the heavy gear bag to his waist, he looped the dangling end of the line around his forearm, then gave the knot a yank. Freed from the line, the skiff floated downstream, towing Fredo behind. After a quarter mile, Clay started the engine and hauled Fredo aboard. The stage was set.

Dr. Jonathan Meade and his son, Chip, were on the dock by nine in the morning, checking the boat's instruments, fuel supply, and life preservers. They hauled the cooler aboard, along with assorted bags of insect repellent, sunscreen, towels, hats, jackets, and all the other paraphernalia required for an autumn day on the river. Dr. Meade pursed his lips and let out a shrill whistle—a signal for the wives to board. Irene and her daughter-in-law of five months, Leigh Anne, waved to the neighbors as they ambled down the pier.

The James River sparkled under a cloudless, brilliant blue sky, the day blessed by temperatures in the low seventies, a light wind, and no rain predicted. The 370-horsepower Mercury engines thrummed as Dr. Meade guided the boat toward the deeper water of the channel. Near its mouth, the James is broad—nearly five miles across as it drains into the waters of Hampton Roads and Chesapeake Bay.

As the boat skimmed over the water, fuel streamed from the worn hose into the engine room. The wind carried away the noxious odor, leaving the family blissfully unaware of any danger. After ten minutes enduring the boat's seesaw motion, Leigh Anne's stomach revolted, and she fled below to the head. She leaned over the bowl, surprised and annoyed because, in years of racing the waters along the eastern Atlantic, she had never before been seasick. She rested her hand on her abdomen, wondering, *Am I pregnant?* Taking deep breaths to combat the nausea, she wrinkled her nose at the smell. *Is that fuel?* She pivoted, cupping her hands around her mouth to yell through the hatch.

At that moment, Dr. Meade turned into the wake of a passing barge, the boat bouncing as it topped the wave. The wad of gum fell from its perch and landed on the nest of wiring. The exposed wire touched the foil of the gum wrapper and sparked, igniting the fuel vapor.

The engine room exploded, propelling deadly shrapnel in every direction. Chip, standing behind his father at the helm, bore the main force of the blast and was killed instantly. A metal shard sliced through Irene Meade's neck. Leigh Anne was blown back by the concussive wave, her head striking the edge of the counter and knocking her unconscious. The smoke and flames consumed the cabin, and Leigh Anne with it. Dr. Meade, burned over 90 percent of his body, was found unconscious in the water, rescued, and transported to the burn center in Norfolk. He died that evening.

Clay and Fredo spent the day in the hotel, listening to reports about the tragedy on the James and waiting to learn the doctor's fate. At ten that night, a grim-faced newscaster reported that Dr. Jonathan Meade had died. Clay made one call, confirming that the job had been accomplished—and with no survivors. On Monday morning, they verified the wire transfer, dropped the rented tank at the scuba shop, caught a flight to Helena, Montana, picked up their cars and fishing gear, and drove north to a campground near Holter Dam. They spent the next week fly-fishing on the Missouri River, waiting for their next assignment.

The investigation determined that poor maintenance—including a worn fuel line and frayed wiring insulation—was ultimately responsible for the tragedy. Dr. Meade's friends and colleagues refused to accept the findings, arguing fiercely that the good doctor was a former Navy SEAL who had been meticulous in caring for his boat. In the face of damning evidence, however, their voices held no weight.

PART THREE

Michael

1993 – 1994

Chapter 27

September 1993
New York City

Six days after leaving Goražde, Zlatan stepped off the airplane at JFK Airport. He presented the passport of Michael Cantrell—birthplace Ketchikan, Alaska—and passed through Immigration and Customs formalities without a hitch.

His earlier stay in Newport News could never have prepared him for the sheer audacity that was New York City. He spent the first day luxuriating in the hotel, with its crisp sheets and fluffy towels and deep bathtub and pulsating shower and commanding view and so many fabulous sights that he became breathless with anticipation for the next wonderful thing. He ate ravenously and was quickly overcome with nausea and vomiting, his malnourished body paying the price of too much, too soon.

He ventured out on the second day, his neck craning upward at the towering skyscrapers and his ears ringing at the cacophony of constantly honking taxis. In Times Square, he sampled the fare at Roxy Deli. He rode the elevator to the top of the Empire State Building and spent forty-five minutes on the observation deck, strolled for two hours through Central Park, and explored the corridors of Grand Central Terminal in the late afternoon.

The following day, he rode the subway to lower Manhattan and, after borrowing a jacket from the maître d', splurged for breakfast at Windows on the World in the World Trade Center. He visited Battery Park and took the ferry to the Statue of Liberty. That evening, he bought tickets to the revival of the musical *Guys and Dolls* at the Martin Beck Theatre on Broadway.

The entire experience was enthralling. He wanted to stand in the middle of Times Square and shout, "I love New York!" As he left the theater, he felt a presence at his side and turned to see Pete walking beside him. His mood soured at the sight of the man, ruining what had otherwise been a glorious day.

"Now that you've had a nice little vacation, we need to talk, buddy," Pete said. "Let's head back to your hotel."

Pete took the big chair, his feet propped up on the ottoman. "So, Michael, how are you adjusting to your new life?"

Zlatan was still uncomfortable with his new name, unaccustomed to people addressing him as Michael or Mr. Cantrell. He stood in front of the window, arms crossed over his chest, trying to make sense of what he was being asked to do.

"You want me to work for this airline, this Transoceanic Airlines, as a flight attendant. But my real job would be to spy on other flight attendants? Is that it?"

Pete pulled his feet off the ottoman, sat up, and leaned forward, his hands folded together, like a salesperson making a pitch. "Flight attendants make perfect spies. We know this because we use them ourselves. They travel all over the world, and nobody blinks an eye. A lot of people just think of them as waitresses in the sky and assume they are not very bright. That's a big mistake. Most of those who fly internationally are educated and resourceful. They have to be. When something goes wrong at thirty thousand feet, it's not like you can call in a manager.

"Most of the crewmembers who do this are collecting a little money under the table by doing pickup and delivery for bigger fish. A few are more than that. They actually gather intelligence. They charm the pants off—literally—a guy who has something they want. Some of them are paid by foreign governments, some are freelancing and selling the intel to the highest bidder. Those are the ones we want to find. We need to learn who they talk to, and either make them work for us or put them in jail."

"Why me?"

"You have already proven yourself as an asset—a very good one. You're observant and personable. People like you, and because of that, they have a tendency to talk, to open up. And your girlfriend, the one who was killed … What was her name, Imela? She was a former flight attendant, yes? I'll bet she taught you some lingo."

Michael turned his head, angry that Pete had pulled Imela's name into the conversation. "How do you even know about her? And what if I say no?"

Pete shrugged. "We know everything about you. And if you don't want in, well, that's your call. But your passport will be revoked, and you'll be back in Sarajevo. And that's the good result. The bad result is that you could end up in the slammer for possession of false documentation."

Michael's eyes narrowed at the implied threat. "How can you be certain that I will even be hired by this airline?"

"We've got it covered, buddy. We can get you the job, put you on any flight, send you to any city. We have, shall we say, a relationship with Trans-O. We're like this," he said, crooking his middle finger over his index finger. "We help each other."

Chapter 28

October 1993
New York City

Six weeks to the day after his conversation with Pete, Michael donned the airline's distinctive gunmetal-gray and gold wings as he graduated from the Transoceanic Flight School near Orlando. Matching his passport, the Transoceanic ID carried the name Michael Cantrell.

The airline assigned Michael to the crew base in New York, where he tried to adjust to the anything-but-routine life of a flight attendant. Newly hired flight attendants were placed on reserve status, to fill in on short notice when crewmembers were needed. They carried pagers and rarely wandered far from the place where they lived. If they spent the night away from home, they always took a packed bag. Their lives had little structure and zero predictability. The uncertainty of whether a call would come, the inability to plan for a specific climate or the number of days away, and the requirement of reporting to the airport within two hours of receiving a call, made life as a new hire stressful. When the low pay was added to the mix, it was not difficult to understand why the dropout rate during the first year was staggeringly high.

Michael, however, faced none of these complications. His assignments came not through the ordinary channels of communication from crew scheduling, but from Pete—and with plenty of advance notice. He carried the pager for effect, but it never buzzed. Living alone, there was no one to witness the lack of pager activity or that he was always suitably packed and never rushing to make a flight.

On Pete's direction, he took a furnished studio apartment in Kew Gardens, a neighborhood in the Queens borough of New York City. The area's proximity to JFK and LaGuardia Airports, and availability of public transportation, made it a popular living choice for airline personnel.

"They call it *Crew Gardens*," Pete said with a laugh. "With all the airline folks there, you'll have more opportunity to socialize, learn airline-speak, get comfortable, and most important, ask questions."

The location also gave the appearance that Michael lived like every other new hire, in a cheap apartment with thrift-store furniture. However, when two of Michael's classmates from training suggested that the three of them should live together in a two-bedroom to ease the cost burden, Pete nixed the idea.

"Roommates get to know too many details about you. Leads to bad juju," he said. "The objective of the game is to get to know people without them knowing a thing about you."

The airline gave him five days to find a place to live and take care of any other necessary business before reporting for work. Michael did not need that much time. He leased the first place he visited, a third-floor studio that was barely bigger than a shoebox. Its size mattered little. After the crushing conditions in Bosnia, the tiny space was warm and welcoming. He laid down the first and last months' rent, plus a security deposit, and moved in the following day.

In the middle of the afternoon, as he was hanging his uniforms and his few clothes in the matchbook-size closet, Michael's intercom buzzed. He was surprised to hear Pete suggesting lunch and, admitting that he had not yet shopped for food, hurried downstairs. They found an outside table at a nearby pub and chatted as they waited to place an order.

Once they had drinks in hand, Pete handed Michael a photograph. "This is your first assignment."

Michael studied the picture. The woman in the photo was likely in her midforties, judging by the few lines on her face and the whispers of silver in her short, dark hair. Her light brown coloring suggested a Mideast or Latin heritage. "Who is she?" he asked.

"Her name is Isabel Alvarez," Pete replied. "She lives near Washington, with a man who works for the government, and commutes up to New York. We have reason to think she could be stealing secrets from her boyfriend. She came to our attention last week, when she was spotted at a pub in London. Sitting next to her was a known Russian agent."

"And what am I supposed to do?"

"She's going back to London tomorrow. We want you to follow her around ... see if she meets up with anyone, particularly this guy."

He pulled out a black-and-white photo of a tall man with a taut face, square jaw, hard eyes, and light brown hair that was graying at the temples. He looked to be in his fifties, although Michael was admittedly a poor judge of age.

"This is the Russian?"

"Yes, although you would not know it. His English, I'm told, is perfect."

"Is he dangerous?"

"He is a colonel who was trained by the GRU, so, yes."

Michael almost dropped the picture. The GRU had been the Soviet Union's main intelligence directorate and its most feared.

"You have a camera, right?"

Michael nodded. He owned a Nikon, a gift from Dr. Meade.

"If you see him," Pete continued, "try to snap a picture of him and anyone he might be with. And pay special attention to Isabel—the Russian might not be her only contact. But do be careful. They are both quite skilled."

Chapter 29

October 1993
London, England

The following evening, Michael joined twelve other flight attendants—including Isabel—for the trip to London. Pete had told him to keep his eyes on Isabel during the flight, to see if he noticed any unusual interactions with passengers or other crew. But Pete did not understand one fundamental rule of the sky: seniority prevails. As the senior purser, Isabel was in charge of the cabin crew. She chose to work the first-class cabin. Michael, as the most junior crewmember, was assigned to the very back of the aircraft. Michael found excuses to visit the first-class cabin several times during the flight, but noticed nothing out of the ordinary. He did learn that she was not particularly well-liked. Most of the crew found her to be overly demanding and strict.

On the bus going into the city, Michael made it a point to sit near Isabel and made casual conversation with the other crew, asking their plans for the layover. Finally, Isabel mentioned that she had shopping to do, and perhaps take in a musical if she could get a ticket. Michael saw an opening and took it.

"I've never been to London before," he said. "Would you mind if I tagged along so you could show me around? In return, I'll spring for the tickets."

Isabel cocked her head, her brow wrinkled in curiosity. "Really? I'm not sure I'm the best London guide. And my choices of what to do are probably not very interesting, particularly for a guy."

"It doesn't matter. I haven't got a clue."

She arched her eyebrows. "Alright, although I can't imagine why you'd want to hang with me. When we get to the hotel, you've got fifteen minutes to change and be ready to go. I'll meet you in the lobby."

"Cool," he said. "What's the musical?"

"*Crazy for You*," she snorted. "Which remains to be seen."

Michael grinned. He had not expected her to have a funny side.

Michael scored two theater tickets from the concierge, charging them to the Amex card that Pete had provided. He was still uneasy about the entire arrangement and was glad that he had not needed to use the card that had come with his Swiss account. While Pete had come through with whatever Michael needed, Michael did not fully trust him. The Swiss credit card remained a secret.

"Spend what you have to spend to do the job, but don't go overboard or we'll cancel it," Pete had warned.

This is worth it, Michael thought. *I'll be close enough to see whatever she does.*

Isabel stepped off the elevator precisely fifteen minutes after checking into the hotel. Michael waved the tickets triumphantly, and her eyes widened.

"That's quite an expense for a new hire. Are you one of those people who lives off a trust fund, or are you just careless with money?"

Michael laughed and shook his head. "No, I just have some money saved."

"What kind of work did you do?"

"I was a journalist."

Her eyes narrowed. "Interesting," she said, turning her back and heading for the hotel entrance.

He slung his camera over his shoulder and followed. Isabel led him to the nearest station for the Underground, London's name for their subway system, telling him that most people just called it the *Tube*.

They got off at Knightsbridge and wove through the crowds toward Harrods. Michael stared in awe, taking in the enormity of the store he had heard so much about. But when they stepped inside, his jaw dropped. Never had he seen such a place. It seemed that anything produced on the planet could be found in one of its dozens of departments.

For two hours, he watched Isabel carefully as she shopped. He could not detect that she had made contact with anyone. She now toted two large shopping bags, their yawning tops seemingly begging for more merchandise. He realized that a person could easily drop an item into one of the bags without being noticed.

A stop at the Harvey Nichols department store added to the bundle. She explained that she liked to pick out special things for her family, most of whom lived in Miami.

"You live in Miami?" he asked.

"No, my family is there. I live in Virginia, just outside of Washington."

She was now laden with three bags, and Michael offered to carry them. To his surprise, she handed them over. He had become convinced that one of the bags would somehow be used to pass something to someone. He knew that if she was truly a spy, he was out of his element. But her actions thus far had not given him any cause for suspicion. To the contrary, she seemed quite normal.

"Tea?" she asked.

"T what?" he asked back.

She laughed gleefully and, in a terrible imitation of a British accent, said, "If one is truly going to do London, one simply must take tea at Claridge's."

They set off through Hyde Park, an oasis of greenery and tranquility in an otherwise manic city, and walked the mile to the iconic hotel in the Mayfair neighborhood. She checked her packages with a porter and, without hesitation, approached the maître d' in the elegant foyer, where afternoon tea was being served.

"I have a reservation, for Isabel ..."

"Certainly, Miss Alvarez. For two."

Contrary to her earlier assertions that she would not be a good guide to London, it was obvious to Michael that she knew it quite well. Had she made the reservation when she got to the hotel? Or had she made it previously, in anticipation of meeting someone else there? His head was swimming with possibilities.

They sat on opposite sides of the table, two people with little to say to one another. The waiter presented dainty, crust-trimmed sandwiches of smoked salmon on rye and cucumber with dill, along with plates of biscuits and a bowl mounded with thick, white cream.

"Scones and clotted cream," she whispered.

He followed her lead, taking delicate bites of the sandwiches and spooning a generous dollop of the cream onto the scone. The sandwiches were not to his taste, but he found the scones to be heavenly.

"These are wonderful," he said.

She gave a slight smile. "Yes, they are."

The waiter delivered a plate of petits fours and offered a selection of tarts and other desserts. Michael sampled everything and, enjoying the luxury, decided he would visit Claridge's again. As he sipped the delicate Fujian white tea, he decided to probe.

"Did you grow up in Miami?"

She pulled a sour face and shoved her glasses onto the top of her head. Without the glasses, he caught a glimpse of what she must have looked like in her twenties. She had deep-set, exotic eyes that had, at one time, probably melted a few hearts. She was still attractive, but her jawline had gone soft, and she had developed a permanent crease between her eyes that made her look perpetually angry. Michael was beginning to suspect that, beneath her sharp veneer, Isabel had a soft side. She had surprised him by allowing him to tag along in the first place. He had expected her to grumble throughout, as she reportedly did during flights. But she had been patient and had infused their walk with colorful commentary. He had the sense that she genuinely wanted him to enjoy his first trip to London, to give him a gift he would remember forever.

"Not exactly," she said, studying him. "Are you still a journalist?"

"Not exactly," he replied.

She glared at him, then relaxed when she realized he was joking. "I don't often discuss my personal life. Whatever I tell you is not for publication. Can I trust you?"

He met her eyes. "Yes. Whatever you tell me stays between us." He wondered if he could keep the promise.

Isabel, he learned, was one of 14,000 unaccompanied children airlifted out of Cuba in the early sixties. In a secret operation code-named Operation Peter Pan, the US government partnered with the Catholic Welfare Bureau in Miami to spirit children off the island as Castro was solidifying his power. Pan Am's two daily flights from Havana to Miami were soon packed with children.

Many of the parents were able to immigrate in short order, whereupon they were reunited with their children. Not all, however, were so lucky. Some were placed in orphanages and foster homes scattered across the United States. Isabel was one of them. She was housed in Miami for several months and then, at the age of ten, sent to Iowa.

Isabel's foster home had, by her account, provided a less than stellar childhood environment. The foster parents were abusive and alcoholic. Her parents, who should have been airlifted to Miami a few weeks after Isabel, did not make it off the island before the operation was halted. Still, she had managed to find her own way, putting herself through college and eventually landing a coveted position as a stewardess for Pan Am—the airline that had brought her to the United States. Like many former employees of the fabled airline, she had found employment with Transoceanic after Pan Am's demise in 1991. It was not until years later that she learned her parents had eventually escaped from Cuba on a leaky fishing boat. They had been looking for her for years. She had become, she admitted, a fervent anti-Castro activist.

That must be the connection. She's involved in a plot to overthrow Castro, Michael thought. *But why would she be in contact with the Russians? It doesn't make any sense.* With a jolt, he realized it did not matter. Most crewmembers in New York found Isabel to be a cross between batty and witchy, but Michael understood her perfectly. She was a survivor. He liked the woman's grit. Whatever she was doing, she had her reasons.

They were standing by the porter's stand, waiting to pick up Isabel's packages, when Michael caught sight of the man from Pete's photo—the Russian. His heart seized, and his instincts started screaming that he should run. It took all his effort not to panic.

He tried to appear calm and relaxed, but then recalled that he had been instructed to take a picture. He felt the beads of sweat break out on his forehead. Shifting his stance to let the camera swing into his hand, he wrapped his fingers over the grip ... and then froze. There was no subtle way to bring the viewfinder up to his face and snap a picture of a man twenty feet away. He relaxed and dropped his arm to his side.

Isabel handed him the shopping bags, one after the other. He wondered if one seemed lighter and another heavier, before realizing that, unless someone had added or removed a lead weight, he would not have been able to feel the difference. He stood where he was, his feet cemented to the floor, as Isabel reached for the final bag.

Out of the corner of his eye, he noticed the Russian approaching. He took a position behind Michael, forming a queue. Michael tensed. He had heard stories of merciless interrogations and outright assassinations by Russian agents. His breathing grew ragged, his armpits flooding as if someone had turned on a faucet. Isabel seemed oblivious. She accepted the bag from the porter and swung it over to Michael, narrowly missing the Russian.

Her expression was immediately contrite. "I'm so sorry," she said. "It was heavier than I realized. Did I hit you?"

The Russian held up his hand and shook his head in a dismissive gesture. "I'm fine," he answered. Turning to present a ticket to the porter, he said in flawless English, "Black Burberry overcoat. And an umbrella as well."

Michael tried to appear nonchalant as he studied the man. In person, the Russian seemed less formidable than the hard face in the photograph—until he turned and looked directly at Michael. While the man's smile appeared friendly, his startling gray eyes held little warmth. Michael felt as if he were being appraised. He felt his skin prickle.

Isabel gave no hint of recognition and, misinterpreting Michael's discomfort, put her hand under his arm and guided him out of the hotel.

"I can see that you are overwhelmed, but I need to make another stop, at Lillywhites, to pick up some golf shoes I ordered for my father. Then we'll go the theater and I think we'll try the Dog & Duck pub afterward. Does that sound good to you?"

Michael merely nodded, his throat as dry as the Sahara and his tongue paralyzed. He tried to quell his anxiety as they strolled down New Bond Street, with Isabel pointing out one luxury store after another. But he kept looking back over his shoulder, terrified that the Russian might be there. The only time he had felt such fear was when the men had abducted his brother and sister. In his darkest moments, he wondered if he was just a coward or merely someone trying to survive. He had not yet found an answer.

The walk to the famous sporting goods store was uneventful, as was their time at the theater. He tried to relax, to enjoy the musical, but could not overcome his feeling of dread—something bad was going to happen.

As they sat in the pub afterward, sipping their ales between mouthfuls of fish and chips, he asked her more about her anti-Castro activities. She was reluctant to discuss the topic, but not so reserved about her opinion of the Cuban government.

"There are some who wish me ill. There are some who want to open the channels of communication between the two countries, to allow citizens to travel freely. But many believe that, as long as Castro is in power, we cannot allow ourselves to do this. Reestablishing relations without acknowledgment of what he has done to Cuba's sons and daughters is not the answer."

"Are the Russians still supporting him?"

She looked at him quizzically. "The Russians? Well, Cuba relied on the Soviet Union for decades. The breakup of the Soviet bloc changed all that. The resulting policy shift was like a gut punch; it left the island reeling. They have no free market and few trade agreements and little sense of how to proceed. Cuba's economy is suffering tremendously. Worse, its citizens are suffering."

"So, wouldn't it be a good thing for the United States and Cuba to normalize relations?"

She closed her eyes and shook her head. "Only after Castro is in jail and the country holds free elections. If we reestablish relations with them, we would be ignoring all the crimes that Castro and his minions have committed. And ignoring those actions is the same as condoning them."

After an all-night flight and a full day walking the streets of London, Michael was dog-tired. He bid good night to Isabel at the hotel elevator and collapsed into his bed, but found sleep elusive. His head spinning, he tried to find connections between Isabel's story and what Pete had told him. The idea that she might be a spy working with the Russians seemed ludicrous. Still, the man in the photo—the Russian—had materialized at Claridge's at the same time as he and Isabel were finishing tea. He felt sure it could not be a coincidence.

Chapter 30

October 1993–January 1994
New York City

Pete had just snoozed his alarm when the phone rang. He picked up the receiver and listened to the hollow echo of an international call. He answered warily, "Hello?"

The voice on the other end said, "He needs more training. Work with him."

Swallowing hard, Pete replied, "I'll take care of it." He was unsettled by the call. He had no inkling of the man's name, nor did he want to know—he had made that assessment on the tarmac in Sarajevo. But the man was obviously a powerful figure, having plotted and then implemented the entire scheme of using Michael to infiltrate the airline's CIA-connected spy ring.

The colonel's next comment made the hair rise on the back of Pete's neck.

"He was nervous from the moment he spotted me. It was obvious that he knew what I looked like. What did you tell him?"

Swallowing hard, Pete tried to explain. "It was important to demonstrate the reality of the situation—that Isabel Alvarez is in contact with the Russians. I told him you were former GRU."

"That was a serious error in judgment. You are to keep me out of the conversation. Is that clear?"

"I'm sorry. It won't happen again," Pete mumbled.

"For now, just keep him on a short leash, and for God's sake, give him some training. I followed them all afternoon and he never spotted me. I have plans for him, but his inexperience could make it very dangerous ... for all of us."

"I'll do my best," Pete managed to say. "But it's not as if we have a world-class training facility here."

"I'm sure you'll find a way," the man said coldly. "I'll expect a report on his progress and your assessment of whether or not he has bought into your story about the Cuban woman."

Pete looked at his watch. "His flight lands in a few hours. I'll send a report after I meet with him."

Ninety minutes after his plane touched down in New York, Michael was back at his apartment building. He found Pete waiting in the vestibule.

"Seriously?" Michael complained. "I need a shower, I need food, I need sleep. Can't this wait?"

Pete showed no sympathy. "I need to get a report in, pronto. What did you learn?"

Michael told him about spending the day with Isabel, about watching her every move, about the packages and being unsure if anything could have been put into or taken out of one.

"It was crowded, people bumping into each other all the time. I can't be sure. But the Russian showed up at Claridge's while we were having tea there."

Pete feigned excitement, letting his eyes widen and his words quicken. "Was he with anyone? Do you think he was planning to meet Isabel there until you tagged along?"

"I don't know. She had a reservation, for two, but I don't know when she made it. Maybe that morning."

Pete shook his head vehemently, dismissing the idea. "It takes weeks, even months, to get a reservation there. No, she was meeting someone. What are the chances that the same guy shows up in both a hotel bar and at Claridge's at the exact same time as Isabel Alvarez, huh? I'll tell you! Zero! Zero, zero, zero!"

He calmed himself a bit, then said, "So what did you talk about?"

Michael shrugged, the lie coming easily. "Not much. I found out she's originally from Miami and has family there. Other than that, we mostly talked about London and flying."

Pete grunted, then said, "We may need to send you out with her again. I'll know more later."

Michael suppressed a smile. He would enjoy spending another day with Isabel. "Whatever," he said. "Now can I get some sleep?"

"Not so fast. Let's go get a bite. We'll talk."

Pete waited while Michael showered and changed, relishing his success with the operation so far. Despite the colonel's comments, it seemed that Michael had followed his instructions and seemed capable of managing an assignment.

Outside, they walked several blocks, finding a cozy Italian restaurant with a formidable selection of pasta dishes. Michael dug into a plate of arancini while Pete absently toyed with the ice in his Scotch.

"Isabel's going back to London. Tomorrow night."

Michael choked. "No way! I just got back!"

"Gotta do it, man," Pete said. "We need to know whatever we can about her."

"Won't it seem suspicious? Me showing up twice at the last minute?"

"Nah. The scheduler tells me it happens a lot. But for this one, you need to get there at the last possible minute, as if they had just called you. The girl you'll replace is going to have a little fender bender on the way to the airport."

Michael jerked his head up. "Whoa. What are you talking about?"

Pete stared at Michael. "We're not going to hurt anyone. It won't be anything serious, trust me. But she won't make the flight."

Michael was still wary. "What exactly am I supposed to do this time? I've already been on her big tour of London."

"Make nice with her. You obviously hit it off. I'll bet she likes having you along."

Taking a sip of beer, Michael grumbled. "What am I looking for this time? What size shoe she wears?"

Shaking his head, Pete looked at Michael as if he were a disobedient child. "Really? You think this is silly?"

"No. But I'm not sure what more I can do."

Pete handed Michael a watch.

"Pictures, Michael. We need pictures. A big camera is fine, but there are too many times when you can't use it without being noticed.

"This thing, however, is almost undetectable. It's good for about twenty feet, no more. Hold up your arm and rest your chin on your fist, so the watch face is pointing straight ahead of you. Slip your other index finger behind the buckle, like it's bothering you because it's too tight or itchy, and just pull the metal tongue on the strap. Shazam. Ultraquiet."

"You're kidding, right?"

"No, Michael. We need this."

Pete spent hours imparting his knowledge of tradecraft to Michael, who lapped it up. Week after week, Michael was assigned to shadow various flight attendants on trips to Istanbul, Dubai, Rome, Bombay, Panama, and Tokyo. In addition, he was positioned on several of Isabel's trips to Europe. He was worming his way into her life—cementing their friendship—with Isabel inviting him to accompany her on her various excursions around the cities she knew so well.

He carried his Nikon frequently, playing the tourist so obviously and so effortlessly that no one gave his watch a second glance. While the big camera captured each city's must-see attractions, the watch on his wrist got its own workout—keeping a record of the establishments the women frequented and the people they met.

"Transoceanic is a nest of spies and traitors," Pete said one morning over coffee. "But with your help, we'll catch them and lock them away forever."

Michael was not convinced. He had written extensive reports and taken hundreds of photos with the watch-camera, but had never seen anything that led him to believe the women were engaged in espionage. He had not spotted the Russian again, had never detected anything unusual in Isabel's behavior—other than Isabel just being Isabel. *A nest of spies and traitors? No way. What is Pete really after?*

PART FOUR

Maggie

1994

Chapter 31

January 24, 1994
CIA Headquarters
Langley, Virginia

Cat picked up the remaining half of the roast beef sandwich, envisioned the fat globules clogging her arteries, and set it back on the plate. The cafeteria offerings were generally pleasing to the palate, but not always the healthiest options on the planet. She picked up the tray and ambled toward the exit, tossing the uneaten sandwich and chips into the rubbish bin. She smiled politely at the two men boarding the elevator with her—young, new analysts, probably—and gave them an encouraging nod when she got off at her floor.

One of the admin staff spotted her and stood, a note in his hand, as she approached her office.

"You had a call," he said. "From Collette Bishop. She wouldn't tell me what it's about."

She took another step before his words registered, then stopped in her tracks, processing the message. She was renowned for her poker face, be it good news or bad, but the admin's words were a bombshell. She blinked.

"Give me the number," she said quietly.

She closed her office door and gave herself a moment to speculate about the reason for the call. The news, she was sure, would not be good. Collette Bishop was Marc Bishop's mother. *It's been a long time,* she thought. *A very long time.*

Marc, the son of an American diplomat and his French wife, Collette, was born during his father's posting in Tehran in the late fifties. He grew up speaking English, French, and Farsi. During his father's assignment to Iraq in 1964, he began learning Arabic. By 1967, when the Six-Day Arab-Israeli War shattered diplomatic relations across the region, he was already proficient in the language. His father's later assignments to Ankara and Abu Dhabi added Turkish to his repertoire and further cemented his fluency in Arabic.

In addition to his linguistic capabilities, he developed a deep understanding of the region's cultures. He was completing a master's in Middle Eastern studies at Columbia University when the CIA knocked on his door. Intrigued, he accepted their offer. Like Cat, he had never looked back.

They were lovers once, having met at The Farm—the CIA's training facility near Williamsburg, Virginia—shortly after joining the Agency. The attraction was immediate and, after smoldering for three weeks, exploded in a passionate weekend at a beach house on Hatteras Island. Their paths diverged, however, when she was assigned to Tehran and he was posted to Saudi Arabia. Still, they managed to maintain a relationship for nearly two years, finding a night here and an afternoon there in some of the globe's least romantic locales.

Then she met Tom Powell. While Marc was intensely sexual, reckless, and daring, Tom was romantic, levelheaded, and measured. An hour with Marc was like being swept up in a tornado, terrifying and exhilarating at the same time. Being with Tom was like a comfortable and soothing day at a spa. Marc picked up women in every port. Tom was the loyal, trustworthy man who would never stray, the yin to her yang. She had made her choice and had no regrets. Still, every so often, unbidden and unexpected, Marc would surface in her dreams.

Over the years, she kept tabs on Marc's exploits, concern for his safety simmering quietly beneath her stoic exterior. He spent most of his time in the field, far from the comforts of embassies and the camaraderie of fellow Westerners, gathering intelligence and recruiting assets to be his sources.

In September of 1990, during the lead-up to the Gulf War, he was dispatched to the Kurdistan region of northern Iraq. He set out on his most dangerous assignment yet, under the cover name of Khalid.

In the months before the war, and for the forty-two days that the coalition bombarded Iraq during Operation Desert Storm, his presence gave the coalition critical, real-time knowledge of the events taking place in the northern part of the country. After the announcement of the ceasefire in late February, he remained in place, still monitoring activities in the region. He was scheduled to rotate back to Langley in mid-April. Then, in early April, the ever-belligerent Iraqi army swarmed back into the region, exacting a terrible revenge on the Kurds. When three days passed with no word from Marc and no sightings of the man the locals called Khalid, his colleagues at Langley suspected the worst.

He surfaced two days later—having escaped the slaughter by running for his life. He had slipped across the Turkish border, making his way to Cizre, where the Agency maintained an unremarkable flat in an unremarkable apartment building. Cat, copied on the message sent to headquarters, breathed a long sigh of relief and made the convincing argument that Marc needed a break. A car was arranged, and he was transported to Ankara for debriefing.

After two comfortable weeks of undisturbed sleep, thirty-minute showers, all the food he could eat, and the replacement of his threadbare clothing, they presented him with another assignment. The United States was entering northern Iraq to provide protection and humanitarian assistance to the Kurds. Since he spoke the language and knew the region well, it was generally felt that he could be of some help. He shrugged and accepted the posting at the base in Silopi.

No one could have predicted that, five days later, he and two others would be gunned down stepping out of the camp's mess tent.

After the shooting, quick action by several of the camp's soldiers, and the talent of a young army surgeon, saved the life of the man they knew as Khalid. The major who had been with him was not so fortunate, having bled out from a gunshot wound to the chest. The third victim, a captain, had taken a bullet to his upper arm, but survived to resume his career in the military. The shooter had never been identified. The initial theory was that some local, infuriated at his lot in life, had taken aim at the three Americans.

A helicopter evacuated Khalid to the big air base at Incirlik, where his ID was entered into the computer. The entry triggered an alert to Langley, where the gods of the clandestine service demanded more answers. They wasted no time in launching an investigation of their own and assigning a team to oversee Khalid's care.

The investigators were initially stymied by the absence of people who could attest to Khalid's whereabouts on the day of the attack. With the exception of the colonel, who had seen Khalid at breakfast, and the captain, who had seen him at dinner, no one recalled seeing him for the entire day. For almost twelve hours, he seemed to have simply vanished.

The interview with the captain, however, was more enlightening. The captain, recalling the incident in detail and describing how someone had called Khalid's name, insisted that Khalid had been specifically targeted. He theorized that he and the major had merely been collateral damage. The team's natural progression of thought was that Khalid's life might still be at risk.

After conferring with the spymasters at Langley, the team announced Khalid's death, fudged the paperwork, updated his information in the computer, and loaded him on a transport aircraft departing Turkey an hour later. The official record attributed Khalid's death to massive head and chest trauma, the result of two gunshot wounds inflicted by an unknown assailant.

The investigative team eventually concluded that Marc had been targeted, but they could not say who or why. His whereabouts that day, and the nature of his activities, remained a mystery. For the last three years, he had been living in his mother's home in Paris, rebuilding his strength and trying to recover the missing pieces of his life.

Fewer than ten people in the world knew that Khalid was still alive. And now, out of the blue, his mother had called. Cat braced herself and reached for the phone.

Chapter 32

Cat cradled the phone to her cheek and responded when the voice at the other end of the line answered the call. "Collette?"

"Bonjour, Catherine. It is good to hear your voice. I am sorry to disturb you, but Marc asked me to call. He has remembered something important."

Frowning, Cat realigned her thinking. She had expected bad news. "How is he?"

She listened as Collette related the anguishing first few weeks after Marc had arrived in Paris. Intubated, medically sedated, and near death for weeks, he had remained in the hospital for two months before waking up one morning and asking for ice cream.

That Marc had survived at all was a miracle, she told Cat. But the traumatic brain injury presented a challenge. It had not only erased some of his memory, it had jumbled some of those things he could remember and played havoc with his short-term recall. On most days, his memory was crystal clear—on others, a hazy mess. He would sometimes mix up people, or dates, or locations—or all three. His rehabilitation had been arduous, but he had worked his way back. Aside from exhibiting a few behavioral quirks, he had progressed beyond anyone's expectations.

Cat's relief was transparent. "I'm so glad that he's doing well. Are these behavioral quirks troublesome?"

"Oh no. Not at all. We have all adjusted."

She went on to say that Marc's most eye-raising oddity was his habit of dressing in a white thobe and wearing a ghutra on his head. And while he would respond to his given name of Marc, he often introduced himself to others as Khalid.

Khalid. Cat felt a cold shiver run down her back. Marc was using his undercover name.

Collette explained that Marc's physician—Dr. Al-Zahawi, who contracted medical services to the clandestine services of the US government—attributed the behavior to the identity crisis Marc was suffering as a result of his forced medical separation from the job he loved. The doctor believed that dressing as an Arab gave Marc a sense of purpose, of being back in the region where he had spent so much of his life. The other factor, the doctor admitted, was that the ghutra concealed the physical damage to Marc's head.

"He asked me to call you because he has remembered something important," Collette said. "He was watching a news broadcast on the television this morning, a piece about the war in Bosnia. He recognized someone and suddenly began to remember things about the day he was hurt. Catherine, I must tell you that, before this, his memory of that day has been blank. I was cooking dinner when he ran into the kitchen, shouting at me that he wanted his boots. I tried to calm him. I told him that his boots were still in the duffel that they sent home with him from the hospital. You know, I actually opened that bag once, not long after he ... there were some clothes, stained with ..." she trailed off.

Cat prodded her gently. "And did you still have the boots?"

"Oh yes. He was so anxious! And then he twisted the heels off. I have never seen such a thing!"

Cat jerked upright. "What did he find?"

"He would not show me. He said he was doing his job, that he could not tell me anything more. Then he looked for your number and asked me to call you. There are some papers he wants you to have."

Cat sat back, her mind racing, wondering how much confidence she should have in Marc's recollections. His memory was no longer reliable, and the notes were three years old. A lot of water had passed under the bridge since then.

"Let me make some arrangements, Collette," she said. "I will call you tomorrow."

Collette returned the handset to its cradle and looked over at her son.

"She is making *arrangements* and will call tomorrow," she said caustically.

"Cat's just being cautious," Marc said. "For now, I need a photographer—a professional, someone who might have a darkroom. Do you know anyone? Someone you trust?"

Collette had met Cat only once, but that single encounter had been enough to make her realize that her son was head over heels for the woman. While he had never shared the circumstances of their breakup, she knew that it had caused him great pain. Therefore, when he had asked her to place the call to Cat that evening, she had understood. He was still very much in love. She was not sure if she should be happy that her son had reclaimed a portion of his memory or mournful about what that memory meant. A tear slipped down her cheek as she nodded and dialed the number of a longtime friend. When the call went to a recording, she left a message.

She replaced the handset and told her son, "I am sure he will help, but he may be away. He travels often. It may be a few days before he responds."

Thrumming her fingers on the desk, Cat considered the best course of action. *Do nothing? Bring Marc to Langley? Send someone to interview him?* She picked up the phone.

Chapter 33

January 25–27, 1994
New York City
Paris, France

On a frigid Tuesday night in late January, Pete showed up unexpectedly, just as Michael was leaving the apartment to meet friends for drinks.

"You'll have to cancel," Pete said.

Michael pushed past him. "I just got back. I'm meeting friends. I need some free time. Come back tomorrow."

"No can do, Michael. It's rather urgent."

Michael went back into his apartment and called his friends, agreeing to meet an hour later than planned. He moved over to the window, looked out, and then turned around and leaned against the sill. "So, what's so important?"

"This one's hot," Pete said.

"What do you mean?"

"Well, not that. Oh, she's a looker for sure, but more than that, we're almost certain that she is engaged in some high-level espionage. Her husband is some kind of star over at the State Department, specializes in Middle Eastern affairs. That entire region is still a powder keg, and there are ongoing negotiations that he's involved in. In the meantime, we believe she's feeding intel to the Iraqis. I smell a divorce in the oven, and arresting her is gonna be the icing on that cake."

He pulled out a picture of a very pretty redhead. "Her name is Maggie. Maggie Marshfield. We need to know who she's talking to. We really need photos. She's on the Paris crew tomorrow night."

Michael put his fork down. "What do you want me to do this time?"

"Same thing, Michael, but take lots of pictures—anyone she talks to, anywhere she goes. You're a natural. Get in her good graces and follow her around like a puppy dog, just like you did with Isabel Alvarez. She'll love it."

Michael was quick to learn that Maggie Marshfield was nothing like Isabel. She was drop-dead gorgeous and possessed an extraordinary skill for dealing with passengers. She had a knack for listening, her manner suggesting that whoever was doing the talking was the center of the universe. Like Isabel, Maggie was a purser. Unlike Isabel, she was adored by her fellow crewmembers. Michael wondered if she was just naturally adept at relating to people, or if her husband—the diplomat from the State Department—had played a part.

She had been in the airline industry for over fifteen years and was still great at her job. She still had *it*, that unquantifiable blend of sophistication, energy, and good looks that were prerequisites for a career in the aviation's international sector. Theoretically, the company also looked for some semblance of customer service ethic, but Michael assumed that was secondary. If you were beautiful and hated people, you might still get the job. If you were great with people but had a face like a dog, you were dead meat. But Maggie was special. She had the face and manners of an angel.

Maggie worked in the back of the airplane on the way to Paris. Michael kept his eyes on her, but it was impossible to know if she was engaged in any secret communication. She could have scribbled a note on a napkin, slipped classified papers under the liner of a meal tray, dropped a metal capsule into a drink, or simply released something from her hand while leaning over a passenger's seat.

Pete had said that she was passing information to the Iraqis. Michaels eliminated the majority of passengers as possibilities because they were American or European. Instead, he focused on several travelers who appeared to be of Middle Eastern descent. Nevertheless, he saw nothing in their communication with Maggie that aroused his suspicion. He became convinced that if any exchange would take place, it would be on the ground, in Paris.

After the dinner service, the crew gathered in the galley, setting up the rotations for dinner and rest breaks. Michael rested his forearms on the galley counter and stared at the ovens, thinking. He was dreading Paris, not wanting to waste his time trailing after another Transoceanic flight attendant on the implausible assumption that she was a spy. *It's stupid,* he thought. *Why would she do it?* He leaned over his coffee cup, absently rubbing the rim with his index finger.

"Michael? Are you okay?"

Jolted out of his reverie, he straightened. The question had come from Maggie, her expression one of concern. On an impulse, he decided to try the same ploy that had worked so well with Isabel.

"Just thinking. It's my first time in Paris, and as much as I want to see the city, I'm not looking forward to seeing it by myself."

He waited for some response from her, but she stood still, looking at him quizzically. He decided to take the plunge. "Would you mind if I tagged along with you? I won't bother you. I would just like some company."

And in this, too, Maggie proved she was nothing like Isabel.

"I'm sorry," she said, the wrinkle between her eyebrows suggesting sympathy with his plight. "But I have plans to meet up with friends. Perhaps next time, if we fly together again."

At the hotel, Michael hurried to his room and threw on a pair of jeans, a lightweight sweater, sneakers, a blue and orange ski parka, and an orange knit hat, then raced back to the lobby. He stopped by the front desk and asked for a map.

"The hotel is here," the concierge said, circling a spot on the map before handing it to Michael. "You will find the Metro station across the street and around the corner."

Michael took a seat in the far corner of the lobby, keeping an eye on the elevator while studying the map. After thirty minutes, he began to worry that he had missed her. After forty-five, he told himself that he would only wait another fifteen minutes. But ten minutes later, Maggie stepped off the elevator and walked straight to the hotel's entrance. He waited a beat and then sprang from his seat to follow her.

She was a fast walker, but he kept pace, staying far enough behind that she would not notice him, but close enough that he would not lose her. The task was made easier by her choice of clothing: she was wearing a strawberry-colored scarf, its ends flowing down the back of her coat. In a sea of bland winter attire, the color was like a beacon. He had a fleeting thought that, as a diplomat's wife, she might have been trained in surveillance detection. He quickly cast the idea aside. *I'm either going to lose her, or she's going to see me and have me arrested for stalking.* As the thought raced through his head, it sparked another. He glanced at his jacket, at the bright orange stripe running down its left side, and hastily took it off, along with his orange hat, wadding them both into a bundle that he tucked beneath his arm.

Trying to ignore the biting cold, he studied her back and became mesmerized by the sight of the leather messenger bag tapping against her left hip as she walked. It looked large enough to fit a ream of legal-sized paper, and he wondered what secrets she might be carrying. He fantasized about somehow stealing the bag, but it had a crossbody strap and a snatch-and-grab would be nearly impossible. By the time she skipped down the steps into the Saint-Lazare Metro station, he was shivering violently. As she neared the bank of ticket machines, he wondered how he could get close enough to see her destination when, subway pass already in hand, she walked past the machines and pushed through the turnstile.

He sprinted toward a ticket dispenser and, with no knowledge of her plan, purchased a day pass with unlimited rides. By the time he went through the gate, she was nowhere in sight. Guessing that she would be traveling inbound, he sprinted toward the platform and caught sight of her boarding the second subway car. He sprinted to the third car and leapt inside just as the doors were closing, grabbing a bar to lean against. Looking through the glass doors separating the cars, he could just make out a sliver of the red scarf. He kept his eyes locked on Maggie and prayed that she would not look his way. He shook out the parka, stuffing the hat in one of the pockets, and put it on, inside out, the navy lining as bland as any other clothing on the train. The only distractions were the now-visible labels, at the neck and on the seam under the armpit. Two women, seated across from him, eyed him curiously, then giggled and whispered back and forth like two conspirators. He ignored them, hugged himself tightly to restore some warmth to his body, and focused on the crowd in the car ahead of him.

Maggie got off at the third stop and, without hesitation, took off for the exit. Michael took a mental note of the station name and went after her. He realized that, wherever she was going, she must have been there before. She was not only already in possession of a Metro pass, she was sure of the route, not needing to consult a map or even look up at the directional signs.

When they emerged from the station, Michael was disoriented until, after two blocks, they crossed a bridge over the Seine. The bridge emptied onto an island in the middle of the river, the Île de la Cité, which housed Notre Dame Cathedral. He had heard much about the majestic structure and, knowing that it was a tourist magnet, imagined that it could make a good meeting place. And, he admitted to himself, he wanted to see it, wanted to enjoy the sights of Paris as he had enjoyed those of London.

She made a left turn at the corner ahead, while he got caught behind a large group of schoolchildren, whose jumping and skipping and interlocking of arms disrupted the otherwise suffocating but orderly flow of pedestrians. When he reached the corner, the street opened into a plaza, and the towers of Notre Dame loomed in front of him. Despite the gloomy winter day, the entire area was teeming with tourists. He scanned the plaza for the red scarf but could not find her.

He spun wildly, confused, until finally spotting a flash of color to his left, behind a wrought-iron gate at the entry to a wide stone building. He broke into a run, knowing that once she entered the building proper, it would be difficult to find her.

Approaching the entry, he noticed the building's name chiseled into the stone overhead: Hôtel-Dieu. *Hotel? Why did she come here?* But as he stepped inside, he found himself transfixed. The structure was massive, comprised of two long, slender, rectangular wings running parallel to one another for at least five hundred feet. An arched loggia ran the length of each, culminating at a portico at the far end. The design gave the building an open, welcoming feel, and allowed natural light and fresh air to penetrate the interior. Between the two sections lay a courtyard and immaculately manicured garden. The effect was stunning in its beauty and tranquility, a classic example of Italian Renaissance architecture.

He looked around, perplexed by the absence of a hotel lobby and the typical legion of staff.

A voice behind him asked sweetly, "May I help you?"

Turning toward the woman, he noticed an array of signs, one in red with an arrow and the word *Urgences*, confounding him even more. He responded with his own question: "What is this place?"

"It is a hospital, monsieur, of course. But you are American, no? You would not know this. The gardens and architecture are very beautiful, and of course you may visit." She put her finger to her lips and added, "And it will be good to be quiet."

He thanked her and found his way to the garden. *A hospital? Is Maggie sick? Visiting someone who is?* He had no answers. He had been lucky thus far, tracking Maggie all the way to Notre Dame. But now she was nowhere to be found. He was thoroughly chilled, his fingers and ears aching from the cold. He found a bench in the damp shadows at the edge of the garden and retrieved the hat from his pocket, pulling it over his head. He kept his hands in his pockets as he fumbled with the map, wondering what to do next.

Chapter 34

January 27, 1994
Paris, France

Marc's hope that Cat might fly to Paris was dashed when he spotted Maggie Marshfield entering the hospital. He had seen her, a stunning redhead, in many of Cat's photos. Watching her approach, he could see that she was equally beautiful in person. He wondered how much she knew about the work he had done—and about his relationship with Cat.

He tamped down his disappointment that Maggie seemed not to recognize him at all, for the first time grasping the reason that they had never met. Cat knew him well. She had been aware of his attraction to beautiful women, had known he would have been interested in Maggie, and she would not have allowed him the opportunity to jeopardize the women's friendship. So why had she sent Maggie now? And then he grasped her reasoning. Cat had gone below the radar, working unofficially, to protect him. To all but a very few at Langley, he was officially dead. She had quietly sent her best friend—someone she trusted without question—to meet with him.

Mentally, he scolded Cat. *You should not have sent Maggie. This is more dangerous than you know. You have put your friend's life in jeopardy.*

He shook her hand in greeting and gave his name as Khalid, then introduced the man beside him as Dr. Al-Zahawi. He led her to the doctor's office, a space that was private, quiet, and comfortable. In the time since his discharge from the hospital, he had frequently experienced issues with anxiety when outside the confines of his mother's home. The hospital was an exception. He could, occasionally, manage a coffee and cake at the patisserie across the street or a visit to the bookstore on the corner, but only in full daylight and never at dusk. Even today, for a meeting of such importance, he had needed the doctor to accompany him.

He handed Maggie photocopies of the notes he had written before the attack in Turkey. He described the circumstances under which he had witnessed an exchange of weapons for money, involving two American soldiers and a group of unidentified foreign nationals. He had included the names of the soldiers who had accepted the money, as well as the name of a colonel who might have been involved.

At the end of the meeting, Khalid offered his hand and Maggie extended hers. But instead of a quick shake, he grasped her fingers. Startled, Maggie started to object, but then he spoke, his voice so soft she could barely hear his words.

"Tell her I still miss her," he said.

Maggie's eyes flew open, and she gaped at him, wondering what game he was playing, until she saw the sadness in his eyes. Maggie made the mental leap, realizing that Cat had once had a relationship with this man. It explained why Cat had seemed so concerned about him, and why she had sent Maggie to the meeting. And a second later, her head spinning, she concluded that Cat must have known him not just romantically, but also professionally, which meant that he had worked in the intelligence community, and perhaps still did. She was stunned that Cat had not shared any of the background with her.

Is Khalid even his real name? Why didn't she tell me about this guy? Had they been serious? What is she hiding?

She turned to go, and then he dropped the bomb.

"There is more," he said. "I took photos. But the film is being developed and won't be ready for a few days. Listen to me. There is a lot of money involved here. You need to be careful."

Maggie frowned, wondering if he was just paranoid. She hid the uncertainty and nodded at him. "Thank you for the warning. We'll arrange to pick them up ... um ... next week."

His eyes bore into hers. "Make no mistake. This is dangerous—for both of you. These are bad people, and they have killed before."

She was taken aback. She had never before been concerned about her safety—Cat would never knowingly put her in danger.

Maggie Marshfield had learned, years ago, that Cat worked for the CIA. It was a secret Maggie had never betrayed. While she knew little about Cat's work, she had witnessed her friend's restraint whenever the "What do you do?" subject came up at social gatherings. Cat vaguely presented herself as a freelance marketing consultant and was adept at deflecting questions, always steering the conversation to another topic. Maggie's husband, Paul, whose clearances allowed him to know much more, revealed only that Cat was *very* good at her job. Subject closed.

Maggie had remained in the dark until nine years ago, when Cat had asked her to collect a package from an asset in New Delhi. "No big deal," Cat had said. "He'll give you a couple rolls of film. Just put them in the bag with your camera. Nobody will give you a second look."

The onetime request had turned into an arrangement in which Maggie helped Cat several times a year. As the frequency of her assignments had increased, so, too, had the responsibility. While she still occasionally couriered items back and forth, she had gradually become more involved in actual intelligence gathering and had made numerous trips at Cat's behest. She had never told Paul about any of it, walling off the secret that only she and Cat shared.

Maggie summoned a brave face and replied, "I'll be fine."

Michael became aware of the murmur of voices, the volume gradually increasing. The words were unintelligible, but one of the voices was female. *Maggie.* The sounds grew louder, and he judged that they must be on the floor above, walking in his direction. They stopped directly over his head, and he froze. The open gallery allowed snatches of their conversation to drift into the garden below.

A man said, "... lot of money ... careful."

Then Maggie's voice, "... pick up ... next week ..."

The man again, his words clear, said, "... dangerous for both of you. They have killed before."

Michael deduced that they must have split up then, because the voices of the two men were fading. But he caught a phrase or two—in Arabic.

He threw caution aside, racing down the gallery until he reached the colonnade that connected the two wings. He took the steps two at a time, up to the next level, arriving in time to steady his arm against one of the columns and snap pictures of the two men walking toward him. The man on the left wore a white medical coat, snaps fastened in the front with the sleeves pushed up on his forearms, and a hospital badge affixed over the right breast. *A doctor,* Michael thought. The dark-bearded man on the right was tall, with a strong jaw and imposing physique. He wore traditional Arab garb, with a long white thobe over his body and a white ghutra on his head.

The men were startled by his sudden appearance, their eyes growing wide. The man in the thobe reacted first, lunging toward Michael, while the doctor pressed himself against the wall and backpedaled.

Michael turned on his heels and leapt down the steps. Reaching the bottom, he ran toward the front of the building, arms pumping, as the tall Arab's shouts carried across the courtyard. He reached the entry and plunged through the doors, into the throng of people. He lowered his head and pulled his hat off, hoping to somehow become invisible. He was afraid to turn around, afraid to walk too fast, fearing that either might attract the attention of his pursuer. He melted into a group of men and women moving away from the cathedral and toward a bridge that led to the opposite side of the Seine. He ambled with them. Only when he reached the other side, what Parisians called the Left Bank, did he turn around. There was no sign of the white-robed man.

He wandered for several blocks, eventually finding a crowded café. He sat, staring blankly at the menu, letting the adrenaline wash out of his system and the warmth of the café seep in, and tried to process what had just happened. After four months of stalking his fellow crewmembers, he had finally hit the mother lode. There was no doubt that Maggie Marshfield was in it up to her pretty little neck.

Chapter 35

January 28, 1994
Washington, DC

Maggie caught a flight back to Washington within ninety minutes of arrival in New York. From the moment she entered the line to clear customs at JFK until the wheels touched down at Washington National and she found a pay phone, she had fidgeted anxiously. She had passed Marc's notes off to a courier the night before, but had not included any mention of the photographs he had promised. That information could only be given verbally, in person. She fumbled for coins, then dropped them into the slot on the phone box and dialed the number. Drumming her fingers on the phone booth's shelf, she waited impatiently for the Langley operator to connect the call.

"Come pick me up," she said when Cat answered. "It's important."

"Thirty minutes, maybe forty-five," Cat said. "I need to close out a few things."

"I'll meet you outside."

Maggie stayed indoors for thirty minutes, savoring the warmth of the terminal, before walking out into the bitter cold. She spotted Cat's car five minutes later. She started talking the moment she slid into the passenger seat.

"He has photographs. Actually, will have photographs. He says he's having them printed."

Cat's eyes grew wide, and her lips parted in surprise. She glanced over at Maggie.

"He has photos?"

"That's what he says."

"And he didn't think to have his mother mention that when she called?"

Maggie looked out the window, not wanting to look Cat in the face. "Actually, I think he was hoping that you would be the one making the trip to Paris. He said to tell you that he misses you."

That made Cat pause a beat. Finally, she said, "It was a long time ago, and I have my reasons for not telling you. It's complicated, but the crux of the matter is that it's better that you don't know anything. When did he say the photos would be ready?"

"Next week."

Cat took a deep breath. She kept her face blank, but internally, she was seething. Marc, or his mother, should have mentioned the photographs during their call. Marc's report was shocking in its detail, made more so by the attempted assassination only hours later. And while the value of a handwritten report from three years ago was questionable, photos added an entirely new dimension.

The pictures also increased the threat level. If anyone were to find out that Marc was alive and that he was holding evidence, Marc would be at risk—and so would Maggie. The incident may have been three years old, but whoever had done the shooting was still out there.

"I need to think about this—and about whether to send you back. It could be dangerous," Cat said.

Maggie looked over at her friend. "He said the same thing."

"Well, there you go."

Ultimately, Cat decided to tread cautiously. While there was little likelihood that the attacker would be aware Marc was still alive, she was wary of call logs showing a string of calls between her office and Paris. She decided to wait a few days before contacting Collette Bishop.

Chapter 36

January 28, 1994
New York City

Genuinely pleased, Pete's face lit up when Michael handed him the tiny spool of film from the watch.
"This is great work," he said. "Now we'll learn who the Marshfield woman is selling our secrets to. I know you're probably ready to take a trip to the islands for a little fun, but don't go out of town just yet. We may need you for some follow-up work. I'll come by in a day or two and let you know our next move."

He left Michael and checked his watch on reaching the corner. It was nearing rush hour. *Subway or cab?* He made his decision upon eyeing the leaden skies and the traffic, and set a fast pace for the subway station, grousing as he walked. He hated the New York subways, thinking that every rider should be required to spend two days each year with a bucket and scrub brush. The stations were filthy, rat-infested, and reeked of sour urine and vomit. The tiles were chipped, the paint was peeling, the walkways were crumbling, and there was trash everywhere he looked. He would never understand why the citizens of New York tolerated such squalor.

He found a working pay phone on the third try—another annoyance—and hesitated. He rarely used the telephone. Phones could be compromised, and he was calling from a nonsecure phone. But it was nearing the end of the day. He wanted to make sure someone would be there to process the film. He dialed.

To the voice that answered, he said, "Richard?"
The voice said, "There is no Richard here."
"Is this 7-4-0-2-1-3-0?"

"No, you must have the wrong number."

The name "Richard" established his identify. The other digits established a date and time for their meeting. If the time had been unacceptable, the person answering would have provided a different number.

He boarded the train into Manhattan, switched lines at 50th Street and again at Columbus Circle, riding to the last stop at Van Cortlandt Park. He emerged from the station to find that the temperature had plummeted and sleet was spilling out of the skies. He spent several minutes trying to hail a cab and finally gave up. Slogging through the mush, he thought, *This had better be worth it.*

Thirty minutes later, he faced the tall, white building and presented his credentials to the guard at the gated entry. Cleared, he stomped up the long drive and into the building. The guard had called ahead. A man in a charcoal-gray suit was waiting. Pete had met with him several times and still did not know his name—everyone called him *G*.

"I have the film," he said to the man. "Can we get it done now?"

The man took Pete by the elbow and led him to the elevator. "This is about the Marshfield woman, yes?"

"Yes."

"She is well-connected. You think there will be something useful here?"

"I think we may have something, yes."

"Very well. Let's go find out."

An hour later, the woman from the Documents section approached them, a large brown envelope in her hand.

"There were only two usable photos on the spool. One of them is quite clear. The other, not so much because the camera was tilted away from the subjects."

She turned her back and walked away while the two men pulled the photos from the envelope.

Pete squinted at the men in the photo, one in a doctor's white coat, the other in a white Arab thobe. Both subjects were wide-eyed, as if startled.

He asked, "Who is it?"

G frowned. "The face is not familiar. I'll send it in. Someone should recognize him. Stay the night—take one of the guest apartments. You can have dinner with us. The answers will be here in the morning."

Pete wasn't sure which option was least appealing: enduring the snow and another subway ride or having dinner with G and his wife. The woman was a terrible cook. He chose dinner.

G's wife acknowledged him with a nod and sequestered herself in the kitchen, eventually emerging with a platter of boiled pork, boiled peas, and boiled potatoes. Pete forced the food down and, being polite, took seconds when she offered them. He snuck a glance at his host and got a knowing wink in return. G was no fan of her cooking, either.

After dinner, Pete and G sat across from one another and tossed back several shots of vodka. They kept their conversation to a light banter, agreeing that Dallas should easily dominate Buffalo in the upcoming Super Bowl. Shortly after midnight, G accompanied Pete to the guest flat. He punched the push buttons on the secure lock, pushed the door open, and instructed Pete to be back in the office at ten o'clock.

At five minutes before ten the following morning, Pete was standing in front of G's desk. He noticed the file in G's hand and asked, "Who is it?"

"A dead man."

Pete's eyebrows shot up. "What do you mean?"

G handed him two photos. "We believe that these are the same man. On the left is the photo you took. The other was taken three years ago, at a US camp on the Iraqi-Turkish border. The thing is, that man was shot and killed shortly after the photo was taken."

The older photo, apparently taken from a distance, was slightly fuzzy. But as he studied the two images, Pete could see the similarity. Both men were tall and muscled, with hard jaws, dark hair, and deep-set eyes. In the photo Michael had taken, however, the man's face was partially obscured by his beard and the ghutra on his head. Pete's forehead wrinkled with uncertainty.

"It could be," he said, handing the photos back to G. "They look a lot alike."

"We need to make certain," G said. "Your man overheard the Marshfield woman say that she would return next week. I want your man to go back, and I want a recording of the conversation that she has with this man. We need to make plans for handling this, because every instinct tells me that the men in the photos are one and the same. Let's figure out our options."

Four hours and several phone calls later, Pete was back on the subway, mentally rehearsing the script for Michael's next assignment.

Chapter 37

January 29, 1994
New York City

Pete had let Michael know how pleased he was about receiving the roll of film. But now, standing in the kitchen, he slathered on a layer of excitement and praise.

"This is great work," Pete gushed. "All that effort has finally paid off. Thanks to the photos, we have learned the doctor's identity and we're working on the other man. Now all we need to do is to learn what they were discussing. That will give us the trifecta."

Michael shook his head, brushing aside the idea. "I was lucky to get the shots I did, and even luckier that I lived to tell the story. That guy," he said, remembering the man in the long white robe, "would have pounded my brains out if he had caught me."

Pete nodded in empathy. "Scary situation."

"Yes," Michael agreed. "Very."

"Well, now that you know where the Marshfield woman met them and what the men look like, you are wiser and more prepared."

Michael looked at him sharply. "What do you mean?"

Pete shrugged. "You heard them mention a meeting next week, isn't that right? Well, we would like a recording of that next meeting. That's where you come in."

"Are you crazy? I only saw them on the walkway. I have no idea where they actually had the meeting. And they have seen my face. I won't be able to get anywhere near them."

"It's not a problem. The photos told us the name of the doctor, and we will have someone plant a recording device in his office. You will fly to

Paris with her next week. All you will have to do is retrieve the device after the meeting. This should not be difficult."

"Why can't that same someone pick up the recorder and send it to you?"

Pete smiled patiently. "To be frank, I don't trust the man. He is an opportunist. If I ask him to pick it up, he will listen to the recording and want even more money. And I cannot be certain that he would even give me the tape. He could try to sell it to an interested third party. His reputation is, shall we say, somewhat sketchy."

This was a revelation to Michael, that the information could be so important that someone would be willing to pay big money for it. He wondered, not for the first time, what Maggie had gotten herself into.

"Let's celebrate your success in Paris. Let's order a pizza and have a couple of beers to celebrate."

Michael pulled two beers from the refrigerator and shared a toast. But he was surprised. Pete had never before wanted to socialize. He would show up, pay for drinks and dinner, give Michael the assignment, and leave. Michael wondered about the change in behavior. *What does he want now?*

Pete paid for the pizza, grabbed two more beers, and sat beside Michael on the worn sofa. He pulled a slice from the box and said, "We're working on a solution to deal with the Alvarez woman. We will need your help."

Michael looked up, frowning. "What do you mean?"

"I want you to go to London tomorrow night. Isabel is on the crew. You'll be home on Tuesday, in time to fly back to Paris for Maggie's next meeting with the Arab."

Groaning, Michael said, "I really need a few days off."

"Soon, Michael. Just go to London and Paris, and then you can have a week."

"What's so important about London? What more can you possibly need?"

"Unfortunately, we know that Isabel is committing treason, but we have no concrete proof. So, we have to be creative. We have come up with a plan to remove her from the playing field."

Michael sat very still, waiting.

Handing Michael a slip of paper, Pete said, "This is a list of what we need."

Michael looked over the list, trying to make sense of it, and gave up. "What is this for?"

"We are building the case against her. The evidence will substantiate our charges against her."

"So you're going to manufacture your own evidence?"

"If she were not endangering national security, things would be different. But we now have an opportunity in which she will have to face the consequences of her actions."

Michael pursed his lips in distaste. "What opportunity?"

Pete ignored Michael's annoyance and offered the explanation. "Recently, there has been some talk of possible changes to America's policy on Cuban refugees. We have learned that, soon, there will be a hush-hush meeting taking place between officials from Cuba and the United States. We don't know which city, yet, but we have a source.

"What interests us is that Cuban officials nearly always travel abroad on Russian aircraft, and never on a US carrier. But in this case, we have learned that, after the meeting, the Cuban delegation is planning to fly to New York on Transoceanic. This may signal a thaw in relations between the two countries.

"For activists like Isabel, this is a hot issue. We're going to arrange for Isabel to hear of this, and provide an opportunity for her to arrange her schedule. She has a history of being disruptive."

Pete was glad he had rehearsed the script. The lies flowed easily, and Michael seemed to buy the fiction.

"So let the police there take care of it," Michael said.

"That's a possibility," Pete replied, "but we like to take care of these things ourselves. We are going to provide irrefutable evidence of her involvement in a conspiracy to disrupt the negotiations."

Michael's stomach clenched. "What are you going to do?"

Pete's voice was barely a whisper. "Are you familiar with the space in the tail? The space that some crewmembers use as a rest area?"

Michael's mouth went dry. Crews had been known to use the space as a bunkroom on long, crowded, overnight flights. It was on just such a leg across the ocean that fellow flight attendant Robert Bailey—known to everyone as Bales—had introduced Michael to what he called "the aft lounge." While the existence of the space was not top secret, Michael was surprised that Pete had heard of it.

"I know about it," Michael said cautiously.

Pete caught Michael's eyes and held them. "On this night flight, Michael, you will need to become more familiar with that space."

"Why?"

"Because, when the time comes, you will place something in the tail of the airplane—something that will have Isabel's fingerprints all over it."

Michael shoved his plate away and rocketed out of his chair. "No! Are you crazy?"

"Sit down, Michael," Pete hissed. "We are not crazy. The device will be harmless. The components will be real, but there will be no explosive material. The threat alone will be enough to put her in jail for a long time."

Michael felt sick. The idea of even a fake device on an airplane was the stuff of nightmares. "I don't care. I'm not going to be involved in this."

Pete ran his finger around the rim of his glass. "Well, I'll give you some time to think about it. Go to London, get the items on the list, and we'll talk when you get back."

Michael realized how naive he had been, never considering that America could support such criminality. For the first time, he began to worry about his own safety. What would they do if he refused? He knew he was expendable, but would they throw him in jail? Kill him? Would they actually go that far? Yes, he thought. *They would. For men in power, it is the same everywhere. They become corrupted.* He hung his head. *I could leave tomorrow, maybe go out west. I have money. America is a big country. It should be easy to disappear.*

That night, Michael tossed and turned, chilled to the bone about the consequences of what Pete was asking him to do and equally fearful about the consequences of just walking away. He finally fell into a fitful sleep and woke up shortly after noon, ill-tempered and famished. He dressed and hurried down the street to a small deli, where he ordered two sandwiches and two drinks. When he returned to his sparsely furnished apartment, he discovered that a manila envelope had been slipped under the door.

As he ripped open the envelope, two photos fell out. He let out an involuntary gasp, the blood draining from his face and his legs turning to jelly. He laid his hand on the wall to steady himself, then stumbled to the sofa and collapsed. The first photo showed his brother Daris, malnourished and unkempt, sitting on a patch of ground with his back against a tree, his hands and feet bound. The other showed his older brother Goran, with his wife and daughter. They looked thin, but otherwise unharmed. The photos were recent, with a copy of last week's International Herald Tribune propped against Daris's chest, the date clearly visible. His infant niece—barely able to pull herself upright a few months ago—had been caught in midstride, running toward the camera.

He pressed the pictures to his chest, ricocheting between tears of joy that his brothers were still alive, grief that he was not there to care for them, and blinding rage over the way the Americans had manipulated him. Pete had known about his brothers all along, kept it to himself, and shown his hand just as Michael was beginning to waver. The implicit threat was terrifying—if he refused to cooperate, his brothers were in grave danger.

There was little choice. He would do as he was told.

Chapter 38

January 30–31, 1994
London, England

T he London-bound flight departed New York at 7:17 p.m., after a half-hour delay. Shortly after takeoff, Michael unbuckled his seatbelt and trudged up the aisle. The mammoth 747 was still climbing, and the incline strained his calves as he made his way forward to the first-class section. Isabel was already out of her seat, opening the galley compartments that held the bar equipment. He pitched in, helping her to unwrap the plastic from the racks of glassware. As they worked, he surprised her by announcing that he had reserved tickets for *Sunset Boulevard*, a musical that had opened in the West End only a few months earlier.

"I just want to thank you," he said, "for showing me around London. I've really enjoyed it." He was surprised to see Isabel blush.

"You are very kind," she responded. "There aren't that many people who want to spend time with me. Most of them think I take this job too seriously, and the rest are put off by my politics. Don't get me wrong, I'm not playing crybaby, just stating facts. And I appreciate that you are an exception."

It was Michael's turn to blush. "To hell with the rest of them," he laughed. "I enjoy your company."

Michael grabbed a paper towel and used it to pick up three wads of plastic wrap that she had discarded, quickly wrapping them in one of the tray table-size cotton napkins used in the first-class cabin. Seeing that other flight attendants were beginning to move about, he tucked the cloth napkin under his arm and returned to the back of the airplane.

Two hours later, after the service was completed, Michael once again strolled up to the front of the plane, this time for his dinner break. He helped

Isabel clean up the remnants of the meal service, poured a few coffees, offered pillows and blankets, helped himself to a meal, and lowered himself onto one of the crew jump seats. He watched Isabel carefully, waiting for her to touch something that might be used as evidence later. When she slipped on the rubber gloves to pull her own meal from the oven, he clicked his tongue in satisfaction. He beckoned her to sit beside him and pretended to show interest while she nibbled at her food and told him about the parts of London they would explore on this trip.

Isabel rose from her seat when one of the passengers, returning from a visit to the restroom, asked for a drink. Michael stood as well, then shoved his used meal tray into the carrier. With Isabel's back turned, he grabbed another cotton napkin and scooped up the gloves.

Getting the lipstick, Swiss Army knife, and cockpit key would be trickier. Isabel had stowed her handbag behind her jump seat, which was directly adjacent to the galley in the forward cabin and in full view of passengers and crew. There was no way he could root around in the bag without being seen. Those items would have to wait.

He studied Isabel for a minute, watching as she used the back of her hand to brush away a stray lock of hair, and felt a sudden pang of regret. He had come to like this woman, to admire her, and he was revolted by the thought of contributing to her undoing. Her life had not been easy. She looked tired, the worry lines on her forehead more pronounced, and he wondered about the demons that haunted her. *But what choice do I have? I have to think of my brothers first.*

He decided to scout the tail halfway through the in-flight movie, when the cabin would be dark and quiet and many people would be asleep or watching the film. There would be few people alert enough to observe his actions. If he waited too long, the movie would end, and the bathroom rush would begin. His nerves were fraying, and he wondered if he would even be able to pull it off. He summoned his courage. *Now or never.*

"I'll be back in a few," he said to the small cluster of flight attendants gathered in the aft galley. No one raised an eyebrow. Crewmembers were human. They needed bathroom breaks.

He walked briskly to the back of the airplane, then turned around and let his eyes scan the cabin in front of him. Assured that no one was watching, and with palms sweating, he raised his hand and slid the overhead panel back. He stepped onto the closet rim and hoisted himself into the tail.

Ninety seconds later, he dropped back to the cabin floor and again looked for anyone whose eyes were glancing his way. He spotted no one. He slipped into one of the lavatories, locked the door, lifted the toilet seat, and promptly threw up.

The next evening, as Isabel and Michael took their seats in the West End's Adelphi Theatre, Isabel placed her purse on the floor between them. The shoulder bag was big and heavy, packed with all the accoutrements of the globe-trotting female flight attendant: passport, flashlight, currency wallet, credit cards, business cards, address book, keys, bottle opener, Swiss army knife, pens, notepads, hairbrush, and cosmetics. Often a crewmember's handbag was so stuffed that the clasp would pop open. Isabel's bag fit that description. Michael waited until after intermission and, when the lights went down, shifted his position so that his hand could reach the bag.

Barely moving a muscle, he pulled his gloves from his pocket and carefully slipped them on. And waited. Ten minutes into the play's final act, he lowered his hand. His fingers found the clasp, and he lifted it slightly, feeling it give way. He waited several minutes to see if there was any reaction from Isabel, if she had heard the sound of the clasp opening or had detected his movements. Nothing. He crossed his legs, allowing his foot to graze the handbag on the floor. The purse tipped over, its contents spilling out. Michael gave the bag an extra nudge with his foot. Isabel's belongings clattered across the floor.

"Mierda!" she exclaimed, the Spanish expletive exploding from her lips.

A few dozen heads twisted toward the sound, annoyed at the distraction. Michael reached down and scooped a mound of the debris into his lap. The couple in front leaned down and retrieved some of the items that had rolled their way, then discreetly passed them back.

As Isabel was trying to jam everything back into the bag, Michael continued to run his hands over the floor. Isabel finally leaned into him and said, "It's fine. Don't worry. We'll look when the show is over."

When the lights came on, the theater patrons passed several additional items their way, including a few coins, a tube of mascara, a gold hoop earring, a roll of breath mints, and even a small coin purse containing fifty British pounds—equal to about seventy-five dollars. At the final inventory, the only things missing were her lipstick, cockpit key, flashlight, and Swiss Army knife.

"The knife and key wouldn't have rolled," she complained. "Somebody just took them. Why would they do that?"

"I'm sorry, Isabel. It's my fault. My foot hit your bag."

She waved her fingers, brushing away the apology. "I just have too much stuff in that stupid purse. My own fault for carrying everything but the kitchen sink."

Mike followed her out of the theater, patting his coat pocket, where the missing items were safely tucked away.

Chapter 39

January 31, 1994
CIA Headquarters
Langley, Virginia

In the week since she had first spoken with Marc's mother, Cat had written and practiced what she would say on the next call. While she would not berate Collette—who did not understand the stakes in the game—Cat could certainly hold Marc's feet to the fire for not following protocol after discovering the old photos. She was still rehearsing as she dialed.

Collette began chattering from the moment she heard Cat's voice. "Oh, it is so good of you to call, my dear! You must be wondering about the film. My friend has been on holiday, in Malta, which is why it took him so long to get back to me. He's quite active, you know, for a man in his eighties. Travels all over, photographing anything relating to World War II—battlefields, graveyards, ruins. Some of them were quite haunting. He published a book, you know ..."

"I'm sure he is quite talented, Mrs. Bishop," Cat interrupted. "But do you have some idea when the photos might be ready?"

"Well, dear, he worked on them last night. He has his own darkroom, you know. He's very skilled. I have no idea how he manages such a thing."

"Yes, I understand it is an art, Collette, but when will be bring the photos to you?"

"Oh! Well, he brought them by this morning. Refused to take any payment at all! Such a gentleman! He was so kind to Marc, saying that Marc might never win any awards for his photography, but he was a hero."

"Collette, may I please speak with Marc?"

"Well ... oh ... well ... of course," Collette stammered.

Cat could hear murmurs as Collette handed the phone to Marc. She held her breath.

"Hello, Cat. Long time."

Marc's voice was more raspy than Cat remembered, perhaps the result of too many surgeries or too many cigarettes. Her eyes misted and her carefully prepared words vaporized. She wanted to ask him if he had quit smoking, how he was getting along, whether he ever thought of her. After a long pause, she pulled herself out of the quicksand.

"Marc. It's good to hear your voice," she said softly.

"I've missed you, Cat."

"Marc ..."

"I know. You're calling about the photos," he said. "I have them. The quality is not too bad, all things considered."

"We need to pick them up."

"Are you coming?"

"Marc ..."

"I know. But a guy can hope. When?"

"Thursday. Same place?"

"No." He told her about the strange incident at the hospital, when the man had jumped in front of him. "He had a camera—in his watch."

"Are you sure?"

"As sure as I can be. I haven't seen him since, but I still think we should switch the location. There's a place called L'Assiette Propre. It's on the Left Bank. I'll arrange to be there at noon."

Cat disconnected the call and, wiping her eyes, dialed Maggie.

"Can you go to Paris again?"

"When?"

"Day after tomorrow."

They chatted for a moment before disconnecting. Maggie waited for the dial tone, then punched in the number for a supervisor she knew in crew scheduling.

"Hey, it's Maggie Marshfield. I need Paris. Wednesday night would be perfect."

"Hang on," the deep voice said.

She listened to the rustling of papers and murmurs of conversation as the arrangements were made.

"Flight One-Zero-Two-Four," the voice said. "Wednesday, the day after tomorrow. You're in luck—it's the only Paris opening on the board."

"Perfect. I owe you."

"Not a problem. Anytime."

"I'll bring back wine. Something good."

"You're the best, Maggie."

Chapter 40

February 1, 1994
New York City

The door buzzer sounded just as Michael was stripping out of his uniform. He was in a hurry, a two-hour weather delay in London making him late for dinner with friends. He knew immediately who was at the door—Pete was the only person who had ever come to visit. Ignoring the buzzer, he stepped into the bathroom. Fifteen minutes later, he emerged from the apartment, clean and shaven. He had walked only half a block before the black car pulled up beside him, Pete in the passenger seat, a stranger at the wheel.

Pete rolled down his window. "Michael," he said, "I need to pick up those items you got in London. And I've learned that the meeting in Paris will take place on Thursday. It's set up—you're on the crew to Paris tomorrow night."

Michael kept walking. "You're an animal," he said over his shoulder.

"That's no way to greet a friend. Come on, now. We have to talk."

Michael turned toward him, anger contorting his face. "Talk? I think your photographs have done the talking. You knew my brothers were alive, but you let me believe they were dead. Now you are threatening to harm them if I do not do as you say? I always believed that America was a special place, that the people here were good people. Now I know how morally corrupt you are, that you are no better than the Serbs, who are intent upon killing every man, woman, and child who happens to be Muslim." He spat at Pete and turned away, resuming his walk.

The car crept along, keeping pace with Michael. Pete turned toward the driver and said something that Michael could not hear, then swiveled back to Michael.

"After you do this thing, your brother Daris will be released."

Michael stopped and turned back toward the car, fury infusing his voice. "And you expect me to believe you? God knows how many other lies you have told me. Is Isabel even a spy? Is Maggie? What about the other women you had me follow? Do you even know how to speak the truth?"

With an icy calm, Pete said, "Sometimes we have to do what we have to do. We needed your cooperation."

"You are a pig."

"I understand that you are angry, Michael. But think of your brothers. You have a chance to save them."

Michael shook his head, fighting an increasing nausea. "Save them? Or condemn them? You only mentioned Daris. What about Goran?"

"He is simply added insurance. You know how it is. We need to be sure that you will not reveal our plans or speak of them afterward. Right now, Goran and his family are safe. When this is over, they will continue to be safe, even prosper, as long as you continue to work with us. But if you do not play along, my hands will be tied, and this will end badly. I will not be able to help you or your brothers."

A sense of defeat washed over Michael, and his stomach roiled. He lurched toward the curb, vomiting into the gutter. He had been trying to devise an escape ever since finding the pictures under his door. It had been an exercise in futility as, one by one, he had discarded every idea that came to mind. He could not go to the authorities—Pete was one of them—and he was in the country under an assumed identity. And if he refused to cooperate, his brothers were as good as dead. It was an impossible situation.

He put his hands on his thighs and kept his head down, waiting for the nausea to subside. He spit into the street, wiped his mouth with his hand, and stood, turning back toward Pete's car.

"I have the things in my apartment," he said.

"Well, let's go get 'em. Time's a-wastin'."

Michael had been careful not to use his bare hands when handling any of the articles with Isabel's fingerprints, dropping everything into one of the hotel's plastic laundry bags and stuffing it into his suitcase. He handed the bag to Pete, who dropped it into a small backpack he had carried upstairs.

"Who's the other guy in the car?" he asked.

"Someone who works with me," Pete replied. "I told him you would make the right decision. He wanted to see for himself."

Pete walked over to the window, opened the shade, and stared at the street below. When he offered no further explanation, a cold shiver of fear prickled along Michael's back. *Was that a signal to the man in the car? Am I in danger? What would have happened if I had not played along?* Michael's temples were suddenly throbbing, and the air in the apartment was stifling. Working to keep his expression impassive, he poured a glass of water from the tap and gulped it down.

Still facing the window, Pete did not notice Michael's anxiety. Michael could feel the sweat pooling in his armpits. He was afraid to ask more, but at the same time, he was afraid of not knowing.

He managed to ask, "W-what happens now?" He heard the quaver in his own voice.

Pete turned back toward him and shrugged. "It's all in motion. Once we find out where the Cubans will be, and when, we'll get you on the crew with Isabel. You will stage the evidence, Isabel will be taken into custody, and you can take a vacation."

Michael's words came out fast and furious. "How can you even be sure she will change her schedule? And about that evidence … she'll figure it out … that I took the knife and the lipstick. She'll remember the other things, too. How are you going to handle that?"

"Michael, it doesn't matter what she says. No one will believe her! She has motive. They will see that she deliberately changed her schedule. Her politics are well-documented. And they will find her fingerprints, not yours." As Pete finished speaking, he jammed his hand into the backpack.

Michael, leaning against the kitchen wall, jerked upright and sucked in a staggered breath, asking himself, *Does he have a gun?* He turned, took two steps toward the door, and reached for the knob.

Pete, his hand still in the bag, looked up. "Where are you going?"

Michael froze. "I thought I heard someone at the door," he stammered.

Pete's face morphed from puzzlement to a sly grin as the truth became clear. "What? You thought I was going to shoot you or something?"

Michael said nothing.

Pete tilted his head, his eyes narrowing and the skin between his eyes creasing deeply, as if he were making a new assessment of Michael and not liking what he saw. He shook his head in admonition, then pulled a map from the bag and thrust it at Michael.

"Take this with you to Paris. After viewing the photographs, we placed a recording device in the doctor's office. We have learned that they are planning lunch at a café called L'Assiette Propre." He pointed out a circled spot on the map. "We believe that plan is firm, but it could change. Thus, the map."

Michael took the map and glanced at the café's location. "It's not far from Notre Dame."

"Right. Close enough to the hospital for the doctor to have lunch there. When they arrive, the waiter will put a special bread basket on their table. When they leave, the waiter will retrieve the basket and give it to you. He's been paid, but he's French. He'll probably want more. Give him another five hundred francs."

"Will that be enough? Are you sure he'll give it to me?"

"He might be greedy, but he's not stupid. If he resists, tell him that if he doesn't want his balls to end up as morsels in the Boeuf Bourguignon, he should cooperate."

Michael was horrified. "Oh, my God! Are you expecting me to ... "

Pete looked at Michael as if he were an idiot. "Of course not. Don't be ridiculous," he said, brushing the idea away with his fingers.

As Michael walked back to the sofa, he spotted the backpack on the table, yawning open and exposing the black metal of a gun. He forced himself to look away, to dismiss what he had seen, yet wondered if the weapon held a bullet that was meant for him if he did not cooperate. He could not help but think that he had just passed some sort of test.

Pete's eyes narrowed, and he stared hard at Michael as he said, "Michael, this will all work out, and your family will be safe. Just don't get any ideas. Don't screw it up."

The implicit threat was terrifying. Michael's chest was so tight that it felt as if he might suffocate. He was trapped. Completely, irrevocably, trapped.

Chapter 41

February 3, 1994
Paris, France

The flight to Paris was uneventful, with the crew jocular and efficient, all the galley ovens operational, no malfunctions in the inflight entertainment system, no unruly passengers, and no turbulence—only the vibrating thrum of the engines powering the aircraft across the Atlantic. *And,* Michael thought, *Maggie Marshfield is still gorgeous—and still a suspected traitor.*

Maggie seemed surprised to see him again. While crews were often scheduled to fly together for a month at a time, it was unusual to encounter the same reserve flight attendant on consecutive trips. Michael worried that the doctor and his companion might have mentioned the incident to her, although he doubted that they could have described him well enough for her to make the connection. He relaxed when she gave no hint of being suspicious. On the contrary, she was friendly and even remembered his previous request to be shown around Paris.

Midway through the flight, he told Maggie that he was not feeling well and asked permission for an extended visit to the aft lavatory. Maggie appeared only mildly concerned—international crewmembers often experience nausea and diarrhea—but found it odd that Michael would choose a lavatory in the rear of the plane. She cocked her head as she nodded her assent, then shook her head in wonder as Michael hurried to the back of the airplane.

For the second time in as many flights, he locked the lavatory door and hoisted himself into the tail. And once again, he waited several minutes before reentering the cabin. This time, he was calmer. If he had to place a device in the tail, he was now reasonably sure he could do it without being caught.

After landing in Paris, he walked side by side with Maggie through Charles de Gaulle Airport—locked in the sterile, glass-paneled corridors reserved for persons entering the country. As they neared the immigration counter, she looked at him sideways.

She asked, "Are you still in the market for a personal tour? I have some business to attend to, but I should be back to the hotel by one o'clock."

Surprised by the offer, Michael hesitated, calculating. *I wonder when the waiter will hand over the recorder. What if I have to wait longer? Can I get back to the hotel in time?*

He hedged. "That sounds great! But could we make it one-thirty or two?"

Maggie blinked, paused a beat, held her smile in place, and finally said, "Sure. Two, it is." But she could not help but think that, for someone new to Paris—and so eager to tag along with her—Michael having a scheduling conflict seemed unlikely. *What is he up to?* she wondered.

This time, Michael was more prepared to follow Maggie, both through his understanding of the city and his attention to attire. He had packed a fisherman's sweater, a charcoal-colored down parka, a dark ragg wool hat, and a pair of gloves, all of which he hoped would keep him warm and blend inconspicuously with the other pedestrians on the streets of Paris. He left his room within five minutes of checking in and made a quick stop at the concierge desk to pinpoint the location of the café on his map. He sped to the Metro station and purchased a day pass, then quickly retraced his steps and took a seat at a small patisserie with a view of the hotel entrance. He paid for a coffee and croissant, and waited. Thirty minutes later, he spotted Maggie, with the same messenger bag slung over her shoulder. But this time she had a sky-blue knitted scarf wrapped around her neck. He followed her to the Metro station and boarded the car behind hers, musing that her affinity for brightly colored scarves was a godsend.

When Maggie got off the train, Michael tagged along at a distance, relaxed in the knowledge that he knew where she was going. She repeated her previous route but, instead of turning toward the Hôtel-Dieu, continued straight, past Notre Dame and across the river—via the same bridge he had used after fleeing the hospital the last time he had been there. He was trailing seventy or eighty feet behind when she vanished. The blue scarf was there, and then it was not.

Despite the chill, the streets in the Latin Quarter were churning with people. He approached the point where she had vanished, took a quick glance at the map, whirled around in the street, and eventually found what he was looking for. He turned left and discovered his destination immediately ahead.

The restaurant was tucked away on a short, narrow street on the fringe of the Latin Quarter. He gave a silent prayer to whatever force had made him follow her—he would have had a hard time finding it on his own, even with the map. It specialized in Mediterranean cuisine, he guessed, judging by the aroma teasing his nostrils.

The restaurant had a covered entry, more like a skinny alcove, in front of the door and windows. The glass door and windows were fitted with iron grills—whether a decorative touch or a security measure he could not tell. Combined with the shadowy recess, it was nearly impossible to see inside. If he could not see their table, he would not know which waiter to approach for the device. He knew that if he entered too soon after Maggie, she would be suspicious, would know he had followed her. He decided to wait.

He paced the street for thirty minutes, then walked up to the glass door and peered in. The restaurant had a long aisle down the middle, with a line of chairs backed against the wall and the others in the aisle, the tables lined up between the chairs. It was all very orderly, even with the throng of people inside. The waiters hustled along the aisle, never having to weave through the usual random chaos of tables. Breathing a sigh of relief that none of the seats faced the restaurant's entrance, he opened the door.

The hum of conversation was one or two decibels over cozy, but not uncomfortably loud despite the stone floor. The upholstered chairs, linen tablecloths, and wall decor probably helped mute some of the noise. The scent of spices and grilled lamb made his mouth water. He approached the maître d', and his stomach growled, loud enough that the man raised his eyebrows.

The man looked Michael up and down, making an assessment, and asked, "American?"

"I am, yes. I don't have a reservation, but ..."

The man waved his hand dismissively. "Just one?"

"Yes. Just me," answered Michael. Out of the corner of his right eye, he spotted a long streak of white. *A white thobe,* he thought. *The Arab is here.*

"We can accommodate you," the maître d' said. "Ghasif will show you to your table."

Ghasif appeared at the elbow of the maître d'. Michael guessed his age at not more than nineteen or twenty, a student perhaps, working his way through the nearby Paris-Sorbonne University. Michael fell in behind him, keeping his eyes fixed on the young man's left shoulder and studiously avoiding the right side of the restaurant where the Arab was sitting. Maggie would be with him, he was sure. He wondered if the Arab would recognize him, but decided it was unlikely. Their encounter had been brief and unexpected, and Michael had been wearing an orange hat that covered the top of his face and most of his hair.

He kept his eyes down and perused the menu. Lebanese, he realized. When the waiter appeared, he ordered a sparkling water and the mezze, an assortment of hot and cold appetizers. As he folded the menu to hand it to the waiter, he stretched his back and neck, taking the opportunity to glance around the room. The Arab was sitting almost directly across from him, his eyes canted down, reading a newspaper. *Le Monde.* The Arab spoke French. But then the Arab looked up, and Michael realized he was not the same man he had seen at the hospital. He looked around the room. Maggie was not there. Maggie was nowhere to be seen.

His heart froze with the thought that perhaps they had led him here, that they knew he was following her. He tried not to panic, concentrating all his effort on trying to breathe normally and maintaining a neutral expression. But his heart was now pounding, and his palms were sweaty. He tried to think. She had probably gone out the back door and headed back to the hospital, but there was no way to know for sure. She and the doctor could be anywhere. He realized that he would have to go to the doctor's office and attempt to retrieve the device, just in case they had met there. But how was he supposed to do that?

As he thought about how the situation had transpired, the fear evaporated and was replaced by anger. Pete and his cronies had known of this restaurant, knew it would be impossible for Michael to find the right waiter without going into the restaurant and revealing himself. In his estimation, it was a situation destined for disaster. It made no sense. He muttered to himself, *What is going on here?*

He was debating his options when Ghasif, the young man who had showed him to the table, appeared. In flawless English he said, "We thought you might also enjoy our baba ghanouj. With our compliments." On his tray was a bowl of pureed roasted eggplant and a linen-lined basket of perfectly golden-brown saj bread. Ghasif set both on the table and gave Michael a wink. "The bottom pieces are very special."

Michael recovered enough to thank the waiter. He was just taking a bite of the paper-thin flatbread when he heard a woman's voice, pitched high, squeaky with surprise.

"Michael?"

He looked up, and there was no need to feign his astonishment. Maggie was standing three feet away.

She asked, "What are you doing here?" She was not smiling.

He coughed into his napkin, giving himself time to recover. *There must be another room*, he realized. *In the back or in the basement.* It was something he had not considered. The speech that he had planned while he was waiting outside seemed to slip from his grasp. An idea popped into his brain and, with nothing else, he looked up.

"I saw this place advertised and thought I would try it. My mother was of Lebanese descent. She enjoyed cooking the recipes she'd grown up with. I think it reminded her of her own mother. I grew up loving their food."

It was a fabrication, of course. His mother had been Swedish. His only exposure to Lebanese cuisine had been a small café in Sarajevo, before the war. His eyebrows lifted in question. "You like Lebanese, too? Would you like to join me?"

Maggie was still not smiling. "I've already eaten. I had lunch with friends. How long have you been here?"

"I just sat down a couple of minutes ago. Is everything alright? You look upset."

He spotted the doctor, who was just behind Maggie and heading for the door. The Arab he had seen at the hospital followed the doctor. Maggie was still there, staring at him.

Maggie eyed the clean tablecloth, the barely wrinkled linen napkin, and the nearly untouched baba ghanouj, and decided he was telling the truth. *At least*, she thought, *the truth about when he had arrived. Not necessarily about anything else. This guy, who says he knows nothing about Paris, now says he just happens to be here because he likes Lebanese food? Not likely. Not even remotely likely. Is he following me because he wants to get into my pants, or is it something else?*

She offered him a wan smile.

"Sorry, I'm not upset. I just have a migraine coming on and it's hard to be sociable when my head is splitting. I hope you don't mind, but I'm going to cancel this afternoon and take a rest instead. I apologize. I'll try to join the crew for dinner."

Michael could see through the lie, but felt a wave of relief wash over him. He would not have to spend the afternoon pretending to be some simpleton needing a tour of Paris.

"I completely understand," he told her. "I hope you feel better. Is there anything I can do?"

"No, I'm fine, thank you. Enjoy your meal."

She turned and walked out the door, where the doctor and the Arab were waiting. She did not look back. Michael stared after them, his eyes focused on Maggie's messenger bag. There was no question about it—the bag was full. Whereas it had hung limply from her shoulder an hour ago, the pouch now bulged and thumped heavily against her hip as she walked.

Michael picked up the basket of bread and moved the saj bread around, as if he were looking for a piece that was crisped to his satisfaction. He spotted the microcassette, cocooned in plastic wrap, beneath the bread. It was only about half the size of his pinkie finger. He squeezed it into his palm with three fingers, while using his thumb and index finger to pick up a fragment of the saj bread at the same time. He dropped the bread onto his plate, lowered his hand into his lap, and slipped the device into his pocket as the waiter laid several additional plates on the table. Ghasif appeared moments later and gave him a knowing smile.

"Is everything to your satisfaction, sir?"

Michael reached into his pocket and withdrew the five 100-franc notes, then slipped them between the bowl of baba ghanouj and the plate beneath.

"Everything is perfect. Thank you," he said as he slid the plate toward the young man.

"It was my pleasure, sir," Ghasif said, picking up the plate and backing away.

Done, Michael thought. The kid had not demanded more money, just hoped for it, and there was no need to threaten anyone. And now he was one step closer to getting out of the arrangement with Pete. He left the restaurant and shuffled toward Notre Dame. *But what are the chances that Pete will keep his word? Not good,* he thought. *Not good at all.*

Chapter 42

February 4, 1994
New York City

P ete's eyes followed Michael's tall frame gliding through the crowd outside the customs clearance area at JFK's International Arrivals Building, commonly called the IAB. Maggie trailed about twenty feet behind, chatting with another uniformed flight attendant. He watched carefully. Michael and Maggie did not speak, nor did they wave to one another. They went their separate ways without a look or a word.

Admittedly, he had been worried. Maggie was an exceptional beauty, and he had been told that Michael enjoyed women. Moreover, Michael had never been fully on board with the operation. None of those factors had bid well for the success of the plan. But when Pete had played the card of the brothers' well-being, the odds had changed, and Michael seemed to have pulled it off.

He followed Michael out of the terminal, watching him head toward the stop for the Q10 bus back to Kew Gardens. He glanced down the length of the walkway in front of the building. Maggie was at the other end, surrounded by a dozen other uniforms *Crew bus stop*, he surmised, *for the crew parking lot*. He shouldered up to Michael without looking at him.

Out of the side of his mouth, Pete asked, "Want a lift?"

Michael turned his head in surprise. "Why are you here?"

"Just offering you a ride."

"Fine. Where's the car?"

"Wait until Maggie gets on the crew bus, then come with me. I'm in the lot—over there." He pointed to the parking lot across the street, an area packed with cars in the center of the airport.

They waited ten minutes, standing quietly on the median, until the crew bus finally appeared, disgorging a gaggle of departing crewmembers and then swallowing those who had just flown in. But as the bus pulled away, Maggie was still there. Pete watched her carefully. She did not appear to be nervous or upset and was not looking their way. Eventually, he figured it out. She was waiting for a different bus—one that would take her to another terminal in the airport. She would be taking a flight back to DC. Sure enough, three long minutes later, she climbed aboard one of the buses circling the airport. Pete gestured to Michael, and they stepped into the crosswalk and headed toward the lot.

Michael asked again, "Why are you here?"

Pete ignored him and asked, "How was Paris?"

"I still don't know what she's carrying in the messenger bag; I couldn't exactly rip it from her body. Otherwise, successful," Michael replied, patting his own bag. "I have the microcassette. But your information was seriously flawed."

Pete raised his eyebrows in surprise. "Our sources have always been good."

"But they had the meeting place all wrong. The address and the name were right, but that's it. It wasn't a simple café, or a place you could blend in with the other diners. I had to go in, and she saw me. There was nothing I could do about it."

"Except lie," Pete responded.

"Exactly."

"Don't worry about it. For now, just relax for a few days. Your next flight is the most important of all."

Michael's expression went slack, the corners of his mouth drooping and brow furrowing. "The next flight. With Isabel," he said. "There must be some other way."

"We have looked at this from many angles. This will assure that she never betrays us again," Pete said.

They reached the car, and Pete unlocked the doors, gesturing for Michael to get in. Pete, however, remained outside the car, held up an index finger in a "wait one minute" signal, and moved a few feet away. Michael could see that Pete had one of the new Nokia cellular phones in his hand.

Michael desperately wanted to hear what was being said, but the car doors were closed, and the power windows were up. For a few seconds, he tried to read Pete's lips, until Pete turned away. Very few people had portable phones, and he had seen them only in advertisements on the television. He wondered how many people in the CIA already had them and if the government versions of the phone were different. *Probably,* he thought, *encrypted, maybe, and some sort of locking feature in case it's stolen.*

Pete opened the car door and slid behind the wheel.

"Neat," Michael said with a smile. "You have one of those new phones."

Glancing over as he turned the key in the ignition, Pete said, "Yes. Useful, at least sometimes. It really depends on where you are; service is limited."

"I thought you could only get those Nokias in Europe."

Pete paused a beat. "We have our sources."

I'll bet, thought Michael. Aloud, he said, "When do I go?"

"We're not sure yet. We're waiting to hear where the meeting is being held."

"And what if something goes wrong?"

"We've thought about it ... about something going wrong. We think it should go well, but you are right. It is best to have a backup plan." His left hand dropped from the wheel, felt around in the compartment on the door, and came back up with a folded manila envelope. He passed it to Michael with a shrug. "We obtained another passport for you. Just in case."

Relieved, Michael let out a grunt. This was not what he had expected, having been convinced that Pete would screw him over at some point. Michael withdrew the envelope's contents, expecting an American passport in another name. But the cover was midnight blue, almost black. Canada.

Continuing, Pete said, "You will need to memorize everything about this identity. Make sure you can answer questions without hesitation. And it would be a good idea to spend some time at the library learning everything you can about Canada. I don't know how much time you have, so use it wisely. We don't think anything will go wrong, but if it does, you should be prepared."

Thumbing through the papers, Michael reached the conclusion that his time with Transoceanic would soon be over. What would they do about the other women he had followed? He was curious.

"What about Maggie Marshfield? Is she going to be arrested?"

With another shrug, Pete said, "Don't worry about her. We're taking care of it."

Maggie stepped off the bus at the American Airlines terminal, directly across the airport from the IAB. She walked to the ladies' room, stripped out of her uniform, and changed into civilian clothes. She packed the uniform and checked her bags at the counter, where the agent advised that flight had several empty seats and that chances of getting on were excellent. If a lot of people showed up at the last minute, there was another a couple of hours later. Maggie looked for the nearest pay phone.

Cat picked up on the second ring. "Powell."

"It's me," Maggie said.

"Did you have a good time in Paris?"

Maggie knew she had to be careful. She was on a public phone. She approached the subject obliquely, leaving Cat to read between the lines.

"I did some walking around. Had a wonderful lunch yesterday. Seems to be a popular place. I ran into some friends there and, just as I was leaving, even saw someone from my crew."

"Is that right? That's quite a coincidence."

"I thought so, too. Small world. And I did some shopping ... picked up some photographs I thought you might like. I shipped them to you last night—you should have received the package this morning."

"We'll talk about it tonight. What time is your flight?"

"It leaves here at five-thirty, but I'm riding on a pass, so I'm space available. Assuming there's an empty seat and no delays, I'll be into National at seven."

"I'll pick you up. We'll grab a bite."

"Deal."

Chapter 43

February 4, 1994
Washington, DC

Maggie pulled her luggage off the carousel at baggage claim, draped her coat over her arm, and headed for the airport's street exit, threading her way through the crowd in the airport rush-hour version of bumper cars. One man hit her particularly hard, knocking her sideways and nearly sending her sprawling. She spun around angrily, but he kept moving, without a word of apology. She pushed through the exit doors and headed for the passenger pickup lane.

Cat had just circled back around the roadway that wound through National Airport when she spotted Maggie exiting the big sliding glass doors. She flashed her lights and released the trunk lid. Maggie waved, hoisted her bags into the trunk, tossed her coat onto the back seat, and jumped in beside her friend. They hugged each other, and Cat pulled away from the curb.

"I made a reservation at Martin's," she said, referring to a popular tavern in Georgetown. "Okay with you?"

"Perfect," said Maggie. "I'm ready."

In fact, Maggie was more than ready. She had been uneasy ever since the encounter with Michael in the Lebanese restaurant. She could not put her finger on it, but there was something about him that made her uncomfortable—enough so that she had not gone to dinner with the crew in Paris. Instead, she had ordered room service and told her friends that she was suffering from a migraine. *Maybe I was just imagining things,* she thought. *Drinks and dinner with Cat is just the ticket.*

Cat asked, "So, who showed up at the restaurant in Paris?"

"A guy on the crew, Michael. It startled me, that he was there. It was just weird. Paris is a big city, and this was not a crew hangout."

"Do you think he followed you there?"

"I don't know. He didn't enter the restaurant until I was leaving."

"What made him pick that place? It's Paris—one would think he'd be looking for French cuisine."

"Exactly. But he said something about his mom being from Lebanon and doing a lot of Lebanese cooking. He had a craving, I guess."

Cat thought a minute. "Unlikely, but possible."

"Yes," Maggie admitted. "But it was still creepy."

Cat steered the car into the left lane, following the signs pointing to the northbound George Washington Parkway. She tapped her finger on the steering wheel, thinking.

"Could he have just taken a shine to you?"

"Maybe."

"Have you flown with him before?"

"Yes, actually. He was called out on standby for the last Paris trip, too."

Cat tensed. Not wanting to alarm Maggie, she had not mentioned the incident in which a man had jumped in front of Marc and taken his picture. She had been puzzling over the incident since Marc mentioned it during their call. She had not been able to make any sense of it. *Did the man snap a photo because Marc was wearing his Arab garb? Was it a random prank? Had someone discovered that Marc was in Paris?*

And now, some reserve flight attendant had shown up on both of Maggie's flights to Paris. Not good.

Maggie asked, "Did you see him after you landed?"

"Yeah, he was waiting for the Q10 bus into Queens. That's it. He didn't follow me."

Cat tamped down her discomfort and kept the conversation light. "It's probably nothing." She paused for a moment. "I could take a quick look at his background ... just to make sure."

"But the airline already does background checks. It's probably just my imagination."

Cat dropped the subject, for the moment. She would get the man's name another way. She already had his first name, *Michael.* "Okay," she said. "And what happened last night?"

Maggie looked confused. "Last night? I never left my room. The courier rang me on the hotel's house phone, just like last time. He came up to my room and showed me his ID. I gave him the folder. You got the folder, right?"

Cat flicked her eyes to the rearview mirror. *Five cars back, same headlights, same speed,* she thought. The car had been with her since leaving the airport, onto the GW Parkway, onto Arlington Boulevard. *Maybe nothing, maybe something. But what are the chances?* She goosed the gas a little and moved from the middle lane into the left lane. Fifteen seconds later, the fifth car back moved left. *Something.* She eased back into the center lane and, as the exit for the Key Bridge came into view, jerked into the right lane and onto the ramp.

Maggie let out a strangled squeak shriek and looked sharply at Cat. "What is it?" she cried. "What's wrong?"

"We have a tail," Cat replied calmly. "Or at least we did. They didn't make the exit."

"Tail? Someone's following us? Who?"

"Good question. I don't know. But they've been behind us since the airport."

"You're sure? There's a lot of traffic."

Cat glanced over at her friend and raised an eyebrow. "Seriously?"

They crossed the bridge, then crawled through the traffic on M Street before turning onto Wisconsin Avenue in Georgetown.

Chapter 44

February 4, 1994
Georgetown, Washington, DC

Parking was always a challenge in Georgetown. Cat circled four times before scoring a space two blocks from Martin's. As was often the case, many of the tables were filled with tourists—heads bobbing and fingers pointing as they imagined Nixon or LBJ as youngsters on Capitol Hill, pounding out policy with a gaggle of politicos, or Madeleine Albright framing a foreign policy initiative, or JFK asking for Jackie's hand in what is now known as *The Proposal Booth*.

Cat and Maggie dined at Martin's frequently—fond of its historical context and its ambience. The hostess smiled in recognition and led them back to a room in the back called *The Dugout*, where Bill Donovan and his crew had often met in the early days of the OSS—the Office of Strategic Services—the precursor to the CIA. They felt it was a fitting tribute.

Maggie ordered the mussels and the pinot grigio, Cat the short ribs and a cabernet. With the small room to themselves, Cat got down to business.

"Tell me about the photos."

"What? I don't understand. You saw them, right?"

"Humor me."

"Crates of weapons in a truck," Maggie answered. "One of those big trucks—a Deuce and a Half, so a lot of crates—and bags of money. The focus was mainly on four guys, the two Americans who were selling the weapons, a third guy who was the leader of the buyers, and an older man—probably the boss. Those two were passing themselves off as Kurds, but Khalid had his doubts. He thought their skin was too light. He told me that they were dressed like Kurds, but except for the leader, they didn't talk at all. And their clothes were too clean, almost new. He thought it was weird—like a bunch of guys who were rounded up to take part in a play."

"What do you think? Could you tell who they were?"

"Not a clue. You know that I've never been that great with ethnicity."

"Khalid took the photos?"

"He did. He said he wore a camera underneath his gear, with a remote shutter that he rigged somehow. He told me he had pegged the two soldiers as trouble. Then they asked him along because they needed a translator for a mission set up by a colonel at the base. He went along, took the pictures, and intended to hand them off the next day, but ..."

"But he was shot," Cat finished, twirling the wine in her glass. She leaned back in the booth, considering how much to share, whether to tell Maggie that the man she knew only as Khalid was, in fact, a CIA veteran named Marc Bishop. She decided that, for now, she would keep that information to herself.

"Okay," said Cat. "Tell me everything you can remember about the men in the photos."

"Well, there was one guy in particular, the leader. This was the same guy that Khalid claimed to have seen on television. He said he had thought it was odd that during the entire transaction, he was the only one of the buyers who spoke. And he spoke English, apparently very well, as Khalid was never called upon to translate. He said there was only one time when the man spoke in anything other than English. His impression was that it sounded Eastern European. I meant to ask Khalid more as we were walking out of that restaurant, but then there was Michael, and ..."

"What did he look like?"

Maggie looked at Cat in alarm. "Why are you asking me this? You saw the photos, right?"

"I never received them. I got a call from our people in Paris just before you called me. Some teenagers found the courier's body last night, in a subway restroom. He'd been stabbed several times."

Shocked, Maggie gasped and cupped her hands over her mouth. "Oh, my God!"

"His wallet and courier bag weren't with the body, which is why it took some time before he was identified. It might have been a robbery gone wrong, but I don't like the timing. I think he was targeted, that someone thought those photos were important enough to justify murder."

Dazed, Maggie sat very still, staring at her friend and processing the implications. If they knew about the courier, they most likely knew of her involvement. That meant they also knew about Khalid and his friend, the doctor.

"What about Khalid? Is he in danger?"

"I sent a team to his home. They're moving him to a safe place until we can arrange to bring him back to the States. I'm praying that he has duplicates or negatives for those pictures. If not, you're the only one who has seen them."

"Aside from Khalid and the photographer, you mean."

"True. We're trying to contact the photographer. But if the negatives are gone, that leaves you to corroborate Khalid's description of the men."

Maggie held her trembling hand over her heart and whispered, "If they find him, they will kill him, too, won't they? Along with Dr. Al-Zahawi, if they haven't already."

"They won't find him."

Maggie closed her eyes and took a few deep breaths, trying to regain her bearings. With her eyes still closed, she searched her memory of the previous day.

She had returned to the hotel, pulled the photos from the messenger bag, and spread them over the bed—a series of thirty-two. The images were reasonably sharp, capturing the men's features clearly. There were shots of vehicles—one big truck and several small vans, shots of crates loaded with weapons, shots of big bags of money, shots of men in a group, and close-ups of individuals, with two images capturing every detail of the two non-American men Khalid had raised questions about. One of the men was inside a car, but it seemed as if his eyes had bored straight into the lens, leaving Maggie to wonder if he had known that Khalid was carrying a camera.

"In the pictures," Maggie said, "there were two men who interested Khalid most. One was probably late twenties and was taller than the two American soldiers, by four or five inches maybe. And the soldiers were taller than the other men by a couple of inches. So maybe he was six-two or three? Just a guess. The photos were black-and-white, but Khalid said he had light brown hair and dark brown eyes. His hair was cropped close—military—and no facial hair, except two-day scruff, like he hadn't shaved for a couple of days. He was wearing a T-shirt and his arms were very muscular."

She glanced up at Cat, a bloom of red in her cheeks. "Yeah, I noticed." She paused, recalling more details. "In one of the photos, he was writing on a clipboard. I'm sure the pen was in his left hand, so left-handed."

"Was he in uniform?"

"No. I mean, he was wearing camouflage pants, but his T-shirt was plain white, and he wasn't kitted out like the Americans. This guy looked more like someone ready for a backyard barbeque than someone negotiating a pricey arms deal."

"Would you recognize him?" Cat asked.

"Him? Absolutely."

"And the other man of interest?"

"That's harder," Maggie sighed. "He was inside a car, so I could not tell you if he was tall or short. He was older, late forties or early fifties. I really only remember his eyes—they were cold, intimidating. He gave me the creeps, and it was only a picture."

Cat paid the check, and they strolled leisurely toward the car. She kept her eyes moving—looking, always looking—while Maggie window-shopped, blissfully unaware. The car had tailed them, that was certain. But she had been tagged at the airport, and that meant someone had been waiting—someone who knew which flight Maggie would be on. She weighed the possibility that the tail had been not on Maggie, but herself. *No*, she thought, *too coincidental*.

Reaching the car, Cat was about to put her key in the door when she noticed the anomaly. The lock on the passenger door was up. She knew she had locked the doors—an action as automated as putting one foot in front of the other—and the driver's side was still locked. Someone had broken in through the passenger door.

"Maggie, get away from the car," she commanded. "Right now! Back the way we came, one block."

Maggie's eyes went wide, but she did as she was told.

Cat reached in her bag and pulled out a new cellular handset, wondering if it would work as advertised. She dialed as she hurried after Maggie. The call was picked up within seconds.

"Accounting," the voice said.

Cat recited a code, then said quietly, "I need a response team. Someone's tampered with my car. Georgetown, on Wisconsin, just off M Street. White Volvo."

The voice was calm. "Probability of explosive?"

"Unknown," she replied.

"A team is on its way."

Within three minutes, the street was a fiesta of emergency lights, with vehicles angled across the intersections at either end to prevent any traffic from entering. The bomb squad arrived nine minutes later. Cat and Maggie watched it all from half a block away.

"The door lock wasn't right," she explained to Maggie. "Better to be safe than incinerated, I always say."

"I thought you lost the tail."

Cat frowned and wrinkled her nose, as if she had encountered an unpleasant smell.

"Me too," she said. "There's a team on its way. They'll handle the bureaucracy, offering up some creative story about national security. After the car is cleared, they'll load it on a flatbed and take it to a secure location. Sorry, but your suitcase is gone for the night."

"I can have Paul come get me. Not sure how I'm going to explain this to him."

"Well, let's not give him the whole story just yet. I've got an idea. Let's just go to my place. When's the last time we did a sleepover? Maybe we could even do a little shopping tomorrow. You'll be back in time for dinner."

Maggie raised an eyebrow. "And what are we really doing?"

Cat shrugged her shoulders. "Looking at photographs. At Langley."

Chapter 45

February 5, 1994
CIA Headquarters
Langley, Virginia

The tech dropped an object on Cat's desk and said, "No bomb, but they did find this." The object was a black plastic rectangle, about the size of a pack of chewing gum.

Cat leaned back in her chair and crossed her arms over her chest.

"Is that an RFID tag?"

"It is. Found it in the pocket of a coat in the back seat. Someone was tracking you."

"In the pocket?"

"Yes, ma'am."

"Black wool, Bill Blass?"

"Yes, ma'am."

Maggie, absorbed in the task of studying faces on the computer, heard the description and looked up in puzzlement.

"You found it in my coat?"

The tech looked at Cat, who nodded, and answered, "Yes, ma'am."

Maggie thought back. She had worn the coat in Paris, but she had put her hands in her pockets on the way back to the hotel. She would have noticed any foreign objects. But in New York, the weather had been mild. She had carried the coat onto the bus, onto the airplane, and through the terminal at National. She opened her lips in a silent *Oh!*

"What?" Cat asked.

"At National, there was a guy who bumped into me. He hit me hard. I almost fell. Could he have ...?"

"Do you remember anything about him?"

Maggie shook her head. "I barely saw him. Just a jerk who nearly ran me over. Dark hair, I think. Black parka. The rest is a blur."

Cat turned back to the tech. "Anything else?"

"Whoever broke into your car was careful. We found smudges consistent with gloves, and the only prints we found are people you would expect to have been in your vehicle."

"And you didn't find anything else?"

"No, ma'am."

Maggie smiled. "When do I get my bags back?"

The tech looked confused. "Bags?"

"My crew bag and suitcase. They were in the trunk."

"Ma'am, there were no bags in the trunk. Just a spare tire and a jack." He handed the car keys to Cat. "We parked it for you."

"Thanks, Fred. We'll take it from here," Cat said, dismissing him.

Maggie was upset. "They took my bags? That's all my travel gear! Now I really have to go shopping, never mind the hassle of ordering a new uniform, crew bag, and handbook. I'm not happy."

"Handbook?"

"Yes, the book we have to carry on every flight—the one with all our procedures and checklists."

Maggie stormed back to the desk, sat heavily in the chair, and with renewed determination, resumed looking at photos.

Cat rested her elbows on the desk and propped her chin in her hands, massaging her neck, thinking about uniforms and handbooks and wondering how difficult it would be for someone to impersonate a flight attendant. *Probably not that hard. But for what purpose?* She picked up the phone for a conversation with the head of security at National Airport.

The man was cordial, but not optimistic when Cat asked for access to the terminal's security footage from yesterday.

"There are cameras inside the airport," he said, "but don't expect too much. Coverage is spotty and quality iffy. Let me have a look. Come on over to my office around four."

She disconnected and called out to Maggie. "When are you flying again?"

"Four days from now," Maggie answered. "To Frankfurt. It's cold, but the food and drink are spot-on."

"That's right ... there's a restaurant there you like, a crew gathering spot. What's the place called?"

"The Baseler Eck."

"Maybe I'll join you someday."

Maggie raised her eyebrows. "Now that could be interesting."

Looking at Maggie, Cat had a sudden inspiration. If Marc could get to Frankfurt, he could ride on the same flight with Maggie back to the States. Maggie could keep an eye on him and, forewarned, should be able to identify anyone on the crew who did not belong. It also meant that he could forgo an escort, which would help keep his movements more under the radar.

She reached for the thick book on the shelf behind her, the OAG—the Official Airline Guide—that listed all scheduled flights around the world. There was a Lufthansa flight at 7:00 a.m. from Paris to Frankfurt, which would connect nicely with Maggie's flight back to New York. But she needed a name for the ticket, and Marc was known to carry several passports. *Which one will he use? Hopefully not Khalid.*

She typed an eyes-only dispatch for transmission to the Paris safe house.

> Subject's travel 11 Feb 07000 via LH to meet wife in Frankfurt is approved. Subject and wife will board TOA to JFK on Feb 11 and meet clients on arrival.

Cat's next call was to the Pentagon. Having requested files on the three names that Marc had mentioned in his written report, she had expected resistance. Instead, a two-star had left her a message that they would be happy to cooperate.

"The files should be delivered to your office shortly. I've included a copy of the CID report," the general said.

The Army's Criminal Investigation Division was known to be smart, thorough, and unrelenting, but its investigators were not infallible.

"Thank you," she said.

"When you read the report, you'll notice that all three men submitted their papers two months after your guy was killed in Silopi, The CID thought the timing highly unusual, but found nothing else to arouse suspicion. I find it curious that, after all this time, you are now asking about those same men. What's changed?"

Cat hesitated. "We're just tying up some loose ends." As the words came out of her mouth, she could envision him rolling his eyes.

"Sure you are," the general said with an edge in his voice that had not been there previously. "I'm sure I don't have to remind you that someone murdered your man, and this case is still open in our books because it happened under our watch. If you've run into some new evidence, it would be in everyone's best interest to share what you have, just as we are sharing our files with you."

Cat composed her answer carefully. The general and CID did not know that her man was still alive, and right now, she had no intention of sharing that fact.

"Does the report say where these men were on the day of the shooting?"

"Yes. The two soldiers took a truckload of supplies over to Zakho, logging out at oh-nine-thirty and logging back in at sixteen-thirty hours. Colonel Garvin remained at the camp all day. CID found nothing to tie them to the shooting."

The mention of the truck made the hair on the back of her neck stand up. Marc's report stated that they had driven west, to Cizre, not east to Zakho.

"Thank you, General. I'll let you know."

"You do that. Good day, Miz Powell."

Cat set the phone down gently and let out a whistle. She pulled up a map, comparing the distance from Silopi to Zakho—where the soldiers said they had taken supplies—to the distance from Silopi to Cizre—where Marc had said they unloaded the weapons. Cizre was a few kilometers farther, but the difference had not been great enough to have drawn the investigators' attention. The discrepancy had gone unnoticed.

As promised, the men's personnel files arrived within the hour. She arranged the stack and started with the first folder.

Staff Sergeant Joseph Roether, originally from Ponca City, Oklahoma, had enlisted after graduating high school. He had spent eight years in the army, including tours in Iraq and the Balkans, and had made his way up through the ranks via time served, rather than through any demonstration of outstanding leadership. He had separated from the service with an honorable discharge two years earlier. There were no red flags in his record, other than the cryptic comment from one superior that *Sgt. Roether would benefit from diversity training.* The statement seemed to jibe with Marc's impressions of the man. Sgt. Roether's last address of record was in Enid, Oklahoma.

Sergeant Donald Allen was a four-year veteran who, like his friend, was originally from Oklahoma. And like his friend, he had left the service two years earlier and settled in Enid. He was a low-profile soldier who had simply done his job and never garnered any attention. His record was as bland and unremarkable as oatmeal.

Cat rubbed her index finger over her lips, thinking about all the cash that had changed hands and how two small-town boys from Oklahoma would have managed it without help. That brought her to the colonel.

Colonel Shreve Garvin hailed from Turrell, Arkansas—a spot in the road twenty-five miles northwest of Memphis. He had joined the ROTC at Arkansas State University in Jonesboro, graduating with honors and a degree in political science. His twenty-three-year career was peppered with commendations and citations that had earned him a promotion to the rank of full bird. He had been, by all accounts, an intelligent and well-respected officer. The unsolved shooting—and the questions raised in its wake—had left a stain on the man's record that could not be erased. Within five months, he had received his army separation papers and returned to his hometown. Two months later, he had been discovered in a Memphis hotel room—a gun in his hand and a hole in his head. The coroner had ruled it a suicide.

She placed a call to the Memphis Police Department and was shuffled through several people before landing at the desk of a detective familiar with the case. When the man picked up, she heard papers shuffling and the buzz of conversation in the background.

"Detective Curtis," a voice said.

She introduced herself and said, "We're looking into the murder of a man under Colonel Garvin's command three years ago. I was wondering if you could fill me in on anything relevant to the colonel's death. Maybe share your impressions about his state of mind, or anything that might lend some perspective to our ongoing investigation."

"Interesting," the detective said. "My personal impression was that it wasn't a suicide."

Cat was expecting a deep drawl, but the detective's voice was crisp and only lightly Southern. "There were some things knocked around the room; I felt there had been a struggle. And I thought the blood spatter was off, smeared where it should have been spray. I had this notion that somebody had helped him put that gun to his head."

"But you were overruled?"

"That's one way of putting it. *Overruled*. Tactful choice of words. I had the impression that somebody didn't want us digging too deep," he replied.

"Who was that someone?"

"Maybe you should mosey on down to Memphis for a couple of days. Might prove to be an educational visit."

Cat pulled the handset away from her ear and looked at it as if it were an alien object. *Did I hear that right? Did he just ask me to fly down to Memphis?* She pressed the phone back against her face.

"Well, Detective, that's an interesting idea. Let me think about it."

At one-thirty, Cat finally threw in the towel. She dropped Maggie at the townhouse she shared with Paul, then watched as the two embraced for a gentle kiss. She smiled, in spite of herself, and wondered how Maggie would explain the missing luggage.

She wondered, too, why she had resisted bringing Paul into the loop—he certainly had the security clearance to be read in on Maggie's activities with the Agency. Maybe, she admitted to herself, it was because she was worried that Paul would push Maggie to quit. Regardless, it was time to bring him up to speed. She made a mental note to arrange a meeting with Paul next week.

As she backed out of the driveway, the earlier conversation with the detective came back to her mind. *Mosey on down to Memphis.* The words echoed in her head. *Could there really be something to learn there?* She made a detour to her house, tossed a few necessities into a bag, and then drove to National Airport. She met with the security chief to dissect the camera footage from the previous day. The police had found the video from Maggie's incident, but the images were grainy, and the man had kept his head down, never looking up at a camera.

There was no question that the man had deliberately run into Maggie. He had sped from one side of the concourse to the other and took direct aim at her. The images did not show him actually slipping the RFID tag into her coat pocket, but watching the encounter on film, Cat had little doubt. She thanked the security team and strolled slowly toward the terminal exit.

All in all, she felt like a dog chasing its tail. The only good news was that Maggie had provided a good description of the mystery man. The soldiers had been identified. But she still did not know who had gunned down Khalid or why. It made no sense. Why take a translator along, then kill him a couple of hours later? Killing him before returning to the base, and casting the blame onto enemy fire, would have raised fewer questions.

Memphis, she thought. *Maybe there's something there.* She changed direction and found the Northwest counter. After booking the next flight, she hustled back to the parking lot to retrieve her bag, located a pay phone, and placed a call to Detective Curtis. "I'm coming in on Northwest, arriving at seven thirty. I'm running to make the flight. Since I don't know the city, would you mind booking a hotel for me?"

"My pleasure," he said. "I'll pick you up. You game for dinner? Best barbeque in the world right here."

"Sure, Detective, as long as it comes with a beer."

"You're on. And call me Dave."

Chapter 46

February 5, 1994
Memphis, Tennessee

Detective Dave Curtis was, Cat thought, a seven, maybe an eight. It wasn't so much his looks, which were more character actor than leading man, but rather his intelligence and affable nature. He picked her up in an old Volvo wagon, with a kid's seat in the back. The floor was littered with crumpled juice boxes and dried-up french fries.

"How old?" she asked.

"Four," he said. "My sister's kid." He noticed Cat's questioning look and added, "She and her husband died in a car crash two years ago—drunk driver. I was the custodian."

Cat was taken aback. "I'm so sorry. I've disrupted your evening. I should have ..." Her voice trailed off.

"No need to worry. Natalie—that's her name—is spending the night with my neighbor. They have a bunch of kids, and she has a great time there."

She nodded, vaguely unsettled by the tragic story, and asked if he was originally from Memphis.

"Chicago, actually," he said. "My best friend took a job down here after college. I tagged along for the ride. Still here."

He pulled into the parking lot of a modest, one-story building with cocoa-brown wood siding and a sign that sported a pig in a chef's hat. As soon as she opened the car door, the aroma tickled her nostrils. Her stomach rumbled, an audible complaint about the single slice of toast she had consumed for breakfast.

"Good, you're hungry," Dave said with a laugh. He opened the trunk and lifted out a box, carrying it into the restaurant.

Dave—obviously a frequent patron—greeted the staff by name, and they were quickly escorted to a booth in the back corner. Dave set the box beside him and patted the top. "Food first," he said. "Then we'll talk about Colonel Shreve Garvin."

They chatted over dinner, a large rack of ribs that Cat devoured in short order. She swallowed the last morsel, shoved the plate of bones aside, took another sip of Sam Adams, and leaned back in the booth. An involuntary belch escaped as she shifted position.

"Oh, excuse me! I'm sorry, but that was fantastic!"

Dave laughed and said, "I'd be offended if you hadn't enjoyed it. There are a ton of barbeque joints in this town, but Corky's is my favorite. If you'd like to stick around for a couple of days, I'd be happy to give you a tour of the other notable eating establishments."

She laughed in return, uncertain if he was serious or simply yanking her chain. She played it safe, saying, "The offer is tempting, but I have to get back. Every day brings another crisis somewhere in the world."

"Right," he said, his grin disappearing. "So, Colonel Shreve Garvin. I brought the file, photos and all."

He rested his forearms on the table, clasped his hands, and leaned forward, his voice just above a whisper. "We got a call from the hotel just after three in the morning. A couple of guests had called down to the front desk, saying that they had heard a gunshot. Lots of tourists and businesspeople visit this town—gunshots in one of our best hotels doesn't help our image, you know?"

Cat nodded. "So, the cops knocked on a few doors and entered the one that didn't answer."

"Exactly. I was off duty, but I got the call. The other teams were still wrapping up a bank robbery gone bad and a couple of drive-by shootings gone worse—multiple victims, little kids. It was an ugly night. They found Colonel Garvin in a room on the fifth floor, at the end, next to the stairwell."

He pulled out five photos and slid the top one, facedown, across the table. "Tell me what you think. And, uh, they're not family-friendly."

Cat scooted into the corner of the booth, her back to the wall, shielding the images from public view, and then lifted the photo. Colonel Shreve Garvin was slumped on the right side of the bed, a blackened hole between his nose and the inner corner of his right eye. There was a red ring around the wound, likely a muzzle imprint, and the skin nearby was peppered with small discolorations, both indications of a close-contact gunshot. Blood and bits of skull and brain tissue were spattered over the pillows and wall. She frowned and said, "He shot himself in the eye?"

"That was the finding. Look at the others."

The second photo was a close-up of the side of the colonel's head. The bullet had torn through the man's brain and left a ragged, pulpy mess in its wake as it exited. The third showed a close-up of the man's face, his eyes open and clouded, with a three-inch abrasion on the skin beneath the lower right eyelid. The fourth photo was of the bedside table lamp. There was a reddish-brown smear on the side of the shade facing the wall, which Cat assumed was blood.

"What is that abrasion under his eye?"

"The coroner determined that the gun must have hit the cheekbone when it fell from the colonel's hand."

Cat's eyebrows went up a notch. "That's an interesting assessment. It looks more like a hard scrape."

"See the smear on the lampshade? But no spatter."

"So, he shot himself in the eye, dropped the weapon on his face, and then moved the lamp? Do I have that right?"

"Just about. The finding was that the lamp must have been knocked over when he got onto the bed, and that one of the first responders picked it up and inadvertently rubbed it against some of the blood."

"Not impossible but sounds like a bit of a stretch. Did anyone admit to touching the lamp?"

"Nope. Did I mention the bruise on his left wrist?"

"Ah. The shoe drops. So, your theory is that someone helped him put the gun to his head?"

"I think there were two other people in that room. I think someone immobilized his left arm, while someone else put the gun in his hand and forced it to his head. I think the colonel tried to pull back, leaving the scrape on his face. I think the lamp fell during the struggle, and that someone put it back afterward."

From the moment she had seen the first photo, Cat had leapt to the conclusion that she was looking at a homicide. No one shoots himself in the eye. She asked, "You have any thoughts about who?"

Dave raised his eyebrows and nodded. "Oh, yeah," he said, patting the box. "My place or yours?"

The Marriott on Poplar Avenue had upgraded Cat to a spacious corner room on the eighth floor, a bonus she attributed to the detective's influence. She rolled her bags into the corner, and they sat cross-legged on the floor, the files spread out between them.

"It had all the markings of a homicide, and that's how we worked the investigation," Dave said. "We narrowed it down to two guys. American, according to the desk clerk. She based that on their flawless English, although they might have had a slight accent—probably not Spanish and definitely not Southern. White skin, dark hair, which narrows it down to a few billion people on the planet. They paid for one night, but the room was pristine—bed made, towels unused, no usable fingerprints. Cameras inside the hotel weren't functioning, which was rather coincidental. But they have separate systems for inside and outside, so we were able to pull images from a camera overlooking the parking lot. A white sedan left the hotel within minutes of the first call reporting the gunfire. Camera angles didn't catch the plates. Whoever they were, they vanished. The clerk sat with a sketch artist, but that went nowhere."

"They were pros. It was an assassination."

"Yep. That's what I think. Two days later, some of the brass from downtown started making inquiries, and we knew the case was going to turn into a pig. The coroner, whose preliminary report stated that the scrape under the colonel's eye was most likely the result of a struggle, submitted a new report blaming the scrape on a dropped gun. He wrote that the bruise on the wrist was at least two days old—again, a contradiction to the original report. It went downhill from there."

"There had to have been rumors floating around."

"The word was that someone from DC slammed the lid on the case. Next thing I knew, the coroner certified the death as a suicide. Case closed."

That got Cat's attention. "Which agency?"

"Dunno. It was very hush-hush."

Cat puffed her cheeks and blew out a stream of air. "That's a lot of nothing to go on," she said.

"Never said it was going to be easy."

"Do you still have the sketches? From the desk clerk?"

He pulled two sheets of paper from a folder and handed them to her. "I made copies."

Cat studied the drawings and shrugged. "European, maybe? Eastern Europe? I'll run them through our database and see if anything pops up." She stood and stretched. "Let's see if the bar's still open. I could use a drink."

"We can toast to dead soldiers, missing hit men, and the all-encompassing excuse that any info we need is above our pay grade," he replied with a wry grin.

"There is that," she sighed.

Chapter 47

February 6, 1994
New York City

Pete checked two pubs before finding Michael at the third, sitting at the bar with a beer in hand, fixated on the television screen. Michael and three other men were watching the New York Islanders going down in flames to the Buffalo Sabres. After four consecutive Stanley Cup trophies and a heartbreaking loss in the finals the following year, they had gone steadily downhill. Pete pegged the three as native New Yorkers, their accents a giveaway. Complaining loudly about the team's miserable performance, they were shouting profanities at every perceived mistake on the ice.

He caught Michael's attention and motioned to an empty booth at the back of the room. Michael frowned in annoyance and remained seated, turning back toward the screen. For a moment, Pete considered yanking him off the stool, but let his anger slide away. Michael knew the consequences; compliance was mandatory. A few minutes later, at the end of the second period, Michael slid into the bench across from Pete.

"It's a go," Pete said quietly. "The Cubans are meeting with the Americans in Frankfurt and are booked on a Transoceanic flight to New York afterward. We slipped the information to Isabel, and true to form, she swapped trips. Everything is working out as planned. You'll just need to practice your part."

They walked to a vacant apartment three blocks away, Pete slipping the key in the door as if he owned the place. Inside, on top of the breakfast table, was a Transoceanic crew bag—slate-gray fabric with gunmetal-gray trim and the airline's gold and gunmetal logo. Curious, Michael watched as Pete unzipped the soft-sided bag. At first glance, he detected nothing unusual, but after peering into the bag, he could see that an identical crew bag was tightly stuffed inside.

The contents of the interior bag appeared to be the usual crew gear, along with a few personal items. Michael recoiled as he recognized items that he had stolen from Isabel: the galley gloves, Swiss Army knife, flashlight, cockpit key, and lipstick. But there were other things, too, including a flight attendant handbook, batteries, shoes, and a hairbrush.

He looked up at Pete. "Are these Isabel's things?"

Pete shrugged. "We paid a little visit to her apartment in Washington."

Michael was dumbfounded until realizing that he should have expected something like this. They had forced him to take only a few items because Isabel would remember the circumstances under which they had been lost and would point her well-manicured nail straight at him.

The greater shock came when Pete revealed the bag's carefully concealed components—the pieces that would become the bomb. On the table was a duplicate set of parts that could be handled without worrying about fingerprints. Michael watched as Pete put the device together, explaining each step, before breaking it back down into the individual pieces. Then it was Michael's turn. The practice session lasted until after midnight—assembling the device, taking it apart, and assembling it again—until Michael could have performed the motions blindfolded.

Expecting to take it with him, Michael put on his gloves and reached for the bag.

"No, I'll deliver it to you," Pete said. "At noon, just before you leave for the airport."

Watching Michael leave, Pete wondered if the kid would go through with it. *Maybe, maybe not. He has a conscience.* He picked up the phone and dialed G.

"He's ready," he said.

G grunted and asked, "Did he buy the story?"

"Of course," Pete replied. "Why wouldn't he? Most of those flight attendants carry the same tools of the trade."

"And he believes that everything belongs to Isabel?"

"Yes. There's not a hint that he thinks otherwise. After all, he knows what he took, and now those things have appeared in the bag. It's a logical progression. Of course, there is always the possibility that he could look inside the handbook or search the interior pocket of the bag and see the name on the crew tag, but I don't think he will."

"I hope you're right."

"It's a good plan. It will work."

"We will find out soon enough."

Chapter 48

February 6–9, 1994
CIA Headquarters
Langley, Virginia

Cat took the early morning flight back to DC and was in her office by ten o'clock. Sundays were generally quiet and it gave her time to think about what to do next. Despite her optimism with Dave, she had a gnawing suspicion that any effort to dig into the death of Colonel Shreve Garvin would be met with a wall of resistance. She assumed that, whichever agency had quashed the investigation in Memphis, they would have had a very important—and very secret—reason for doing so. Despite her misgivings, she requested a meeting with her boss the next morning.

On a hunch, she went looking for Marianne Riel, a longtime employee of the Agency. Marianne had a pretty face, a matronly physique, a quiet demeanor, and over the years, had evolved into a fixture who was more wallflower than bouquet. She went about her business at will and largely unnoticed. Cat had realized early on that, beneath that drab exterior, lay a whip-smart, tenacious, and devious mind.

She was only mildly surprised to find Marianne at work—the Agency was her life. She laid the two sketches, facedown, on Marianne's desk and said softly, "My car was compromised the other night. These two might have been involved. I was hoping you might help identify them."

Marianne did not even blink. She gave Cat a sideways glance and said, "Give me a couple of days."

Cat met with her boss, a cautious and pedantic man named Jeff Keely, the next morning. While they were not always of the same mindset—she preferred action, he preferred deferral—they tolerated each other. After fifteen minutes of explanation on her part, one two-minute phone call on his part, and thirty seconds of "the matter is closed," she was back at her desk. She had known what his reaction would be and never mentioned the sketches. She would continue her own investigation.

On Wednesday, Cat was in the cafeteria, nibbling at a salad, when Marianne sat down across from her. They made small talk over soup and salad and waited for the crowd to thin.

"I queried the usual suspects and came back with zilch. Then I recalled an operation we were running several years ago. I was gathering info on contractors, and there were two guys—code names Clay and Fredo—under consideration for the job. The file on that op is closed so I cannot confirm, but my recollection is that they resembled the men in your sketches. They weren't American, so we had deniability. Eastern European as I recall."

Cat nodded. *Well, well,* she thought.

Chapter 49

February 10, 1994
En route from New York City to Frankfurt, Germany

Michael leaned on the galley counter, cradling his coffee cup and trying to work out an alternative course of action. *How am I going to get out of this? What are they really going to do? Will they arrest Isabel when we get to Frankfurt? Will they figure out she's being set up? Will they come after me?* Try as he might, he could not shoo away his feelings of impending disaster. In the days since the practice session, Michael had been overcome with anxiety, eating little and sleeping less. There seemed to be no way for him to escape Pete's control without risking the lives of his family. But the enormity of what he would have to do to save them was crushing his soul.

"Michael! Earth to Michael!"

He blinked and looked up. Isabel was staring at him. He jerked his brain back to the present. "Sorry. I was thinking about something else. Want me to do the walk-through?"

"Sure," she said, her eyes twinkling in amusement.

He swallowed the last of his coffee, then parted the galley curtains and peeked out at the half-empty aftmost cabin of the Boeing 747.

Transoceanic Airlines flight 366 was the day's last US-carrier flight out of JFK bound for Frankfurt, Germany. The aircraft could seat a total of four hundred twelve passengers, with sixty-five in the first- and business-class cabins, and three hundred forty-seven in economy—and more if lap-held infants were included. Tonight, however, the load was light—a mere one hundred ninety-three travelers—typical of February, typical of a Thursday night. Tomorrow would be another story altogether.

After an all-nighter across the Atlantic and the landing in Germany in the early morning, the aircraft would welcome a new load of passengers and head back to JFK. Friday morning flights back to the States were generally full, and this week would be no exception. Businessmen, military personnel and their wives and children, tourists on excursion fares ... everyone wanted to get to their destination by the weekend. Michael had looked up the flight on the computer, learning that it was oversold by twenty-one seats. But a different crew would handle the mass of humanity flying back to the States; he and his fellow flight attendants would be transported into the city for a day of rest before returning to New York the following day.

Drawing the curtains closed behind him, preventing the blaze of light from disturbing nearby passengers, he stepped into the aisle and walked slowly toward the airplane's tail. In the past, passengers had been known to die quietly in their seats while the crew, unaware of the crisis, swapped war stories in the galley. The company now required that flight attendants take regular strolls through the cabin—at fifteen-minute intervals, according to the manual—to check passenger needs and ensure that no one was in distress. In practice, no one set a timer. Thus, twenty or thirty minutes might elapse before someone raised the question, "Has anyone done the walk-through lately?"

The cabin was dark; the overhead and sidewall lights were turned off to encourage sleep, and the movie had flickered the last of its credits some time ago. Tonight's film offering was a loser. The few who had rented headsets had tuned out and fallen asleep long before the end of the show. Taking advantage of the extra room provided by the abundance of vacant seats, most of the passengers were resting in nests fashioned of pillows and blankets. He ambled down the aisle—his head swinging back and forth as he waved his penlight over the rows of seats—taking stock of the sleeping bodies and checking for anything out of the ordinary. Flight attendants were required to have flashlights available, and Michael had two: a flimsy penlight with two AA batteries that ran out of juice after one or two flights, and a stronger Maglite with two C batteries. And like most flight attendants, he always carried spare batteries in his crew bag.

The only exception to the inky aft cabin was the glow cast by two reading lights. One reflected off the balding pate of the seat's occupant, a middle-aged man pecking laboriously at his laptop computer. Instead of pillows and blankets, his space was strewn with file folders and yellow legal pads. Michael picked up the man's now-empty coffee cup and offered a refill. The guy never spoke, simply nodding in response to the inquiry while he continued to type. Michael calculated that the man had consumed at least a dozen cups—black, one sugar—since the beginning of the flight.

Continuing aft, Michael reached the back of the cabin, checked the lavatories, and then turned to walk forward through the aisle on the opposite side of the airplane. He paused at row 48 and studied the elderly woman in the window seat. She seemed to have dropped off while reading. Satisfied by the rise and fall of her chest that she was indeed alive, he leaned over to extinguish the reading light shining onto her snow-white hair. She did not stir.

He slipped back into the galley, and three sets of eyes looked up expectantly.

"Need anything?" asked Isabel.

"Just another coffee for the computer slave," he replied affably.

"He's going to float into Frankfurt. I'll take it out for you." Isabel rose from her perch—a metal rack she had removed from an oven and draped with a blanket. After hours on their feet—with no seats in the galley and no other illuminated space in the cabin—flight attendants would resort to any measure to relieve their swollen legs. She poured the coffee, swept up a sugar packet and napkin, and disappeared through the curtain.

The two remaining flight attendants, Tom Kaiser and Linda Clendaniel, returned to their banter, spinning a yarn from Pan Am's glory days. They, and Isabel, had been hired by Transoceanic shortly after Pan Am's demise in December 1991. As a newcomer to the industry, Michael often found their stories wildly entertaining and listened attentively. Many of the tales were familiar, having earned a place in global airline lore, but sometimes the teller would offer a delicious new slant. Tonight, Tom's narrative was a tired retread.

Occasionally, his fellow flight attendants—having shared their own history—would ask about his life prior to Transoceanic. He gracefully deflected the inquiries, revealing only that he was a small-town boy who had joined the airline a few months ago. They would never have understood his earlier life, would never have suspected his background.

Michael checked his watch and glanced up as Isabel reentered the galley. "Time to switch," he said.

Isabel presented him with a tolerant smile and consulted her own timepiece, a filigreed gold pendant hanging from her neck. She nodded inclusively at Tom and Linda, giving her assent to a break. "Go ahead and wake up the others," she said. "Take forty-five minutes. We'll want everything set for breakfast to go out an hour and fifteen from now." She issued the orders matter-of-factly, trusting that each member of the crew would meet her expectations.

While strictly against company regulations, sleeping on nighttime international flights was common practice. On light flights like this one, the majority of flight attendants elected to enjoy the comfort of a seat at the back of the first-class cabin, or on the upper deck—upstairs—in business class.

Tom and Linda responded in unison, "We'll go upstairs."

Michael had rehearsed his line a hundred times. "Actually, my stomach is bothering me. I'll take a book and go to one of the heads in the back. If I start to feel better, I'll let you know where I am."

Isabel was mildly surprised that he would choose a lavatory in the back, rather than a less-trafficked spot at the front. But over the last few months, she had observed that Michael had a number of unusual idiosyncrasies. *To each his own*, she thought, although she found the idea of spending any length of time in a foul-smelling, germ-laden bathroom completely disgusting.

Chapter 50

Michael stepped out of the galley and again made his way aft, past the nameless reclining bodies and the still-slumbering elderly lady in seat 48A. This time, he kept his flashlight turned off and his eyes averted, his brisk pace and body language declaring him to be unapproachable. Upon reaching the jump seat at the aft left door, he turned around and looked forward through the cabin. Still dark, still quiet ... only the computer man with a light on. He quickly grabbed his crew bag from the closet shelf. It was heavier than its appearance implied.

Standing outside the lavatory door, he pulled the bottle opener from his pocket. He slipped the pointed tip into the slot on the plastic indicator displaying the word *Vacant*. Sliding the indicator to the *Occupied* position locked the door, just as if someone were inside. The mechanism, designed to allow the crew to enter a locked bathroom when a person inside was in trouble, was more useful for preventing entry when the toilet malfunctioned—a fairly common occurrence. With a final look toward the front of the airplane, he stepped on the support at the bottom of the closet, slid back the overhead ceiling panel, and hoisted himself and the bag up into the tail of the airplane.

Michael slipped the ceiling panel back into position and turned on the penlight. While he could not stand upright, the area was surprisingly roomy.

While he worried that he could be spotted by another member of the crew, he had made three nighttime trips since his first flight to London with Isabel—making an unobserved entry into the tail on each occasion. He had the motions and timing down pat, and no one had been the wiser, but this time was different. This was not just a trial run. This was the real deal, and if he were caught, he could spend the rest of his life in prison.

He played the light over the space. Wall and ceiling panels—used for aesthetics in the passenger cabin—were absent here, and the beam illuminated a catacomb of insulation, ducting, and bundled electrical wiring. A splash of color in a case mounted on the hull distinguished itself from the otherwise drab space: the infamous "black boxes." There were two, a flight data recorder and a cockpit voice recorder. Interestingly, they were not black; they were florescent orange, making them more readily visible to searchers following an accident. A great deal of research had gone into selecting the location for the boxes; the tail of the 747 was generally considered the section most likely to survive a catastrophic event.

He placed the bag in a recess just behind the access panel and unzipped it. He had stuffed some of his own gear between the two bags: three packs of cigarettes, a razor, a toiletry kit, two paperback novels, a small tool bag, a coil of copper wire, a roll of adhesive tape, and his own copy of the Transoceanic flight attendant manual. The only item that might raise an eyebrow was the copper wire, but flight attendants were known to carry an array of unusual objects.

He also carried a small package of latex gloves. Ever since the AIDS epidemic had exploded a decade earlier, flight attendants had become more cautious. Finding a volunteer to perform mouth-to-mouth resuscitation on a stranger was almost impossible, and handling passenger waste had become a tricky business. Long expected to handle discarded barf bags, diapers, bandages, and tissues saturated from a nosebleed, and with the airlines supplying little in the way of protection, crewmembers now either carried their own gloves or simply refused to take such items from passengers.

He slipped on the protective gloves and pulled the interior bag free, setting it beside him. Using a screwdriver from his tool kit, he pried open the tucked seam in the base of the interior bag—Isabel's bag—exposing a thin, flattened, plastic-wrapped package labeled *Semtex,* above the words *Training Use Only*. The plastic wrap around the explosive was the same wrap that he had snatched while helping unwrap glassware on the London flight. It had Isabel's fingerprints all over it—proof of her involvement.

Semtex, a plastic explosive with a consistency similar to modeling clay, was originally developed in Czechoslovakia and was the Eastern Bloc's answer to the West's tightly controlled C-4. Semtex was readily available to any purchaser with a fistful of money. A small quantity had found its way into Serbian hands to be used against the residents of Sarajevo. Michael had witnessed, firsthand, the results of its destructive power.

He handled the package cautiously. Despite assurances from Pete that they would use imitation Semtex, Michael was not taking any chances. While Pete had told him that Semtex was very stable and would not spontaneously detonate—explaining that soldiers had fired bullets into blocks of the explosive, and had even used it as fuel for campfires—Michael had no way of determining whether Pete's words were fact or fiction. He knew that Pete manipulated people by telling them what they wanted to hear, not by telling them the truth. Yet he was putting all his trust in believing that Pete's promise to release his brothers would be fulfilled—while harboring a feeling of dread that everything Pete said was a lie.

He gently pressed the explosive into place, behind the blanket of insulation and against the top of the aircraft frame, as near to the tail assembly as possible. Pete—or his cronies—had prepared the detonator in advance, disguised inside the gold-colored lipstick case Michael had stolen from Isabel's purse. Michael had practiced the final assembly, but now his fingers trembled as he set about constructing the arming device. Again, he was trusting Pete's assurances that the blasting cap was a dummy. Michael wondered for the umpteenth time, *How would I even know the difference?*

Many international crewmembers carried a second alarm clock as a backup, and Isabel had apparently been in that group. The display on the second clock was blank and could easily be explained away as a dead battery, its true purpose disguised. He unclipped the cover, pushed a new battery against the contacts, and watched it come to life. Pete had explained that it was a pressure altimeter, purchased anonymously in one of the myriad electronics shops in the Akihabara district of Tokyo. It could never be traced.

The altimeter was capable of registering two distinct, user-specified settings. In ordinary use, the device could warn of dangerous changes in pressure at altitude, offering a yellow warning light at the first setting and a red light at the second. He detached the tiny contact from the red light and twisted it onto a short strip of wire. He tore off a piece of the adhesive tape, using it to secure the other end of the wire to a contact on the clock. He set the clock's timer for three and a half hours but did not activate it. He taped one end of another section of wire to the contact for the timer's ringer, and twisted its other end onto the wire protruding from the blasting cap.

The atmospheric pressure at sea level is 14.70 psi, providing the perfect amount of oxygen for human life. Michael thumbed the setting on the first altimeter to 14.40—a rough measure of the air pressure in Frankfurt, which sits a few hundred feet above sea level. He set the second dial to 12.00 psi, similar to Denver—the mile-high city—at 30 degrees Fahrenheit. As altitude increases, the pressure decreases and there are fewer molecules of oxygen in a normal breath of air.

Nearly all climbers of Mt. Everest require supplemental oxygen to survive. Airplanes, which can easily fly a mile or two higher than the highest mountain in the world, keep people alive by pumping air into the cabin and pressurizing it. Passengers are comfortable, but breathing less oxygen, as if they were sitting in Denver or Colorado Springs. And with the reduced oxygen in the air, one cocktail has the effect of two.

The altimeter's yellow light would click on as the airplane approached Frankfurt. After landing, the plane would take on a new load of fuel and passengers for New York. As the aircraft climbed out of Frankfurt, pressure in the cabin would eventually drop below 12 psi. But instead of triggering the red light, the electrical pulse from the altimeter would initiate the clock's timer. Three and a half hours later, the countdown would hit zero. At that moment, the final strip of wire would send a pulse to the blasting cap, which—if it were functional and the Semtex real—would ignite the explosive.

The more that Michael had learned about their plan, the more uneasy he had become. He had tried to put his doubts aside, to ignore the building suspicion about their true intent, but his discomfort had only increased. *After all,* he had wondered, *a bomb is a bomb. When the authorities find the device and learn the identity of the fingerprints, they will arrest Isabel, regardless of how simple or complicated the device is. So why go to all this trouble?*

He had then reached the only logical conclusion. *They are going to use a real bomb. And they are going to blow up the airplane.* The mere thought had made his body quake. And then that same logic fought back. *Why would they bomb one of their own airplanes, killing their own citizens?* He could find no plausible explanation, which then circled back to the conclusion that they would never use a real bomb.

Pete had seemed to sense Michael's unease. "We want the realism," Pete had said. "And the complexity of the device will help convince investigators that she was working with professionals. It underscores the scope of her planning and deadly intent."

Still, Michael thought the entire concept seemed far-fetched—even for Americans, who were known for pushing the limits. What he knew for certain was that the tail, known as the "empennage" in aviation-speak, provided vertical and horizontal stability, controlling the up-and-down motion called pitch, and governing the left-and-right motion known as yaw. The blast from a high explosive, such as Semtex, would rip the entire structure apart. The aircraft would instantly become uncontrollable, fall out of the sky, and plummet into the ocean. Nobody would be able to save it ... or, if it went into the North Atlantic, even find it afterward.

He tossed Isabel's rubber galley gloves back into her bag, dropping her knife on top of the pile. When someone eventually discovered the fake explosive, the evidence would connect Isabel to the materials. He performed a final inspection of his handiwork and hesitated, his stomach knotting. *This is wrong,* he told himself. *Airplanes and explosives, even fake ones, do not mix.* He shook away his misgivings, rationalizing his actions. *I am doing this for my brothers. The Americans would not blow up their own people.* He took a deep breath and quickly returned the remaining items to the bag. Flashing the penlight on the face of his watch, he saw that eleven minutes had elapsed since he entered the tail.

Moving quietly, he worked his way back to the access panel and hunched over it, his heart starting to pound. *Go back and disarm it. Let Pete figure out another way,* he told himself. But then he flashed on the photos of his family, and before he could change his mind, he flicked off the flashlight and noiselessly slipped the panel back a bare two inches. This was the trickiest part of the plan: reentering the cabin unheard and unseen. Relief swept over him ... the space below was still and dark. Sliding the panel back farther, he lowered his head to survey the cabin. From this vantage point he could see the full length of the aisle as it stretched forward, blocked only by the curtain separating the first-class seats from the more modest seats in the back. All clear. He grabbed his own bag, lowered himself back into the cabin, adjusted the ceiling panel, unlatched the door to the lavatory, stepped inside, relocked the door, lowered the toilet seat top, washed his hands, and sat until it was time to serve breakfast.

Chapter 51

February 11, 1994
Frankfurt, Germany

Reaching to pull a heavy bag from the overhead bin, Michael said, "Let me help you with that." The elderly woman he had noticed earlier seemed frail and exhausted. "Do you have family meeting you here?"

"My son," she replied with a wan smile. "He is stationed here, in the army." She tilted her head, squinting, and said, "You're such a kind young man. Thank you."

"My pleasure. I hope you have a nice visit." It was odd, he mused, that he actually cared about his passengers—strangers he would never see again. He really did want her to enjoy her time with her son.

He waited patiently for the remaining laggards in the rear of the plane to gather their belongings, then pulled his own bag from the closet, slipped into his coat, and trailed behind the stragglers as they made their way to the front of the aircraft. The cleaners had begun attending to the first-class cabin and the caterers were already off-loading used equipment and provisioning the galleys for the return flight.

He stopped at the front entry door and exchanged pleasantries with the oncoming crew—several of whom he knew from previous flights and others whom he had never met. He wondered how they would react, later, when Isabel was arrested and they learned of the phony bomb in the tail.

Spotting Robert Bailey among the new crew, Michael grimaced inwardly. Bales had introduced Michael to the "aft lounge" and was known to be a habitué of the space—someone who might find the device. Michael tried to reassure himself that the likelihood of Bales making the discovery was almost nil. It was a daylight flight, the aircraft was fully booked, and the crew would have little opportunity for sneaking a rest break.

Michael arranged his face in a grin. "Bales, you dog!" he said, extending his hand. "What's shakin'?"

Bales leaned in, his voice low, and groaned. "Ugh. Everything, man." He held out his hand, fingers trembling.

"Too many pear brandies, or late night?"

"Both, man. Need coffee."

"Who was the lucky girl?"

"I never kiss and tell."

"You're a true gentleman," Michael said with a grin. He turned to leave, then pivoted back. "Have a safe flight."

"Always," Bales said, giving a thumbs-up.

Michael stepped into the Jetway, went through the door into the terminal, and froze. There were no police, no guard dogs, no commotion at all. There was no sign of any Cuban delegation traveling to the United States. And at the service desk, talking to the gate agent and in full uniform, stood Maggie Marshfield. Twenty feet away, waiting to board, was the man from Paris—the man he had captured in the photo at the hospital. The Arab. He was wearing a business suit—not the long white thobe he had worn at the hospital and in the Lebanese restaurant—but Michael was sure it was the same man. The suspicion was confirmed when the man's head came up, looking at Maggie, and she turned and gave a little wave.

Michael's legs turned to jelly. The terrible truth washed over him, burning into his skin as if someone poured a bucket of acid over him. This was not about Isabel at all. They wanted Maggie gone and they were going to use a bomb to do it.

Maggie glanced up and spotted Michael, concern flooding her face. "Michael? Are you okay? You look awful!"

"Something I ate. Have a good flight," he mumbled before fleeing to the men's room and losing his breakfast.

The alarm in the hotel room went off at three o'clock that afternoon, jarring Michael out of a deep sleep. He stretched and reached for the television's remote. Then, remembering the device he had rigged on the incoming flight, his heart began to hammer. *It wasn't real Semtex,* he told himself. *It was imitation. Everything is fine.* Flipping through the channels, he searched for the BBC and AFN, both of which were good sources of news for English speakers living in or visiting Germany. As the minutes ticked by without an indication of important breaking news, his concern began to ebb, relief taking its place. No story about a plane crash, not a peep about a missing airliner. For the first time in weeks, he relaxed. *It really was fake. I was just being paranoid.*

Grateful to learn that he had not initiated a catastrophe, he fell back onto the bed, letting his heart rate return to normal. Unable to get back to sleep, he threw the bedcovers to the side and padded into the shower, where he rinsed off the residual stink of the airplane—an odor that flight attendants jokingly referred to as *Eau de Boeing* or *l'Air du Bus*. Leaning over the sink, razor in hand, he stared at himself in the mirror.

All the winter flying had taken its toll. The tan on his skin had faded, and his normally sun-streaked, tawny-blond hair was now a boring light brown. He had taken to wearing his hair spiked, the length at the sides just brushing the top of his ears. As he shaved, his gray eyes followed the blade as it rode over his chin and throat. He realized that he still had an ear tuned to the television, continuing to listen for a breaking news story. He shook his head hard, trying to clear away the lingering worry. *Everything is fine. The plane is fine.*

Opening the blackout curtains, he was momentarily surprised by the precipitation spitting against the hotel room's window and the layer of snow on the street below. He retrieved a plastic bag from the closet, tossing in the latex gloves, the copper wire, and the adhesive tape, and tied it closed. He dressed warmly in a thick sweater, lace-up suede boots, knit ragg wool beanie, and topped it with the parka he had bought for the flight to Paris with Maggie.

He checked his watch and left the hotel. Three blocks away, he dropped the plastic bag into a rubbish bin.

Chapter 52

Michael spent the remainder of the afternoon wandering the streets of Frankfurt, and it was well past six-thirty by the time he returned to the hotel. The lobby was devoid of crewmembers, suggesting that they had already left for dinner. No matter; he knew where to find them. While there were occasions when he preferred to keep his own company rather than engage in the typical airline revelry, this evening he knew he had to join them. If the explosives had been discovered, someone would have information. There were few means of communication faster than the flight attendant gossip line.

He hurried three blocks to the Baseler Eck, a favorite hangout of Transoceanic, Pan Am, and other international air crews. The place was popularly referred to as the Gas Station, the moniker having been bestowed due to its location directly behind a recently demolished petrol station.

Entering the restaurant, Michael's throat clenched as he spotted Bales, Maggie, and several other flight attendants who, by now, should be landing in New York. Seeing them, he knew instinctively what had happened. *The flight to New York was canceled. Why?*

Working to control his anxiety, he pasted a wide grin on his face, appropriated an empty chair from a nearby table, and wedged it into a narrow space between Maggie and Bales.

Forcing a laugh, he cracked, "Didn't get enough schweinshaxe last night? You had to come back for seconds?" The schweinshaxe—roasted pig knuckle—was the house special.

Bales laughed and raised his glass in greeting. "I do love their food, but the rumblings of my stomach don't hold much sway with crew scheduling. Actually, the airplane had a mechanical. We taxied out, and some electrical system went haywire. Parts were supposedly coming down from London this afternoon. They said they'll have it fixed by morning."

Michael's mouth went dry. Struggling for composure, he turned toward Maggie and blurted out, "Are we still on pattern?"

In crew lingo, a "pattern" was the block of flights that a crewmember was scheduled to fly from departure from home base until returning. If they remained on pattern, they would fly back to New York in the morning, most likely on the same airplane he had brought into Frankfurt. A chill rippled down his back.

Maggie leaned his way. "Bales and I, and Susanna," she said, tilting her head toward a statuesque blonde at the next table, "are headed to Munich on Lufthansa at five in the morning. Rumor has it that one of our crews rented a car on the layover and got into an accident. Nothing serious, they tell me, but we're picking up their leg to London. Lucky you—you and the rest of your crew get to deadhead back to New York."

Deadheading meant that he would fly as a passenger, on company business, rather than as working crew. Better still, deadheads often rode first class. It was a rare treat, and flight attendants were usually delighted when they were scheduled to ride instead of work. Michael forced a smile, outwardly demonstrating that he was pleased by the news, but his stomach had dropped. He would be riding on the same airplane he had rigged. The realization prompted a host of questions. *Do I really believe that they gave me phony Semtex? Do I trust them enough to risk my life?*

Maggie stabbed a forkful of the pork and waved it admonishingly. "It's supposed to be a full flight back. You might be deadheading, but it wouldn't hurt to offer your help with the service."

He was struggling for an appropriate response when the Baseler Eck's owner appeared at his shoulder, waiting for his order. "Ein bier bitte," he said—*a beer, please*—one of the few German phrases he knew. "And Wiener schnitzel," ordering the breaded veal cutlet that was another popular item on the menu.

Turning back to Bales, he took a gamble. "I wouldn't mind taking the London leg for you. I could use the extra hours, and I have a friend in London I haven't seen in a while."

Bales grinned wickedly. "And so do I, Michael. She's cooking dinner and breakfast."

Michael shook his head in mock amazement. "Only you, Bales." The guy seemed to have a babe in every port.

"Here's to renewing old acquaintances," Bales said, laughing and raising his glass in a toast.

His thoughts swimming, his stomach queasy, Michael clinked glasses with Bales. But the words had reminded Michael of the Arab. The man had obviously been scheduled as a passenger on the canceled flight—presumably traveling with Maggie—but he was not at the restaurant. Would he be on the airplane tomorrow, or had he found another flight? It suddenly felt important to find out.

"Maggie," he said, leaning into her space, "at the gate this morning, I noticed you waving at a guy. Was that your husband?"

Maggie stiffened, and her smile disappeared. She laid her fork on her plate and turned to face him. "No. Why? Are you spying on me?"

Michael felt the color bloom in his face. "No, no, I'm sorry," he sputtered. "I was just curious. I heard he's a diplomat, that he travels a lot. I just wondered. Sorry."

Her expression softened. "No," she said. "My husband is in the States right now. That was just an acquaintance."

Michael nodded and turned back to his plate. He could feel Maggie's eyes still on him. *I went too far. Never should have mentioned that guy.* He pecked at his meal, finished the beer, and left the restaurant well before the others—claiming the onset of a migraine. It was not, he thought, far from the truth.

Back in his room, Michael considered packing his bag and exiting the hotel, simply walking out and leaving his disappearance as a mystery for the authorities to solve. He dismissed the thought, knowing that if the airplane really did fall from the sky, he would quickly become the most hunted man in Europe. No, there had to be another solution.

He pulled down the bedcovers and lay naked on the crisp sheet, pondering his options. Finally, he realized that with all the extra flight attendants and cockpit being rerouted, no one would be exactly sure who should be where. Bales and Maggie would be on their way to Munich and London. For the others, the morning departure would be chaotic, and he would never be missed. Even Isabel, who knew him better than most, would be busy with the full load of people and would not immediately realize he was not on board. He would then have several hours after departure to concoct a story. It was flimsy, but it should work. *What's the worst that could happen, that they would fire me? Better to lose the job than take the risk of becoming fish food in the North Atlantic.*

He turned off the bedside light, rolled onto his stomach, and was asleep within seconds.

Chapter 53

February 12, 1994
Frankfurt, Germany

Michael climbed aboard the crew bus and settled into a window seat, burying his nose in the morning's *International Herald Tribune* while the remaining twenty-four flight attendants and six cockpit crew boarded. The gaggle was a mix of uniforms and deadhead business attire, blond and auburn, short and tall, thin and not-so-thin. The two most junior flight attendants from his crew were in uniform, having been assigned to work rather than deadhead.

Michael wore gray dress pants with a pinstripe pale blue shirt, and a navy sport coat complemented by a gray knit merino wool tie—all topped by his charcoal parka. Except for the presence of his company-issued carry-on bag, he could easily pass for a successful businessman—which was exactly the point.

Tom Kaiser and Linda Clendaniel, engaged in deep conversation, had lagged behind while everyone else boarded the bus. They took the only available seats, one on the aisle beside Michael and the other in the row just in front of him. They continued talking in hushed tones, which suited Michael just fine.

Tom was probably twenty-six or -seven and had been flying for only three months. Tall, lean, muscular, and naturally blond, he had an acerbic wit that provided constant entertainment. He was also a nice guy who made no secret of his homosexuality. Fifteen years ago, someone like Tom would probably have been promiscuous, receiving offers on every flight, in every city. Now, with the AIDS epidemic, he and thousands like him maintained monogamous relationships.

Tom's current arrangement suited him well. Being the significant other of a leading network news broadcaster had afforded him a life of prosperity that would otherwise take years to achieve. While they did not publicize their relationship, it was certainly no secret. Still, they were both acutely aware that, should the nature of their friendship become common public knowledge, the network would drop him like a hot potato. Public perception dictated ratings, and ratings dictated employment. No one was quite sure why Tom continued to fly ... it certainly wasn't the money. Maybe each just needed space.

Linda, on the other hand, should have quit long ago, like on day one as far as Michael was concerned. She was cute enough, with curly short blonde hair, deep blue eyes, and a great set on her chest. She was also one of the most unpleasant people Michael had ever encountered.

Those who knew her well insisted that Linda had—at one time—possessed a great sense of humor and had been pursued by a number of the airline's pilots. She had turned them all down and remained true to the love of her life, a talented actor who had finally begun to experience some success. After ten years of marriage, he had dumped her—exiting the relationship only two days after filming wrapped on a picture generating Oscar buzz.

Her husband's income—previously negligible—had skyrocketed after the Academy bestowed one of its statuettes on the suddenly famous actor. Despite having supported her husband both monetarily and emotionally for over a decade, Linda received almost nothing in the final divorce decree. The judge had sided with the actor's lawyers in awarding him half the proceeds from the sale of their condo in Manhattan, based on his assertions that her travel had been a major factor in the deterioration of the marriage, that he had been the only full-time resident, and that he had personally performed all maintenance on the place. Never mind that her salary had financed the down payment and paid every mortgage installment thereafter, while his maintenance chores had consisted only of fixing a squirrely light switch and a running toilet. The decision earned him a fat profit and left Linda financially devastated.

As the bus pulled away from the hotel's entrance, Michael lifted the newspaper higher and tried to avoid engaging in the normal crew banter. It would be an excruciatingly long twenty-minute ride to the airport. Today was not a day to think about friendships or remember faces.

"Pay attention, everyone," Isabel commanded, her voice rising over the chatter. Faces turned her way, and as the bus made its way toward the airport, she led the working crew through a no-nonsense preflight briefing. Isabel's hallmark was to give the crew a pop quiz on emergency procedures, and she stayed true to form, reinforcing their obligations to passenger safety and reminding everyone to stay on their toes. Michael tried to tune her out and failed. Feeling a pang of regret, he realized how much he had come to like her.

At the airport, the entire contingent breezed through the immigration control checkpoints, flashing their Transoceanic badges and making their way to the departure gate. Isabel approached the gate agent, who gave her the flight paperwork and boarding passes for the deadheads.

Deadhead seating was awarded according to seniority, with the most senior of the crew being issued first class, and the most junior relegated to economy. Michael and Linda had seats beside each other in business class. Tom glanced at his boarding pass and unconsciously wrinkled his nose. His seat assignment was in the back cabin.

This is perfect, thought Michael. "Tom, you and Linda seem to have a lot to talk about. Why don't we switch? I don't mind sitting in the back," he said.

Tom was surprised, but delighted, a wide grin lighting up his face. "Wow, that would be great. Are you sure?"

"Absolutely. Enjoy," Michael replied.

The deadheading crew boarded with the working crew, waving their boarding passes at the agent and taking advantage of the privileges bestowed by an airline employee ID. They tucked their baggage into overhead compartments and closets normally claimed by paying passengers and, having unloaded, set about making themselves comfortable. Most removed their coats and stowed them overhead. A few, including Michael, kept them on. With plenty of time remaining before departure, a number of the crew exited the aircraft to visit the duty-free shop.

Michael left his crew bag on the airplane and trailed along, carrying a leather pouch with his identification and cash. He looked over the merchandise but purchased nothing. As the group wandered back to the gate to board the aircraft, Michael lagged behind and veered away from the gate, slipping into a nearby men's room.

He had considered his options carefully. The restroom offered the best choice for a hiding place. There would be a steady stream of people entering and exiting. Airport cleaning staff do not have the most glamorous job, but they are trained to notice certain peculiarities: a person acting abnormally, a carry-on bag or briefcase left abandoned, a stall that remains locked for an extended period of time. He planned to move from stall to stall, waiting for at least an hour after the aircraft departed. The wait would also give him time to rehearse his stories: one for the immigration officials at the passport control point, and another if he were somehow recognized and caught.

Michael spent over two hours in the restroom, changing stalls every few minutes and going over and over the details of the passport that Pete had given him. He could not afford to stumble. He left the final stall at twelve thirty, washed his hands, and stepped out of the restroom. The first passengers were just beginning to deplane from the Lufthansa flight from Toronto. He stepped back into the restroom, washing his hands again and allowing the congestion at the gate to build. Finally, he exited the men's room, opened his leather pouch as if searching for something, and hurried to the Lufthansa jet's arrival gate.

"Excuse me," he said to the woman at the counter. "I seem to have misplaced my arrival card. Could I have another?"

"Of course, sir," she said. "I have them just here." She rifled through a drawer, then another, eventually retrieving the document and handing it to him. "Do you need assistance in completing it?"

"No, thank you. Oh ... wait ... what was our flight number?"

"One-zero-two-nine," she said with a smile.

He stepped out of the main flow of passengers and held the card against the wall to fill it out. He swallowed hard and inked the entries: Last Name: *Stadler*, First Name: *Graham*, Nationality: *Canada*.

He walked on, following the river of people, his heart thumping madly. *Stay calm*, he told himself.

The line at passport control was twenty deep. He reminded himself to relax, to avoid exhibiting any signs of anxiety. The last thing he needed was to be detained for suspicion of smuggling drugs. He stood patiently, shifting his weight occasionally, just another passenger bored with everyday bureaucracy, until he reached the front of the line and the officer waved him forward.

"What is the purpose of your business?"

"Tourist," he replied.

"How long are you staying?"

"A week or so. I'm visiting friends."

"And where do they live?"

"Near Ramstein."

Ramstein was the big US air base some seventy-five miles southwest of Frankfurt—a frequent destination of American and allied military and intelligence personnel. The officer looked him up and down, then took the card and handed the passport back. "Enjoy your visit."

"Thank you," he said.

Four minutes later, with no luggage, he passed through the Customs line and entered the nonsecure area of the arrivals level at Frankfurt Airport. He found a small coffee shop and took a seat at a back table—just another weary traveler taking a break from the crowds—and faced the reality of his situation.

He had nowhere to stay, no transportation out of Germany, nothing to wear but what was on his back, and a limited amount of cash. The credit card was out—at least for now, and forever if the airplane fell into the Atlantic—because Michael Cantrell would be dead. He was now Graham Stadler, a citizen of a country he had never seen.

He needed to get to his bank in Zurich—fast. He was kicking himself for not having planned for this possibility, for having believed that Pete would never use real explosive material. Now he would have to wing it, and he had only a brief window of opportunity. If the plane crashed, it would take at least a day before any names were released. And, while the Swiss were quite comfortable in dealing with clients of dubious reputation and even more dubious identity, he was not willing to take the chance. Some civic-minded banking official might have a sudden spasm of guilt about handling the funds of a man who had supposedly died in an airplane crash.

He counted the bills in his wallet. With the two fifty-dollar bills in a slot in his passport holder—his emergency cache—he had a total of $195. *Enough to pay for a train ticket,* he thought. *Not enough for a hotel room once I get there.*

For the moment, his bigger concern had to be Pete and Pete's employers. They had supplied him with the Canadian passport; they knew the name. They were not stupid—they would know he had found a way off the airplane. They would be looking for him. Without question, the fastest, easiest thing to do was catch a train to Zurich. He sipped his coffee and considered his fate.

A young woman wheeled her baggage to an empty table six feet away from Michael. Well-dressed, stylishly coiffed, tall—five-nine or -ten—and moderately overweight, she was also an emotional wreck. She sat without ordering, her hands on the table and her eyes downcast, tears slipping down her cheeks. Her eyes were red and puffy and her mascara badly streaked. He watched her carefully, as she appeared to be waging an internal debate about whether to stay or go.

An idea began to take shape. There was no question that Pete's cronies would be looking for him. They would know what he looked like, and probably had photos of him. But they would be searching for a single male among the thousands of people in Frankfurt Airport. *What if...*

Eventually, the woman looked up and caught him staring. She looked down quickly. She brushed her face with her sleeve, trying to wipe away the tears. Michael could not help but notice that she was quite pretty—smeared makeup and blotchy skin notwithstanding. He rubbed his face and pressed his lips together, unsure of his next move and worried about making another mistake. Finally, he stood and walked over to her table. Without an invitation, he sat.

"You seem upset. Can I help?"

She shook her head vehemently.

"Look," he said quietly. "I don't know your situation, but here you are in the arrivals hall with two suitcases and no one to meet you. That can't be good."

She raised her eyes and glared at him.

"Hey," he said, raising both hands in mock surrender. "I have a situation of my own. Maybe we could help each other."

"How?" she asked.

Thirty minutes later, two twentysomething women appeared in front of a ticket window and paid cash for tickets on the next train to Zurich. The taller of the women wore a billowing long gray coat and open-toed flat shoes, her hair hidden under a thick gray beanie and a woolen scarf that covered half her face.

The cashier suspected that the taller woman was a man dressed as a female, but hardly raised an eyebrow. She had a gay nephew. She knew they could be quirky. She handed the tickets to the shorter woman and called for the next in line.

Chapter 54

February 12, 1994
New York City

After listening to the phone ring incessantly for forty-five minutes, Pete finally reached out and lifted the handset.

The voice demanded, "Give me the status!"

"Our scheduler was out of town, out of contact. We had no idea that the same plane would go out today, or that Michael would be on it. There is nothing to be done. The flight has already left Frankfurt."

"So you have no idea where he is?"

"He was seen going into the terminal and through passport control with his crew this morning. Our watchers did not see him leaving the terminal."

"There is no way he would get back on that airplane to New York—he was never fully on board with placing the device anyhow. He would have devised some way of getting out of there."

"It's possible. We still have people at the airport and the train station."

"This is a complete clusterfuck. Just find him."

After disconnecting the call, Pete made a second pot of coffee and wondered about the Russian's obsession with Michael. No other flight attendant had roused such interest. *It feels personal*, he thought. *There is something special about this kid.* Pete had been well trained and his instincts were nearly always spot-on.

In another life, he had gathered intelligence for the CIA, working undercover in the Middle East. He knew, particularly after his last stint in Iran, how the best-laid plans could go terribly wrong. He had a gift for anticipating situations that no one else saw coming, and was seen as a rising star. But in the fall of 1977, he found his name on the list when the new director took an axe to the Agency's roster of clandestine personnel. Poof! No job, no income.

Finding other work had been problematic. His work had been classified, and despite his facility with languages, his skill set was narrow. *Lie, cheat, steal, blackmail.* Hardly the qualifications one included in a résumé. Then, during a visit with a former colleague in New York, he had stumbled upon a tryout call for a new off-Broadway production.

"Why not?" his friend had asked. "We've been trained by the best acting school in the world."

He got the part, his friend did not, and he was now a professional actor—at least, he liked to think of himself as one. In truth, he could barely eke a living out of the bit parts that came his way. He was forty-eight years old, crushed by debt, and still hoping for the big break that would make him a star.

He blamed his ex-wife for much of his financial misery—her expensive taste, always trying to keep up with the Joneses. He had come home one night to find the apartment empty, except for the divorce papers on the kitchen counter.

Now he was stuck with child support and alimony and lived in a roach-infested studio smaller than a matchbox. He could hardly argue child support, but he had lived with that bitch for fifteen years and she never spent a dime on their kid. On Fridays and Saturdays, she hustled tips at a bar in midtown. That income went straight to her personal shoe and wardrobe collection. And alimony? While he waited tables during the day and tended bar five nights a week, she spent her days at the beach or shopping—leaving the kid with the grandmother over in Brooklyn.

He had pled his case in court, but the judge had been unsympathetic. He had kept his anger in check, even when the pompous ass had suggested he try to find another job.

But then the judge had sneered, "You're an actor. You should try the CIA. At least it's steady work."

Pete had exploded, yelling, "I was there for eight years, you fuck. Until they cut nine hundred people."

The outburst had earned him a night in jail and a contempt of court citation—one more expenditure to add to the mountain of bills. It had also attracted the attention of his current employers.

When the stranger had approached him one night and offered him $60,000—cash—to play the part of a spy for a few months, Pete had jumped at the opportunity. In a period of three months, he had built a network of seven Transoceanic flight attendants and two crew schedulers. None of them knew about the others, and all believed that they were performing important services for the US government.

He had initially found the role to be a fun gig—until it wasn't. They had sent him to fucking *Bosnia*, for God's sake. That was when he had figured out—too late—that he was taking money from the Russians. He had finally figured out that the glamorous group of flight attendants, unbeknownst to him or them, had been transporting some of America's best-kept secrets to Europe—passing them to Russian agents and bringing back doctored papers that had no significance whatsoever.

The assignments for Michael, however, were different. He had not carried any secret documents, nor had he been asked to meet with any assets abroad. Pete had come to the conclusion that the Russian was using Michael to locate something—or someone—of particular interest. The Russian had wanted Michael to trail Isabel and Maggie specifically.

Pete could not make any sense of the assignments until learning that Maggie was married to a rising star at State—and discovering that she was having secret meetings in Paris. Certainly, the man she had met there was of interest to the Russians. That discovery had lit a freaking fire. There had long been rumors that some of the airline's flight attendants actually did perform errands for the CIA. Pete was now almost certain that Maggie was one of them, and probably Isabel as well. *Am I engaged in treason?* he wondered. *Oh yeah.*

But that was the least of his worries. He was a participant in a conspiracy to take down an American airplane. If he did not find Michael soon, he was a dead man. Either the American authorities would send him to death row or the Russians would dump him in a landfill in New Jersey.

Plagued with worry and frustration, he pounded his fist on the table. *Michael, where the hell are you?*

Chapter 55

February 12, 1994
North Atlantic, South of Greenland

Transoceanic flight 367 reached its initial cruise altitude at 11:46 a.m., as the flight attendants were handing out peanuts and preparing drinks from the bar carts. Two hours later, following the meal service and after the last of the meal trays were picked up and stowed, blankets and pillows were offered, and passengers pulled down their window shades.

Isabel dimmed the cabin lights and started the first of the two movies that would be offered for viewing. The screens lit up with the opening credits of *A Few Good Men*, a box-office hit released just over a year earlier. Fittingly, she thought, it was about the trial of a corrupt commandant at Guantanamo. Headset rentals were brisk. The cabin grew quiet and passengers settled in, kicking off their shoes and making themselves comfortable as they watched the film, read their books, or drew blankets over themselves and slept.

The aft galley morphed from mealtime frenzy into a refuge for those seeking conversation or simply a place to stand or stretch. The galley occupied a large space centered between the L4 and R4 doors, so designated because they were the fourth doors from the nose of the aircraft, with one on the left and one on the right. Flight attendants dutifully patrolled the cabin, delivering drinks when requested and otherwise simply confirming that all was well with their charges.

Four hours and five minutes after takeoff, as superstars Tom Cruise and Demi Moore were embroiled in a battle of wits with costar Jack Nicholson, Isabel slipped into the cabin and meandered toward the tail of the airplane. Reaching the last row of seats, she paused briefly, stooping to pick up a pillow that had fallen into the aisle. Her fingers brushed the pillowcase, a familiar papery feel, and then ... nothing.

The timer on the device ticked off the final second. The blasting cap flashed and burned into the block of Semtex, igniting the plastic explosive and instantly releasing gases that expanded at the rate of over twenty-six thousand feet per second. In less than the blink of an eye, the blast ripped through the tail of the aircraft. It punched a large hole in the fuselage above and behind the L5 door, tore away a massive section of the empennage, destroyed key hydraulic systems, and created a pressure wave that buckled the floor and ceiling structures in the rear of the plane.

Like a pin puncturing a fully inflated balloon, but on a much larger scale, the jet's pressurized air found its escape through the jagged opening. The violent rush of air took with it everything that was not tied down: newspapers, articles of clothing, pillows, shoes, and people in the vicinity of the blast's epicenter.

The force of the explosion slammed Isabel against a row of seats, breaking her back. She managed only to open her mouth in terror, her primal scream drowned out by the roar of air, before being sucked out of the aircraft.

Tom and Linda, sitting just aft of the first-class cabin, heard a muffled *whhhmmmppphhh* and exchanged a startled glance as the air rushed out of the stricken plane. Their expressions turned to horror as several seconds passed without the oxygen masks deploying. Tom reacted first, unbuckling his seat belt and intending to dash for one of the oxygen bottles stored in overhead bins and at jump seats throughout the cabin. He was too late. Thirty seconds after the explosion, a lack of oxygen rendered him incapable.

Alarms went off in the cockpit, and within seconds the highly experienced crew donned oxygen masks. Having trained relentlessly on the procedures for an explosive decompression, the captain instantly clicked off the autopilot. He pushed the control yoke forward to send the nose down and descend. They needed a lower altitude—one with enough oxygen to sustain human life. But with the empennage and hydraulics fatally compromised, the doomed aircraft failed to respond. As the crew began to comprehend the situation, they frantically tried to keep the plane aloft. With only the four engines functioning, they applied various combinations of thrust to control yaw, airspeed, and altitude—all to no avail. In a final insult, the massive 747 pitched down, rolled to starboard, and fell of its own accord.

Chapter 56

The captain of a British Airways 747, cruising high over the North Atlantic some thirty miles to the right of Transoceanic 367, was mindlessly staring out the cockpit window when he spotted an anomaly.

Gesturing excitedly with his left hand, he shouted at the first officer, "Did you see that?"

The response was instantaneous. "Jesus! Was that ... was that ..."

The captain pressed the mic button on his control yoke that keyed the selected HF radio. "Gander Radio, this is Speedbird 213." Gander Radio was the communications conduit for Gander Centre, which was the OACC—the Oceanic Air Control Center—for this area of the North Atlantic. Speedbird was the call sign for British Airways.

"Speedbird 213, Gander Radio. Go ahead."

"Uh, there appears to have been an event slightly below us, at our ten o'clock," he said, referring to the position of the hands on a watch face. With the nose of the British aircraft at twelve o'clock, ten o'clock was to the left and somewhat forward.

"We saw a flash, like an explosion," the captain continued.

"Speedbird, confirm your position and say again."

The BA captain repeated the message and gave the controller his position in latitude and longitude.

Almost simultaneously, a KLM pilot keyed his microphone. "Gander Radio, KLM 617 confirms explosive event at our two o'clock."

"KLM 617, Gander Radio. Confirmation received. Report your position."

The adrenaline was now pumping wildly in the traffic controllers managing the air corridors across the North Atlantic. They immediately began the process of confirming aircraft known to be navigating along tracks parallel to the BA and KLM aircraft. Transoceanic 367 failed to respond.

Within minutes, the Gander Centre controllers cycled through the initial phases of their emergency procedures and reached the critical level. They contacted the Halifax Rescue Coordination Centre. Other flights following the same path across the ocean were quickly diverted to more southerly or northerly tracks, clearing the way for the search and rescue effort.

Aircraft pilots were requested to attempt radio contact with the missing plane and to report any visual sighting. With a mounting sense of dread, cockpit crews across the North Atlantic scanned the skies and set their radios to VHF 121.5—the aircraft emergency frequency known as Guard.

BA led the effort with the first call, "Transoceanic 367, this is Speedbird 213 on Guard." KLM followed, as did Air France, Alitalia, Lufthansa, Delta, and many others. With a heavy heart, the BA captain made a final, desperate plea, "367, please respond." There was no answer.

The airline itself was notified. Transoceanic, within seconds of receiving the shocking news, implemented its own emergency protocol and began to notify and assemble appropriate personnel. Concern escalated to dread, and as word spread, hundreds of Transoceanic employees closed their eyes and prayed for a miracle.

Holding out hope that the airplane was suffering from some recoverable malfunction, controllers held their collective breath and hoped for communication from the aircraft. A missed call did not necessarily mean disaster, they told themselves. In an emergency situation, flying the aircraft takes precedence over all other tasks. Pilots are trained to first aviate, then navigate, and finally, communicate.

With little radar coverage over the vast ocean, airplanes crossing the North Atlantic are required—at specific waypoints along the route of flight—to check in with controllers from Gander Centre (to the west) or Shanwick Centre (to the east) to confirm altitude and position. When the flight missed the first check-in, and then another, reality set in. Transoceanic Airlines 367 had gone down over the North Atlantic.

Every oceangoing vessel in the vicinity turned full throttle toward the coordinates supplied by the BA and KLM cockpit crews. The *Tulugaq*, a Danish artic patrol cutter stationed in Greenland—and on that day docked at the southwest of the island, in Kangilinnguit—was hastily issued new orders. But with a top speed of only thirteen miles per hour, it would take nearly twenty-four hours to reach the site.

The US Navy called out several ships, including the USS *Grapple*—a rescue and salvage ship based at Norfolk. The *Grapple* was known for its heavy lift equipment, making it ideal for recovering aircraft wreckage from the ocean depths. It also boasted manned diving and remotely operated vehicles, although winter conditions in the North Atlantic would preclude use of most diving operations. The USS *Annapolis*, an improved Los Angeles-class nuclear submarine already conducting operations in the North Atlantic while en route to Norway, was diverted to the site. Its mission: find the airplane's voice and data recorders.

A second ship from the Danish Royal Navy, an ocean patrol vessel named *Triton*, set a course toward the site at twenty-one knots—about twenty-four miles per hour—and would arrive just before sunrise. The Canadians immediately called upon the *Edward Cornwallis*, a high-endurance, multitasked vessel based in Dartmouth, Nova Scotia, which would arrive in three days.

The US Navy and the US Coast Guard dispatched aircraft, sending two P-3C Orion aircraft and two C-130s. One of the C-130s was currently deployed to the International Ice Patrol, which scours the North Atlantic and the Grand Banks for iceberg hazards from February through July.

Canada provided air support by sending two long-range CP-140 Auroras and one C-130 Hercules aircraft from their base in Greenwood, Nova Scotia.

The initial search grid was formulated from the missing plane's last confirmed position and the coordinates provided by the KLM and BA crews.

Due to the distances involved, three hours would elapse before the first search plane arrived in the area. Because of the shortness of the days at northern latitudes during the winter, the sun would set at 4:39 p.m. local time. The searchers would have only about ninety minutes of usable daylight.

Chapter 57

February 12, 1994
London, England

After waking long before dawn, flying to Munich, and then working a flight to London, Maggie Marshfield was ready for a nap at the hotel. Instead, taking advantage of the gloriously clear sky and mild temperature, she set out on a brisk walk through Hyde Park. Feeling refreshed upon reaching Piccadilly, she turned west and headed for her favorite store in the world: Harrods. She could wander forever through the iconic establishment and, on this day, spent three hours browsing its many departments and famous food halls. It was late afternoon when she returned to her room.

She tossed her packages on the bed, flipped on the television, and was stripping down as she stepped into the bathroom. The words of the BBC news reader took a moment to register, and when they did, her legs turned to rubber. She lurched toward the bed and sat, stunned, her eyes riveted to the map displayed on the screen.

"... disappearance of a Transoceanic 747 in the North Atlantic, two hundred miles off the Greenland coast. Flight 367 was en route from Frankfurt to New York. An extensive search is underway ..."

Maggie barely heard the remainder of the report. *I would have been on that plane ... I would have been on that plane.* She fought to catch her breath, to control her racing heart. *If not for that car accident in Munich ...*

She picked up the phone and, hands shaking, dialed her husband. At the sound of his voice, she began to cry. "Paul ..."

"Thank God," he breathed. "I've been frantic. When I didn't hear from you ... I thought ... I thought ..."

"I was going to call you tonight. I got rerouted ... I'm in London. I just turned on the television."

"London? What ... it doesn't matter. I only care that you're safe. Oh, thank God!"

"Paul, I just turned on the television. The BBC is only saying that the plane is missing, nothing more, but planes don't just disappear. Oh, my God! I went out, enjoying the day, having fun shopping. It's crashed, Paul, and most of my crew was on that plane! And I've been out, just having a good time, and I had no idea. All those people, Paul, people I knew! And I wasn't even supposed to be here. I was supposed to be on that plane!"

As he listened to Maggie struggling with a jumble of thoughts and emotions, her words tore at his heart. He slipped into the skin he wore whenever confronting a crisis, his words calm and soothing. "Maggie, what you're feeling is normal—if I'd done this, if I'd done that, why them and not me. It's perfectly normal to feel this way. But listen, sweetheart, it was just a regular day for you. Crews get rerouted all the time."

"I know, but ... what if ..."

"You'll have these feelings for a while, the what-if thoughts. It's normal! Look, I know how these things go. I think it might be a good idea to talk with a professional—someone who might be able to help you work through this."

Maggie's tears were running freely now, spilling down her face and onto her chest, leaving irregular dark splotches on her blouse. She studied the spots absently, listening to Paul and analyzing her reaction. *Am I crying for the people on the plane? Or out of relief that I wasn't among them?* Paul's suggestion—that she talk with someone—might be a good idea. He had dealt with people who had been through similar life-shattering events. "S-s-sure," she said, her voice breaking. "The airline has people, too—the Critical Incident Response Team. But they probably have enough to handle already."

They talked more, Paul consoling her and sharing the few details that had been released to the media. Finally, he asked, "Are you going to be okay tonight?"

"Yes, I think so. I'm safe; I'm fine." She paused, wanting to put on a brave face for Paul's benefit, then admitted, "Well, not fine right now, but I will be. I'll be home tomorrow."

Paul said, "I'll fly up to New York and meet you; I'll go ahead and book a hotel. You may need to stick around—for a few days, anyhow. You know how thorough these investigations are; they may want to interview you."

"Interview me? Why? Who?" But as soon as the words were out of her mouth, she knew what his response would be. She was one of the last to have seen many of the crewmembers alive—they had eaten dinner together the night before. Like it or not, she would be caught up in the investigation.

"FBI, certainly," he said. "Given that an explosion was reported, it's going to be a criminal investigation. The NTSB will participate, for technical expertise and evaluation of safety-related issues. And there could be foreign agencies involved. If it crashed in international waters, the United States would lead the investigation. The lead would typically fall to Canada if it crashed in their territorial waters, and to Denmark if it crashed within Greenland's waters. But given the circumstances, I doubt that the FBI will take a second seat to anyone. Let's just plan to stay in New York and take the temperature of the situation."

"I wish you were here. It's just so … I don't know … there aren't any words. This is horrible. Horrible. It's like Lockerbie all over again," she said, referring to the 1988 terrorist bombing of a Pan Am 747 flying over Scotland. The airplane had split apart and tumbled to the earth, six miles below. The center section of the fuselage and the wings—laden with fuel—tore into a residential area in the town of Lockerbie, generating an enormous fireball. The crash killed all two hundred fifty-nine passengers and crew, and eleven more on the ground. Both Maggie and Paul had lost friends in the tragedy.

Paul was quiet for a moment, then said, "I've been thinking the same thing. It feels eerily familiar. But let's not jump to conclusions. They haven't released any details yet. Nobody knows what happened."

"Paul, we both know that airplanes don't just fall out of the sky."

He sighed. "I'm just hoping that …" Paul did not finish the sentence.

"That what? That it was something like a mechanical failure?"

"Yeah," he said, slowly drawing out the word. "It's just somehow easier to take when it's an accident, and not murder. I'd give anything if I could beam myself to London. Just hang in there for a few more hours."

"I'll be okay," she said with as much confidence as she could muster.

Paul knew better. "By the way," he added, "Cat's been calling every fifteen minutes ... she's worried as hell."

Cat. Maggie collapsed against the pillows piled at the head of the bed, thunderstruck. Cat Powell was her closest friend. The tiniest of notions, simmering just beneath the surface since she had heard the terrible news, exploded into conscious, horrible thought. *Was I targeted?*

"Tell her I'm okay," she finally said.

"I will," Paul said. "Actually, I wouldn't be surprised to see her show up in New York. You know her; she's going to be digging for details."

Maggie paused before responding. "Why? Do you think she knows something?"

Paul hesitated before answering. "I don't know. There could be reasons. It's hard to say. Maybe her interest stems from your personal connection."

"I hope that's all it is. I would hate to think ..." She left the thought unspoken. She and Cat knew everything about each other and shared everything, *or almost everything*, she admitted to herself.

The mention of Lockerbie took Maggie back to the days and weeks following the tragedy. The Pan Am 747 had broken up over Scotland. Organized teams combed the land, gathering the tiniest of fragments—scattered over eight hundred forty-five square miles of countryside—and eventually logging thousands of pieces of debris into their database. They discovered evidence of the blast and determined that the explosion had occurred in the forward cargo hold; they even pinpointed the specific baggage container. They found parts of the suitcase that had held the bomb, along with bits of clothing and shards of a portable radio, and discovered that all bore explosive residue.

In a massive effort to determine how the explosion had resulted in the 747's loss of structural integrity, specialists reconstructed sections of the airplane—by piecing the wreckage back together.

And now, more than five years later, two Libyans had been indicted and were supposedly under house arrest in their home country. She and Paul had speculated about the odds of the accused men being brought to trial ... and whether the evidence against them was strong enough for a conviction. Maggie leaned back against the bed's headboard, thinking about the possible causes of the Transoceanic flight's disappearance. There were few plausible explanations.

During the Lockerbie investigation, a fragment of circuit board—reportedly part of a timer—had also been turned in, leading many to wonder why it would have been set to go off while the flight would still be over land. Various parties had long theorized that the person planting the explosive device would have wanted it to go off while the aircraft was over water, thus making it exceedingly difficult to recover evidence. Maggie could not help but think that this time, a bomber might have done it right.

Her thoughts turned to Paul's comment that Cat might show up in New York. The skin on her arms prickled, and she shivered. At the time of the Lockerbie bombing, several Islamic groups had claimed responsibility, some plausible, others not. But other rumors had flourished. One of the most persistent was that the bomber had targeted American intelligence personnel on board, including a CIA officer on temporary duty with the Beirut station, an officer from the Defense Intelligence Agency, also assigned to Beirut, and two members of the Diplomatic Security Service.

Is the CIA somehow connected to the Transoceanic flight? Am I a target? Holy God, let it be something else.

After composing herself, she dressed and made her way to the hotel bar—reluctant to be in anyone's company, yet knowing it was a journey she had to make. What she really wanted was to just curl up in a ball in her bed. But there were other crew to think of—pilots and flight attendants alike—who would be reaching out to one another, sharing the latest news, seeking comfort. All of them would be suffering.

The bar was packed, but strangely quiet—the normally raucous crews from Transoceanic forgoing their typical revelry. Sorrow hung heavy in the air. None were immune, because every person present knew at least one person on the ill-fated flight. The previous day's flight cancellation meant that the victims included leftover pilots and flight attendants who were deadheading home. *Horrible term,* she thought. *How many? At least twelve. Maybe thirteen.* It all added up to over thirty Transoceanic colleagues on the downed flight, a staggering number. Most of them had been together at dinner the night before, at the Baseler Eck, and she recalled the laughter and gaiety on the last evening of their lives. *Michael, Tom, Linda, Isabel, all the rest ... gone.*

Chapter 58

February 13, 1994
North Atlantic, South of Greenland

B y the following morning, the worst was confirmed. The *Global Caller*—a container ship registered in Panama and on course for Oslo—reported encountering a debris field some 250 miles southeast of the Greenland tip. The wreckage appeared to be scattered over a wide area and included the shredded remnants of life vests, luggage, seat cushions, small pieces of the aircraft itself, and pieces of bodies—all consistent with an airplane striking the water.

The captain of the massive 950-foot ship commanded his crew to scan the ocean for survivors and to retrieve all possible wreckage before it was claimed by the sea. It was a daunting task. The behemoth was incapable of navigating nimbly, and the captain was fearful that any movement of his ship would only inflict further destruction to the flotsam.

With the discovery of the debris, the planned search grid shifted east from Transcontinental 367's original surmised position. The area was extended even farther outward when an Iceland-bound trawler recovered a floating chunk of the doomed aircraft's vertical stabilizer—the tall fin at the plane's tail—almost sixty miles to the east. With the discovery, one thing became clear: the airplane had experienced a catastrophic event at altitude. It had broken up while still aloft, with the tail hitting the water at one point and the main body propelled westward to another.

Formidable at any time of year, the North Atlantic is particularly brutal in winter. Frigid temperatures, gale-force winds, and towering waves make it an inhospitable place for human life. While both the seas and the skies were unusually placid on this particular day, the calm would not last. Neither would usable daylight. Time was of the essence.

Experts weighed in on the possibility of survival. They generally agreed that, with an explosion at altitude, it was unlikely that the airplane's occupants would have been able to don life vests. Even if they survived the impact, they would have been thrown into the ocean—where the water temperature hovered around thirty-one degrees Fahrenheit. Under the best of circumstances, loss of consciousness would likely occur in less than fifteen minutes, and death would follow less than thirty minutes thereafter. Immersion in cold water numbs the face and extremities to the point of uselessness, making it impossible to hold on to floating debris or even close one's mouth to keep out seawater. The wave action only exacerbates the effect. Any survivor without a flotation device would quickly drown.

Although aware that the likelihood of finding survivors was remote, the searchers were nonetheless hopeful that the rescue component of their mission would be successful. They searched with an intensity born of having witnessed miracles at sea, scanning the water for any trace of life. They found none.

With the primary debris field in international waters, the government of the United States of America quickly assumed authority over the investigation, dispatching go-teams from the FBI, NTSB, and other agencies. Investigators have a moral imperative to keep open minds, examine every detail, and consider all options when faced with an aircraft accident. Investigations can take months, and time and again, initial speculation about the cause of an accident has proved to be inaccurate.

Regardless, two factors shaped the opinion of the aviation industry and the flying public: first, airplanes did not simply fall out of the sky midflight, and second, the Lockerbie disaster was still fresh in everyone's mind. Those in the aviation industry leapt to an almost unanimous conclusion: bomb. A few aviation experts, when cornered by the media, suggested the possibility of structural failure from metal fatigue or a faulty repair, but insisted that the possibility was extremely remote. All emphatically agreed, however, that the investigators would eventually uncover the cause.

The *Triton* arrived just before dawn. Commissioned by the Royal Danish Navy only three years earlier, it was the largest and best-outfitted military vessel in the immediate area and had a medical team and one Sikorsky helicopter.

The importance of recovering the human remains and returning them to their loved ones could not be overestimated. The *Triton*'s helicopter crew flew from ship to ship, gathering the victims' remains and delivering them to the *Triton*. The P-3Cs and C-130s followed a search grid, noting the location of still-floating remnants of the crash. Coordinates were relayed to the various vessels, with orders to retrieve any flotsam.

The *Triton* also worked a grid of its own, using the original coordinates called in after the explosion and the distribution of the debris encountered thus far. The Triton's sonar was on a hunt for the airplane's recorders.

The flight data recorder and the cockpit voice recorder were both constructed with an attached underwater locator beacon. Once immersed in water, the beacon would emit a very short ping approximately once per second. Under normal conditions, the ping's range is only about one to two kilometers. Locating the device in shallow water is relatively easy if its approximate location is known. A single vessel can search approximately seventeen square miles per hour. The search area for Transoceanic 367 initially reached out over sixty miles in each direction from the central debris field, an area of over eleven thousand square miles, with not a speck of shallow water.

Personnel on board the ships faced the grim task with solemnity, respect, and grit. Tears streaked the seaworn faces at the sight of a torn and soggy teddy bear with a missing eye and no arms. They wept openly upon discovering the torso of a young woman, recognizable only by the mound of her pregnant belly. And yet, racing against the clock and the leaden skies that promised heavy weather to come, they worked furiously, gathering any and all remnants of Transoceanic 367 from the unforgiving sea.

With each passing hour, the debris field widened, carried by the unrelenting motion of the ocean swells. What remained on the surface were lightweight fragments of the fuselage, strips of insulation, torn seat cushions, and severely disfigured body parts. Some hand luggage was plucked from the water—bags with trapped air and light enough to prevent immediate sinking. Checked baggage had been loaded into containers that were then secured to the aircraft floor. The force of the impact would have destroyed the floor and ripped the containers apart. While a few pieces of luggage might have broken free, their sheer weight and density would have doomed most to the seafloor.

A part of an engine pylon was recovered, as were a small section of galley bulkhead and a side panel with a window. It would later be determined that both were from the area aft of the L2 door, leading some to surmise that the airplane had rolled to the right as it went in, allowing some sections on the left side to pop free and briefly remain afloat. The nearly complete disintegration of the fuselage told a different story. Most believed the worst-case scenario: the aircraft had nose-dived from altitude.

As the sun set on the second day, it became apparent that no survivors would be found. Further search efforts would concentrate on retrieval of human remains and crash debris.

With the portent of heavy weather, officials made the difficult decision to release the commercial vessels that had diverted to assist. Collected wreckage would be tagged and transported to Garrison St. John's, a Canadian base in Newfoundland, where it would be examined by investigators and scientific experts.

The Americans, as the coordinating authority for the search, announced that Transoceanic flight 367 had crashed in the North Atlantic and that all aboard were presumed lost. The search and rescue effort's designation was officially changed to search and recovery. The president of the United States promised an exhaustive investigation.

Chapter 59

February 19–24, 1994
Northern Virginia

Over the next few days, pressure to find the bomber reached a fever pitch. The public, demanding answers and largely convinced of Middle East involvement, unleashed its verbal outrage at Congress for not taking retaliatory action. Members of the US Senate and House railed at the intelligence community for their failure to detect the plot in advance. The United States and its allies tasked their intelligence and investigative agencies with finding the bomber, insisting upon daily updates.

Those on the front lines were doggedly pursuing every lead and leaving no stone unturned in investigating the passengers, crew, and anyone who had been within sneezing distance of the airplane in the days prior to the catastrophe. Analysts in the various intelligence agencies quietly stroked their chins in thought and ultimately offered no answers.

The media scoured the list of victims for newsworthy names to feature in their reporting. Revelations about Tom's relationship with his well-known partner found traction among religious conservatives, who demanded the anchor's resignation and threatened to boycott the network.

Linda's ex-husband displayed his acting chops as, seemingly stricken with grief and eyes misting, he told the cameras how much he still loved her.

On the fringes, fingers pointed at Isabel, painting her as a dangerous anarchist. Anonymous sources confided that she had been furious about impending changes to US-Cuba relations and had become unbalanced as a result. Other fingers pointed at the Cubans, insisting that they had brought down an airplane to be rid of her. No evidence was provided to support either accusation.

Rumors circulated about the presence of US government employees aboard the flight, insinuating that they were covert operatives returning from some mission in the Middle East. The presses hummed with speculation about retribution being sought by a foreign power. Iran, Iraq, Lebanon, and Syria were most frequently mentioned, but America had no shortage of enemies.

One name on the list of victims—Marc Bishop, US citizen and resident of Paris—caught the eye of several members of the intelligence community. Most dismissed the name as coincidence, given that Marc had been dead for almost three years. A handful of seasoned officers, however, raised their collective eyebrows and wondered what was afoot.

Cat had not slept in days. She leaned back in her chair, squinted her eyes, drummed her fingers on the armrest, and peered at the man sitting across from her, the very-much-alive Marc Bishop.

As planned, he had been booked on the flight. But when the flight was canceled and Maggie was rerouted, Cat had canceled his reservation. She had arranged transportation to a more secure facility: the American air base at Ramstein. He stayed on the base, in the visiting officer quarters, for nearly a week before finding space on an Air Force transport to the States. Thus far, no one had made a connection between the Marc Bishop who perished in the North Atlantic and the Marc Bishop listed on the Air Force's manifest several days later.

"You can't go back to Paris," she said. "And you cannot contact anyone, including your mother. Later we might be able to work out a story, like you were backpacking in the Amazon rain forest with no communication." She waved her hand like a wizard with a wand.

Marc Bishop smiled at the gesture. On numerous occasions he had witnessed Cat work her magic—she could spin gold out of cow dung.

She continued, "I'm just grateful that the airline screwed up and kept your name on the passenger list, because it buys us some time. I cannot dismiss the fact that both you and Maggie were supposed to be on that flight. My instincts are screaming that you were a target, maybe the only target. But if I'm wrong, they may still try to come after Maggie. For the time being, we err on the side of caution. You need to be invisible. You're staying at my house until we come up with a better solution."

Marc Bishop's eyes widened in surprise, and he tilted his head in an unspoken question.

Cat gave him a hard stare, then walked around the desk, placing her hand gently on his shoulder. Softly, she said, "Marc, I am glad to see you ... you have no idea. But that is where it ends. Tom doesn't know about our past, and we are going to keep it that way."

Marc lowered his head, massaging his temples with the heels of his hands. Finally, he looked up, his face composed. "Agreed," he said.

She turned back to her desk and picked up the phone, dialing her husband. "I'll be home early. And I'm bringing a guest. He needs to lie low for a while, so he'll be with us until we can determine a course of action."

Tom, accustomed to Cat's frequent and sudden changes to their plans, gave no indication of being surprised. "That's fine," he said. "But remember that Arnie is spending the weekend."

Cat had completely forgotten about Arnie's visit. She thought about it for a moment, then smiled to herself, thinking, *This could work out quite nicely.* Aloud, she responded, "Perfect. We'll be there soon."

She picked up her bag and jacket, then opened her office door. "Let's go," she said.

Cat introduced Marc to Arnie and Tom, saying, "Marc is an old friend. He needs a place to stay for a bit, and since we have plenty of room, I suggested that he stay here."

The men shook hands and waited for more details from Cat, who turned her back and opened the refrigerator. With nothing more forthcoming, Tom looked over at Marc and said, "Want a beer?"

Marc threw back his head and laughed. "Sure."

Cat turned back toward her husband. "Maybe something imported? Beck's, perhaps? And then maybe all of you can watch football together—or something equally manly."

Tom rolled his eyes. "Beck's we have. But football season is over, dear. Super Bowl was almost three weeks ago. I seem to recall that you even watched the game, screaming obscenities at Dallas as they trounced Buffalo yet again."

"Well, baseball, then?" she asked brightly.

Tom shook his head in mock disgust and gestured for the men to follow him. "Rangers are playing the Whalers tonight."

Arnie called back over his shoulder, "Hockey, Cat. It's winter. They play on ice."

She picked up a wooden spoon and waved it threateningly. "Watch out, big boy, or you'll end up in my next batch of goulash."

The men hit it off, finding common ground in their travels throughout the Middle East. Over dinner, they regaled each other with tales of their adventures, each becoming more exaggerated. Cat, sipping a glass of Bordeaux, relaxed and enjoyed the repartee.

By Sunday night, Arnie and Marc had become fast friends. Upon learning that Marc was looking for a more permanent living arrangement, Arnie offered Marc a room in his townhouse in Boston.

"Come stay at my place! I have lots of room, and I guarantee that it will be a lot more fun than sticking around here with Tom and Lady Gloom and Doom."

Marc glanced furtively at Cat, whose eyes sparkled in amusement. His brow wrinkled in thought as he weighed the idea, while at the same time wondering if Cat had planned this exact scenario. Finally, he nodded. "How could I pass up an offer like that? I'm in!"

After three days of debriefing, Cat escorted Marc to Union Station, and with a sense of foreboding, put him on the Amtrak train to Boston. She could not shake the feeling that the murder of Colonel Shreve Garvin was tied to Marc. And the killers were still out there. Despite her efforts to learn more about Fredo and Clay, she had found only dead ends. With nowhere else to go, she had shelved the file.

"Be careful, Marc," she said, the worry creeping into her voice. "Keep your head down, your mouth closed, and your eyes open. If you see anything, anything at all, I'll get a team to you right away."

Marc nodded. "Thank you," he said. "I'll be fine. I'm getting better every day."

"I'm glad. You'll like Boston, and there are terrific medical facilities there. But just be careful. There are eyes everywhere."

He hoisted his bag over his shoulder and climbed up into the business-class car. He watched as Cat turned to go, then called out after her, "You know that I still love you."

For an instant, Cat froze. Then she pulled her shoulders back and kept walking.

Chapter 60

Seven Months Later
September 1994
Northern Virginia

Cat set the coffee to brew, shoved the egg casserole into the oven, and arranged several croissants and pastries on a plate. She had briefly considered serving up bloody Marys or mimosas, but had pushed the idea aside. For this visit, alcohol was a bad idea.

It was Saturday, a rare day off, and she had called Maggie the previous evening to ask about getting together this morning. Although they talked frequently, they had seen little of each other since the Transoceanic catastrophe seven months before. Cat had been stretched to the limit with Agency business, while Maggie had gone back to flying after a three-month leave of absence that included regular appointments with a therapist.

Spotting Maggie's car pulling into the drive, Cat stepped out and greeted her with a firm hug. "I'm so glad to see you," she murmured. "I've been incredibly busy, and it's making me a bad friend. I'm sorry."

Maggie kissed her friend on the cheek and said, "You know you don't have to apologize to me. Getting the bad guys comes before anything else."

"Indeed," said Cat. "Let's go inside and have a chat." She preferred to be inside her home or office, which were specially constructed and regularly swept for bugs, when engaging in any discussion related to the crash. Prying eyes and ears were everywhere. The media was still clamoring for information and the FBI was chasing every imaginable lead, but no suspects had been identified.

Cat poured two mugs of coffee and sat across the table from Maggie, who pulled a croissant from the plate and took a bite.

"Delicious," Maggie said.

"I got up early and drove over to Antoine's. Their pastries are from heaven!"

"You went all that way? Wow! But worth it, thanks!"

"So, how are you doing?"

"Much better. I still think about it a lot, you know … the *what-if*. But not like at the beginning. Dr. Morales has really helped. I'm not sure where I'd be without her."

Paul had put Maggie in touch with Dr. Sofia Morales, a therapist who was well-known for her work with victims and survivors of terrorist attacks.

"I'm no shrink," Cat said, "but I think these traumatic events bear great similarity to losing a loved one. At first, it gnaws at you every waking second and invades your dreams. The anguish fades over time, but never completely goes away. It's always there, lingering just below the surface and ready to burst through at the most unexpected moments."

Maggie nodded. "It's a lot like that. I guess my biggest hurdle is accepting that we may never know exactly what happened, and more than that, who was behind it."

Cat puffed her cheeks and blew out a long breath. "We're still looking. It's exceedingly difficult and terribly frustrating for anyone working on it. I can only imagine what it's like for you … waking up every day with no resolution." She got up to make more coffee—and gather time to think.

The US government was sparing no effort in trying to determine the cause of the disaster. While experts agreed that a high explosive was almost certainly involved, there was still much to discover before they could establish a trail of evidence leading back to the bomber. An underwater crime scene, the depth of the water, the treacherous condition of the seas in the North Atlantic, and the inhospitable climate were all contributing to the challenge.

The US Navy had been assigned two critical tasks: finding the aircraft's data and voice recorders and locating areas with a high concentration of debris. They were highly interested in the fragment of the vertical stabilizer that had been recovered by the Iceland-bound trawler. The distortions in the metal and the fact that it had been found some sixty miles from the primary crash site meant that the separation had not been a result of impact with the water—it had separated from the aircraft while aloft, probably at cruising altitude. Burn marks on the metal and the pattern of the deformities supported the theory that it had been subjected to an explosive event.

Following the initial search and rescue effort, three ships and a submarine had been dispatched to search for the recorders, which, when submerged in water, are designed to emit a pinging sound detectable by sonar. Finally located in mid-March, they were heavily damaged but salvageable. In the millisecond before its connections were severed, the data recorder noted sudden anomalies involving a sudden yaw and a change to the aircraft's pitch. The cockpit voice recorder simply cut off at the same moment. The findings were consistent with the stress forces of an explosive event in or near the tail.

Deep submergence vehicles, capable of sophisticated underwater photography and equipped with robotic arms, performed the grim assignment of exploring the wreckage. After weeks of examination, they had succeeded in retrieving only two hundred twelve of the four hundred twenty-nine passengers and crew—some of whom were found still strapped to their seats. The tangled and crushed remains of the engines and fuselage bore the expected characteristics of high-speed, uncontrolled impact with the water, and therefore, only fragments deemed crucial to the inquiry were brought to the surface. In total, these pieces represented less than fifteen percent of the aircraft. The remaining wreckage was photographed but remained on the seafloor.

Analysts pored over images from thousands of square miles of seabed, looking for pieces of evidence and anything thought to be inconsistent. Because the explosion had occurred at altitude, most of the small or lightweight fragments would have experienced wind drift and, once in the water, would have been carried for miles by ocean currents. The task was like trying to find a specific grain of sand on a beach.

Cat looked thoughtfully at Maggie and made the decision to tell her. "They found something," she said. "It hasn't been released to the public yet."

Maggie's eyes widened. "When? What?"

"A piece from the tail, two weeks ago—several miles from where they found the vertical stabilizer, well away from the main wreckage. Somebody with good eyes noticed something unusual—probably someone fresh who hadn't been looking at images for days on end. The lab results came back yesterday. I can't give you all the details, Maggie, but there was definitely a bomb in the tail."

A submersible had retrieved the object, a rectangular section almost two square feet in size, tangled in a wide strip of aircraft insulation. Embedded in the insulation were small fragments of black plastic and tiny pieces of wiring. The entire package had been shipped to the FBI Laboratory at Quantico, Virginia, where the piece was identified as part of the aircraft tail cone. Its curled edge indicated proximity to an explosive event. One of the plastic pieces, about the size of a fingernail, bore three numbers that were eventually determined to be the model number of an altimeter manufactured in Japan.

Maggie drew a sharp breath. "So, not a passenger, not a piece of luggage. You're saying someone on the inside, someone with access to the airplane."

"That's where the evidence is leading, yes."

"Someone from maintenance? A mechanic, you think?"

Cat pursed her lips. This answer was going to hurt. "Well, the aircraft did have a mechanical problem in Frankfurt, but it was an electrical problem in the avionics bay at the front of the plane. The maintenance people were on the tarmac and in the cockpit. No one went near the tail."

"How can you be sure?"

"These guys work together, Maggie. Think about it. Someone would have had to disappear for quite a while, and it would have been noticed."

"Ground staff. Someone could have walked onto the airplane while it was at the gate."

"But when they discovered the engine problem, they moved the airplane to the hangar. All the ground staff were off and have been accounted for."

"You think it was a crewmember." She shook her head like a petulant child. "I don't believe it."

Cat sat quietly, letting Maggie process the new information.

Maggie suddenly lifted her head. "Wait! Everyone from the original crew got back on the airplane. They are all dead!"

"That's true."

"Are you saying that one of them did that willingly? Decided on suicide and took an airplane full of people along, too? That's insane!"

"We're trying to figure it out, Maggie. They tell me there's a space in the back, above the toilets, where they think the bomb was placed," Cat said. "Tell me about it. In all honesty, can crewmembers get up there?"

Maggie blinked and took in a deep breath, letting it out slowly. "It's against company policy, but sometimes the crew might take a nap up there. But there are no steps or anything—you have to climb up from that closet by the lavatory and ..." She stopped talking and squeezed her eyes shut.

"What?" Cat asked. "What are you thinking?"

"On the way to Paris, one of the flight attendants—the guy who showed up at the restaurant when I met with Khalid—claimed he was sick and spent his entire break in one of the aft toilets. I thought it was the stupidest thing I'd ever heard. Why would he go all the way to the back? There are hundreds of people using those toilets ... they get really disgusting. And then ... and then ... oh, my God. When the airplane arrived in Frankfurt ... when I was at the gate, getting ready to board ... he asked me ... he asked me if Marc was my husband. Why would he have even noticed that Marc was there? He was sitting with all those people in the boarding area."

A shiver crept down Cat's spine. "Who was it, Maggie?"

"Michael. Michael Cantrell. But that's ridiculous. Why would he do such a thing? And get killed in the process? It makes no sense."

It took all the control Cat had to keep her expression neutral, to cover up her reaction to the name. She stood suddenly, threw her hands into the air, and twirled around the kitchen. "You know what? We need to forget about all this for a little while. Let's ditch the eggs and go into Georgetown for lunch. We'll do a bit of shopping ... have a good time together. We haven't done that in months. Are you game?"

Maggie blinked, startled by the sudden change in topic. Then she started to laugh. "Why not? Let's go have some fun!"

"I'll get my jacket," Cat answered. She fled to her bedroom, wanting to scream, wanting to throw up. *Stop it,* she told herself. *Look into it later. It can't possibly be the same person.* For the remainder of the day, she would keep Maggie's attention—and her own—diverted from the crash and the name Michael Cantrell.

Chapter 61

September, 1994
Northern Virginia

Despite Cat putting on a good front, Michael Cantrell's name gnawed at her for the entire afternoon. When Maggie finally left for home, Cat jumped in her car and headed to Langley. She had become involved with the investigation into the Transoceanic crash because of her close friendship with one of the crew—Maggie—and because there had been three CIA employees aboard the plane when it went down. Two of the CIA people had been working in Pakistan, the other in Yemen. She had become intimately familiar with all aspects of their lives: their spouses, their current projects, their bank accounts, and their habits—good and bad. She had found nothing to suggest that they had been targeted.

She had paid little attention to the names of the crewmembers on the aircraft, with the exception of Isabel Alvarez. Isabel was a Cuban refugee and nearly everyone possessed some degree of paranoia when it came to Cuba. But they had found nothing that would tie Isabel to the bombing. Michael Cantrell presented a different problem.

The CIA kept an extensive archive of newspapers on file, and she pulled up a mountain of articles listing the names of the crash victims. The information was always the same: name, age, and place of residence: Michael Cantrell, 32, New York. The only photographs of passengers were people of note: a Wall Street financial genius, a pharmaceutical company's CEO, a well-known actor, a concert pianist from San Francisco, the aircraft captain.

She sat back, thinking. As part of the investigation, the FBI had been building files on anyone connected with the flight, including passengers and crew. She could certainly ask for the information, but she had no legitimate reason for the request—and she would leave a trail. Then it hit her. The airline had probably published some sort of memorial document, information that would not have found its way into the Agency's files. She closed up her office and got back in the car. Speeding toward Dulles Airport, she considered her approach—nothing demanding, nothing official, nothing that would give away the urgency.

Before getting out of the car, she took a tissue and wiped most of the makeup off her face. She spat into her hands and ran her fingers through her hair, dampening and shaping it just enough to look somewhat less expensively cut. She stuffed her scarf in her bra, giving her a more matronly bosom, tossed her jewelry into the glove compartment, and slipped on a light overcoat and a pair of flats that she kept in the car. She gave herself a glance in the rearview mirror and, satisfied, made her way into the terminal.

Cat stood in the long line, finally receiving a wave from an agent at the counter. Adopting a meek voice, she said to the agent, "I'm sorry to trouble you. I'm not sure who to contact. I'm a schoolteacher. I've been working down in South America for several months, and I just learned that a girl I used to teach in Florida, Isabel Alvarez, was a stewardess on that terrible flight. I thought that perhaps ... uh, I was wondering ... I thought perhaps Transoceanic might have published something about the crew and that you might have a copy."

The agent's expression morphed from friendly to sad as Cat made her pitch. She looked sympathetically at Cat and said, "You know, I think there might be a copy of the newsletter in the back. Let me look."

Less than five minutes later, the woman was back, a manila envelope in her hand. "I did find it. I've just put it in an envelope for you. Um ... could you keep it in the envelope until you leave the terminal? We don't want to make passengers nervous."

Cat blinked at the agent's words but managed to reply, "Of course not. I understand completely. I won't open it here at the airport. Thank you very much for your trouble."

"I'm glad to be of help. I'm very sorry for your loss."

Cat thanked her again and, envelope in hand, turned away from the counter. She was sorely tempted to defy the agent and rip the envelope open right there, but managed to control her impatience. Instead, she walked slowly and deliberately back to her car.

She tore off the flap of the envelope and pulled out the newsletter, seeing the bold, black box on the front page. The entire issue was devoted to the memory of the Transoceanic employees who had perished in the crash. She flipped through the pages, with the first few devoted to the cockpit crew and pursers. Then, in alphabetical order, the flight attendants. She found the picture of Michael Cantrell on the fourth page and drew in a sharp breath.

She had no answers about why Michael Cantrell would plant a bomb on a US aircraft. But Michael Cantrell was not who he seemed. Michael Cantrell was an invention—a passport with a solid legend and history behind it—for an unidentified young man from Eastern Europe.

Returning to her office, Cat pulled the file. She leaned back in her chair and read, recalling how Clyde Banks had requested the passport four years earlier. She remembered it well, having been the one who pitched the value of the asset and requested approval for the documents. And then the asset had disappeared.

Cat nibbled at a fingernail. It was rarely good when an asset went underground and resurfaced. It was difficult to rebuild trust once it had been breached. But Michael Cantrell had taken that to a new level. He had bombed an airplane. She was sure of it. Even more disturbing was the possibility that he had not perished in the crash. His name was not on the list of recovered bodies.

She studied the file, looking for incongruities that might give her a clue about his whereabouts. Yes, he had been in Bosnia, but that did not establish his ethnicity. Sarajevo was a diverse city. His real name had never been documented—a fairly common procedure because the identities of assets were zealously protected. She would have given almost anything for a conversation with Clyde Banks, but that secret was sealed forever. Clyde had died in a boating accident last year at Tahoe over the July Fourth weekend— a silly, stupid accident involving too much alcohol.

Cat twisted her head back and forth, working out the kinks, working to come to a decision. Technically, an investigation into Michael Cantrell would fall under the purview of the FBI rather than the CIA. But the Agency and the Bureau were wolfish in marking their territory and notorious for butting heads. But in big investigations like Transoceanic, it was all-hands-on-deck. She picked up the phone.

Chapter 62

September, 1994
CIA Headquarters
Langley, Virginia

A voice answered, "Terry Nichols."
"Terry, it's Cat Powell."
She liked Terry. He was a big guy, a natural athlete. After an illustrious four years of college ball, he had been a certainty for an early pick in the NFL draft. Instead, he had gone to law school and later joined the FBI. Still, talking to him was a risk. He was smart, intuitive, and unequivocal in his respect for the law. She would have to play it carefully.

"Cat? It's been a while," he said. "How are you?"
"All's well. How's the family?"
"Doris is great; she does a lot of work with disadvantaged kids now … finds it satisfying. Our daughter is a sophomore at UVA, majoring in chemistry, of all things." He paused. "But you didn't call to check on me. What's up?"
"Transoceanic."
"Big subject."
"Indeed. I would not want to be in your shoes." As the FBI lead on the investigation, Terry was under tremendous pressure to find the person or persons who had orchestrated the bombing. Cat did not envy his position.
"I'm sure you know of Maggie Marshfield," she said. "Maggie is the purser who ended up in London on the day of the crash. She's also a close friend."
"Yeah, I'm aware. How's she holding up?"

"As well as can be expected. Three months of therapy have helped. We had lunch together today ..."

Interrupting, Terry asked, "What did you tell her?"

"Only that a piece of the tail has been found, no details—only that we are now convinced there was a bomb planted in the tail. But I asked her about the space in the ceiling. She told me that she has heard of people using it as a rest area, but that it isn't that easy to get up there and therefore isn't an everyday occurrence. She did, however, remember that Michael Cantrell, one of the flight attendants on the crew, had spent a considerable amount of time in the aft lavatory on a previous trip. He said he was sick. But it seems that most crewmembers would much rather use the facilities in the front of the plane. She thought his behavior was odd."

Cat heard the intake of breath. *He already knows,* she realized.

Terry said, "We heard about that a few days ago, from another flight attendant who was at dinner with them the night before—name's Robert Bailey. He seemed to know Cantrell fairly well. He confirmed that Cantrell was familiar with the ceiling space in the tail, having been the one who showed it to him."

"Hmm. Feel like sharing what you've found out?"

He groused, "There hasn't been much to find. Only child, parents deceased. Onetime freelance journalist, spent a couple of years in Bosnia ... actually put out some decent stories, so I've heard. According to his employment application with Transoceanic, he became disillusioned with eking out a living as a writer and joined the airlines. We talked to a number of his friends, nothing that set off any alarms there. He was a serious type, a bit of a loner, but friendly and bright and well-liked. We've found zip for motive. Nada.

"We swabbed his apartment. There was already someone living there, so of course it had been cleaned, but we tested the place anyhow. No trace of explosives.

"Oh, and one of the bags recovered just happens to belong to him—a crew carry-on. One of the ships found it the first night, ripped up and soggy, but floating pretty as you please in the middle of the ocean. It didn't yield anything of interest. Bottom line? Michael Cantrell checked in, boarded, and stowed his bag. End of story. I thought we had something. I really did. Now we're back to square one."

Cat could picture him: head hanging, mouth turned down, shaking his burly head. "I'm sorry to hear that," she said. "Or honestly, only somewhat sorry. The prospect of crew involvement didn't sit well with my friend."

"Yeah, I can imagine she wasn't pleased." He sighed and added, "Well, I'm sorry I don't have more to share, but tomorrow is another day."

"The truth will come out eventually."

"It would be nice to still be alive when it does," he said.

She hung up, digesting the conversation. Michael's cover identity had held firm, as had the articles that the Agency had written and published under his name. But the bag was new information. If Michael's carry-on was on the plane, surely he would have been on board as well.

Cat should have felt relief, but could not let go of a nagging dread. Michael Cantrell had disappeared for two years and then entered the United States—on a passport that she had authorized—and she hadn't known a thing about it.

She picked up the phone and dialed an internal line.

"I have a project," she said. "It may take a few days, and it can't wait. Can you handle it?"

"I'll be right up," the voice replied.

Five minutes later, Marianne Riel appeared in Cat's office and took a seat.

"New look. I like it," Cat said, taking in Marianne's noticeably slimmer figure and the stylish, short, spiked hairdo. Marianne had worn her hair in the same, dated, pageboy style for every one of the thirty-plus years that she had worked for the CIA. Obviously, something had changed.

"New beau," Marianne said with a grin. "He's younger than me. I think I'm now what they call a cougar."

Cat laughed. Marianne had a playful demeanor that belied her intensity. She was still one of the sharpest and most tenacious researchers in a building full of such people.

Leaning forward, Cat folded her hands and rested her elbows on the desk. Her smile faded. "Four years ago," she said, "we issued a passport, under the name of Michael Cantrell, to an asset in Sarajevo. He fed us info for about two years and then dropped out of sight. Frankly, we assumed he was dead. But it has recently come to my attention that this same Michael Cantrell was one of the flight attendants on the Transoceanic flight."

Marianne's eyebrows rose slightly, but she showed no other reaction.

Cat went on. "The FBI has investigated him and found no evidence of involvement in the bombing. And our cover story held together. But I flagged his passport after he went silent. I should have been notified when he entered the country, but that didn't happen. So how did he get in? And how did he use that passport on his international trips with Transoceanic?"

A little crease formed on Marianne's brow. "Hmmm."

Cat looked intently at Marianne. "He checked in, boarded, and they found his carry-on bag floating in the debris. Everything points to him having died in the crash. But we thought he was dead once before. I just don't like loose ends."

"I'll have a go at it. Quietly."

Cat watched her leave, turned back to the file, and fingered Michael's photo. *Where are you?* she wondered.

Long after ending the call with Cat Powell, Terry Nichols was still staring at the phone. *What is she not telling me? Damn spies have too many secrets.*

To be fair, he had not been entirely forthcoming with her, either. In the same area of ocean where they had found the section of the tail cone, they had also recovered another badly damaged Transoceanic crew bag. But one of its pockets had survived remarkably intact—a pocket that contained a metal crew baggage tag, a tag imprinted with Maggie's name. Maggie had been hundreds of miles away when the bomb went off, but somehow her custom-engraved tag was found among the wreckage. He and the team had dug deep into Maggie's life and were reasonably convinced that she had nothing to do with the bombing. Still, he felt certain that she was entangled somehow. And that Cat Powell knew more than she was revealing.

Yes, he thought, *the truth will come out.*

Two hours later, he picked up the phone and called Cat.

Chapter 63

September 1994
FBI Headquarters
Washington, DC

Terry Nichols gestured at Cat and pointed to a seat in the corner of the office. "Have a seat. I'll be back for you in a few minutes. Roy here will keep you company," he said, jerking his head at a solid-looking, white-shirted, Windsor-knotted, every-hair-in-its-place, thirty-something man standing in the center of the room. Then Terry turned to Maggie and said, "Come with me."

Maggie, eyes wide and concerned, followed him obediently. She looked back over her shoulder at Cat, mouthing, "What does he want?"

Cat spread her hands and shook her head. "I don't know," she mouthed back.

Terry Nichols led Maggie into a small conference room. Two other agents, both already seated at the table, stared at her with neutral expressions. A third agent, sitting at the end of the table, was turning knobs on a recording device.

Maggie suddenly felt cold. There were no smiles, no warmth, no greetings being exchanged between the people in the room.

Summoning every ounce of her courage, she asked, "What can I do for you gentlemen?"

"Well, you can start by telling me all about how you avoided being on that airplane," said Terry Nichols.

Her confusion apparent, she asked, "What do you mean? I was scheduled to work the flight. Then the plane had a mechanical. They sent me back to the hotel. That afternoon they called with a reroute to Munich and London.

I took a Lufthansa flight to Munich the next morning, and then worked the Transoceanic flight to London. I told you this before."

"Who is 'they'?"

"Flight operations. When there's a problem, they coordinate with the crew scheduling people in New York to figure out who should go where."

"Flight operations in Frankfurt?"

"That's right."

"And what did you have with you? Luggage? Purse? Anything else?"

A sliver of annoyance, in the form of a crease between her eyebrows, crept into her otherwise flawless face. Her voice brittle, she said, "Purse, suitcase, and my crew bag. And a coat over my arm. And gloves. And shoes on my feet. And bra, panties, and pantyhose under my uniform skirt, blouse, jacket, and scarf. I think that about covers it."

Terry Nichols remained unperturbed, catching her gaze and holding it for nearly a minute before she blinked. "Let's talk about your crew bag for a minute."

"What about it?"

"You had it with you the entire time?"

"Of course ..." she started, without finishing. She sat up straighter, lifting her chin. Her lips parted slightly, and her eyes went wide. She dropped her chin and focused on the table, her index finger tapping at the air.

"Maggie?"

"Wait ... wait ...," she said, continuing to tap. Then she asked, "What about my bag? Did you find it?"

The question stunned Terry Nichols. He leaned forward. "Was it missing? You said you had it with you."

"Yes, but it was new! A few days before, after a trip to Paris, Cat picked me up at the airport. I put my bags in her trunk. We went to dinner in Georgetown. When we got back to the car, someone had broken in. My bags were gone."

"Your bags were stolen? From Cat's car?"

"Yes!"

"Was anything else missing?"

"I don't think so. You would have to ask Cat. I had to get all new things ... bags, uniforms, cosmetics, supplies, everything!"

Comprehension dawning, Terry Nichols tapped his pencil on the table. Someone had known Maggie was scheduled to take the flight out of Frankfurt. Someone had stolen her bag and placed it on the doomed aircraft. If he were a betting man, he would wager that her bag had held the bomb. Unfortunately, the seawater had washed away any traces of explosive residue. He pulled a clear evidence bag from a pile of objects on the desk and showed it to her.

"Is this yours?"

Maggie gaped at the crew baggage tag inside the bag, the one she had bought for herself on a trip to New Delhi two years earlier—a brass tag engraved with her name. A single tear dripped out of her left eye and started to snake down her cheek. She absently brushed it away with the back of her hand.

"Yes," she said. "It was on the bag that was stolen."

He showed her a second package, this one containing the section of the bag's pocket that had held the crew tag.

"And you kept it inside the bag?"

She frowned in confusion. "No. That doesn't make any sense. The tag goes on the outside, on the handle."

Terry Nichols nodded again. Whoever had set this up had taken precautions in case the tag was ripped off during the crash. Placing it in the pocket had protected it—and ensured that the bag would be identified as Maggie's.

"That's it, Ms. Marshfield. Thank you for your time and your cooperation. We'll just want a few words with Ms. Powell and then you can go."

"Are you going to tell me what's going on? I have this horrible feeling that my bag is somehow associated with the crash. Am I right? Where did you find it?"

He studied the hurt in her face and made a decision.

"We found it in the Atlantic Ocean, Ms. Marshfield. Near the site of the crash. Now we just have to determine how it got there."

Horror flashed in her eyes, and she put her hand to her mouth. "I can't believe it! Who would do this? And why?"

"I'm asking myself the same question. I'm sorry, Ms. Marshfield, but that's all I can say at the moment. And I'm asking you to not openly discuss this conversation. I'm sure you can appreciate our need to keep this under wraps until we know more."

Maggie gave him a silent nod and started to stand. Her legs felt shaky. She put a hand on the table for balance and swayed unsteadily.

"Are you alright?" he asked.

"I'm fine. Just ... just ... I don't know ..."

"Get her some water," he said to one of the other agents. "And a candy bar or something. Quick!"

He turned back to her, trying to be reassuring, and said, "I've given you a shock. Just sit here for a few minutes. Take your time."

Ignoring him, she propped her elbows on the table, cupped her head in her hands, and began to cry.

Terry had no words to comfort her, and after offering a meager "I'm sorry," left her in the care of the two remaining agents. He walked back to his office, gesturing for Cat to follow, and dropped into his chair. He swiveled his chair to face Cat.

"We've found some additional evidence. I'll tell you about it, but first, tell me about picking up Maggie at the airport a couple of weeks ago. Tell me what happened that night."

It took Cat a moment to register that he must be talking about the incident in Georgetown.

"My car was broken into," she replied.

"And?"

"And I had it picked up and checked for devices—explosive, tracking, audio, whatever."

"And were there any?"

"No. They didn't find anything."

"And was anything missing?"

Cat realized what he wanted to know. "Yes, as a matter of fact. Maggie's luggage was stolen. A suitcase and a crew bag."

"Nothing else?"

"Nope, that's it."

"Kinda strange, don't you think?"

"I wondered, at the time," Cat mused, "how difficult it would be to impersonate a flight attendant. However, they did not get Maggie's ID, and she reported the theft to the airline. What's this about?"

Terry told her about the crew tag. The information hit her like a thunderbolt. He had just confirmed that someone had targeted Maggie—or, more probably, Marc.

"Any idea why someone would want her dead?" he asked.

She let her posture sag, clasped her hands loosely, and let herself appear relaxed—like someone with nothing to hide. Marc's name could not become part of this conversation. Not yet, maybe never.

"No," she replied.

He knew that she was lying—and that she knew that he knew. Whatever she was keeping to herself, it had to be pretty damned important.

"Nothing else you can tell me, then?"

"Like I suggested yesterday, I thought maybe Michael Cantrell might deserve a look. But he's the only lead I have, and you've already cleared him."

Chapter 64

September, 1994
CIA Headquarters
Langley, Virginia

M arianne was back in Cat's office two days later, a thin folder in the crook of her arm. She started speaking even before she sat down.

"Michael flew into JFK in late September of 1993, arriving from Zurich. The address he gave on his customs card was the Marriott Marquis in Times Square."

Cat's eyebrows shot up. "Well, there's an interesting, and pricey, residence. Of course, he could have said the Bronx Zoo. With a US passport, nobody's going to question where you say you live."

"And with his cover story of having been out of the States, reporting from Bosnia ..."

"Right."

"But how did he get in without my receiving a notification?"

Marianne tapped the folder with her index finger. "Two days before Michael flew into New York, a man named Robert Wiggins accessed and edited Michael's records. He was a twenty-year supervisor with the INS," she said, referring to the US Immigration and Naturalization Service. "I believe he purged the flag you'd placed on the passport."

"He worked for INS? What's the connection?"

"I can't answer that without throwing up flags that would alert the FBI. Wiggins was a US citizen and a federal employee ... clearly not in our mandate. But he had a mortgage, two kids in college, another in high school, and he died of lung cancer just a month after Cantrell started working for Transoceanic."

Cat steepled her fingers against her lips. "You think that he got something in exchange? Like money?"

"I know it's a jump," Marianne admitted.

"Yeah, but a short one."

Cat pulled the bottle out of the drawer and dry-swallowed two aspirin before meeting with her boss, knowing it would not be an easy discussion. Resigned to the task, she went to his office, laid out the facts, and argued for FBI involvement.

"We have to make sure," she concluded.

He read her report again and peppered her with a series of questions designed to distance the Agency from any appearance of wrongdoing.

Finally, he said, "Let's just let it rest. We'll give the FBI some time to develop a suspect, and we'll revisit this as circumstances warrant. As you pointed out, there's no evidence suggesting that he blew up that airplane."

Cat left his office knowing he would never revisit the investigation, would never expose the Agency to the scandal that could erupt. She wasn't sure if she was supposed to feel furious or relieved, admitting to herself that she felt a little of both. She pulled the bottle of Scotch from the cabinet in her office, poured two fingers into the glass, and savored the peaty burn as the liquor hit her palate.

He's right, she thought. *There's no real evidence of involvement. You're only hanging on to this because Maggie could have been on that flight. You need to let it go.*

Reluctantly, she closed the file.

PART FIVE

Maggie

Four Years Ago

Chapter 65

October, Four Years Ago
Sarajevo, Bosnia and Herzegovina

Goran Terzić stood in the cool shadows at the back of the coffee and tea shop, absently rubbing the cloth over an intricately hammered copper samovar. The two small sitting rooms buzzed with soft, but lively, conversation. *At least four languages*, he thought. *German, Swedish, Italian, French.* He caught a few guttural intonations in Dutch and upped his count to five, trying to place the source. Sometimes the Dutch came back; he wasn't sure why. *To atone for their inaction as his countrymen were slaughtered? To satisfy some unscratched curiosity?*

He let his eyes wander over the men and women relaxing in the courtyard, enjoying the warmth of the morning sun. His family catered to the tourist trade, a somewhat eyebrow-raising way to make a living, considering his bias against the West. Not that he admitted his sentiments to the infidels who fouled his property—they were, after all, useful both as a source of information and as a camouflage for his real business.

His gaze rested on a tall burly blond in his midtwenties. Goran pegged him as the Dutchman. There was a time not so long ago, he mused, when a Dutch battalion—assigned to the United Nations peacekeeping mission during the war with Serbia—had profoundly failed to stay a moral course. The massacre at Srebrenica had occurred under their watch. In the worst case of mass murder in Europe since World War II, some eight thousand Muslim men and boys from the town of Srebrenica had been separated from their families and herded into busses—much like the Jews had been herded onto Nazi trains on their way to Auschwitz and Treblinka—and were summarily executed and dumped into mass graves. While it was true that the UN forces were under strict orders regarding what they could and could not do, and that most were unarmed, Goran had little use for men who excused their actions—or inactions—by claiming that they were just following orders.

Interrupting his reverie, a female voice behind him said, "It's beautiful!" *English. Six.* "I think so," he remarked over his shoulder.

He placed the vessel back on the shelf and turned to face the woman. She was middle-aged—standing apart from the Gen-X and Gen-Y crowd who frequented his store—and uncommonly attractive and well-dressed. The Hermes scarf spelled money, although she seemed to wear it more as a matter of respect—her self-styled version of the Arab hijab—rather than to flaunt. Wisps of ginger hair, fading to white, peeked out from the fabric around her forehead.

"Where did you find it? Istanbul?" she asked.

The friendly smile revealed perfectly aligned, perfectly white teeth. If her speech had not identified her as American, the teeth certainly would have. The smile reached her eyes, crinkling the corners, but it was their astonishing color that drew his interest: a peculiar brownish-green, similar to the nut of a pistachio peeking from its shell.

The realization hit him like a sledgehammer: he recognized this woman. His heart thudded wildly, his chest heaved, and he doubled over in a coughing fit. *Calm down,* he ordered himself. *Give her nothing to raise suspicion.*

"Are you alright?"

He remained bent over, gathering his wits. *Be polite. Answer her questions.* He kept his head down, trying to control the cough and his racing pulse. "I am fine," he finally managed to say. "I am sorry for the interruption. Gaziantep ... the urn is from Gaziantep."

"Antep?" She used the old name of the city, implying a familiarity with the area.

"Yes. I visited a few weeks ago. You know it?"

A look of surprise fluttered across her face—a crease of uncertainty appearing between her eyebrows, her eyes penetrating, her head cocked to the left. "Your English is quite good."

She had spoken the remark as a statement, but he sensed the question behind it.

He fed her a well-practiced response. "Thank you. My mother was a teacher. She knew English and instructed us as children. It was years ago, but my customers give me the chance to practice."

He detected a microscopic relaxation in the woman's frown.

"Ah. The things you learn as a child stay with you forever—languages, skiing, riding a bicycle. Sorry, for a moment, you reminded me of someone I once knew." She waved her hand in front of her face, as if to clear away a cobweb.

He stood awkwardly, his unease escalating. "I see," he mumbled.

"I'm sorry; I've made you uncomfortable."

He shrugged. "It is nothing."

"Well, I'm sorry anyhow." She hesitated, staring at the samovar, and then said, "You asked if I know Antep. I visited once, but only for two days. Someday perhaps I'll go back. I remember the Bakircilar Çarşısı," she added, referring to the city's renowned coppersmith bazaar. "Is that where you found the samovar?"

"I am not certain. It was a gift," he replied.

Her smile dimmed. She was disappointed.

"But probably," he added.

The smile brightened again. "How is the city now?"

Goran thought for a moment, straining to find the right words.

He was not particularly fond of Turkey, preferring the dense forests and cooler climate of his native Bosnia. He found, too, that when away from Sarajevo, he missed its hilly terrain and the mountains overlooking the valley. Gaziantep sat on a dusty, parched plateau. Outside the city, fields of drought-hardy pistachio trees broke the monotony of the brown landscape. There were a couple of meager rivers that irrigated a strip of fields before wandering southeast and feeding into the Euphrates to the east. But when he thought of the area, the images that came to mind were invariably brown.

Gaziantep was close to the ancient trading route known as the Silk Road, and was one of the oldest cities in the world. It had greatly enhanced its economic base since the early 2000s, polishing its image and expanding foreign trade—all while still maintaining the exotic flavor that appealed to the foreign traveler. It had become, for a time, one of the *in* places to visit. The Bakircilar Çarşısı mentioned by the woman had become a favorite destination. But while the bazaar still thrummed with the metallic beat of artisans working their craft, the once-blossoming tourist trade had all but vanished.

The majority of foreigners now seemed to be journalists, misguided adventure seekers, or displaced citizens of the country next door. While the city continued to bustle with commerce, a sense of discomfort—of foreboding—scented the air. A mere thirty miles from the Syrian border and just sixty miles north of Aleppo, Gaziantep had become a haven for thousands of refugees fleeing the war—and a transit point for recruits of the Islamic State.

He kept his thoughts to himself, finally offering a simple observation. "It is still dry and dusty, but it has changed. More people. I prefer Sarajevo. It is much more beautiful."

She nodded. "That it is."

The woman ordered a salep, a hot drink reputed to have medicinal properties. The source of its healing power supposedly stemmed from wild orchids, their tubers ground into flour and mixed with milk, sugar, and a dusting of cinnamon. Goran gave little credence to the belief, but it was a popular drink among the shop's customers, so he kept it on the menu.

As he prepared the salep, she asked, "What took you to Antep? Do you have family there?"

"Business," he replied easily. "I import pistachios. The region around Antep is perfect for growing them. I use them in my bakery and sell the rest to the local markets."

Her eyes widened. "You have a bakery?"

"It is a very good one." He forced a laugh, trying to portray an amiable shopkeeper. "Would you like to try some of my baklava?" He pointed to a tray of pastry on the counter behind him. "It is as good as what you would find in Antep."

She accepted a thumb-size triangle of the pastry and took a dainty bite, following quickly with another. She closed her eyes, savoring the explosion of sweetness and flavor from the phyllo-pistachio concoction.

"Mmmm," she purred, "ambrosia of the gods. This is absolutely delicious," she pronounced, opening her eyes. "Greek baklava is nothing like this."

He turned to attend to another customer who had stepped up to the counter, while the woman swiveled to admire the assortment of mugs and decorative tins lining the shelves on the wall. From the corner of his eye, he noticed her pause. When he saw the object of her attention, he felt a prickle at the nape of his neck. She was eyeing a simple pewter coaster that encased a round white tile. The tile was emblazoned in red with a representation of an eagle, its wings spread and talons stretched menacingly. *Frankfurt* was printed above the bird. Beneath, in bold letters, were the words *Baseler Eck*. He held his breath, then watched her spine stiffen and her shoulders roll back.

Still facing the shelves, she asked, "Have you been to Germany?"

"Germany? Never. Why do you ask?" He managed to speak the words innocently and, for effect, paused and frowned as if wondering why she would ask the question. He then stepped beside her. Laser-focused on the coaster, she had not moved.

"Oh, that," he continued, pretending that he had just realized why she was asking. "A gift from a customer. Years ago." The half-lie slipped easily from his lips, but his mouth was as dry as the Sahara. "Customers occasionally give me gifts to use for decoration." He spun around, gesturing toward the displays. "I have many such things."

She cast her gaze at the collection, taking in the souvenirs and bric-a-brac planted among the mugs. "Your clientele appears to be well traveled," she observed.

"Those who visit Bosnia have often seen much of the world," he agreed.

She nodded, as if accepting his explanation, but her ramrod-straight posture said otherwise. Turning back to face him, she handed him the half-full cup of salep. "Thank you. It was delicious, but I must be going."

Despite her politeness, it was evident that her mood had soured. "I hope you enjoy your evening, and perhaps you'll come back to visit," Goran offered, intuitively grasping that her hurried departure from the shop meant trouble.

"I'm leaving tomorrow for Istanbul," she replied. "But thank you. Good luck with your bakery."

She turned abruptly and left the shop. He watched her cross the street and turn left. He considered following her but could not leave the shop unattended. He thrummed his fingers on the counter, trying to soothe his mounting anxiety. *It is only a coaster,* he told himself. *She knows nothing.*

An hour later, as he was cleaning off one of the outside tables, he spotted her again—half a block down, starting to turn away, her gaze cast downward, shoulders hunched forward, hair tucked under a different scarf. But there was no mistaking her profile, or the hand—clutching a camera—falling quickly to her side. He muttered a curse and shooed the remaining customers from the shop. Pulling his cell phone from his pocket, he shivered, and his skin turned to gooseflesh, as if a cloud had passed over the sun. *No good can come of this,* he thought. *It will not end well.*

When the voice answered, he hurriedly blurted out the events of the afternoon. "The red-haired flight attendant from your picture—she was just here, in the shop. She left, then came back to the place across the street. I caught her taking a picture of me. It was all because of that coaster from the restaurant in Frankfurt; I told you it was a bad idea. I could feel her suspicion; she knows something is not right."

Goran listened for a minute, then said, "She leaves for Istanbul in the morning. What do you want to do?" Nodding in wordless agreement with the voice at the other end of the line, he finally said, "I will take care of it." After disconnecting, he hit a speed-dial number.

"We have a problem," he said. He related the events of the afternoon and asked, "Where are you?" At the response, he breathed a sigh of relief. "Good. I'm coming. I will call when I land."

His next call—this one to Turkish Airlines—secured a seat on the last flight to Istanbul that night.

The final call was to a well-placed Turkish official in Istanbul—a man well-known for his depraved and expensive sexual appetites, and for the finesse with which he negotiated the bribes to support his perversion. Tomorrow, he would receive a particularly handsome payout. As an official in the Directorate General of Migration Management, the man had access not only to the records of foreign nationals residing in the city, but also to the centralized databases of arriving and departing passengers at Istanbul Ataturk International Airport.

Chapter 66

*October, Four Years Ago
En Route from Amsterdam, Netherlands,
to Toronto, Canada*

T he call from Sarajevo had come as the man was boarding the flight. His shock had been so great that his hand had trembled when presenting his boarding pass.

The gate agent had looked at him with concern. "Are you feeling ill?" she had asked.

"No," he had assured her. "I have just received some bad news from home. I will be fine."

In truth, he had not been fine. Questions had flooded his brain. *What had brought her to Sarajevo? Could her visit to the café have been planned? What were the chances that her visit was merely random? Could she be picking at a thread, or could she have found a connection to what happened over twenty years ago?* Nauseated by worry, he had rushed to the lavatory, slammed the door behind him, raised the lid of the toilet, and vomited.

Now, staring at the ocean churning thousands of feet below his window, he imagined the terror of the airplane disintegrating midflight. *Had everyone screamed? Could they even have been heard above the howl of air rushing violently through what remained of the fuselage? What thoughts had gone through their minds? Would they have known they were doomed? Did they pray? Call for their mothers? Cry for their children? Did they even have time to realize what had happened before their oxygen-starved brains tumbled into unconsciousness? As they plunged through the air, did they eventually awaken and see the earth growing larger beneath them? Would they have felt the impact?*

He leaned back against the headrest and closed his eyes, willing his brain to erase the images of hundreds of innocent people tumbling through the sky. *Well,* he rationalized, *some were probably not so innocent.*

The aircraft shuddered for several seconds and then suddenly dropped. He tried to swallow his fear but, unbidden, beads of perspiration broke out on his brow. He was fully aware that the rough air was analogous to a car driving over a rutted road or hitting a pothole, but at this altitude, logic escaped him. He swept his arm over his forehead, his sweat spotting the sleeve of his navy blue shirt, and tried to relax. The effort was pointless. His mind played these games every time he boarded an airplane. He had once been comfortable with flying—before the ghosts that haunted his sleepless nights, before the nightmares of death. Now, he preferred to keep his feet planted on terra firma.

The bile rose in his throat and his mouth twisted in self-revulsion as he struggled to regain control. If the prophets were to be believed, Judgement Day would determine his fate—depending on which interpretation of the scripture held true. He would surely face a day of reckoning, but not today. Today, he would continue about his business. The internet may be rife with conspiracy theories, but he had covered his tracks well and there were no survivors to tell the tale.

Chapter 67

October, Four Years Ago
Sarajevo, Bosnia and Herzegovina

Maggie Marshfield put the camera aside and nibbled at the half-eaten lamb kebab on the plate beside her. For her last evening in Sarajevo, she had planned to dine at a highly recommended restaurant near Baščaršija, the bazaar in the historic district. Instead, she had locked herself in her hotel room and ordered room service.

The trip was originally planned as a "girlcation" with her best friend, Cat Powell. When Cat had canceled because of some unspecified crisis somewhere in the world, Maggie had opted to travel by herself.

"Not a good idea, Maggie," her husband, Paul, had said upon learning of her decision. "Sarajevo might be an interesting place to visit, but there are lingering issues from the war. It's risky from a security standpoint. I was okay when you and Cat were traveling together, but I'm not comfortable with you going by yourself."

"I've traveled all over the world; I think I can take care of myself," she had argued. "I was in Sarajevo during the Winter Olympics in '84. I've always wanted to go back. We have everything reserved, and I don't want to lose this opportunity."

Begrudgingly, he had eventually relented, under the condition that she stop by the US embassy when she arrived. She had done so, instantly recognizing that Paul had paved the way. There were offers of breakfast and lunch and dinner and sightseeing. She declined them all, thanking the staff and offering assurances that she would be fine. She could almost see them breathing sighs of relief. They were busy enough without also having to play babysitter.

During her stay, the city had seemed friendly and safe, its citizens kind and helpful. But the encounter with the man in the coffee shop had left her deeply unsettled. As she had walked away, the reality set in: she was traveling solo in a city she did not know, in a country with a long history of problems. Paul might have been right, she admitted to herself. Independence and resourcefulness aside, she was well outside her comfort zone.

She was reasonably sure that the man had seen her snap his picture. She had been half a block away, but he had turned directly toward her. *If he is who I think he is, going back to take the photo was an incredibly stupid thing to do.*

At this moment, she was unnerved to the point that she was considering calling the embassy's duty officer. She picked up her mobile phone and toyed with it. *What am I going to say? That I think I met a ghost? They'll think I'm delusional.* She placed the phone back on the nightstand.

She moved the room service tray to the desk and shoved the chair to the door, jamming it under the handle to supplement the deadbolt. Looking at her handiwork, she shook her head in disgust. *This is ridiculous. I'm leaving in the morning. I'll be out of here and safe with friends in Istanbul before noon. Get a grip.*

She returned to the bed, folded her legs like a pretzel, and for the hundredth time, stared at the image on her camera. She zoomed in and out, in and out, examining each pixel of the man's crinkled and weathered face.

Everything about him seemed straight out of a Hollywood casting call for eccentric characters. Beneath the deep tan, he was fair-skinned. He was tall and rail-thin, with a sinewy physique that spoke of a hard life of outdoor labor. The dichotomy between his physical appearance and the nature of his employment left her wondering where he actually spent most of his time. *Certainly not in the shadows of a coffee shop,* she thought. He had an untamed tumble of wavy white hair that brushed his shoulders. His facial characteristics were partially obscured by a thick, salt-and-pepper beard and mustache. With a mule and a plow, he might have been a struggling farmer. With a robe and a wand, he could have passed as a wizard in a fantasy series. With a shave and a custom-tailored suit, an eccentric billionaire. But she could imagine no scenario that included full-time work in a bakery or coffee shop.

Maggie had a talent for remembering faces. But it was his pewter-gray eyes, and the absentminded manner in which he had been rubbing the samovar with his index finger, that had caused the little hiccup in her heartbeat. The simple motion had triggered the memory of a long-dead male flight attendant leaning on the counter in an airplane galley—a testosterone-pumped guy who, she was sure, had wanted nothing more than to get into her pants. His eyes had been exactly the same color. The timbre of his voice was the same, too: distinctively deep and sonorous. But the man in the photo was fifty pounds lighter and more than two decades removed from the man in the airline uniform. Still, he looked so much like him. She frowned and looked again at the picture. *A strong resemblance, to be sure, but how could it be him?*

Yet she had sensed something evasive, something not quite right, from the moment she had mentioned his command of the English language. And when she had spotted the coaster among the items he had on display, a chill had run down her spine. The Baseler Eck was a restaurant near the Frankfurt train station and a hangout for airline crews—definitely not a tourist attraction. And it was in that restaurant that she had seen Michael Cantrell for the last time.

She stared at the photo and shivered, an ominous feeling creeping over her. *Coincidence?* She bit her lip. Years of hanging out with Cat and living with Paul had taught her that there was no such thing.

What if he somehow steals my camera? The thought came out of the blue. Some of her friends had experienced the loss of a purse or camera and had been shocked at how fast it happened—the thief slicing through the shoulder strap with a single swipe of the razor and deftly grabbing the booty.

The thought crossed her mind that she was just being paranoid, but she decided not to take any chances. She transferred two of the photos to her phone, then pulled the tiny SD card from the camera and popped in a spare. After tucking the card deep into a pocket of her carry-on, she sat back on the bed and typed a short email to Cat.

> Miss your company, not as much fun going solo. When I get back, let's talk about this guy.

She read the short message, deciding that the content was sufficiently cryptic without being alarming, and attached the two pictures. Cat would likely assume that there was an amusing story about the man in the photos. No sense in shouting that the sky was falling until she knew more. Her finger hovered over the *Send* button for a split second, but she tapped the *Drafts* folder instead. She told herself that tomorrow would be soon enough, after she arrived in Istanbul and had more time to process her thoughts. At this moment, however, she wanted nothing more than to get out of Sarajevo.

She closed the laptop and, still fully dressed, slipped between the sheets and drifted into a fitful sleep.

Chapter 68

October, Four Years Ago
Istanbul, Turkey

Mahmud Erbakan spent a restless night. He shifted from side to side, thinking alternately about the quickest way to get the requested information and what he would do with the money. As a senior official in Turkey's Directorate General of Migration Management, Mahmud Erbakan had access to the documents of refugees and foreign nationals residing in—and visiting—the city of Istanbul. His status also gave him authority to monitor the activities in the arrival hall at Istanbul Ataturk International Airport.

The request had come at an opportune time—his funds were nearly depleted. Had this been a routine request, he would have waited a few hours and then checked the databases for details about the woman arriving from Sarajevo. The lure of a large sum of money, however, made him eager to obtain the information quickly. He instructed his secretary to cancel his morning meetings, telling her that there were pressing matters at the airport.

In the morning, he drove to Ataturk and parked his car in the lot reserved for official use. He exchanged pleasantries with staff, visited with two minor officials, and entered the arrivals area shortly after eleven o'clock. He spent an hour wandering from booth to booth, ostensibly observing the officers' interaction with passengers. His presence generated some initial surprise among the staff—it was not often that a high-ranking official chose to rub noses with lowly employees—but he was handsome, well-dressed, and personable, and did not seem to be on a mission to destroy careers. The staff calmed, but kept a sharp eye on him. One never knew.

Mahmud positioned himself near the immigration booths and occasionally posed his own questions to the travelers entering his domain. He checked his watch regularly, awaiting the noon arrival of the Turkish Airlines flight from Sarajevo.

Maggie Marshfield entered the arrivals hall at 12:14 p.m. Mahmud spotted her instantly. Few women traveled alone in this part of the world, fewer still had red hair, and only one matched the picture on his mobile phone. Goran, the man who had called him last night, had driven to the Sarajevo Airport before dawn. After finding an unobtrusive spot with a good view of the check-in counters, he had waited for the woman to show up for her flight. The half dozen photos he sent to Mahmud's phone had captured the woman perfectly.

Had Maggie Marshfield been accompanying her husband on a trip involving official state business, she would have presented her black diplomatic passport, and that would have been the end of it. But she was traveling solely for pleasure and, following government guidelines, had presented her blue personal passport. For this trip, she was an ordinary citizen passing through ordinary channels.

Mahmud knew nothing of Maggie Marshfield's status and, if he had, might have reconsidered his participation in the scheme to learn of her plans while in Istanbul. But given his presence at the airport throughout the morning, no one paid particular attention when he approached the booth where the woman stood.

He picked up the woman's passport from the desk and examined the photo, comparing it to the woman in front of him and memorizing the name. He visualized the woman in the picture on his phone: red hair, navy leather jacket, marine-blue scarf around her neck. There was no question that this was the woman he sought.

He cocked his head, adopted a stiff posture, and asked, "What is your business in Turkey?"

Well-accustomed to the vagaries of immigration control, Maggie answered the official's inquiry with a patient smile. "Tourist."

"What other cities are you planning to visit?"

"Only Istanbul, unless we make a side trip to Gaziantep."

"Why would you go there?"

"I was there once before, years ago. I'd like to see it again."

"How long is your stay here?"

"A week to ten days."

"Where will you be staying in Istanbul?"

"With friends in the Arnavutköy neighborhood."

"And their name and address?"

Maggie hesitated. The question was unusual in its detail. While some countries require that visitors provide the address of their accommodation during their stay, Turkey did not usually ask this of Westerners. Frowning, she supplied the address and told the man that their names were Louise and George Burke.

Mahmud handed the passport back and bowed slightly. "Enjoy your visit, madam."

"Thank you," Maggie said, and then added, "I truly love your city."

He smiled back, liking her. She had a presence. Americans would have said she was classy. He waited until she disappeared through the exit doors, then threaded his way through the terminal and back to his car. Once inside, he stabbed at his phone. The call was picked up on the second ring.

"I have the information you asked for," Mahmud said.

Chapter 69

Daris Terzić lowered the car's window, relishing the tang of the salt spray and inhaling the spicy, smoky scent that permeated the air of Istanbul. His chin sported a trendy four-day stubble that could leave an observer wondering if the scruff was intentional or just an indication of nonchalance toward personal grooming. The ruddy bloom of his cheeks and the creases around his eyes hinted at years spent squinting into the sun.

He was stocky, average height, with deep brown eyes, earthy brown hair, and an olive-toned complexion. His coloring and stature seemed to be simply an extension of his father's chromosomes—not at all like his brothers, who had won the genetic lottery from their mother and grown up to be tall, athletically lean, and fair-skinned. In his youth, he had cursed the physical attributes that set him apart from his two older siblings. Later in life, he had found those same traits to be an advantage. He could thread his way through a crowd, slip casually into restaurants and bars, and wander the streets without drawing attention. In his homeland and its Balkan neighbors, he was an ordinary, unremarkable, everyday man. He *blended*.

He followed the directions he had been given, eschewing the O-1 beltway and opting, instead, for the route over the Galata Bridge and up the west bank of the Bosphorus. The ocean strait, which he had once thought to be a river, separated two continents and divided the city into its corresponding Asian and European sectors. The Bosphorus connected the Black Sea to the Sea of Marmara and, beyond, the Aegean and the Mediterranean.

From its ancient origin as Lygos, and through later incarnations as Byzantium and Constantinople, Istanbul was a thriving port of trade and flourished as a cultural and intellectual mecca. But it was the city's strategic geographical position and formidable defenses that sealed its fate as a city to be conquered, and reconquered, and conquered again. Persians, Athenians, Spartans, Romans, Arabs—all battled for the crown jewel over the centuries. And all, in some measure, contributed to the hash of its cultural state today.

The wind swept through the window, splaying strands of hair across his face. Veined with silver, his long hair gave the impression of being untidy—despite a recent visit to his barber. He reached up and tucked the stray locks behind his ear. The illusion of ordinary vanished as the gesture revealed a malevolent band of scar tissue that stretched from high behind the earlobe and down his neck before disappearing beneath the band of his T-shirt. In his homeland, a land torn by war, such disfiguring injuries were not out of the ordinary. Yet people invariably reacted to its ugliness. For years, he had tolerated the stares, the pointing, the gasps of strangers and children, finally growing his hair to conceal the old wound. More often than not, he wore a turtleneck. Today, however, Istanbul was unseasonably warm, and he would look out of place in a long-sleeved jersey. He needed to fit in.

Traffic slowed to a crawl in the bustling Karaköy district just north of the bridge, where tourists and locals mingled easily in the multitude of shops and cafés lining the streets. The commercial area was packed with vehicles and pedestrians, while its shoreline boasted a thriving maritime trade. Hundreds of pleasure craft, passenger and car ferries, and cruise ships floated nearby, with an armada of fishing boats packed among them. Nearing the docks, Daris found the air heavy with the odor of the day's catch.

He chose the route closest to the water and noted with interest the two cruise liners docked at the Yolcu Salonu passenger terminal. The first—with only half a dozen decks—was most likely used for tours around the Black or Aegean Seas, or into the Mediterranean. The second was almost double the length of its smaller companion—with perhaps sixteen or more decks—and probably held over three thousand passengers. While the smaller ship might hold only a third as many people, he thought, chances were that it catered to a wealthier crowd. He committed the ships' logos and names to memory and decided to look them up on the web later.

Away from the port and the business district, traffic thinned, and he let his gaze wander as he drove. He swung his head toward the seaside promenade that hugged the shoreline, a popular diversion for the city's fourteen million inhabitants. He compressed his lips into a thin line as he swallowed his contempt for the couples strolling arm in arm, the bare-shouldered mothers wheeling infants in hooded carriages, and the immodest comingling of male and female office workers setting a brisk pace to their destinations. *Unholy*, he thought, *women believing they are equal.*

His view of the Bosphorus was interrupted by the Dolmabahçe Mosque, and eventually gave way to a canopy of stately trees and the high walls guarding the ornate Dolmabahçe Palace. He had attended prayer in the elegant mosque only once. Finding the swarm of Western tourists offensive, he had never returned.

He continued up the coast, past the parks, shopping areas, universities, and palaces of sultans long dead, finally sighting the Bosphorus Bridge. At the time of its completion, the first-constructed span across the strait held a place in the top five of the longest suspension bridges in the world. Its position had eventually been usurped by newer engineering marvels, including the third bridge over the strait.

His eyes drifted upward as he passed beneath the bridge. Staring up at the beams and columns supporting the travel deck, he could not help but think that a few well-placed blocks of explosive could produce dramatic results. He could imagine the entire structure crumbling into the sea, throwing road transportation into chaos and creating a navigational hazard for one of the busiest waterways in the world. It was something the authorities had obviously considered as well, given the abundant concertinas of razor wire enveloping the structure's supports. But the defenses were far from impregnable, and he wondered if others had deemed the bridge an exceptional target. *Worthy of consideration*, he thought.

The greenspace known as Cemil Topuzlu Park came up on his right, and midway down its length, on his left, he spotted the familiar logo of one of Turkey's largest suppliers of automotive fuel. In a deferential nod to its moneyed neighbors—who required fuel for their vehicles but winced at the unsightly intrusion of the facility—a line of palms and cedars shielded the vulgarity of the pumps. *A possibility*, he thought. Much of the area's traffic funneled through this road. Those in the military would likely see it as a choke point, but to him, it represented an opportunity. He signaled a turn and pulled into the station.

He took his time topping off his tank, making mental notes of the layout. He took it all in—the arrangement of the pumps, the covers for the underground tanks, the convenience shop, the light poles, the electrical transformer box at the rear of the lot, the air hose, the drainage grates, the absence of cameras. He clicked the app on his phone, and pretending to be absorbed in a call, recorded a 360° video of the location. Satisfied, he got back into the car and pulled back onto the roadway, continuing north.

Entering the neighborhood of Arnavutköy, he was struck by the obvious signs of prosperity. Aside from the fastidiously maintained homes and the abundance of BMWs lining its streets, he noted the gated entries, decoratively barred windows on residences' lower levels, high walls deterring access to the properties, and even the occasional display of razor wire. He would need to explore the streets with a careful eye ... cameras would most certainly have some presence here.

The area was home to a number of influential Westerners who, despite requiring extensive security precautions, nevertheless declared it to be a safe and charming location. The neighborhood's narrow cobblestone streets hugged the contours of the hilly terrain and boasted an abundance of small restaurants and shops. There was nothing flashy here, nothing to draw attention. It was simply a quiet, relaxed community—albeit with the unmistakable scent of money.

It was also an area that refused to lend itself to easy navigation. One-way streets were the norm, and he missed several turns before finding the compound. He drove past twice, scanning the area without turning his head—just another driver seeking a parking spot in the congested neighborhood. He spotted three cameras on the first run, another on the second pass, and was sure there were more. The dark blue BMW peeked from behind the gate, along with a Chevy Suburban—most likely of the armored variety. None of it mattered, really, because the plan had begun to take shape at the moment he had seen the petrol station. But he was a firm believer in preparation; ignoring the small details could be catastrophic. Knowing about the Suburban was critical, and they could prepare accordingly.

He found an open space for the car—near enough to the house that his drive-by would not seem out of place—and walked a block and a half to a park facing the Bosphorus. The stamp-size space was dominated by a statue of Atatürk, Turkey's first president, but provided a number of benches for enjoying the view. He bought a fresh-squeezed orange-and-pomegranate mix from a juice stand on the corner and found an unoccupied bench. Ten minutes later, his brother joined him.

Chapter 70

Goran was seething with frustration. "We cannot sabotage the car or invade the residence. Both are too well protected. The guards are South African, and they have military training. I walked by twice, and their eyes were on me the entire length of the street. The only way to get close would be to create a diversion in a public place. Even that is a terrible idea—we would not get out alive."

Daris laid his hand on his brother's shoulder and spoke calmly. "Not a diversion—we will create an accident."

"An accident? And how are we going to arrange that?" Goran asked petulantly.

"There is a petrol station down the road. They drive by it every time they go into the city." He outlined his idea.

"And where will we get a tanker? And who will drive it?"

Daris waved his hand impatiently. "I have already thought of these things. All can be arranged. We have made many friends here who are eager to help."

Unhappy, Goran shook his head. "We should let it go. She has left Sarajevo. She has only a vague suspicion and nothing to support it. It was years ago, and her memories cannot be that clear. She knows nothing."

"And yet you called me and boarded an airplane. You were worried, and with good reason. You know that she is not going to forget. She will come back, and she will bring people with her. No, it is best that we take care of the problem now."

Goran nodded in reluctant agreement. His brother was the smart one, the one who could devise the most complex plan and steer it to completion without leaving a trace. To Goran's knowledge, Daris had never failed a mission.

Daris did not tell his brother, but he had overheard the woman mention the possibility of a flight to Gaziantep in two days. Time was running out. He had already set his plan in motion.

For three days, he had been shadowing Maggie Marshfield. He was becoming familiar with her habits and her schedule. That was not to say that she would not do something out of the ordinary, but he did not think so. For a diplomat's wife, she seemed cavalier about security protocols. She kept to a schedule, taking a strong coffee with her friend at eight each morning, always at the same local café. They would chat about the day's itinerary, and they took a predictable path while walking—or when riding in the car. She favored the drive along the Bosphorus.

In three days of watching her, she had not once tripped to his presence. Tomorrow the women planned to visit the Grand Bazaar after having their morning coffee. Daris thought it a fortuitous decision, since the petrol station was directly in the path of their route. He clapped his brother on the shoulder and said, "We must go. There is much to do."

They drove to Alibeköy, in the northern part of Istanbul, well away from any area of the city where they—and the man they were meeting—might be recognized. They arrived midmorning and found their man—twenty-five years old and the father of two—leaning against a concrete wall topped with razor wire. Eighteen months earlier, Abdul Attia had gathered his family and slipped out of Syria and into Turkey. They were safe, but Abdul's status as a refugee made it impossible to find work in his profession as an accountant. Their savings depleted and living in squalor, Abdul had scraped out a meager living by performing odd jobs.

When a friend suggested that a group of Bosnians might be able to help, Abdul had jumped at the chance. He was introduced to Daris, who talked of offering Abdul a new life. But first, Abdul would have to work hard and prove himself worthy. The following day, he was hired as an apprentice maintenance technician for a large petrol distributor. He had learned the trade, worked his way up, and now scheduled the fuel deliveries. When they were short a driver, he filled in.

Daris had his own plans for Abdul. His organization needed someone with financial skills, someone who could be trusted. He had kept an eye on the young man, and a few weeks later, offered him an opportunity to supplement his salary. Abdul quietly accepted the job—tallying income and expenditures and pointing out anything unusual. Abdul had examined the books and understood why it would be dangerous to ask questions. He kept his head low and his mouth shut, both traits that pleased Daris immensely.

Abdul kept his side job secret, working the books at night when his wife was asleep. He stashed the ledger in a pocket of the backpack he carried to work every day, away from prying eyes.

Then, a few weeks ago, Abdul's younger son fell while playing—his leg just crumpled beneath him. A few days later, he could no longer throw a ball. He lost his appetite. When Abdul found bruises on the boy's body, he was concerned that his child was being abused. A visit to the doctor's office said otherwise; the boy was diagnosed with lymphoblastic leukemia. Treatment was available, they told him, but very expensive.

Abdul was a hard worker and dedicated family man who was bearing his circumstances with grit and grace, but his son's illness was the final insult. Desperate and angry, he railed against those who had destroyed his homeland, his life, and his son's opportunity for survival. Word got back to Daris.

Daris gazed at the young man, almost sorrowful that he was going to lose someone so valuable. "Is there a place where we can walk while we talk?" Daris asked.

"There is a park ... five minutes from here."

Goran got out of the car and moved to the back seat, relinquishing the front passenger seat to Abdul. They drove in silence to the park's entry, locked the car, and began walking.

"I have a task for you, my friend," said Daris. "You will not like it, but it is for the greater good."

Abdul's eyes widened. "I am eternally grateful for all you have done for me. What is it that you want me to do?"

"I want you to cause an accident—with a gasoline tanker."

Abdul's mouth went dry. "You mean to cause an explosion? An attack?"

"Yes. Accidents with gasoline tankers do happen, is that not true?"

"Yes, but not often. Usually from striking another vehicle on a motorway."

"Exactly. There is a very specific car that would be involved."

Abdul played the possibilities in his mind. "Will there be people in the car?" He asked the question, already knowing the answer: *There is no reason to blow up an empty car.*

"A driver and two women. One of the women has stumbled into something she should not have seen. It jeopardizes our entire network—all the people who have helped you and others like you."

Abdul was horrified. *Murder!* He had never subscribed to the fundamentalist point of view. His father, and his father's father, taught him that it was a sin to take a life.

"I cannot kill someone!" he exclaimed.

Daris stared at him coldly. "Even if it means an opportunity to save your son?"

"What ... what do you mean?" Abdul stammered.

"If you do this, I will make arrangements for your family ... transport to France and medical care for your son."

"The police will question me."

"Perhaps."

Suddenly, Abdul grasped the situation with nauseating clarity. They intended for this to be a suicide mission. The women were likely Westerners, he realized. Muslim women would be dealt with in a different manner. "I need some time to think about this," he said.

"I'm afraid that is not possible. This must happen tomorrow."

Abdul was stunned. "Tomorrow?"

"You will take the place of the driver who is regularly assigned to deliver fuel to the station in Arnavutköy."

A chill went up Abdul's spine. "What will happen to him?"

"I will need his address so that we can have a talk. I am sure he will cooperate."

Abdul hung his head. He wanted to believe the words but knew in his heart that the driver would be dead tomorrow. And what was he to do? Say no and walk away? He would be dead before they returned to the car. And what would happen to his family then? If he did as they asked, at least he might have a chance of survival. His stomach churned wildly.

Finally, he looked into Daris's eyes. "You will take care of my family? I have your word?"

"Yes, my friend. You have my word."

With Daris listening attentively, Abdul suggested several methods for destroying the car and its occupants. From his own point of view, all the options were likely to fail. Nevertheless, Daris eventually settled on a plan that, he believed, held the greatest hope for success.

As they parted ways that afternoon, Daris said, "There is one more thing. You must tell no one, not even your wife."

Chapter 71

Abdul slept little that night, his brain on overdrive, mentally weighing his options. If he did not do as Daris had asked, death was a certainty. If he drove the truck, death was still a gamble, but the odds were better, and his family would be looked after. If he went to the police, what could he tell them? He had no idea who the target might be and no proof that there was a target, or even a real plot. And if his actions were discovered, he—and probably his family as well—were doomed. Left with no good choice, he finally abandoned any further attempt at sleep.

At three-thirty in the morning, he drove to the fuel terminal in Cekisan, in the Avcilar district—at the far western side of Istanbul on the Sea of Marmara—where his company maintained its fleet of thirty-one tanker trucks. He waved to the security guards, gratified to see that none of the other workers had yet entered the facility. He unlocked the office and pulled up the planner on the computer. As he did every morning, he studied road closures and other factors that might affect delivery schedules. He made changes to several routes and, buried in the middle, included adjustments that would position a tanker at the Arnavutköy station by 8:45 a.m.

Abdul had reached the conclusion that he would need to use one of the company's older tankers if he were to have any chance of success. The newer tankers had certain safety features, such as roll stability systems and elliptical tanks, that lessen the chances of catastrophic failure. There were two such tankers available, to be used only when a newer truck was unavailable. The key, then, would be to disable the normally scheduled truck, removing it from the equation.

After ensuring that the security detail was out of sight, he found the truck and removed its electronic control unit. He flicked the exposed computer with a spark from a welder's rod—effectively frying its electronics—and reattached it to the truck. He glanced at his watch: 4:45 a.m. The workers would begin to arrive within thirty minutes. He hauled himself into the truck's cab and stuffed the ledger into the deep, little-used pocket behind the passenger seat. If he lived, he would retrieve the book early the following morning. If not, someone would eventually find it. He wasn't sure what that someone might do with it; perhaps an investigation would ensue, bringing Daris to justice. But only after his wife and sons were safe.

Shortly after six o'clock, Abdul's manager hurried into the room. "The driver on the Arnavutköy route has not shown up, and he is not answering his phone. You'll have to take his place."

Abdul's stomach clenched. The possibility that Daris had harmed the driver was staggering. *Did he kill him? If I survive, will he kill me, too?*

Without thinking, he blurted out, "But I was going to ask to leave early today! My son has an appointment with the doctor," Abdul protested.

The boy truly did have an appointment, but his wife generally tended to such things. The excuse was born of desperation. If the plan went forward, the police would later learn that he had not wanted to take the route. If he was still alive at the end, his reluctance to drive today might save him. And if his boss assigned the route to someone else, Abdul could escape any involvement.

His boss was having none of it. Thrusting a fistful of paperwork toward Abdul, he said, "I need a driver, and you're the only one here. Take the delivery route or find another job."

Abdul snatched the papers from his superior and left the office, striding angrily toward the line of trucks. If he lived through this, he would still need the job.

He climbed into the truck and put the fob in the ignition, praying that his sabotage had done the job, and breathed a sigh of relief when the engine refused to fire. He tried again, for good measure and a good performance, before hollering to one of the mechanics, a man he had come to regard as a friend.

"This engine is dead!"

"I'll take a look," the man responded.

The mechanic raised the hood and peered inside, looking for loose wires or other abnormalities. "I don't see anything. I'll run some diagnostics."

"That will take too long. I'm already running late. It's better if I just take one of the old trucks."

"Boss won't like it," the mechanic said.

"Well, I don't like being late," he replied. "It causes you to hurry. That's when things go wrong."

The mechanic nodded and pointed at the nearest of the two older trucks. "Take that one. It has an intermittent problem with the starter, but if you try a few times, it will work. The other is a piece of junk."

"Thank you. Wish me luck when the boss finds out."

"You will need it!"

Abdul put his hand on his friend's shoulder and said, "Take good care of my truck. I trust you to take care of everything."

Abdul pulled into the queue of tankers, eventually filling two of the tanker's compartments with regular gasoline and the third with diesel, according to the planner's spec sheet for the two deliveries on the route.

It was seven o'clock before he pulled out of the terminal, and he spent the next hour and fifteen minutes traveling into the city at a crawl. Upon arrival at the Arnavutköy station, he presented the paperwork to the manager and went about dropping the load of fuel into the underground tanks. By a quarter of nine, he was finished, and the truck was half-empty.

Climbing back into the truck, Abdul easily spotted Daris on the sidewalk on the opposite side of the road. He wore a bright, mustard-colored turtleneck and was leaning against a light pole, his chin cocked against his cell phone. Abdul wanted desperately to hear what was being said, but cell phones were never used when driving the tankers. Urban legend claimed that a spark from a cell phone could ignite the gasoline vapor. Despite numerous documents debunking the claim, he had never been willing to take the chance.

He assumed Daris was talking with Goran. According to the plan, Goran would be positioned near the house where the woman was staying. It was Goran's responsibility to alert Daris when the car left the residence.

Chapter 72

Maggie Marshfield and her friend Louise Burke finished their coffee at the street-side table and waved at the owner as they stood and turned to walk back to the residence. Strolling up the hill, they shared a laugh about the antics of the guests at last night's party, before turning to local politics and Turkey's president.

Louise stopped walking and turned toward Maggie, saying, "We just don't know how this will all play out. He has an iron fist. Just you wait ... his hard-line tactics are going to be a problem."

Maggie turned to face her. "A problem as in a fracture with the West? Turkey's been an ally for a long time and ..." She caught something in her peripheral vision, stopping mid-sentence as she turned to look fully behind her. *That man that just turned down that street ... he had the same white hair as that man in Sarajevo. No, that's crazy.*

"What's wrong?" Louise asked, alarmed.

Maggie shook her head. "I'm not sure. I thought I saw someone, but it was probably my imagination. I'm just a little spooked by something that happened in Sarajevo."

Louise grabbed her hand. "Let's jump in the car and get going. You can tell me all about it on the way."

Shuffling paperwork and pretending to fill out documentation, Abdul sat in the truck and kept his eyes on Daris, waiting for the signal. At five minutes before nine, he saw Daris clasp his hands behind his neck and stretch mightily, as if relieving a troublesome muscle kink. Abdul jerked upright, the shot of adrenaline surging through his veins. He slammed his hand against the start button ... and nothing happened. His heart racing, he tried again. And again. Finally, the engine caught.

As the car turned onto the road paralleling the Bosphorus, Louise stretched out her long legs and melted into the BMW's cushy leather seats. "So, tell me about Sarajevo."

Maggie told her about the visit to the coffee shop and her strange encounter with the owner.

"He looked so much like someone I knew years ago. But he died in the crash ... the one that went down off Greenland."

"And yet you think you saw him this morning?"

"I'm not sure. Maybe."

"Excuse me," the driver said. "What did he look like?"

Maggie recalled his face. "Tall. White hair, long and scraggly. Weathered skin, very tan. Salt-and-pepper mustache."

"I'm going to call for backup. We have seen that man a few times over the past couple of days."

Maggie's eyes grew wide with fear. "He's here?"

"Yes, I think so," the driver responded. He looked in the rearview mirror and glanced at the steering wheel, finding the button for the phone. "I think we should ..."

He had been concentrating on the conversation taking place in the back seat and, as a result, was a second late in recognizing the danger. The tanker truck shot out of the petrol station, flying across the two southbound lanes and starting its turn into the northbound lane.

Louise and Maggie's driver slammed his foot on the brakes, the heavy BMW's tires shrieking in protest as he desperately pulled the steering wheel to the right in hopes of somehow avoiding the inevitable. In the span of a heartbeat, the women opened their mouths in horror as the realization struck. Their screams died as the car slammed into the middle of the tanker, pulverizing its hood, shattering the windshield, blowing the front tires, and crushing the passenger compartment. The force of the impact lifted the BMW's rear wheels off the ground and crumpled the center compartment of the tanker.

A Mercedes in the northbound lane plowed into the tanker's cab, killing its two front-seat occupants instantly. A black Honda slammed into the rear of the Benz, bending the frame and trapping the driver. The rig tipped on its side, releasing the vapor from the half-full tank and spilling the remaining fuel onto the BMW and the street below.

In less than the blink of an eye, the street erupted in an intensely orange wall of fire.

Chapter 73

October, Four Years Ago
CIA Headquarters
Langley, Virginia

The rap on the door of the secure space was soft but insistent, demanding attention. The faces of the room's nine occupants were lifted toward the screen, intently watching the live video feed from a midnight hostage rescue op in a village north of Kabul. Cat heard the knock and shoved her chair back. As a matter of procedure, one of the more junior attendees should have answered the summons, but Cat rarely stood on protocol and was nearest the door. She cracked the door open and saw the dour face of her assistant, Oscar Fuentes.

"Traffic from Istanbul," he said in his raspy voice. "Eyes only," meaning that whatever the news, it was not intended for general consumption. He gave no clue about the topic, no hint of the devastation that lay ahead. He left unmentioned that the subject was pressing—there was no need. No one interrupted these sessions unless the matter was supremely urgent, meaning that something had gone to hell in some corner of the world. Istanbul sat squarely in her domain: South Asia and the Middle East.

Cat pushed her chair under the table and gathered her belongings. A few sets of eyes darted her way, their curiosity aroused, but just as quickly slid back to the action on the screen. She slipped wordlessly from the room and found herself nose-level with Oscar's armpit. She was five-seven; Oscar was a foot taller. She tilted her head back to get a better angle on his face, knowing instantly that something was very wrong. Oscar's unfailing ability to maintain a poker face had made him the butt of many jokes about inscrutability, but on this occasion, pain registered in his dark eyes.

"What's up?" she asked as Oscar led her toward the elevator.

He inclined his shaggy head toward her ear. "There's been an incident in Istanbul. Arnavutköy, to be precise."

Her heart skipped a beat. Maggie was visiting friends in Istanbul—and the friends owned a residence in the Arnavutköy neighborhood.

She followed Oscar to a windowless anteroom, where his neat-as-a-pin workspace guarded the door to her office. A trim, dark-haired woman in her early forties sat in a chair across from his desk. Pindar Aydin, whose ageless skin was the envy of every female in the building, looked up at Cat with deep, sorrowful eyes. Ten years old when her family had immigrated to America from Turkey, Pindar Aydin was now a senior analyst of Middle East affairs.

Cat swiped her card in the lock for the interior entry and beckoned them inside, closing the door behind them. Still standing, she looked at Oscar and asked, "What is it?"

Oscar's jaw clenched before he spoke. "The consul general in Istanbul called for you. It's Maggie Marshfield, Ms. Powell. There's been an accident. We don't have all the details."

Cat's stomach clenched. "Is she alive?"

"She died at the scene. I'm so sorry."

The blow was crushing. The air rushed from Cat's lungs, all sense of normalcy incinerated in a flash. She crossed behind the desk and collapsed in the big leather chair, agony contorting her features, refusing to accept the unacceptable. *Not possible. Not dead. Like the Transoceanic crash in '94. Maggie could have died, but didn't. Could not be dead now. This is a mistake.* And then, from some unknown kernel of her brain, came the question: "Was it PKK?"

To the well-informed employees of the CIA, it seemed a natural question, given that Pindar was an acknowledged expert on the Partiya Karkerên Kurdistanê—in English, the Kurdistan Workers' Party. A Kurdish political organization primarily operating out of Turkey, the PKK had been engaged in a conflict with the Turkish government for over three decades. Many of the recent bombings in public places bore evidence of their involvement.

"No, ma'am," Pindar responded. "She was riding in a car that collided with a gasoline tanker. Preliminary reports point to an accident."

Cat focused on the woman's tightly clenched hands and forced herself to think. "An accident? Tell me what you know so far."

Pindar shared the little information she had. "Mrs. Marshfield was in a private car. The car belonged to a Mr. George Burke." She looked up. "She was visiting his wife, I believe."

Cat nodded. "We are friends."

"We believe that Mrs. Burke was the other occupant of the car and also died at the scene," Pindar continued. "They were passing a petrol station at the same time that a tanker was pulling out. Witnesses stated that the tanker seemed to lose control for a moment. It rolled onto its side, hitting the Burkes' car, and spilling fuel on the roadway. The driver of the tanker was consumed in the explosion and fire. We have word that Mrs. Burke's driver attempted to rescue the women but was forced back by the fire."

"He is alive?"

"Yes, but badly burned."

Cat took a deep breath. "Oscar, start looking at flights to Istanbul. Let's find her husband, Paul."

Oscar was quick to respond. "He's here—in DC. Flew in two days ago by way of London."

That surprised her; she had assumed that Paul was out of the country. It was unusual for him to fly into town and not contact her beforehand. "I'll call him. If he decides to travel to Istanbul, I'll want to be on the same plane."

She focused on Pindar. "Keep me informed. If this was an accident, then so be it. But we also need to consider that it might not be that simple. Any little thing that seems off-center, I want to know. Keep your eyes and ears open."

"Of course, Ms. Powell. Um, do you have a communication preference?"

Cat considered the question. Pindar was asking, obliquely, if Cat would prefer to use an unofficial method for sharing what she learned ... a burner phone, a private mail account. Something off-the-books. She leaned back in her chair, massaging her temples with her long, slender fingers. Regardless of whether or not they fully approved, Langley would know—would expect—that she would look into the circumstances of Maggie's death. Depending on what she found, they might or might not be supportive of continuing involvement. This was particularly true given that other agencies would be conducting their own investigations. Turf wars. Toes might get stepped upon, egos bruised. She sighed at the absurdity of the game.

"For the moment, let's just use regular channels until we see how this plays out. If you find anything remotely suspicious, use the word *chocolate* in your message. We'll take it from there."

Cat watched Pindar and Oscar leave and then slammed her fists into the desk. *I was supposed to be there. If I'd been there ... then what? It wouldn't have happened? I would have saved the day? All that woulda, shoulda bullshit? Pull yourself together. You can cry about it later.* She pulled out her government-issued, heavily encrypted BlackBerry. She pressed the number 3 and held it, engaging the speed dial for Paul's mobile phone.

Chapter 74

October, Four Years Ago
State Department
Washington, DC

P aul Marshfield, respected statesman, former US ambassador, and current special envoy, was accustomed to dealing with tragedy. He had witnessed the carnage of atrocities committed in the name of religion, provided solace to the wives, husbands, sons, and daughters left in the wake, and attended memorials for unnamed Americans who lost their lives in service to their country. But while he may have been the leader who took charge, managed the aftermath, and comforted the victims' families, the deaths had always lain heavy on his heart. His wife was the one person who could console him, the one person who could lift his spirits during his darkest hours.

From the first news of the crash, Paul had found himself on the receiving end of being managed. With the Secretary of State out of the country, the notification had fallen to the Deputy Secretary, a well-respected career diplomat with a reputation for getting things done. Paul was assured of a thorough investigation.

"We'll get to the bottom of this, Paul," the deputy promised. "And if this incident was anything other than an accident, we'll get those responsible and bring them to justice."

Incident, Paul thought, annoyed. *You could not simply say explosion, stabbing, shooting, bombing, or any term that might imply homicidal intent because it's important to protect Turkey's sensitivities. Everyone is going to treat this like a live grenade, tossing it around and hoping to be far from ground zero if it explodes. And "bring them to justice"? What a load of horse hockey.*

Instead, Paul thanked the deputy for his efforts, and for taking the time out of his busy day to give the notification personally.

He had been almost relieved to learn that the crash appeared to be accidental, but the feeling had been short-lived—rather like swallowing a couple of aspirin tablets to combat a bad hangover. He could not escape the notion that Maggie's death might ultimately be his fault. Representing the United States on foreign soil had often been compared to pinning a target to one's back. Everywhere one turned, there were always ideologues hell-bent on retribution for some perceived American slight.

When the deputy left, he asked the secretary to hold his calls, closed his office door, opened his computer, and pulled up the files he had hoped never to need. As the printer relinquished the pages he had selected, he closed his eyes and leaned back in his chair—whispering the lyrics to *America*, the old Paul Simon song. *Let us be lovers, we'll marry our fortunes together.* It had been a favorite of Maggie's, somehow fitting of their life as a couple. He allowed the tears to slip down his face, waiting for the phone in his shirt pocket to vibrate, knowing it would not be long before the news reached Cat. The government could send a hundred highly qualified people to Istanbul, and maybe they would learn the cause, and maybe they would release their findings. But there was no one whose instincts he trusted more. If there was a truth to discover, Cat Powell would find it.

Oscar worked his magic and secured two seats on a Lufthansa flight leaving shortly after ten that night. Paul accepted an offer of accommodation at the residence of the consul general, an estate located in Arnavutköy and just up the hill from the site of the crash, while Oscar had made other arrangements for Cat's stay.

"Rosalie Marchesani owns a flat there," Oscar suggested, referring to a former Agency colleague. "It's a short walk to the consul general's residence. It's small, but reportedly has a magnificent view of the Bosphorus and, more important, a street-level garage on the bottom floor. I'm told that the convenience more than compensates for the cramped living space."

"Perfect," Cat had replied, not arguing the point. She would spend little of her time there and needed only a place to bathe and sleep. She checked her watch. "Get me her bank's routing info. I'll try to have the payment wired before I leave."

A phone call later, Oscar tapped on her door. "No worry about the rent. I told Rosalie about the circumstances of your visit. The place is yours for three weeks, no charge. But it's booked after that."

Cat wrinkled her nose and frowned. "I didn't know Rosalie very well. She was solid, right? Nothing questionable about the offer?"

Passing her a sheet of paper, he said, "Here are her particulars. She's solid as a rock. Still does occasional work when we need someone local."

She raised her eyebrows. "Is that right? Well, hopefully this was really an accident and there's nothing to find, but I'll keep her in mind."

Oscar had chosen Cat's seat with some care—on the opposite side of the aisle and a few rows back from Paul. If one were snooping to see who was seated next to Paul at departure, the airline's reservation system would show that the seat was occupied by one Enrique Velazquez, a businessman from Madrid with no known association to Paul Marshfield. While Cat was not advertising her visit to Istanbul, neither was she traveling under an assumed identity. Her name was on the passenger manifest—one just needed to look a little farther than the immediate vicinity of Paul's assigned seat. After takeoff, Cat switched seats with the accommodating Mr. Velazquez.

To the unpracticed eye, Paul appeared as polished as ever—posture erect, immaculately dressed, and polite. But Cat took note of his pallor, the exhaustion in his eyes, and his uncharacteristic silence during the journey. Pen in hand, he spent the first hour of the flight reviewing the documents that he and Maggie had prepared in advance of their first posting abroad. Always one to plan ahead, he had updated the files with each subsequent assignment. Thus, the folder he now handed to Cat bore only a few edits and reflected his ability to anticipate the unexpected. She read through the papers, ticking off those items she or his staff could handle without Paul's personal involvement.

Left unspoken was the assumption that Cat's presence should be low-key. While others would handle the actual details of the investigation, she would stand on the sidelines, listening and observing, detecting hesitancy and watching for signs of deception.

Chapter 75

October, Four Years Ago
Istanbul, Turkey

After a short stopover in Frankfurt, they flew on to Istanbul, arriving just after six in the evening. Paul was met at the aircraft door by a small contingent of Turkish and American officials. Cat lagged behind, casually adjusting the large designer glasses on the bridge of her nose and draping the forest-green scarf over her head and neck. While allowing a buffer of other passengers to crowd ahead of her, she studied the faces in the greeting party and committed them to memory. She wrinkled her nose in distaste on sighting a familiar face, an undercover officer from the Defense Intelligence Agency named Nate Carr.

She had met Nate a few years earlier, while observing a training session at The Farm, the CIA's training facility near Williamsburg. His file painted a picture of a well-educated man with a sharp mind and tactical expertise, but she found him to be clearly lacking in his grasp of human nature and cultural affairs—the breadth of which could be measured on a pinhead. Cat, organizing a joint DIA-CIA operation on the Arabian Peninsula, had crossed his name off the list of those to be considered. Arrogant enough to believe he was well-equipped for the job, Nate had reached out to his uncle—a three-star at the Pentagon—thereby confirming both the assessment in his file and Cat's evaluation. The mission had been a success overall, but the after-action reports were less than complimentary about Nate's performance. Cat's initial take on the man had not even scratched the surface. Though few were willing to put their opinions in writing, one longtime operative stated—off the record—that Nate was like a dirty cop: he had no sense of honor or integrity. Another whispered to Cat that if Nate ever showed up on one of his teams again, he would personally stake the man over an anthill.

Now—particularly given Turkey's strategic importance to the region and to the United States—Cat wondered how Nate had risen to a position where he would be involved in the highly sensitive investigation of the death of an American diplomat's wife. *Would not have been my choice,* she thought. *And he'll figure out I'm here soon enough, if he doesn't know already.* He glanced her way but gave no sign of recognition. *Good boy, Nate. Stay away— far, far away. You may not have invited me to the party, but I'm here and I play by my own rules. Don't get in my way.*

Cat edged into the stream of deplaning passengers, joining the throng flooding the arrival hall. As she moved into the long line for those with non-Turkish passports, Paul was whisked through immigration and customs formalities and shepherded out of the building.

Thirty minutes later, Cat emerged into the chaos of the Atatürk Airport terminal and found the car rental counters. Oscar had made her reservation at Hertz, but she bypassed the blaze of yellow and black, veering instead toward a European agency she had used previously. If anyone had tracked her presence on the plane, they might also have found the car reservation. While hiding out in Istanbul was not part of the plan, she was not eager to announce her presence. *Better to at least make this a little troublesome,* she thought.

The agent was attentive, spoke nearly flawless English, and valiantly attempted an upsell to a red Nissan. Cat declined, politely but firmly, opting for the less conspicuous gray Hyundai, and set out in evening traffic for the drive through the city. Having visited Istanbul on several occasions, she had a general familiarity with the city and knew its major arteries. She made several abrupt moves, to the ire of blaring horns of other drivers, but detected no cars risking the same crazy turns. And while the abundance and similarity of the automobiles jamming the roads were making it more problematic to identify a tail, it also gave her an advantage: the same difficulties would apply to anyone attempting to follow her car.

The traffic was even more congested than she remembered from her last visit—a seemingly impossible feat—and she endured the nine-mile crawl for over an hour. Relying on Google Maps to guide her through the maze of streets that made up the Arnavutköy neighborhood, she located Rosalie's building with only one missed turn. Not nearly so predictable were the hundreds of people on foot, leading to three pedestrian near misses, a stream of profanity, and a craving for alcohol.

Cat found the key as promised, tucked into a hollow in one of the planks of a white Adirondack-style chair in the courtyard, and let herself into the apartment. After tapping the code into the alarm panel, she stood still, letting her senses test the space. The air was slightly musty, as if the place had not been used for some time, but with the lingering odor of disinfectant, suggesting a recent cleaning. She caught the trace of a woman's scent—*shampoo or body wash?*—mildly reminiscent of citrus with a hint of basil, and knew she could recognize the smell if she encountered it in the future. Stepping farther into the apartment, she checked the bedroom, closets, and bathroom. Assured she was alone, she began a more thorough inspection and was mildly surprised to discover several discreetly positioned sensors, interior cameras, and a small screen cycling through views of the building's exterior. *Interesting. What type of side business is Rosalie running?*

She rearmed the alarm, found a hanger for her simple black dress—the requisite all-occasion garb for female travelers—and shed her travel clothes. She stepped into the shower and rinsed off the stink of the airplane before pulling on tights, sneakers, and a bulky sweater. The other belongings remained folded in her single suitcase, a habit ingrained from years of sudden unscheduled departures. She swiped her teeth with a toothbrush and was rinsing her mouth when she heard the soft chime of the doorbell.

Automatically reaching for the gun tucked into the holster at her waistband, Cat cursed silently at the realization that she was unarmed. She padded softly back to the viewer and watched as the screen cycled through the exterior camera shots. At the front door, face in profile, was the DIA operative Cat had seen at the airport. Annoyed, she considered ignoring the intrusion, before accepting the inevitable. She was going to have to deal with him sooner or later. She deactivated the alarm and opened the door.

Nate Carr was only slightly taller than Cat, shorter when she was wearing heels. Height aside, he was acutely handsome, and his hairstyle (short undercut, top slicked back) and wardrobe (dark denim, silk scarf, leather biker jacket) made him a poster boy for hip and edgy. Unknowing passersby often mistook him for an actor or model, and as she had witnessed on several occasions, women buzzed after him like flies to honey. At first blush he seemed pleasant enough, even charming, until the night wore on and his self-absorption ultimately revealed itself. Even now, he wore a lopsided grin that belied his spiteful nature.

"Miz Powell," he drawled. "Nice to see you again."

Cat raised her eyebrows in mock amazement and decided to let her irritation show. "Really? Honestly, Nate, I doubt it."

His face clouded in resentment at the exchange, but he recovered quickly and pasted on a complacent smile. Cat could almost hear him thinking about the wisdom of being on her bad side and how it might affect his career. After a pause, he shrugged.

She shook her head in disgust. "What did you do? Hack all the rental car agencies?"

"Not quite. We had a spotter outside customs; he saw you at the rental counter. The young lady was very eager to help us, by the way."

"Oh, I'm sure. Or maybe it was just your Southern charm," she said, wondering if Nate had threatened the woman. He had a reputation for stepping right up to the ethical line, and sometimes crossing it. Not that she had never crossed the line, but there was a difference. Cat found him to be bright, but morally lazy—achieving results but via questionable methods. The man was more bully than white knight.

"You used the car's GPS system to find me?"

"Easy-peasy," he said, looking around the apartment. "Nice digs you've got here."

"And may I ask why you felt it necessary to track me?"

He gave her a hard look. "Because I'm wondering why you've really come to Istanbul. Is it because you feel the need to play detective? Is there some reason you think this was anything but an accident?" He paused for dramatic effect before continuing, "Or was this one of Langley's blown operations, and you're here to erase any evidence of your involvement?"

Anger surged through her. *No sense in giving him the satisfaction*, she thought, brushing aside an urge to kick him in the balls. She took a deep breath. Her voice steely, she responded, "Not that I'm required to give you any reason for my presence here, but Maggie and Paul Marshfield are my closest friends. I owe it to them and I owe it to myself to look around and ask questions. I need to be satisfied about what happened. To suggest that I have some nefarious motive is beyond the pale."

He stared at her for a moment, as if trying to determine his next move. Finally, he nodded. "I know you're good. I also know you have a reputation of being a team player. So, in the spirit of cooperation between agencies, I'll expect you to let me know if you uncover anything. I, of course, will do the same."

Cat lowered her chin slightly, as if assenting, although she knew that any information provided by Nate would be suspect—he had never been one for sharing. And for her part, she would participate in the masquerade of teamwork—but give him only the information that would best serve Langley's interests.

She walked him back to the entry and, as he stepped over the threshold, was tempted to slam the door on his ass. Instead, she said, "See you around."

He looked back over his shoulder and gave her a sly smirk. "That you will, Cat. I'll be in touch."

Closing the door, she pressed her head and back against the cool wood and clenched her fists. She shuddered and pushed away from the door, heading for the kitchen and a strong drink.

Chapter 76

Given Paul's position, concerns had been raised regarding the possibility that Maggie had been targeted and, as promised, the formidable investigatory powers of the United States government were brought to bear. The FBI dispatched a team, counterterrorism experts were sent to weigh in, and forensic analysts flew to Turkey to examine the wreckage. All assured Paul that they would leave no stone unturned in their pursuit of the truth.

Cat followed their progress with a critical eye. She had to admit that the teams were thorough, examining every detail and every nuance—almost to the point of obsession. They worked backward through the events on the morning of the accident and, twelve hours after her arrival in Istanbul, Cat found herself at the fuel terminal where Abdul had been employed.

She had tagged along with an FBI agent named Wayne. As the investigative contingent met that morning, she had overheard Wayne complaining about the strong Turkish coffee. She had stepped outside, slipped several bills to a waiting taxi driver, and asked him to perform a miracle. Ten minutes later, as the teams were piling into an assortment of rental vehicles, the driver had come running over, cup in hand. If nothing else, Cat knew how to curry favor with the Feds.

Now, along with a translator sent by the consulate and a policeman sent by the Turkish authorities, they were meeting with the manager of the facility where Abdul had worked. She stood a few steps back, along with the policeman, while Wayne and the translator conducted the interview. Although she was fluent in Arabic and Farsi, and had some knowledge of Pashto and Urdu, Cat's grasp of Turkish was nearly nonexistent. She could pick up an occasional word but was forced to rely on the translator's interpretation. Over the course of many interrogations, she had learned the hard way that not all translations were accurate. She put her hand in her pocket and pressed the button to turn on the micro recorder.

"What kind of employee was Abdul?" Wayne asked.

The manager seemed momentarily flustered until the translator explained the question.

"Oh, yes, I see. He was a very good employee. He worked hard. We promoted him three times." The translator's English was good, but a bit stiff, and she seemed to struggle with anything other than short pieces of conversation.

"And how long ago was that?"

The manager's head bobbed as he made the mental calculation. "I think almost two years."

"Is that unusual? Three promotions in such a short time?"

The man shook his head vigorously. "No. He was a smart man. It was better for us to make use of his skills, and at a very low rate of pay."

The FBI agent lowered his gaze and looked the manager in the eye. "You mean that because he was a refugee, it was easy to take advantage of him."

At the translation, the manager blushed and looked away. "I do not make the rules."

Neither did most of the people of Nazi Germany, Cat thought. *And look where that ended up.*

"How was he on the morning of the accident?"

Knitting his brow, the manager said, "He did not want to go on the route. His son had an appointment with a doctor. He was unhappy that he had to drive."

"What do you mean?"

"The regular driver did not come to work. Abdul took the route for him."

Wayne glanced at Cat, who raised her eyebrows.

"Where is the regular driver? We would like to speak with him."

The manager lowered his head. "I am afraid that is not possible. He is dead."

Wayne's posture changed abruptly. "Dead? How?"

"The police said he slipped in the shower. He hit his head. It is a terrible thing."

"Terrible, yes," Wayne agreed, but his worried frown spelled concern. "What does his family say?"

"That, I do not know."

"Is there anything else you can tell us? Anything else out of the ordinary that happened that day?"

"There is nothing more. I am sorry that he has died. He was a good man, and fire is a terrible end."

Wayne and Cat went through the desk where Abdul had worked before the accident. There was nothing of note aside from the usual items accumulated by someone who works in an office: a few coins, a photograph of his sons, and a notebook where Abdul kept names and phone numbers. Wayne snapped pictures with his phone, capturing the information. There were only a few names, Cat noted. Abdul apparently did not have many friends. It should take only a day or two to check them out.

Wayne thumbed through the remaining content, written in Turkish, and stopped at a page where Abdul had scribbled a number of English phrases.

"I think he was trying to learn English," Wayne remarked. "I wonder if that's important."

"It's something to consider," offered Cat. "Maybe he was bucking for another promotion. Or maybe he just wanted to learn a few phrases. Or he wanted to go to America. Maybe his wife can answer that."

"Let's go see her first, and then check on the original driver. It's just weird that he's dead, too. I'm not big on coincidences."

"Neither am I," said Cat. "Neither am I."

Wayne started to walk away with the notebook, but the policeman held out his hand. Wayne reluctantly handed it over, and muttered to Cat, "Think we'll ever see it again?"

"You think it's important?"

"I don't know."

Cat watched the policeman drop the notebook into his leather messenger bag.

They left the office and were walking toward the car when the manager came trotting toward them. He seemed out of breath and, Cat thought, a bit nervous.

"I thought of something else," he said.

"We're listening," Wayne said.

"The truck. He took one of the old trucks. The drivers are only supposed to take an old truck when a new truck is in for repair."

Cat and Wayne shared a glance.

"Why?" asked Wayne.

"The new trucks are more fuel-efficient and safer."

"Do you know what happened to the new truck?"

"The mechanic said the engine was dead."

"Let's go talk with him."

They found the mechanic, a swarthy man in his midforties with a gap between his two front teeth, struggling to place a new battery in one of the engines. He said he remembered the morning perfectly and that, yes, Abdul's truck had refused to start. Abdul had taken one of the older trucks instead.

"What was the problem with the first truck?" asked Wayne.

The mechanic shuffled his feet at he spoke, looking at the ground and then glancing up at his boss. He seemed nervous, and Cat wondered if he was afraid of speaking openly with his boss present.

"Excuse me," Cat said, turning to the manager. "Would it be possible to have a glass of water?"

The manager gave an apologetic nod and hurried off.

Cat turned back to the mechanic. "You were going to tell us about the problem with the first truck," she said.

The mechanic let go with a torrent of Turkish, which their aide summarized in a single sentence.

"It was a computer malfunction and took a long time to fix," she said, translating. After another burst from the mechanic, she went on to say that the mechanic had warned the driver about the second truck. "It had a problem with the starter. He was assigned to fix it last week but was too busy. He does not want his boss to know."

At least that explains his nervousness, Cat thought. *Job security is everything in a country where the economy is tight and where there are so many unemployed.* "We will not say a word," she said.

Chapter 77

The originally scheduled driver of the tanker had lived in a comfortable apartment near Istanbul University's Avcilar campus and the Pelican shopping mall. The widow, whose puffy and red-rimmed eyes could not disguise her pretty face, opened the door. Wayne introduced the team as FBI. Cat saw no reason to clarify.

Cat took in the furnishings, noticing a table with a framed photograph surrounded by votive candles.

In a low voice, Cat asked, "This is your husband?" The photograph showed a man in his midfifties. His wife was younger.

The woman nodded as a fresh stream of tears ran down her face.

"Could you tell us what happened?"

The translator started to speak, but the woman said, "I speak English."

The woman explained that she had been at work and had come home to find her husband on the bathroom floor. "I am a nurse; I work nights at Avcilar Hospital. He took medication for his heart, but I did not expect this."

Wayne asked, "Did you try CPR?"

The woman put her hands to her face and shook her head. With tears welling in her eyes, she murmured, "CPR would not have revived him. I touched him; he was ... cold."

"I am so sorry for your loss, and I regret the intrusion, but I must ask you a few questions. Did you notice anything unusual? Anything out of place or missing?"

"Like a robbery?" she asked, dismayed. "I do not think that is possible. There is nothing missing from the apartment."

"So, nothing to indicate that there was anyone else in the apartment."

"No, but why are you asking these questions?"

Wayne took a breath. "There was an accident in Arnavutköy two days ago that killed seven people. Your husband was scheduled to drive the truck that day."

The woman clasped her hand over her mouth, and her eyes went wide.

"And do you think my husband's death is related?"

"We don't know, ma'am. We're just investigating the circumstances."

"He called to tell me that an old friend had come by shortly after I left for work. They were having dinner together. He probably had a glass or two of raki, although he would not have told me that. He is not supposed to take alcohol."

"Raki?" Wayne asked, puzzled.

The translator explained that raki is an anise-flavored liquor, similar to ouzo.

"An old friend," Cat repeated. "And they had drinks together. Do you know who it was?"

"He did not say. You can ask our neighbors. Perhaps someone saw him."

"Did you talk with your husband afterward?"

The woman's jaw quivered. "No. We were busy at the hospital. I called later, but he did not answer. I assumed he had gone to bed." The tears fell freely now, leaving streaks in her makeup. "I never got to tell him I loved him."

The team knocked on several doors, but none of the neighbors remembered seeing anyone visit the driver's apartment. They left contact information, just in case, but knew the effort was futile. Locals were suspicious of the police; there would be no calls.

Abdul's apartment was in the same district, no more than two miles from the original driver, but the neighborhood was considerably less affluent. While the first widow had been alone in a large flat, more than a dozen mourners were crowded into the tiny apartment Abdul had shared with his wife and sons. Disturbed by the appearance of the four officials, one dark-haired man exchanged sharp words with a man with wild white hair. When the translator said nothing, Cat patted herself on the back for having already turned on the recorder.

The man with the dark hair turned to face them, talking angrily in Turkish. "What do you want here? Have you no respect?"

The translator said, "He is saying that this is not a good time. It would be respectful to wait."

I will bet that isn't exactly what he said, thought Cat, watching the man's facial expression. But upon hearing the translation, Wayne whispered to Cat, "I'll take it."

Cat gave a barely perceptible nod, and Wayne stepped into the man's personal space.

"Seven people have been killed," he said, his voice hard. "We are investigating the circumstances. Is there something you are trying to hide?"

The man's eyes widened. He looked toward the policeman before sliding his gaze back to Wayne. "Of course not," he said in perfect English.

It was Wayne's turn to be surprised. "You speak English."

"I should hope so. I have a degree from Michigan," he said.

Wayne tipped his head in apology. "I regret the intrusion. We would like to ask his wife a few questions. We will not take up much of her time."

The man gestured at Cat. "She is with you?"

"Yes."

"It would be best for her to speak with his wife."

"We can manage that. What is your connection to the family?"

"I'm with a group that provides assistance to refugees. We help them find employment, a place to live, ensure their children get schooling. I helped this family." He held out his hand. "My name is Daris."

With the man named Daris hovering nearby, Cat and the translator sat beside Abdul's widow, who was introduced as Haya. Cat listened intently, trying to pick up a sense of the conversation, but was quickly lost. She followed the body language which, to her disappointment, gave away little.

Haya was initially quiet and withdrawn, surely still in shock. She had little information to share, saying only that her husband had seemed distracted and had not slept well on the night before the accident.

"He was so worried about our son's illness. We could not possibly afford the treatment." She glanced at Daris and then buried her face in her hands and wept. "Now, there is no hope, and I can only watch my son die."

Cat rarely let her emotions get in the way of her work, but she felt sorry for the woman. The family had been barely scraping by, and with Abdul's death, they were now in an even more precarious position. With no source of income, Cat knew that things would not go well. She had few words of solace for the grieving woman and felt a pang of regret that there was little she could do to ease the situation. *Impossible circumstances,* she thought.

The woman, her face tear-streaked and creased with pain, raised her eyes to Cat in a silent plea for exoneration. "My husband was a kind man. He loved his family. He would never cause harm to anyone, not like those monsters who drove us out of our home in Syria. He would not harm another."

The only reply that Cat could find was the trite and stale phrase she had already used too many times. "I am so sorry for your loss."

Cat continued talking with Haya for another fifteen minutes, dropping seemingly mundane questions and hoping to catch a whiff of something amiss. Nothing caught her attention. Cat eventually stood to leave, popping a final question.

"We found some English phrases in your husband's notebook. Was he trying to learn the language?"

"He dreamed of one day going to America. He was an accountant, you know. He was very smart."

Cat bit her lip and bowed her head. *An accountant who could only find work scheduling fuel runs. It's the same everywhere—refugees barely stand a chance.*

The team left the apartment no more informed than when they had arrived.

"Your take?" Wayne asked Cat.

"The wife is obviously devastated. If her husband was somehow involved, she didn't know about it."

"They have a rough road ahead."

"Yeah."

Wayne turned toward the policeman and the translator.

"Thank you both for your help today. We may need you again tomorrow. We'll be in touch."

Standing beside the policeman, Cat nodded her agreement and then swiveled toward the car, bumping into him and nearly losing her balance. He reached out his hand, helping to steady her, until she said, "I'm fine, just lost my footing. Thank you again for your help today."

Cat settled into the passenger seat, thinking that Wayne, being FBI, would probably not approve of what she had just done. The CIA had taught her certain skills, which she had honed over the years. She had no qualms about employing a little pickpocketing when necessary, and the policeman's messenger bag had presented an easy target. She tucked Abdul's notebook under her belt at the small of her back, thankful that she had worn a jacket that day.

Goran and Daris stepped out of Abdul's cramped apartment and walked to the street corner.

"We should get rid of Haya," Goran said to his brother. "You told Abdul you would get them to France; I'm worried that Abdul may have told her. And she may have told someone else. That is what women do."

Daris marveled at his brother's naivete and lack of foresight. *Of course Abdul had told his wife,* he thought. The knowledge was on her face, as clear as day, when they had shown up at her apartment two hours earlier. Abdul was not a stupid man. He may have thought that by telling his wife about France, she would be able to pressure Daris into keeping his promise. At one point, as she was speaking with the FBI agents, she had looked directly at him. He was equally convinced that she had not spoken of the secret to anyone. One slip could mean that the FBI would come for Daris, eliminating any chance of saving her son. Haya would stay quiet, of that he was certain.

"We will wait until the FBI people have gone, when no one will be watching," Daris said. "Then we will pick up the family for their journey. Sadly for them, the trip will be short."

Chapter 78

A week after their arrival in Istanbul, the members of the investigatory team convened at the US consulate, a massive fortress in the northern outskirts of the city. Following dozens of interviews, reviews of the few cameras near the crash scene, examination of the wreckage, postmortems on the drivers involved, and thorough probes into the financial records, political profiles, and social media histories of all concerned, there was nothing to suggest that the crash was anything other than a terrible accident. Cat was not convinced.

"What have you found out about this Daris character?" she asked.

One of the senior officers from the consulate responded, "He's from Bosnia, although he spends quite a bit of time here in Turkey. He appears to have found a calling helping Syrian refugees resettle; he even facilitates relocation to Bosnia for some. Our embassy in Sarajevo took note of all those trips and decided to take a look at him, but nothing stood out. According to their reports, he and his brother run a bakery and coffee shop. Supposedly his baklava is not to be missed. They import their pistachios from Gaziantep, which explains his frequent visits to Turkey."

"He supports this philanthropy with proceeds from a coffee shop and bakery? That seems a bit of a stretch."

"Like I said, Sarajevo has already checked him out, so that's what we have to work with. It's unclear how deep the dive was. I'll concede that it wouldn't be the first time that one of our missions missed the mark. So, if the Agency wants to pursue it, that's your prerogative. I just don't see anything that ties him to the crash."

Cat nodded, understanding the problem. There certainly was little to support State pursuing the matter further.

"Understood," she said quietly, turning her full attention back to the factual review of the case.

The tanker driver had fled Syria in search of a safe haven, had been an exemplary employee, had a wife and two sons, was educated, had no known ties to extremism, and was otherwise unremarkable.

George and Louise Burke, the couple Maggie was visiting, had lived in Istanbul for nine years. Originally the regional director for a multinational food conglomerate, George had become disenchanted with the company and resigned. He had found a failing seafood export business, purchased it, and grown it into a thriving, lucrative business. His wife, Louise, had once been a flight attendant for Pan Am and was a close friend of Maggie. Cat had met them on several occasions and liked them both. Delving into the couple's life and finances had revealed nothing that would paint George as a murderer or Louise as suicidal. And with George devastated by Louise's death, all agreed there was nothing suspicious in the relationship.

The BMW's driver, Pieter, was a longtime employee of the Burkes, having also worked for them in their previous posting to Johannesburg. While the Burkes were very generous with all their employees, they went to extra lengths with Pieter and frequently invited him to join them for dinner. The remainder of the security detail took the friendship in stride, regarding him as someone who was protective, highly capable, trustworthy, and whose character was above reproach.

The occupants of the Mercedes, a bank executive from Germany and his wife, and the driver of the Honda, a plant manager from Japan, were thoroughly investigated and found to be innocent victims in the crash.

Working with the available evidence and dozens of interviews, they reasoned that the problem with the new truck's starter may have been a contributing factor. Witnesses stated that after dumping the fuel load, the truck sat in the petrol station for at least ten minutes. Based on Abdul's anxiety about missing his son's appointment with the doctor, they theorized that he may have been in a rush and abandoned normal caution.

With no evidence to the contrary, those present agreed to classify the death of Maggie Marshfield as accidental, the result of the car in which she was riding having struck a fuel tanker pulling out of a petrol station. But in a room of intelligence agents and law enforcement investigators, the word *coincidence* hung like a dark cloud over the gathering. Despite their best efforts, they had been unable to determine any causal connection between the death of the original driver—or the original tanker's malfunction—to the explosion. Studying the faces of those seated around the table, Cat felt in good company; few appeared to be completely on board with the decision. In the end, however, all confirmed the finding.

After the meeting adjourned, Cat was headed out the door when she heard her name called. She recognized the voice at once and turned around, chiding herself for not having left the building sooner. Nate Carr was striding toward her, wearing his usual smug expression. As he walked by a group of young female office assistants, he slowed his pace, smiled, made eye contact with a shapely blonde, and winked at her. Cat rolled her eyes and waited.

When he reached her, Cat asked, "Been dipping your wand in the consular talent pool?"

"Always interested in someone who can make me stand up and salute."

"You're disgusting."

"And you've forgotten how to enjoy life's little pleasures. But enough chitchat. The team all agreed that Maggie Marshfield's death was accidental. You haven't shown us anything to the contrary, and ultimately, you concurred with the final assessment. May I assume you're done here?"

"You may assume whatever you like, but we all know that there is more to this story. One of these days, I'll find out what."

"It's over, Cat. There's nothing to find."

Cat gave him a feral grin. "You've been pushing that story from the beginning. Makes me wonder why. See you around, Nate."

She turned on her heel and walked out the door.

Chapter 79

Cat returned to the apartment and, as she did every night, checked for any disturbance of the furnishings or her belongings. The place seemed reasonably safe, but she had been unsettled ever since landing in Istanbul. As an accomplished practitioner of old-school tricks, Cat had positioned two hairs—just so—amidst the contents of her suitcase, prepared the floor near the door with a light and nearly undetectable dusting of powder at the door, and set a perfectly arranged stack of papers on the desk before leaving in the morning.

Such techniques were well-known among the senior members of the clandestine services—and mostly abandoned by those coming of age in the technology era. Foolish, however, was the person who underestimated her, because those methods were only part of her arsenal. An enthusiastic devotee of technology, Cat possessed a number of everyday items, such as the electric toothbrush in the bathroom and the phone charger plugged into the socket on the kitchen wall. Both served a dual purpose in that they were perfectly functional for their advertised use but also held tiny, motion-activated cameras that could livestream an intrusion.

Cat preferred using both systems—high-tech and no-tech—in partnership. The person who spotted one type might overlook the other. And on this day, she was right. Someone had been in the apartment, as evidenced by the faint footprint at the door and the displaced hairs in her luggage. But whoever it was must have found a way to compromise her electronics, and those of the apartment as well, because there were no recordings from the cameras—nothing to indicate there had been an intrusion.

Wondering if bugs had been planted, she searched each room, knowing that the effort was probably futile. Whoever it was, he must have state-of-the-art equipment that she would be unlikely to find.

She poured a good splash of vodka over two cubes of ice and took a long swallow. Savoring the burn, she could feel the warmth of the liquor doing its work, relaxing the tension as she set about packing for the trip home. It would be an early night; she and Paul were booked on the 6:00 a.m. flight to Washington.

The idea formed just as she was stuffing a pair of shoes in the bag. She picked up her phone, went outside to the courtyard, and dialed Rosalie.

"I wanted to thank you for the use of the flat," Cat said. "It's lovely."

"My pleasure," Rosalie replied. "I'm glad you liked it, especially under the circumstances."

"You speak Turkish, don't you?"

"Well, yes," Rosalie responded. "Not quite native level, but fluent enough."

"Would you be willing to take on a little project?"

"Of course. When?"

"How about now? Meet me at the café on the corner?"

"Give me fifteen."

Fourteen minutes later, Rosalie ordered a coffee as she took a chair across from Cat. They huddled at the table and Cat gave her a quick summary of the investigation. She pulled out her recorder and cued it to the first interview, explaining that they had gone to the fuel distribution center and talked with Abdul's manager and a mechanic who had talked with Abdul that morning.

Rosalie popped in the earbuds and listened attentively. On hearing the words of the mechanic, she stopped the recorder.

"I don't know if this means much," Rosalie said. "But the translator said the new truck failed because of a computer malfunction."

"Right."

"What the mechanic actually said was that the computer was fried. There's a difference."

Cat's eyes narrowed. "Like a power surge?"

"I don't know. Not my area of expertise. But he had to replace some of the electronics. And it sounds like he and the driver were pretty tight. He said he promised to take care of the truck, that the driver trusted him."

Rosalie listened to the interview with the original driver's wife and learned nothing of interest. When the recording from Abdul's apartment started to play, however, Rosalie's eyebrows shot up.

"What?" asked Cat.

"The men talking in Abdul's apartment ... who are they?"

"One is named Daris. He's from Sarajevo."

"Ah, that explains the language. They're speaking Bosnian."

That caught Cat's attention. "That makes at least two people from Bosnia. What are they saying?"

"The first man asked if the book had been found. The other told him not to speak of it."

Cat frowned. "This book? Abdul's notebook?" She held up the small green notebook she had lifted from the policeman.

Rosalie cocked her head. "You have his notebook? Should I assume the police misplaced it?"

Cat grinned. "Something like that."

"Ah," said Rosalie. "But no. I said *book,* but that's not exactly the right word. He definitely didn't say *notebook*; it's something more like *diary*. No, wait, wait, um ... *ledger*. That's it," she exclaimed. "*Ledger*."

"Ledger? Are you sure? This could be important."

"Yes! That's the accurate word. Sorry, it just wasn't coming to me."

Cat sat back, thinking. *Abdul had previously been an accountant. Was he doing work on the side? For whom? Daris? And where? Here in Turkey ... or in Bosnia? And where is the ledger?*

She rubbed her forehead. "We've officially closed the investigation, but ..."

Rosalie finished for her. "You can't get past the feeling that you've missed something. I know that feeling quite well."

"I'm flying back in the morning," Cat told her. "I'll have a couple of analysts take a look at all this, see what they think. And it will give me some time to clear my head."

"Sometimes it really helps to step away from it for a little while."

"True enough. If I end up wanting to dig a little more, I'll need help. What's your availability for a little contract work? I would pay you directly."

Rosalie lifted her eyebrows in surprise, then nodded. "I could do that."

"Good. But there are a couple of things you need to know." Cat told her about the intrusion in the apartment and that the electronics had been compromised.

"I suspect it's this DIA guy," she continued. "He's here on the team, but I'll bet my right arm that he's working another agenda. I just don't know what that is. Anyhow, I don't want him to know I'm still digging around. If he sees you, well ..."

"Got it. I'll be a ghost."

"Get a burner phone and send me the number, but not from your computer. If I'm right ..."

"Yeah. They've already killed seven people."

"Exactly. Be careful."

Chapter 80

October, Four Years Ago
Washington, DC

For Paul, the flight back to DC seemed interminable. He tried to busy himself by writing notes to the Istanbul staff, thanking them for their kindness during his stay.

Since arriving in Istanbul, he had barely spoken with George Burke. Inconsolable and unable to bear even the thought of being near anything that reminded him of Louise, George had checked into a hotel—length of stay undetermined. Paul had wanted to talk about the night before the accident, to learn about Maggie's final hours, to hear a story that made her laugh, to live her last hours through George's recollections. Instead, he had spent his time in Istanbul fighting demons, imagining the unimaginable. Sedatives had not helped; he'd awakened in delirium every night, sweat-drenched from a dream of Maggie screaming in terror and agony.

Five days after the accident, George had finally made arrangements for Paul to visit the house and collect Maggie's belongings. Paul had set about the task reluctantly, secretly wishing that he had asked someone else to do it. But as he packed her bags, he found the activity of folding her clothes both comforting and agonizing—her familiar scent still present.

Maggie's phone was gone, as was her camera, both lost in the fire. Her wedding ring, as well as the sapphire pendant she had worn day and night, had been recovered. They were safe in his carry-on, along with her laptop.

He felt as if he was mired in quicksand, flailing and sinking deeper into its clutch. He had read the report. The decision to declare Maggie's death as accidental should have come as a relief but had the opposite effect. He wanted, he *needed,* someone to blame. He glanced over at Cat, napping in the window seat beside him. While her signature was on the report, she had not spoken with him about it. They had known each other for a long time. She had something stuck in her craw.

After landing, she said, "I want to borrow Maggie's laptop."

Paul squinted, now more sure than ever that Cat had misgivings about the investigation. "What have you found?"

"Just a feeling that I can't explain. It's probably nothing."

For the first time in days, Paul wanted to laugh. When Cat said something was probably nothing, it invariably meant that something catastrophic was about to happen.

"You have her passwords, right?" Cat asked. They had both witnessed the cyber-havoc that ensued when a loved one died or became incapacitated and no one had the person's passwords. It made for its own special kind of hell.

"Yes," Paul said. "I'll give you access to her password generator. And you'll keep me advised about whatever you find?"

"That depends. Probably. Maybe."

Strangely, her noncommittal response comforted him. Maybe there was an answer—a way out of the abyss.

Chapter 81

October, Four Years Ago
CIA Headquarters
Langley, Virginia

Cat paid three expert translators—Arabic, Turkish, and Bosnian—to create transcripts of the recorded interviews and Abdul's notebook. While they worked, she went through her copy of the thick file on Maggie's death. She put sticky notes on the pages that she felt demanded another interpretation or further clarification. She compiled a document with her own thoughts and concerns about the seemingly coincidental death of the original driver, the computer problem in the scheduled truck, and the starter problem in the replacement truck.

A week later, with results in hand, Cat approached Dwayne and Cheryl Sykes. The two were a match in so many ways: same short height, same chunky build, same pale coloring, similar light brown hair—it was rumored that they used the same hairstylist—and the same towering intellect. She had known them for two decades and had enlisted their acumen on numerous occasions. They had a stellar reputation for insightful analysis.

"There's something there. I can feel it," Cat told them. "I can't put my finger on it, but my gut rarely fails me."

The couple looked at each other, a silent message being exchanged. There were limits—the investigative team had reached a conclusion, and that should be the end of it. But they respected Cat; her skills as an operative were legendary.

Cat pulled Maggie's computer from her shoulder bag and handed it to Dwayne. "Everything is here," she said, pressing a thumb drive into Cheryl's palm. "All my files and Maggie's passwords."

"We'll do it," Cheryl said. "But this takes a back seat to Agency business."

Cat nodded. "Understood. And thank you."

The call from Cheryl Sykes came a week later, suggesting that they meet for a drink after work. Cat proposed a nearby pub that was frequented by Agency personnel. Cheryl readily accepted.

"You found something," Cat said, sliding into the booth across from Cheryl and Dwayne. "Tell me."

Cheryl looked over to her husband and nodded. Dwayne cocked his head and studied Cat for a moment before speaking.

"All the coincidences certainly made us curious, but like you, we found nothing tangible. It's more about what we *didn't* find."

Cat sat up and asked, "What do you mean?"

"This Daris guy—his name is Daris Terzić, by the way—is not on anyone's radar. Yes, the folks in Sarajevo did a flyby on him, found him clean, and shoved his name in a drawer. We've checked with the friendly intelligence agencies and probed several nonfriendlies; there's not a whiff of interest."

"I was sure there was something there."

"It would be helpful if we had access to the missing ledger; it would give us something more concrete to go on. But, like you, we're uneasy about him, so we went ahead and opened a file and flagged his name. He flew out of Istanbul two days ago, back to Bosnia. He doesn't have much flight history, which leads us to think that he normally travels overland or by boat. For the ordinary person, that would be enough to grab our attention. But we think it makes sense if he's escorting refugees. We'll let you know if anything else turns up."

"Good," Cat said with a smile.

"The other thing we didn't find has to do with Maggie."

Cat's smile faded. "How so?"

"We checked her Google account. Location tracking on her phone was turned on, but there's no activity for her last full day in Sarajevo. Nor are there any pictures. We know that she primarily used a camera, rather than a smartphone, but she also had a daily routine of backing up her photos at night.

"Her activity then mysteriously restarts upon her arrival in Istanbul. Did her phone die? Did she just sit in her hotel room during that last day in Sarajevo? Doubtful. So, what are the odds that someone wiped her data versus this being just another coincidence? We're leaning heavily toward the former."

"Not everyone has the skills to erase data."

"Ohhh, very few have those skills. Whoever it was, they were good. *Very* good," Dwayne said. "And it begs the question of where Maggie went that day and what pictures she took. Someone doesn't want that information in your hands. Why? Did she see something? Or someone?"

Cheryl squinted, watching Cat's face and gauging her reaction. "You have someone in mind, don't you?"

Visualizing Nate from the DIA, Cat replied, "I do."

Cheryl frowned and said, "You're going to need someone with exceptional skills if you hope to learn more. Even then, recovering the data might be impossible. Of course, you probably know people, but we have a name—someone we trust. We can put you in touch."

Cat thought for a minute. "He's good?"

"*She's* the best," Cheryl said, handing Cat a slip of paper with a name and phone number.

Cat caught Cheryl's eye. "Biased thinking. I think I've met only one or two females from IT in my entire career." She shrugged and read the name on the note. "Melodie. Is she Agency?"

Dwayne smiled wolfishly. "Nope. NSA. You'll need a code word to contact her. We chose *Surfaris*."

Cat cocked her head, squinting in confusion. "Safaris?"

"No, *S-U-R-faris*. It's the band that played *Wipe Out* in the sixties, like what happened to Maggie's data."

Cat rolled her eyes. "Geeks," she muttered.

Chapter 82

When Cat tapped Melodie's number into her phone, the call went straight to a message announcing that the mailbox was full. She tried again the following day with the same result. Immediately after the third call, Cat's phone rang, with a blocked caller ID. She almost let it go, then answered.

The computer-generated voice on the other end said, "You called my number—three times."

Biting back her annoyance, Cat arched her left eyebrow and said, "I'm looking for some expert assistance with a special project. Mutual friends suggested I contact you."

"Mutual friends?"

Cat's impatience flared. While she had long been accustomed to code words and other tradecraft for establishing a person's identity, this woman was getting under her skin. "The Surfaris told me that you're very smart. Have I been misinformed?"

The robotic voice laughed. "I guess you'll have to judge that for yourself. You've been using a throwaway phone instead of your private number. I didn't recognize it, so I didn't answer."

"You have my private number?"

"Are you really surprised?"

Cat shivered, thinking, *NSA people are spooky.* She asked, "When can we meet?"

"How about now?

"Now?"

"Bingo. I have the day off. I took a drive over to Langley. I'll be at the gate in three minutes."

Seriously spooky, Cat thought.

Melodie was not at all what Cat expected. First, she was female, and second, she was a *black* female—an almost unheard-of combination in the male-dominated world of high-tech. She wore her hair in short natural twists, sported a bright pink headband, and had a sometimes-annoying habit of saying "Bingo," to confirm a statement. She was also stunningly smart. Cat liked her immediately.

Cat laid out the circumstances of her request, cocked her head, and asked, "Can you help?"

"That would depend on the skill of the person who wiped the data. DIA has some serious talent in its ranks, and if they were involved, as you seem to think they were, I'm not optimistic. I'll take a look and let you know."

Chapter 83

October, Four Years Ago
Istanbul, Turkey

Rosalie was ready to call it a day. There was nothing more to learn here. She glanced up at the window that had once been the home of a promising young accountant from Syria and stepped into the flow of pedestrians. She had only gone a few yards when she felt her phone buzz. She moved closer to the building and stopped. She pivoted, her eyes measuring her surroundings, as she lifted the phone to her ear.

Cat's voice was crystal clear, her words hurried. "I'd like for you to visit Abdul's widow," Cat said. "Try to find out if she knows anything about a ledger. Her son is sick, so a monetary incentive should work. Ten thousand is a good start, and take it up to fifteen if she balks. Even if she takes the ten, give her the full fifteen. I have a soft spot for sick kids."

Rosalie swallowed hard. "I wish I could," she responded. "I started watching her apartment yesterday and came back early today. I waited all morning and never saw anyone coming or going. About an hour ago, I finally knocked on a couple of doors. She's gone, moved out, four days ago. One of the neighbors thought the family was headed to France, to get medical treatment for the boy."

"France? Just like that? From worrying about money to a trip to France? And what about Daris?"

"No sign of him."

"France, huh? That means I'm going to have to burn a favor with one of my contacts at the DGSI," Cat growled, referring to the General Directorate for Internal Security, the French service tasked with monitoring terrorism and other threats against the country.

"I should have checked on them earlier," Rosalie said.

"No. I'm the one who told you to stay away. I didn't want you exposed. Frankly, I'm still concerned. I'm not sure who we're dealing with, and you still need to watch your back."

"I'm good. No one following me, nothing unusual has happened."

"Stay alert. I have a proposition for you. If I locate the widow, would you be willing to take a little trip?"

"To Paris? Well, I wouldn't mind a bit of shopping."

"Pack your bags. I'll call you to confirm."

Rosalie's mood lifted. She started humming the tune to "I Love Paris."

Cat chuckled in response. Hearing the sound, Rosalie smiled. Cat had probably not laughed since Maggie's death. *A good sign*, she thought.

As they said their goodbyes, Rosalie noticed the sky and realized the sun was setting. She knew she should get moving, but the long day had worn her out. She needed a jolt of caffeine. She glanced at her watch and then at the café just across the street, not twenty yards away. There were only a few customers: an elderly woman, a young couple, two men reviewing a folder of papers, and a bearded male in his early twenties—smoking a cigarette and deep into his phone conversation. He had been sitting there yesterday, too, making notes in what appeared to be a textbook. He was probably a student.

Rosalie was a keen observer of people, and nothing raised an alarm. The men and women at the café looked no different than the thousands of other people who lived, studied, and worked in Istanbul.

The man on the phone listened intently to the person on the other end. When he spoke, his voice was soft as a whisper.

"You should know that there is a woman," he said. "She has been asking neighbors about Abdul's family. She just got a phone call."

He waited for the response, and when it came, replied, "She will find nothing. We have searched every corner of the apartment. The ledger is not there."

Again, he waited for the other person to speak, then replied, "I will take care of her. I will find out what she knows."

He watched as the woman took a seat in the corner farthest from the street, away from the other patrons. He watched her lips form the syllables as she ordered. Something short, like coffee. He debated his next move. He could leave and try to find her car—he had seen her leave the previous afternoon—but he did not know where she had parked today. Better to follow her.

He gathered his books and stuffed them in the backpack, patted the knife under his sweater, and sat back to nurse the remaining drops in his cup.

The sidewalk had grown dark when Rosalie finally pushed her cup aside. Realizing she had lingered longer than intended, she nodded to the waiter and set out toward her car. Her step was lethargic, the coffee having done little to ease her fatigue. She was going to crawl into bed early tonight, sleep late in the morning, and pack for Paris when she woke up. Paris! It would be work, of course, but she would stay for a couple of extra days and enjoy the city.

She pressed the button on the key fob and heard the muted squawk as the lock released on the driver's side door. She pulled the door open and turned to slide into the seat. She never saw him coming. She felt a hard punch as something struck her breast, followed by a firestorm of blinding pain. When her mouth opened in a fearful reflex, the man planted his own mouth on hers, suffocating the scream. Her brain registered the coarse beard and the taste of ash mixed with coffee. She had a fleeting sense of recognition, realizing too late that she had made a terrible mistake in judgment.

As she tried to wrestle free, the man wrapped his arms around her in an immobilizing hug and pulled her with him into the car. Then his fist hit her jaw, and the world went black.

Chapter 84

October, Four Years Ago
CIA Headquarters
Langley, Virginia

Cat phoned her contact at the DGSI, a fellow intelligence officer she had known for more than twenty years, who promised a quick answer to her query. The response was not as speedy as she hoped, however, and it was three days before the email came in. His reply was a disappointment. There was no record of Haya, the truck driver's widow, entering France. There had been no young Arab boy admitted for treatment of lymphoblastic leukemia. Abdul Attia's wife and his two sons had vanished.

A video call from Melodie came moments later, and Cat steeled herself for another letdown. Melodie confirmed that the data had, indeed, been compromised. The source of the intrusion, however, remained a mystery. On a brighter note, she had made some headway in recovering part of the missing information.

"First," Melodie explained, "I was able to reconstruct a good portion of her whereabouts in Sarajevo. She connected to various cellular and Wi-Fi networks there. I did a bit of sleuthing and have come up with a reasonably good approximation of her path that last day. It looks like she was playing tourist—the tunnel that supplied the city during the siege in the early nineties, the old bazaar, the area they call 'Sniper Alley,' a café where I assume she ate lunch, several small shops, and another place where she presumably took a break for coffee. Nothing unusual in her movements. She seems to have gone back to the hotel late in the afternoon and stayed there until leaving for the airport in the morning."

"That's not like her. She would have found a good place for dinner. She wasn't a stay-in-the-room type."

"Maybe she was tired? Or not feeling well?"

"Maybe," Cat said, unconvinced. "Anything else?"

Melodie sighed. "One odd thing. I found an email in her drafts folder. Or to be more precise, in an online backup of the folder. It wasn't actually in her email. I'm sending it to you now."

Cat's email dinged. Her heartbeat accelerating, she opened the message.

> Miss your company, not as much fun going solo. When I get back, let's talk about this guy.

Cat knew her friend well. This was important. "Who's the guy?" Cat asked.

"That's the million-dollar question. There were no photos attached. There are several possibilities as to why, including that she never attached a photo to begin with. But the suspicious thing is that this draft was only in her backup and not in her actual email. She was a typical user—a zillion drafts and a zillion sent emails that she never cleaned out—so it's doubtful she would have singled this one out and deleted it."

"So someone else ..."

"Bingo," Melodie said softly.

Cat took a deep breath. "Where do we go from here?"

"With regard to her computer, I can't squeeze any more water out of that stone." Melodie paused for a moment, then asked, "Have you gone through all her belongings?"

Cat's brow knitted. "What do you mean?"

"There is another possibility," Melodie said. "People who sense danger will often try to squirrel things away—trying to protect important possessions, like jewelry or even notes to family. The behavior is not that uncommon. Have you done a thorough search of her belongings?"

"Her daypack, camera, and phone were lost in the fire. Aside from that, she had a small carry-on tote and a suitcase. Not much to go through. There was nothing unusual."

"I'm sorry, Ms. Powell. Truly. If you find anything else, I would be more than happy to take a look."

Cat stood and began to pace, trying to figure out if she had any moves left. So far, the entire investigation had been a series of dead ends. There had to be an answer somewhere.

She reached for the phone and dialed Rosalie, expecting her cheery voice. Instead, a man answered, identifying himself as an investigator with the Istanbul police. Cat's heart leapt into her throat.

"I am her friend," Cat told the man. "I live in America."

"And what is your name, please?" the man asked.

Cat paused for a half-beat, instantly aware that she would need to proceed cautiously. She recited a long-abandoned alias.

"I am sorry to deliver this news," the man said, his English surprisingly good. "Your friend was killed."

Cat's legs turned to rubber, and she grabbed the desk with her free hand. His words made no sense. The man on the other end of the line remained silent, and she could sense that he was gauging her reaction. She closed her eyes and prayed silently that this had no connection to Maggie's death. Her voice caught as she asked, "What happened?"

He responded with a question of his own. "How well do you know Madame Marchesani? She has many security devices at her home. Why? She is rich?"

Cat's mind worked quickly. It was almost always better to stick close to the story. "She was comfortable, but not wealthy. I believe that she occasionally conducted background investigations—mostly for Americans looking to hire people in Istanbul."

"I see. And nothing more?"

"Not of which I'm aware. Why are you asking these questions? What happened to her?"

"I regret to say that your friend did not have an easy death," the man said. "I want to find the person who did this."

Cat listened, confounded. *Not an easy death?* Her throat tight, she blurted out, "What do you mean?"

"It is rare that we see such a thing."

"What do you mean? What happened to her?" Cat realized that she was shouting.

"I'm sorry, madame, to tell you. Your friend was tortured."

Cat had no need to fake a reaction; her shock was real. *Tortured?* The sweat popped out on her brow, and her stomach roiled. She could barely manage to speak. "Tortured?" The word came out in a high-pitched squeal.

"Can you think of any reason why this would happen?"

Only one, Cat thought. Her voice quavering, she said, "I'm sorry. I don't know anything." Her mind was racing, wondering how to get more information without revealing her relationship with Rosalie. She asked, "Has her family been contacted?"

"We have notified the American consulate. They will contact her family."

That was good news. She could get more details from them. Something niggled at the back of Cat's brain. "I just talked with her three days ago," she said. "When did this happen?"

"Three days ago. This number, *your* number, is the last call in her phone log. You were the last person to talk with her. You must have some idea what she was doing. Was she investigating something for you?"

The man was hitting too close to home. "No, I'm sorry. I was thinking of visiting Istanbul. She had an apartment for rent, and she was going to check available dates. That's why I called back today."

"I see," he said after a long pause. "In that case, I am sorry for your loss."

Cat ended the call. In an explosion of pent-up grief, rage, and frustration, she swept her arm across her desk, sending a cascade of papers and electronics tumbling to the floor. Curling into the chair, she laid her head on her knees and sobbed.

Chapter 85

November, Four Years Ago
Toronto, Canada

Zlatan leaned back into the soft leather of the executive chair and tried to focus on the presentation on the screen. The presenter, a director in the finance department, was blathering on about risk analysis. The two computer geniuses in the room were red-faced, blaming the financial wizard for upper management's denial of their budget request. He wanted to scream at them, wanted to fire them all.

If the call from Sarajevo last month had unnerved him, the deaths of the women in Istanbul had nearly sent him over the edge. He had sensed—no, had *felt*—the earth tremble under his feet, their carefully laid cover beginning to unravel. Then there was the woman, Rosalie something, asking questions. He still did not understand her involvement, but sensed that the Americans must have discovered something. What could they possibly know?

Daris had streamed the interrogation live, and he had watched with a queasy combination of fascination and horror. The woman, after a long and difficult night, had revealed little. She was either one of the bravest liars he had ever seen, or she was exactly what she said she was: a nobody. Tuning out the argument going on in front of him, he mentally replayed what he had seen.

Daris had leaned into the woman, his face close to hers, asking softly, "Who sent you? What do they want?"

Her voice shaky, she had attempted to lie. "I ... I j-just wanted to know ... what happened, w-what happened to that family."

Daris had pressed the vegetable peeler against her shoulder and swept it down to her elbow. The woman's earsplitting scream dissolved into a flood of blood and tears and snot.

Leaning in again, Daris had whispered, "Tell me. Who sent you?" Then he had drawn the peeler down her arm again.

Through her agony, the woman had burbled that she had been hired by a friend of Maggie's. The friend was concerned about the sick boy; she wanted to help.

Watching the woman on the screen, he could have almost believed what she was saying. Americans could not abide the suffering of a child, unless the child just happened to be in the path of one of the bombs they routinely dropped from the sky.

The interrogation had gone on for some time, until she had finally described the friend as Maggie's college friend, now a marketing consultant. But she had given up the name too easily, which made him suspect that she was lying. The real name had taken longer, coming out only as they used the vegetable peeler to flay the strips of skin from her back.

"Karen Powers!" she had screamed through her sobs. "Oh God! No more! Karen Powers! Her name is Karen Powers! She lives in Boston!"

This time, he had believed her, thinking that all he had to do was find this Karen Powers. But thus far he had nothing. *Who is she? Marketing consultant or something else? How much does she know?* The last few weeks had been nerve-racking, every noise exaggerated, every stranger a threat, every second on the clock one step closer to the American FBI knocking on the door.

He shifted in his seat, forcing his attention back to the verbal brawl taking place in the conference room. A voice of reason was essential, at least for the duration of this meeting. There was simply too much riding on the outcome. But he had already felt the first stab of pain. It was no use; he had to get out of there.

"Gentlemen," he said, his voice carrying over the men's raised voices, "let's take thirty minutes, an hour, two hours, if you need it. But you'd better shove all this squabbling aside and pretend that you are competent. I want a solution on the table—one that you can both live with—and I don't care if it takes you all night."

He stood and strode out of the room, toward his office with its wraparound windows and commanding view of the city forty-two stories below. He wondered if anyone noticed he was sweating, if they could sense that his pulse was racing. His secretary jumped up as he approached, her face etched with worry. He waved her off and swung his office door closed behind him—too hard, the door rattling in its frame. He rotated the blinds on the interior of the office, shutting himself off from the heads that had popped up at the cubicles and desks nearby.

Flopping into his chair, he reached for the desk drawer and rummaged for the pill bottle. He swallowed two of the orange tablets, flushing them down with half a bottle of water, then pressed the remotes to close the exterior blinds and kill the lights. Anything to ward off the oncoming pain. He stumbled to the sofa, kicked off his shoes, lay down, closed his eyes, and tried to relax. Sometimes the migraines dissipated within fifteen minutes, but the ones that hit hard could last for hours.

Zlatan tried to remember when he had last eaten, when he had last had a full night's rest since the nightmare with Maggie Marshfield had started.

PART SIX

Cat

August, Present Day

Chapter 86

August 16
Sarajevo, Bosnia and Herzegovina

P at Desmond grilled the lamb kebabs while Cat steamed the rice and chopped the cucumber and tomatoes for the shepherd's salad. They spoke little, both digesting the horror of Toni Swanson's murder. Cat cleaned up the kitchen and set a pot of coffee to brew while Pat attended to some urgent CIA business. At about nine, Pat poked her head around the corner, said good night, and disappeared.

Cat hunched over the counter, waiting for the coffee to finish its cycle. She drummed her fingers on the counter, her impatience spilling over. *I've been chasing answers for four years and hitting walls at every turn. Now three women are dead—Maggie, Rosalie, Toni. How many others? Someone here is responsible—someone who can tell me why he held their lives in such little regard. But even if I find him, is there any measure of justice that can atone for the lives lost?*

At last, she pulled herself from her reverie, poured the coffee, and sat, opening the tablet computer on the table in front of her. *Here we go.*

Pat had said that many of the bakery employees were immigrants from Syria. In Istanbul, during the investigation into the accident that had killed Maggie, they had encountered a man from Bosnia who helped Syrian refugees. The man had been present—as had Goran—when she and Wayne had interviewed the widow of the truck driver. Cat remembered the man as someone who took charge, whose authority seemed to extend over everyone present in that apartment. *What the hell was his name? Started with a D.*

The official files could only be accessed from either a secure CIA workstation or her agency-provided laptop. Since she had left her laptop in

France, she would need to visit the embassy to view them. But she had kept her personal files—her own notes and observations. Technically, these were files that should have been turned over to the Agency at the end of an operation. But she had kept them, knowing that sometimes the most insignificant piece of information could later be the key to a solution.

She kept these files online, on a heavily encrypted platform that her security-conscious team had recommended. After authenticating, she opened the folder labeled *Blue*—named for the Blue Mosque in Istanbul and her emotional state after Maggie's death. Most were written in her own shorthand, a nearly illegible scribble that others would have found difficult to decipher. She scrolled until she found the pages she wanted:

> DARIS, BOS, Eng fluent. Mich grad. Rec w others (2 BOS? more?) Ledger not yet found. ?? Contents ?? Where is it ??

That's right. His name was Daris, from Bosnia, very fluent English and a degree from the University of Michigan. The recorder had captured a conversation that Daris was having with another man. *What was his last name? Did I ever hear it? And where is that mention of the bakery?*

She kept scrolling, and there it was.

> Daris Terzić. BAKERY w bro.

Terzić! Bro! My God, she thought as the pieces popped into place. *Daris is Goran's brother. How did I miss it?*

She closed her eyes, reliving the visit to Abdul's widow in Istanbul. Daris had been sitting there, dark-haired, dark eyes, black turtleneck, conversing with several other men, all deferring to him. Arrogant, outspoken, contemptuous—until her FBI colleague, Wayne, had pushed back. She replayed the encounter, remembering it distinctly. The man she now knew to be Goran had said something to Daris, and had been harshly rebuked. And she recalled that their translator had not offered the complete conversation. Rosalie had caught the discrepancy, the mention of the ledger, and had also added some clarity to their interview with the mechanic—the man responsible for Abdul's truck.

She scrolled back, reading through the entire file, taking a fresh look at the events surrounding Maggie's death—a look four years removed from the trauma. When she came to Rosalie's translation of the mechanic's comments, she stood up, her heart beating wildly.

> Abdul tight w/mech & trusted him.

Abdul and the mechanic were tight, Abdul had trusted him. Of course! The mechanic has the ledger.

She glanced at her watch: 2:00 a.m. Wrapped up in the old notes, she had lost track of the time. With a six-hour time difference, it was 8:00 p.m. in DC. She pecked out a quick note to Melodie.

> ASAP Get Arnie and Adrian here with equipment. Send Marc and Jones to Istanbul. On arrival have them contact me for instructions.

Cat woke up shortly after eight, groggy after only five hours of sleep. She fumbled for the phone, wondering when the team would arrive, and squinted at the message from Melodie.

> Borrowed a jet, Dep 0300 local, Arr 1800 your time, fully equipped. J LHR→ and M CDG→ will arrive IST approx 1230 your time and will call on arrival.

The team would be here at six this evening. Jones and Marc were flying to Istanbul—Jones from London's Heathrow Airport and Marc from Charles de Gaulle in Paris. They would be in the air until at least noon.

There was a second text, from Pat, saying that she had gone to her office and would check in around lunchtime. The plan was to have dinner delivered for this evening, but she needed to know when and how many. Keys to the second condo, which could sleep six in a pinch, were in the kitchen.

Cat tugged at her sleep mask and buried her head under the covers. *Just two more hours!* She lay there for fifteen minutes, trying to lull herself back to sleep. The effort was futile. Her mind had started racing with the first text and was not going to stop anytime soon.

She pulled on her jeans and a comfortable Henley shirt and stumbled into the kitchen, started a pot of coffee, and fired up the tablet. After taking a moment to focus her thoughts, she began typing.

The phone vibrated at a quarter past one. *Jones.*

"Hang up," Cat said as she answered. "I'll call you back."

She hurried into Pat's secure tent and closed the hatch, then used Pat's phone to dial Jones. When he answered, she asked, "How was your flight?"

"Uneventful," he answered. "I'm here with my new friend from France. What's the assignment?"

"You'll need to rent a car and go visit a mechanic at a petrol distributor outside the city, today if you can manage it. If he has gone home for the day, get his address from the manager. I believe the mechanic has something we need—a ledger—but do not mention that to anyone other than the mechanic. If anyone asks why you're looking for him, tell them that it's in regard to the accident four years ago that killed the American women. Tell them that some questions have come up about the circuit board that failed. That's all they need to hear."

"I'm assuming my friend is my translator," Jones said.

"Correct. He may be rusty, but he'll be good enough. And remember that you have no authority there, so you need them to be cooperative. You know the drill: be friendly but intimidating, but without being a bully. I'm sure the mechanic has the ledger. Your job is to convince him to give it to you. Talk to the facility manager. If it's the same guy that I talked to, you'll find him helpful. I've sent the name of the company and the name of the mechanic to your Tor box."

"What's this about, Cat?"

"Maggie's death was no accident," said Cat. "I'll fill you in when you get here. And Jones? Don't let your guard down and don't trust anyone. People have died because of that ledger. Once you have it in your hands, take the first flight to anywhere that will get you out of there and closer to here."

Jones could hear the tension in her voice—could picture her sitting on a desk, right foot tapping the floor, right hand squeezing the life out of the phone while the left drummed its fingers on the desktop. "Got it," he said. "I'll be in touch."

Cat disconnected, stared at the phone in her hand, and finally made the call that she had long avoided.

Paul listened in stunned silence as Cat told him everything.

Finally, she said, "I would never have knowingly put Maggie in danger. The first job was a favor—a one-off. Then she asked for more. I think she wanted to make a contribution to her country, like we try to do. It was always simple stuff."

"Until Marc Bishop," Paul said flatly.

Cat hung her head. "Until Marc. That should have been simple, too—and then it wasn't."

In a hollow voice, Paul said, "You should have told me."

Cat winced. "Probably. I'm so sorry, Paul," she said.

"She never told me either; that's hard to take. Just find the bastards who killed her, and we'll go from there."

Chapter 87

August 17
Istanbul, Turkey

Marc and Jones found a locally branded rental car counter, filled out the paperwork, and walked away with the keys to an economy-size Hyundai.

"Who's driving?" asked Jones.

"I had a head injury some years back," said Marc. "Occasionally I get the brake and the gas confused. I think it might be better if I navigate and you drive."

Jones turned to look at Marc, thinking he was joking, but one glance told the story. Marc was as serious as a mongoose facing a cobra. He decided to make light of the admission. "Well, your excuse is better than the one I was about to make up. I'll drive—assuming the car is big enough."

Trailing behind Jones, Marc marveled at his size—and at the way travelers in the airport instinctively moved out of his way. He was an intimidating figure. At six-four and just shy of three hundred pounds, the man was the size of a defensive tackle in the NFL—and still impressively fit.

They squeezed into the car, Jones whining about the confined space, and set the destination in the GPS system. They headed out of the airport, and within minutes, hit a wall of traffic.

"Driving in Istanbul is like swimming in molasses," said Marc. "One of the worst places in the world."

"Probably in the same bracket with Mumbai, Manila, and Bangkok," said Jones. "Nothing remotely pleasant about driving in any of them."

"Oh, if you've driven in Manila, Istanbul is going to be a cakewalk," laughed Marc.

The ten-mile trip to the fuel distribution center took thirty-five minutes. By the time they pulled abreast of the facility's security post, Jones's patience had worn thin. They showed their credentials to the guard, who picked up his phone and gestured for them to pull the car to the shoulder.

Ten minutes later they spotted a small utility vehicle speeding toward them. A short, skinny man hopped out of the driver's seat, introducing himself. Marc's grasp of the language was still strong and he turned to Jones.

"He thinks we are here for some sort of inspection. He wants to know who we are."

"Tell him we have a few more questions about the accident four years ago."

Marc translated. The manager paled, and then let out a torrent of Turkish.

"He said he is still haunted by that crash. He is worried that we have come to take him to jail," Marc said.

"Reassure him. Tell him we just have questions for the mechanic who was on duty that day," Jones said.

The manager's eyebrows shot up, followed by another torrent of words. Then he motioned for them to follow him.

"He thinks we are here to arrest the mechanic," Marc said.

It was Jones' turn to look surprised. "Really? Everyone thinks that they're headed to the slammer. Are they haunted by guilt? Well, at least we know the mechanic still works here. Look, when we get inside, we need to talk to the mechanic alone. Figure out how we can get this guy out of the way for a few minutes."

"Oh, that should be easy. I'll just have a seizure."

Jones's jaw dropped.

"I've had practice," Marc said. "Sometimes the brain problem comes in handy. Get him to run to the car. My pills are in the little red bag on the floorboard."

"What? He doesn't understand English."

"You'll figure it out. Just make sure you catch me."

As they entered the maintenance bay, the manager pointed at a man dressed in slate-gray coveralls. The man turned, and Jones saw a flash of fear in his eyes.

Friendly, Jones reminded himself. He held up his hands, signaling that he meant no trouble. He began asking routine questions, with Marc translating. Five minutes into the conversation, the men were becoming annoyed—they had answered the same questions four years ago.

Marc was halfway through his next question when his words came out in a slur and his eyes lost focus. His right hand started to tremble, quickly followed by his leg. He collapsed into Jones's arms.

Both the mechanic and the manager froze in place, horrified by the sight of the trembling man. Jones cradled Marc in his arms and lowered him to the ground.

Jones tossed the car keys to the manager, shouting, "Get his pills." Unable to understand what was being said, the man's face was a mask of confusion. Jones pointed at the keys, pantomimed taking a pill, drew a rectangle with his index fingers, and added the motion of grabbing a handle at the top of the rectangle. Then he pointed in the direction of the car and yelled, "Go!" The manager seemed to grasp the meaning and took off running. Jones waited until the man was out of sight and then said to Marc, "He's gone."

Marc calmly rolled over, looked up at the mechanic, and told him they had come for the ledger.

All the color washed out of the mechanic's face as understanding set in.

"I knew this day would come," he said. "I found it a week after the crash. Abdul was a good man. I knew he was in trouble. Those Bosnians were up to no good."

The mechanic walked over to a large tool cabinet, removed the bottom drawer, then lifted the false bottom. Inside was a well-used, bound book with a dark blue leather cover. He handed the book to Jones.

"I am glad to be rid of it," he said.

Jones quickly realized that he could not simply walk out of the facility with the book under his arm. He lifted his shirt and sweater, then stuffed the book behind his back, under the waistband. He pulled his shirt and sweater down and looked down at Marc, who nodded his approval.

"Thank you," Jones said, nodding at the mechanic.

The manager ran in moments later, the red bag in his hand. He held it out to Jones, who extracted the pill bottle and feigned placing a tablet in Marc's mouth.

"Thank you," he said. "He will be fine in just a few minutes. We just need to get him to the car." Again, he pantomimed, two fingers for walking and two hands for gripping the steering wheel. Marc, pretending to be groggy, gradually sat up, and then stood with the men's assistance.

Five minutes later, Jones and Marc were in the car. Jones drove until no longer in sight of the building, then pulled over.

"Don't ever do that to me again," he said, getting out of the car. "Scared the shit out of me. I couldn't tell if you were faking it or if it was real. Now, take a look and tell me what's so all-fired important about this book."

Jones pulled the book from behind his back, handed it to Marc, and got back behind the wheel. As he pulled onto the road, Marc began thumbing through the pages of the ledger.

"We're lucky. This is written in Arabic, not Turkish," Marc said. He spent a few minutes studying one section of the ledger and added, "My accounting skills are rusty, but I think we just hit the mother lode."

After spending another half hour in traffic, they were back at the airport, returning the car. The agent looked at them curiously, wondering why anyone would rent a car for just three hours.

Winking at Jones, Marc turned to the rental agent. "Too much traffic," he said. "We're going to take a bus or a taxi."

They went up to the Turkish Airlines counter and booked the next flight to Sarajevo, a nonstop departing at 6:05 p.m. Tickets in hand, Jones sent the encrypted email to Cat.

Got it. C U tonight 8:00

Chapter 88

August 17
Sarajevo, Bosnia and Herzegovina

Wrapped up in the old files, Cat lost track of time and almost jumped out of her skin when the door buzzer sounded. She peeked through the viewer and scowled. Her team was here—and her sister, Lindsey, was with them. They stacked their substantial load of baggage in the foyer, leaving only a narrow path to the door.

Cat embraced her sister, but was annoyed that she had come. Lindsey's near-fatal encounter with terrorists had resulted in a long, difficult, and ongoing recovery. She still needed rest and care—at home, not here. She held her sister at arm's length and laid down the law.

"There is probably no way I can convince you to go home, so I'll just set the ground rules." She looked around the room, ensuring she had the attention of all. "Lindsey does not leave this apartment, for any reason," she said. "Admin tasks only."

Glaring at Cat, Lindsey crossed her arms over her chest. "I'm doing great. It was my decision to come," she said.

Not wanting to engage in the tussle between the two sisters, the other members of the team held up their hands in surrender and sank into the sofas. Adrian, Lindsey's beau from the FBI, ran his fingers through his dark hair and suppressed the urge to laugh. Lindsey busied herself with setting up a private network for the team to use.

Arnie, the cousin of Cat's husband, had earned his position on the team through his genius in electronics. He spotted the coffeepot and helped himself to a mug, then asked, "Got anything to eat?"

Ignoring the question, Cat asked, "Why was Jones in London?"

Arnie's eyebrows shot up. "Nice to see you, too," he said. "Flight was long, got no sleep on the plane, and we're famished."

Cat's brow creased. She took a long, deep breath. "Glad you're here, glad you're rested, food is coming. Now, what was he doing in London?"

Arnie was bemused. "Visiting Smith's soon-to-be-married daughter. She asked Jones to walk her down the aisle."

Cat had forgotten about the upcoming nuptials. Her face softened, her lips curling into a bittersweet smile. "That's really wonderful," she said.

Smith and Jones had been colleagues for over thirty-five years, and Cat thought of them as family. She could only imagine how proud Smith would have been, could only imagine how his heart would have swelled. His death three years ago still left an ache in her heart, and her hatred of his killer ran deep.

She pulled herself out of her reverie as Pat, laden with food parcels, opened the front door. The team, drawn by the heavenly aroma, hurried to help.

"The bearer of dinner is Pat Desmond," announced Cat, introducing the station chief to the team. "This is her place. Adrian can stay here with Lindsey. There is another apartment two streets down where the rest of you can stay for a couple of days. Since we are here officially, we will read Pat into this operation. But let's try not to burn her if it goes south."

Arnie asked, "Why is Jones in Istanbul?"

She turned to face him. "I had Jones meet up with Marc Bishop. I've asked him to join us on this operation."

At the mention of Marc's name, Arnie choked on his coffee, dumbfounded. Marc had lived in his Boston townhouse for almost fifteen years. He had never revealed any details of his past life or given any hint that he had been an operative.

Adrian shot a questioning glance at Arnie and asked, "Who is Marc Bishop, and why is he involved?"

"Let's all adjourn into Pat's office. It's cramped, but the facilities are better," Cat said.

The team followed her into the office and squeezed into the tent. Glancing at Pat, Cat wordlessly begged forgiveness for appropriating the woman's private space. Pat merely shrugged, as if to say, "It goes with the territory."

"Marc Bishop is one of the primary reasons you are all here today," Cat said, "Years ago, he was a CIA operative working undercover in Kurdistan. A sniper tried to assassinate him. He still has some memory issues. This isn't ordinarily a problem, but you need to be aware. He was an exceptional operator and has been living a secret life ever since the attack. You can trust him to keep cool and keep quiet—just ask Arnie."

Arnie studied his shoes, mentally kicking himself. He had, over time, picked up on some of Marc's challenges, concluding that the man had been forced out of the CIA due to some medical condition. He was comfortable with not knowing the details, certain that Marc would share them when he was ready. That time had never come. Marc had been a closed book, and Arnie had never pried.

Looking up at Cat, Arnie spread his arms wide. "Man, I never had a clue."

Cat spoke again. "On the day Marc was injured, he overheard a man speaking a language he did not understand. He became obsessed with trying to figure out what he had heard. He was convinced it held the key to why someone wanted to kill him, so I put him with some analysts at Langley. Turns out the language was Serbian. Since then, he has studied the language and become quite fluent. He knows Bosnian, too."

Gabe blurted out, "Aren't they the same?"

"I'm told that they are very similar—speakers of one can easily understand the other. But they are classified as separate languages. Beyond that, I've no idea."

Adrian was not satisfied. "Why not just hire a translator?"

Cat hesitated. If she started any piece of the briefing now, it would not stop. Before she went down that path, Jones and Marc needed to be present. Everyone needed to hear the same message, the same questions, the same answers.

"I will explain everything once Jones and Marc arrive," she said. "They are scheduled to land at eight. In the meantime, we are going to proceed with dinner. You can eat now, or stash your gear and come back. Whatever you do, be sure to save enough for Jones and Marc. It's been a very long day for them, too."

Chapter 89

The Turkish Airlines flight carrying Jones and Marc landed ahead of schedule. The pair wound their way through government formalities in record time and arrived at the apartment before nine. After introducing Marc to the team, Cat nudged Jones and led him into the kitchen. He handed her the ledger, and while piling food on his plate, offered his assessment of the encounter with the mechanic in Istanbul.

"No problems at all," he said in a hushed voice. "The guy seemed relieved to be rid of that book. I think it had been eating at him for a long time."

"Did you have a look at it?"

"No, but Marc did. He is not sure what everything means, but feels certain that we will find it of interest. He called it the 'mother lode.' I'm not sure what that means."

"So, an accountant—one who is fluent in Arabic—would be helpful?"

"Correct. But it will also require some sleuthing. Some of the names and places are in some kind of code, like using the letter 'A' for Aleppo or an alias for someone's name. So, you're going to need help with that part, too."

Cat flinched. "Always something," she said.

"By the way," Jones added, "I don't know Marc's history, but his performance today was Oscar-worthy."

She grinned. "Oh yeah, he's something else. Now grab your food, and let's get this meeting underway."

Pat initiated the videoconference with the stateside team, Paul from his office at the State Department in Washington, and Melodie from her NSA office in Ft. Meade, Maryland.

Now or never, Cat thought. She took a deep breath and said, "Earlier tonight, I told you that we would be joined by Marc Bishop. You asked me why. I came to Sarajevo because of recently discovered information about Maggie Marshfield. Marc is here because there is a connection between him and Maggie. And I am convinced that the connection is central to her death and central to the crash of Transoceanic 367—and that the answers to both are here."

After letting the shock of her pronouncement wear off, Cat spent the next ninety minutes explaining the timeline and the relationship between seemingly random events. She started with the weapons-for-money deal that Marc had witnessed, Maggie's meetings with Marc, and how she now believed those meetings had led to the downing of the Transoceanic aircraft—a plane that Maggie and Marc should have been on.

Gabe asked, "As I recall, Maggie got rerouted. That's why she wasn't on the airplane. What about Marc?"

Cat almost smiled at that. Gabe was so perceptive. She said, "He was booked on the flight. When they were delayed until the following day and Maggie was rerouted, we canceled Marc's reservation and sent him down to the air base at Ramstein. I felt that a US base was more secure than a hotel in Frankfurt. He was there for several days, then hopped on an Air Force transport back to the States. But the airline screwed up—his name was never taken off the passenger list."

Turning to look at Marc, Gabe said, "So you've actually already died twice. Once in a hail of bullets and another time in an airplane crash over the North Atlantic. Man, you need to find another line of work!"

Marc chuckled. "I thought I had—and then Cat called."

The team laughed at that. When the noise subsided, Arnie asked Marc, "Why were you going back to the States?"

Marc pointed at Cat. "Ask her."

Cat's cheeks puffed, and she blew out a grunt of resignation. *Here we go,* she thought. She told them about Marc's photographs and the meetings with Maggie, the murder of the courier, and the arrangement for Marc and Maggie to bring the negatives back to the States.

"Maggie had told me that the photos were not great quality, so I was eager to get the negatives into the hands of our own technicians. When the flight was delayed, I arranged for a courier. Unfortunately, he died in the crash."

Marc held a large manila envelope over his head and waved it. "But I kept copies of the photos," he said.

Adrian's face wrinkled up like a Shar-Pei puppy. "So your theory is that someone took down an airplane just to kill Maggie and Marc and destroy a bunch of old photos? Seems a bit of a stretch."

"Not just someone," Cat answered. "I believe it was a Transoceanic flight attendant named Michael Cantrell."

She explained how Michael had sought out Maggie on several occasions, how he had seen her with Marc, and that he had the means and opportunity to plant the bomb.

Adrian pressed further. "And yet he was on the airplane when it crashed? Is there any evidence that he was manufacturing bombs? Was he suicidal?"

Cat suppressed a smile, secretly pleased at his persistence. He was like a bloodhound, following the scent—wherever it led—until he discovered the truth.

"I take your point," she said. "But there is more to this story. Yes, he was listed on the flight manifest, but like many of the others on the plane, his body was never found. You have to consider the era—things were much more loosey-goosey back then. He was a crewmember. He knew his way around airplanes and airports. I believe that he got off that airplane, without being noticed, before it left the gate."

Gabe asked, "But why? If there was nothing in his background to invite suspicion, what's his motive?"

This was the part Cat dreaded: owning up to her unwitting part in the catastrophe.

"I cannot answer to the motive. But the background raises questions. He was once an asset of ours—in Bosnia," she responded. "In exchange for his information—and it was very good information—we rewarded him with a US passport and christened him with the name of Michael Cantrell."

She expected a barrage of questions, but all sound in the room evaporated, the team shocked into silence. She quickly moved on.

"Clyde Banks, whom some of you knew, was the only one who knew Michael Cantrell's real name. A year and a half before the airplane went down, Clyde came to me, saying that the asset had gone dark, and he had made the assessment that Michael must be dead. During that time in Sarajevo, the population was bombed continuously—much of it directed at civilians. The loss of life was staggering, so we could not dispute Clyde's logic. Still, as a cautionary measure, we put a watch on the passport. If the passport was presented at a US port of entry, I would be contacted. Since I never received a notification, the premise of the man's demise was never questioned.

"Later, we discovered that a computer administrator in Immigration illegally removed the alarm tag. Michael Cantrell entered the country, unchallenged, two weeks later. The computer guy died of lung cancer shortly thereafter, with his family receiving a hefty life insurance payment for $250,000. Turns out the insurance company was a shell company within a shell company within a shell company. And it issued only one policy—to the computer guy. I considered going after the money, but the man had two kids in college, a mortgage on the house, and twenty years of presumably loyal service until he got sick, so what was to be gained? It was not the family's fault that Dad had made a terrible decision."

Adrian glared at her. While he had been a youngster at the time of the Transoceanic crash, the FBI's failure to find those responsible still loomed large. His voice was harsh as he said, "Never mind the questions it would raise. Is that why you never reported any of this to the Bureau?"

She leveled her gaze at him. "To be perfectly clear, Adrian, I did not know any of this until months later. When I found out, I called the lead investigator at the Bureau. In the course of that conversation, I gave him Michael's name—spoon-fed it to him, as a matter of fact. But they had already investigated Michael Cantrell and found nothing tying him to the crime. And then, I reported the matter internally. The decision was made to keep the information in-house. It's complicated."

"Lies usually are," Adrian countered bitterly.

Cat blinked again, and her eyebrows shot up. Packed with eight bodies and too few chairs, the tent had become hot and uncomfortable, and the occupants were becoming short-tempered. She tilted her head to the side and squinted, her eyes hard. When she spoke, her voice was steel.

"I understand your anger." she said. "It was not our finest hour. But we cannot undo the past; we can only try to correct mistakes that were made. And right now, I could use your help in finding Michael Cantrell, because I know that he bombed that airplane. That one deliberate act is at the epicenter of everything I am sharing with you today."

Adrian wrinkled his nose, as if confronted with a foul odor, and then sighed. "Alright," he said, biting down his anger and offering a small nod. "We take the cards we're dealt."

Cat's head gave a small shake, her frustration evident. "I've had an analyst looking for Michael since a few months after the crash. He simply vanished."

She told them about Marianne Riel, who had spent the remainder of her CIA career looking for Michael Cantrell.

"As Marianne was nearing retirement," Cat said, "she kept her eyes open for someone to continue the search. She zeroed in on an analyst named Consuela Calderon, who is bright, extremely tech-savvy, and a whiz with facial recognition software. I remain hopeful that he will be found."

Cat thought back to her first meeting with Consuela, when the mere mention of locating a suspect in the bombing of an American aircraft had made the young woman shiver with excitement. Cat's eyebrows had gone up, but so had her expectations for finding Cantrell. *Any day now,* she mused.

"He could really be dead, you know," Gabe observed.

She shrugged and said, "Possibly, but I don't think so."

Adrian asked, "So, how is this tied to Maggie's death?"

"I went to Istanbul, with Paul, after the accident," Cat explained. "I met with the widow of the truck driver who hit Maggie's car. There were also two men there, speaking in Bosnian. I talked to the one who seemed to be the alpha dog. The story was that he was helping Syrian refugees find work—sometimes in Bosnia. The truck driver was one of them.

"When Lindsey found that SD card in Maggie's bag and sent me one of the photos, I recognized the face. He was one of the men at the widow's apartment in Istanbul. But the photo was not taken in Istanbul. It was taken here, in Sarajevo, at a coffee shop. His name is Goran Terzić, and he owns the coffee shop and a bakery. His brother, Daris, is the alpha dog who was with him in Istanbul.

"And there is another man, a local asset of the CIA station here, who I believe to be involved. His name is Mirko. I met with him today, and there is something about him that just seems off."

Her nose twitched, and she gazed up at the ceiling, as if seeking the answers there. "Interestingly, the minute our meeting ended, this Mirko guy went straight to the coffee shop. He picked up the owner, Goran, and they drove out of town and disappeared into the hills."

Cat handed the photos to Adrian and said, "The photo of Daris is from the Sarajevo station's files. While I have not seen him, that does not mean he's not here."

Adrian studied the faces intently before passing the pictures to Jones.

Cat then told them about the conversation she had recorded in Istanbul regarding a missing ledger, and how the dead driver had been an accountant in his native Syria.

"I hired a woman to try and track it down. She was tortured and killed while trying to find it. That told me the book was important, but it was only yesterday that I finally realized where the ledger might be. As a result of Jones and Marc visiting Istanbul today, the book is now in our hands.

"There is one last thing you need to know about."

Cat recounted how she had decided to play the part of a photojournalist as a cover story for visiting the coffee shop, and that she had borrowed another woman's press badge.

"I snapped a number of photos. I unknowingly captured two GRU officers—a man and a woman, sitting at separate tables. The woman was perched, all nice and cozy, across from a guy who works over at DIA. Was it a planned meeting or a chance encounter? I don't know. We're looking into that. But the woman who owned the badge was murdered later that night, and her camera was stolen."

She finished by issuing a warning. "These are extremely dangerous people. Don't let your guard down for even a second."

Adrian stroked his chin, thinking, and said, "There are a lot of bones there. A little skimpy on meat ..."

"You're right," interrupted Cat. "But all these bones belong to the same skeleton. We just have to flesh it out."

Adrian waited for her to finish and said calmly, "I was going to say that I get it. I see how it ties together. Where do we start?"

Cat rubbed the back of her neck, exhaustion creeping in. She glanced around the tent and stopped at Marc. He looked as if he had seen a ghost.

"Marc?" she asked. "Are you okay?"

"Mon dieu!" he shouted. "This is him! The man who bought the weapons on the day I was shot!"

Cat gaped at the photo in Marc's hand: *Mirko*.

Chapter 90

August 18
Sarajevo, Bosnia and Herzegovina

Cat, puzzling over the extent of Mirko's involvement, found sleep elusive. Having compared the two photographs of Mirko, one from two decades earlier and one from yesterday, she could not be certain that they were the same man. Marc, however, had been adamant. He pointed out that in his old photos, the man buying the weapons held a clipboard in his right hand and a pen in his left. In the photos Cat had taken, Mirko wore a watch on his right wrist. Ergo, Mirko was left-handed. Marc had looked deep into Cat's eyes and held them, intent on convincing her.

"This is the guy. It's him. Trust me," he had said.

She had assigned Melodie two tasks: first, to analyze the two photos, and second, to perform a deep dive on Mirko's background. If Marc was correct, then Mirko had been acting a part at the Sarajevo station—reading from an unknown party's script. While Mirko had not been privy to any classified data, he had been an asset that the station trusted. They would now have to reexamine all the information he had provided over the years. The revelation was not sitting well with Pat Desmond.

Cat finally tossed the bedcovers aside and stepped into the shower. She leaned her head against the tiled wall, closed her eyes, and let the spray of water work its magic. *Who was behind the weapons deal? Probably not Bosnia. They simply were not sufficiently funded, organized, or well-connected. Who would have realized the greatest benefit if Bosnia had been overrun by the Serbs?*

She pumped a shot of pale-blue shower gel onto the loofah and snorted at its label: *Caspian Breeze*. The Caspian Sea might conjure images of beaches and pristine waters, but the reality was far different. The Caspian was a cesspool of industrial and nuclear waste, raw sewage, and by-products of oil extraction and refining, generated primarily by the former Soviet countries that, along with Iran, shared its shorelines. She would not put even a toe in that water. She worked the gel into a lather and began scrubbing her back, then froze. *The Soviets.*

Certain factions within the former Soviet Union had been infuriated by the dissolution of the bloc in 1990, including many of Moscow's elite. Loss of pay, position, power, and prestige had driven an already corrupt system into even greater criminal enterprise—and they had focused their blame on the West. Under the guise of maintaining friendly relations, Russia had been undermining Western interests ever since.

She vaguely recalled instances in which the Bosnians had accused the Americans of supplying the Serbs with weaponry, with the US government vehemently denying the charges. *Had Russia actually purchased American weapons and used them against the citizens of Sarajevo? Had they really gone that far?* Cat let out a long, perturbed sigh. *Of course they had. Is there proof? Good luck with that. So how had they enlisted Mirko to help? And why him?*

The shower offered no more answers. She turned off the water, wrapped herself in a towel, and sat at a small desk by the window. She had roughed out a plan for the team, but now there were questions about Mirko that needed to be addressed. She remembered that, during their meeting, Mirko had mentioned that other local bakeries had failed while Sretna Kafa had thrived, that there had been some animosity. That was good, she decided. Angry people often had loose tongues. But all this had happened a long time ago. Would anyone remember the circumstances? Yes, she thought. The failures would have left emotional baggage in their wake.

She stifled a yawn, added to her notes, and went through the list of assignments once more. Satisfied, she dressed and went to the kitchen in search of coffee.

The sun was bursting from behind the mountains when the team reconvened. Cat glanced at her watch: 6:24 a.m. Most of the team was suffering from jet lag and had slept as badly as Cat. Nevertheless, they were eager to start working on the case. She split them into four pairs and issued assignments. Arnie and Jones would drive up into the mountains and surveil the bakery, while Gabe and Lindsey would spend the day in cyberspace—learning as much as possible about the bakery, its owners, and the true nature of their business. But their first task would be to track down the names and whereabouts of the people who had been forced out of business by Sretna Kafa.

Cat turned to Adrian and said, "I want you and Marc to visit those people. You'll do the talking; Marc will do the translating. Find out what they remember about Mirko and how he fits with Goran and Daris Terzić. You have a gift for observation and for asking the right questions." She chuckled and added, "And you are not easily dissuaded. You are like a dog with a bone."

She and Pat, both proficient in Arabic, would remain in the apartment and begin looking through the ledger. They would scan the book and send it to the experts at Langley and NSA for translation, but first, Cat wanted a peek. Her hope was that one of the entries might help point the team in the right direction.

She swept her eyes over the group. "There is a thread, somewhere, that ties all these events together. Once we pull that thread, we'll have our answers. And we'll have Michael Cantrell."

Pat beckoned to Arnie and Jones and keyed the computer to call up the aerial imagery of the bakery. She pointed to the satellite dishes.

"Cat's the one who spotted them," she said. "I think it's safe to say that three dishes, camouflage, and portability trailers are rather unexpected accessories for a bakery."

"So they are accessing more than one satellite feed. How old are the images?" asked Arnie.

"Two months—a routine pass. We're mainly looking for equipment buildups, military movements, that kind of thing. We missed this entirely, although I will admit that we probably wouldn't have thought much about it anyhow."

"I'd like to get a drone up there for a look," Arnie said.

Pat's eyebrows shot up. "Well…"

Arnie waved her off. "I don't need yours. We have our own. But I need to find a closer launch location, preferably within a mile of the place so I can conserve battery time. We can also use it to help scout out approach routes. I'm assuming that at some point we will want to take a peek inside. Gabe will be particularly interested in their computer network."

On hearing his name, Gabe ambled over, studied the satellite images, and canted his head.

"With three dishes, they have to be running something big. Everything we learn tells me that they are smart. They have managed to stay under the radar for a long time, so they probably have some interesting security. I'll bet their most sensitive computers are air-gapped. So, yeah, a look inside would be good. Maybe I could drop off a little viral present that would help us find out what they're up to. All I would need is a way to get into the building without being seen."

Arnie studied the image and pointed at a clearing about two hundred yards from the building.

"We'll use the drone to reconnoiter the surrounding land and find the best approach to the building," he said.

Pat waved her hands wildly. "Whoa! Whoa! Whoa! This entire country is still littered with mines from the war. You cannot go wandering around the countryside. The only safe approach is to follow the paved road right up to the front door. One of our locals keeps a cabin up there, about three-quarters of a mile from the bakery. You could use it to stage the drone, but do not even think about going in there on foot."

At the mention of land mines, the entire team seemed to freeze in place. The thought was sobering—and terrifying.

Adrian wandered over and squinted at the screen. "Big building," he said. "This is, what? A bakery that delivers a few dozen pastries around Sarajevo every day? Back in the States, a building that size would be producing thousands of pastries every day and distributing them to every grocery store within three hundred miles. And it certainly would not need more than a single satellite dish. So, what are they up to?"

"That's what we're going to find out," Cat said.

Chapter 91

Gabe made short work of tunneling into the government database that documents businesses in Sarajevo. He discovered that the registration application requires each business to list its primary activities. It gave him an idea. With the text from Sretna Kafa's application, it was easy enough to script a search and find the records of other similar businesses. The query served up over five dozen entities that described themselves as a coffee or tea house, café, or bakery. Only two dozen were still in business.

The server holding the tax records proved to be a more formidable opponent, and it took Gabe a little over thirty minutes to find a backdoor into their network. He and Lindsey examined the tax records of seven similar establishments that had gone out of business in the first half of 2004, which fit with Mirko's description of Sretna Kafa's competition having been eliminated. The names of the principals were included on the tax documents, along with their contact information.

They then performed a series of searches to verify, to the extent possible, the current whereabouts of the people involved. He and Lindsey compared notes, cobbled together a list of likely candidates, and fed their addresses into a program that worked out the most expedient routing.

Adrian and Marc went on foot to the first destination, a five-minute walk north of the Latin Bridge. The address was a storefront, relatively new and with no outward signs of the war that had damaged most of the buildings in the old section of the city. The ground floor was occupied by a tour company. The woman in charge looked at them curiously and presented a brochure listing the tour options. Marc explained that they were looking for an occupant on the floor above.

"I am sorry," she said in accented English. "Mr. Sidran is traveling. He will not be back until Friday."

Adrian asked if it would be possible to reach Mr. Sidran by telephone. The woman shrugged her shoulders.

"I will give him a message. If he finds time, he will call you. But I must tell him why you wish to speak with him?"

She ended her statement in the manner of a question, her voice taking on a higher pitch at the end. Marc explained that they were performing an investigation and wished to ask him about his former business, the café. Her eyebrows shot up in surprise.

"That was long ago. But I will give him your message. Perhaps he will call." She shrugged her shoulders again.

They thanked her and walked several blocks to the next address on their list. They found the apartment on the third floor with no trouble, but there was no answer to their knock. The third address was two blocks away. The drab four-story building was in ill repair and pockmarked with the wounds of war. Someone had slapped stucco around the windows—the only sections of wall that could be reached without scaffolding. The main entry was unlocked, and they climbed the narrow staircase to the second floor.

They paused at each door until finding a placard with the name: HARUN GUDELJ. Marc knocked on the door and waited. The door cracked open, and a wizened old woman poked her scarf-wrapped head into the hall.

Speaking Bosnian, Marc introduced himself and Adrian. He asked if her family had owned a café a number of years ago. To their surprise, the woman nodded her head and answered in English.

"Yes, my husband, Harun, owned a café. You would like to hear about it?" She pulled the door open and said, "My name is Emina. Come in and have some tea."

The apartment was small and, unlike the building itself, as neat as a pin. Half the walls were painted a dusty rose and the other half a rich cream color. The floral curtains captured the pink and cream and threw garden greens into the mix. A faint scent of lilac lingered in the room. The furnishings, like the woman, were old and faded but clean. Family photographs paraded across the walls and were perched on every available flat space—a gallery of men, women, and children going back a hundred years or more. The place transported Adrian back to another time, when he was a boy visiting his grandmother during the summer.

Adrian and Marc sat next to each other on the small settee while she prepared the tea, impatient to find out if she had something to offer and yet not wanting to offend.

She poured the tea and slid into a finely carved rocking chair. Adrian wondered how it had survived the winters during the war, considering that many possessions had been burned for heat.

"Our café was just over there," she said, pointing at the window. "A short walk, three minutes. Our food was good and it was popular with tourists, especially Americans. They like to eat," she said with a laugh. "But my husband had a stroke and could no longer work. I could not manage it by myself; I had to let it go."

"So, you got out of the business because of your husband's health, and not because someone was pressuring you," said Adrian.

The woman looked at him quizzically and said, "Another bakery was trying to buy us out, and we did not want to sell. But when my husband fell ill, we had no choice. You can talk to others who had some real trouble. Are you investigating them? It's about time somebody did. The owners, Goran and Daris Terzić, were decent people. What happened to them was very sad, losing most of their family during the war—a mother and sister and two brothers, I believe. But then many of us lost loved ones."

She picked up a photo of a young man in his late twenties or early thirties. "This was my son. He was standing in line to get water. Just to get water. The Serbs murdered him." Her voice trailed off, and her eyes went vacant. She sat, unmoving, lost in a past memory.

Adrian waited for a respectful moment and then said, "I am sorry about your loss. Losing a child is a terrible thing."

She turned to him, nodding. "I think my life ended at that moment." She shook her head, as if to clear her thoughts, and continued, "But back to Sretna Kafa. They were good people, as I said, until they got involved with that Russian. Those Russians just breed corruption, you know. It is part of their DNA. He thought he could fool us by pretending to be Bosnian, but my husband knew better. My husband was no fool; he spent several years in Moscow, and he knew immediately. They had an argument. That is when he had the stroke."

Adrian kept his expression neutral but took a sideways glance at Marc. Their eyes met with the same questions. *That Russian? Stroke?*

Adrian asked, "This man, would you recognize him?"

"Recognize him? Of course," she said with a flick of her hand. "Sniveling rat. But he got what was coming to him—lost his leg to the murderous Serbs. I have heard that he still lives here, in Sarajevo, even after all this time. I do not understand why he does not go back to Moscow where he belongs."

Showing her the picture of Mirko, Adrian asked, "Is this the man?"

She squinted, studying the photo. "It looks like him, but my eyes are not what they once were. You should talk to Imran Kurjak. He will tell you about what happened to his bakery—how they strangled his business. I will give you his address, but we must call him first so that you do not waste your time."

"That would be very helpful, thank you," said Adrian.

Imran Kurjak lived with his wife, Lejla, on the outskirts of Sarajevo—west of the airport on the lower slope of Mt. Igman. They had a comfortable Mediterranean-style home of cream-colored stucco and a red tile roof. The couple were in the garden, unearthing plants from the soil and piling them into large baskets. Beside them, a flat trolley was loaded with a variety of potted plants.

As Adrian and Marc stepped out of the taxi, Imran greeted them with a smile and beckoned them to the rear of the house. The courtyard looked out onto the fields that blanketed the land, right up to the base of the mountain.

"Please excuse the chaos," Imran said. "We are preparing for winter. All the delicate plants and bulbs go into the basement." He sighed and added, "And then we do it all again next year. Please have a seat. We will wash our hands and gather refreshments."

He reappeared ten minutes later, his hands and face scrubbed and bearing a tray of bottles. Lejla followed with a tray of glasses.

"Beer? Wine? Something soft?" he asked. "Personally, I could do with a cold beer."

"We would love to join you, but unfortunately we are working," Adrian said. "Could we take a rain check?"

Imran looked momentarily confused. Marc translated the idiom into Bosnian.

"Ah! Rain check! Why, of course!" Imran exclaimed. "I love these crazy American phrases!"

Adrian smiled and selected a cola, while Marc opted for a soda water with fresh lime.

"I am sorry to disturb you at home," Adrian said. "But we are investigating an incident that happened a number of years ago, involving an American woman. Certain details have only recently been uncovered relating to a bakery here, Sretna Kafa. Your name came up during our visit with Madame Gudelj. We are hopeful that you can help us."

"It was long ago," he said, rubbing his chin. "This American woman, what did she do?"

"She was murdered, Mr. Kurjak."

The man's reaction was almost visceral. His hand fell from his face, his expression hardened, and his eyes narrowed into slits. He turned to his wife and said, "Old Harun was right. Those men were killers."

Adrian's jaw twitched. He straightened and said, "Please tell us what you remember, Mr. Kurjak."

According to Imran Kurjak, Goran Terzić had moved to Sarajevo shortly after the war, uprooting his wife and child after his mother and siblings were massacred in Goražde. The story went that he had come to search for his remaining two brothers. He had found work as a cook and eventually located Daris. The two founded Sretna Kafa in 1999 or 2000.

"We liked them," Imran said. "And they settled into the community. But a few years later, something changed. They fell into company with a man who claimed to have been their brother's best friend. There was an infusion of money—no one knew where it came from—and in 2004 they bought property in the high hills east of the city.

"They built a big bakery, marketing their products to all the hotels and restaurants in town. We had served some of those businesses for years, and suddenly, they were dropping us. We lowered our prices. Some of our customers told us they would come back, but they did not. We later learned that they were threatened. One of our customers had a huge fire. Another was hit by a car and severely injured. We reported these things to the police, but we had no evidence.

"Then they tried to buy our businesses. We were losing money, and they wanted our shop at a very low price. When they came to me, I told them I would not sell. A week later sixty of my customers got sick. The authorities said that my food was contaminated. That was the end—I could not regain our reputation. So, I sold my shop for a third of what it was worth. I was very angry. But now, I am older, and the past is past. The café was a dalliance, a younger man's dream. I had studied engineering and found a good job with a well-respected firm. But I knew I would always just be a cog in someone else's success. I wanted to carve my own path. After we sold the shop, my old firm took me back. I eventually ended up with an office in the executive suite, and I give two lectures at the university every week. Fate." He shrugged his shoulders.

"What can you tell me about those men, the ones who threatened you?" asked Adrian.

"My clearest memory is of the one who told me he was a friend of Goran's brother. I have occasionally seen him in the old town. He lost a leg in the war—a bombing, I believe. He was on crutches for a several years, and then he received a prosthesis. This was quite surprising, because with all the people injured by mines, there was a very long waiting list and very little money to pay for such devices."

"Do you think he was Russian?" Adrian asked.

"All I know is that he was not originally from Sarajevo, but that was not unusual. The country has such a mix of Croatian, Bosnian, and Serbian that it can be difficult to distinguish one from another. I did not recognize him as Russian, but old Harun was convinced."

Adrian held up the photo of Mirko. "Is this the man?"

Imran took the photo in both hands and stared at Mirko's face.

"Oh yes, he is the one."

"And the others? Could you describe them?"

"One was big, physically intimidating, strong, with a flat nose and large ears. The third was also quite muscular, but much shorter, with a nose like the beak of a hawk."

Adrian's brow puckered in thought. "Why do you think they needed your shop? Why did they need such a big bakery? I do not know anything about the business, but that building looks huge—like it could feed the entire city."

Imran chuckled at that. "There is an art to making bread. There are multiple steps, each requiring special handling and a fixed amount of time. You must have enough space to handle many loaves in each stage. Some commercial bakeries are huge, with automated conveyors on several levels. But here, more of the work is manual and on a single floor. And if you add more products, like pastries, you require even more space."

"Did any of your employees go to work for them after you sold them your shop?"

Imran shook his head vehemently. "They did not hire locals. All their employees came from out of the country—mostly Syria and Iraq. They kept to themselves, living up there on the mountain."

Adrian sat up straighter. "None of their people ever came down the mountain to work in the city?"

"I never heard of anyone doing that. It was odd."

Marc, listening intently, held up a finger. "Hang on," he said. "Maybe baking is not the real business. Maybe the people are the business. On the surface it all sounds very philanthropic, providing jobs, food, and shelter for refugees. But why keep them so isolated? Apart from making bread, what were they doing up there?"

Adrian massaged his forehead with his right hand. *Of course. The commodity was not the baked goods. The commodity was people.*

Chapter 92

Jones and Arnie, armed with the drone, topographic maps, and two satellite phones equipped with GPS, headed into the mountains. The cabin's owner had offered the use of his vehicle—a rugged and weathered old Jeep that was more at home in the wilderness than in the city.

"Be cautious," the man had warned. "The land around the cabin has been demined, but there are still thousands of mines buried in the ground around Sarajevo. Do not go beyond the fences. There is no internet, and cell service is spotty. Your cell phones will not work up there."

Arnie, having insisted on including satellite phones in their gear, had looked at Jones and winked.

After leaving the highway, the roads became progressively rougher as they followed the winding roads deeper into the wilderness. They were expecting the cabin to be a spartan affair and were surprised to find a comfortable and well-equipped chalet atop one of the hills overlooking the valley. The bakery sat on the crest of a hill three hundred feet above and a half mile away as the crow flies, hidden from view by the surrounding forest. To reach it by road, they would have to return to the highway and follow a different route—at a minimum, an hour's drive.

The cabin was private, open to the view of the hills in the front and, to the sides and rear, obscured by the forest. It was perfect. They would be able to stage the drone in a location where few could observe their activities.

In the United States, most drone operators are limited by regulations designed to protect aircraft: under four hundred feet and within visual line of sight. Arnie's license, and the nature of his contract with the government, gave him greater latitude during operations having to do with state security. For this mission, Arnie intended to take the drone high, well beyond visual line of sight. Bosnia, as a sovereign nation, would probably take a dim view of his activities on their soil. But the team had decided to forgo the formality of asking permission and would, instead, ask forgiveness if caught. Paul had assured him that—in this case—Bosnia would sputter but would ultimately bend to the will of the Americans.

After looking over the satellite imagery, and now, with eyes on the site, they concurred that the likelihood of being discovered was remote. The bakery sat alone, away from any other buildings. There was minimal risk to aircraft—the location was well removed from the airport's flight path—and the drone's control system was equipped with the latest detect and avoid technologies.

Jones pressed the binoculars to his eyes and brought the distant hill into focus. Although he could not see the grounds, there was no activity on the road that led up into the property. This was Tuesday—not a holiday, not a weekend—and yet the entire hillside seemed deserted. No cars, no bikes, no people, no cloud of steam from the factory.

He pulled the binoculars from his face and said, "Let's get that thing flying. Something's not right."

Arnie looked up. Jones rarely expressed concern. He was always calm and in control, one who could assess a situation and take measured action without panicking. If Jones was worried, there was good reason. But Arnie had to be careful with the drone, a piece of hardware with a price tag upward of five figures.

The aircraft came with its own carrier that morphed into a small camouflaged tent for work in the field. Designed for quick assembly and easy transport, it had telescoping supports and featherlight, waterproof, synthetic fabric. Its sole purpose was to protect the control console from sun and weather; protection and shelter for the human operator was secondary. Arnie popped the last of the support posts into place, secured the cover, and unfolded the drone.

After a thorough inspection of the machine, he said, "I'm ready. Let's get her launched."

He flipped on the power for the control panel, then the drone. He gave the two components a moment to recognize each other, sync, and connect to the satellite that would communicate the controller's commands. He ran through a systems check, then worked the joystick. The drone rose a hundred feet into the air, buffeted by the wind sweeping across the high terrain, and

Arnie worked the controls to keep it steady. He sent it farther aloft, a thousand feet up, and directed it across the valley that separated the two hilltops. Two minutes later, the drone was hovering high over the bakery.

The imagery was crystal clear. Arnie navigated the drone around the circumference of the property, noting that the satellite dishes were still in place. He found nothing moving. The place seemed deserted, devoid of cars or other vehicles.

"Could they have closed for the day?" he asked Jones.

"Why would they?" Jones asked back. And then, as if in answer to his own question, pressed his lips together and hissed through his teeth, "Unless they knew we were coming. That thing has heat sensing capability, right?"

"Yes, but I'll have to take it lower. It also eats up the battery, so we'll only make one pass. Here we go."

Arnie lowered the drone until it was just twenty feet over the treetops. The two men watched the streaming video intently, hoping for a heat signature, but the grounds were cool—no people, no machinery running. It was as if all the electrical power had been turned off. On its pass over the outlying buildings—the living quarters—he spotted an anomaly in the ground at the rear of the living quarters, close to the woods. The ground was uneven and the soil was a different color, as if it had been freshly dug. At ground level, it would probably not be noticeable, and it would be unlikely that a visitor would walk behind the buildings. In another two weeks, autumn leaves would blanket the site, hiding the disturbance. He felt a chill go up his spine.

"What do you make of that?" he asked.

Jones took one look at the scene on the screen and winced. "Call the bird back. Let's get over there before anyone else stumbles in there."

He pulled out the satellite phone and called Cat.

"We have a big problem," he said.

Chapter 93

Visibly unhappy with the idea and pursing her lips in distaste, Cat said, "We have to report it."

Pat held up a finger. "I agree, but it would be better to be on-site when we make the discovery. That way, we avoid explaining the drone, and we can buy some time. I have a friend in SIPA. He will give us some latitude, as long as we give him credit if this turns out to be something of importance."

SIPA is the acronym for the State Investigation and Protection Agency, Bosnia and Herzegovina's equivalent to the FBI. When the agency started, many of their people had trained with the FBI at Quantico. In their short history, they had managed to participate in several international efforts and had gained a reputation for thoroughness and tenacity.

Cat nodded. "I can live with that."

Adrian felt the buzz in his pocket and knew instantly that the call was trouble. He picked up the phone, mouthed a polite "I'm sorry" to Imran and Lejla, moved to the far corner of the patio, and took the call.

"I'm with some folks. What's going on?" he asked.

"Are you close?" Cat asked.

"Other end of town. Thirty minutes."

"Get moving. We'll wait for you here."

Adrian moved back to Marc's side and explained that an urgent matter had come up. He punched in the number to call another taxi.

"No, no," said Imran. "Hang up. If you are in a hurry, I will take you. It will be faster."

Moments later, they were speeding back into the city.

"Thank you for the diversion," Imran said with a chuckle. "I hate gardening. I hate baking, too. Lejla was the one who wanted the café. I lost money, but it was a relief to be rid of it."

Marc and Adrian dropped all pretense of formality and roared with laughter.

Imran was suddenly horror-stricken at having confessed a deep secret to an American FBI agent. He glanced sideways at Adrian. "Please do not include that in your report!"

"Our lips are sealed," chuckled Adrian. "And as long as we are telling secrets—and at the risk of sounding like a stupid American—I have to confess that I have been wondering about your flawless English. Did you study in the States?"

"Thank you for the compliment," Imran replied with a grin. "But no. I did spend a year in London, so perhaps that smoothed over the rough edges. But English is taught at an early age here, and all classes at the university are conducted in English. One must be proficient to stay employed."

He kept his foot hard on the gas pedal, and equally hard on the brakes, and dropped them at the foot of the Latin Bridge, a short walk away from Pat Desmond's flat. Adrian phoned in as they hustled up the street.

"We're here," he said.

Cat, Gabe, and Pat Desmond spilled out the door, lugging Arnie's equipment bags. Cat pointed at Marc.

"Stay here. Work on the translations and give Lindsey a hand. She's digging up more info on the bakery, but it's all in Bosnian. Don't leave the apartment."

"Yes, ma'am," he said, rolling his eyes.

"I mean it. Just stay put until I know more."

They clambered into Pat's small sedan and sped out of the city and up into the hills. They were half a mile from the bakery when they spotted the old Jeep, straddling the center mound on a rutted dirt road. Jones lumbered toward them and leaned into Cat's window on the passenger side.

"How do you want to handle this?" he growled.

"First, let's confirm that no one is actually there; then we'll go in."

"We're going to need equipment. You brought the gear bags, right?"

Cat nodded. "In the trunk."

"What about the dig site?"

Cat closed her eyes and tried not to think about what might lie beneath the dirt.

"Maybe it's just a garden that they turned over for the winter," she said quietly.

Jones bowed his head. "Unlikely."

"I'm uneasy about all this," Pat said in a low voice. "What are we walking into here?"

Cat clicked her tongue and bit her lower lip. "Good question. It's making my skin crawl."

Jones returned to the Jeep and took off. Pat followed.

The bakery sat in a clearing at the end of a winding dirt road, hemmed in by trees on all sides. Nothing about the place suggested that visitors were welcome. The parking lot was tiny, the sand-colored paint was faded and peeling, and the clearing itself was a tangle of grass and weeds that had not seen a mower in weeks. The main entry appeared to be a door that faced the parking area. The faded red lettering over the door read *Mountain Kafa*. Pat recognized the word beneath—*Pekara*—as the Bosnian word for bakery. One third of the way down the length of the building was a silo, perhaps five feet taller than the building.

After trying the front door and finding it locked, they split into two teams and walked the perimeter of the building. The only windows were narrow, twenty feet off the ground, and ran along three sides of the building. Looking up, it was impossible to determine whether the windows were simply decorative or could be opened for ventilation. The back of the structure was just a vast expanse of wall, with no windows or doors. Near the parking lot, next to the silo, was a loading bay that could accommodate two trucks. It, too, was closed and locked. Two smaller doors—Cat guessed that they led to office space—were at the far end. Each had a weather-protected box for a keypad.

"Well, this should be in your wheelhouse," she said to Arnie. But when he lifted the cover of one box, her eyes went wide. "Fingerprint scanners? No loaf of bread needs that kind of security."

"Gabe and I could probably hack it," Arnie said.

Jones cut in, "But we don't know what other measures they might have taken. We already know that these people are dangerous. The doors could be wired and I'm not gung-ho on the idea of being taken apart by some explosive device." He looked up at the roof. "The only option I see is the windows."

"Can you use the drone?"

"No," chimed in Arnie. "It can't get close enough to see inside."

They moved farther back, into the clearing, to get a better view of the roof. They stood with their backs to the outbuildings—about fifteen feet away—and looked up.

Cat asked, "What would it take to get in that window?"

Arnie followed her gaze. "Assuming you can get up there, it depends on whether or not you can pry it open or if you just have to break it. Either way, the best thing I have in the equipment is a pry bar."

"How much rope do we have?" asked Jones.

"Thirty meters," Arnie replied. "What do you have in mind?"

"What do you think about those vent stacks? Strong enough to support my weight?"

Arnie looked up at the vent columns protruding from the top of the building. He puffed his cheeks and blew the air out with a whoosh. "Man, I don't know," he said, looking at Jones. "You're what, two-fifty or -sixty?"

"Close enough."

"I'm about half that," said Cat. "Bring the rope and let's get Pat's car over to the silo." She took a step forward, then stopped and turned around to face the row of buildings behind her. There were three identical one-story structures, each about forty feet long and punctuated with doors spaced eight feet apart. Windowless and austere, they reminded her of self-storage facilities in the States, but with regular doors instead of roll-ups.

She trotted over to the silo and kicked off her shoes. "Jones and Arnie can help me get inside the bakery." She looked over at Pat and Adrian. "You two should check out those buildings. If the staff lived there, maybe there is something to find." To Gabe, she said, "Hang loose and keep your eyes and ears open for any visitors."

"Do we have radios?" Gabe asked.

"And maybe a harness and gloves?" Cat added.

Arnie nodded his head. "Comms and gloves, yes—harness, no. But I can rig you. He rummaged through the bag and found two pairs of gloves. He passed one set to Cat, but the other pair was too small for Jones wide hands.

"Sorry, man," he said. "But I had no idea you were coming to the party."

Jones shrugged it off and went to work helping Arnie fashion a chest and waist harness for Cat. Jones slipped the pry bar into a bag and clipped it to the harness. Arnie passed out earbuds and clip-on microphones to Cat, Jones, Gabe, and Adrian.

Cat asked, "What am I forgetting?"

Jones looked her over from head to toe. "Shoes," he said. "For inside." He picked up her shoes from the ground and tucked them into the bag with the pry bar.

Cat tested the radio, then played out several feet of line and handed the coil to Jones. The bottom of the silo's ladder was about eight feet off the ground, a discouragement to vandals, so Pat nosed the car as close as possible to the structure. Jones pulled himself onto the hood, leapt over to the ladder, and hoisted himself up. Cat followed suit, and the two climbed until they were level with the roof.

"Ready?" Jones asked.

Cat looked at the three-foot gap between the silo and the building and took a long, deep breath. It was a narrow gap, but from a stationary position, not a simple jump—particularly with nothing to grab onto on the other side. *No big deal*, she told herself. If she missed, Jones had a grip on the rope and would stop her fall.

"Ready," she said, steeling herself.

Jones secured the coil of rope to the ladder and wrapped his right arm around the rail. He gripped Cat's forearm with his left hand. She extended her left foot over the chasm, taking advantage of his strength to keep her balanced, and they swayed in tandem to build momentum. With one final push, he propelled her onto the roof. She stumbled and went down on her left knee, her right leg dangling over the edge.

"Pull!" Jones yelled.

Cat clawed frantically, finally dragging her leg up. Her heart was beating wildly, but she pasted on a smile as she rolled over. Giving Jones a thumbs-up, she said, "Just wanted to get your heart pumping. Now it's your turn."

Jones climbed a rung higher on the ladder, tossed the coil of rope onto the roof, and then flung himself sideways. He flew across the gap, landing at Cat's side.

"I'm not totally comfortable with heights," he said with a grimace. "Let's get this over with."

Cat crawled to the edge of the roof and looked down. The edge of the roof was flush with the wall, but the windows were three feet down—too far for her to see into the building. Jones nudged one of the vent pipes with his boot, then kicked a little harder. It seemed sturdy, but there was no way to know if it would hold. He wrapped the rope around it, did the same with a second vent, and went back to Cat. He was big, strong, and perfectly capable of hauling Cat's weight. But the sudden force of a fall would likely pull him, too. He needed a brace. Aside from the vent pipes, the only other structure on the roof was a four-inch lip at the edge that directed water toward the downspouts. He moved a few feet away and kicked at another part of the lip. A few bits of material flaked off, but it did not crumble. He sat next to Cat, braced his feet on the lip, and looped the slack in the rope around his massive forearms.

"I've got you," he told Cat.

"I know. You always do," she replied, then slipped on her gloves, turned over on her stomach, and slid off the edge. Jones held the rope taut, then felt the sudden pull of her drop. He held steady, resisting the urge to jerk back. He played out the slack, a little at a time, the friction burning his hands.

Cat called out, and Jones tightened his grip. She ran her fingers along the edge of the window, hoping to find a way of prying it open, but the window was sealed. She cursed under her breath and pulled the pry bar from the bag. Gabe and Arnie were standing below her, real concern on their upturned faces. She yelled at them to get out of the way. Cradling her face in her left arm for protection, she used her right arm to give the pry bar a mighty swing. The glass shattered on impact, spraying shards of glass in every direction.

Cat shook her head and shoulders and started to wipe her face with her sleeve, then stopped. Tiny flecks of glass sparkled in her sweater. She ran the pry bar around the edge of the window to clear away the remaining shards, gripped the ledge, and hauled herself onto the window frame. She hitched one leg over and sat astride the sill.

"I'm good," Cat said into the microphone, even as she felt the bits of glass still in the frame scraping against her thigh.

She looked down, orienting herself. She was perched about ten feet above a row of metal racks. Shelves, ovens, mixers, and other equipment lined both walls, with a single aisle between. She frowned. The building seemed narrower than she had expected. But, she realized, the scrum of machinery took up a lot of space. It was probably just an optical illusion.

She studied the racks below. They looked fairly sturdy but were dusted with glass, and the shelves would probably collapse under her weight. The rack frame, however, could provide a measure of support until she reached the floor.

She activated the radio. "Hey, Jones! I'm sitting on the windowsill. I need to get to the floor, maybe twenty feet more. I'll get positioned, and then I want you to lower me."

"Roger," he replied.

Cat swung her other leg into the room and sat precariously on the sill, the jagged remnants of glass stabbing into her buttocks. She winced in pain, then told Jones to give her some slack. She pushed herself off the edge, dropping several feet in a heartbeat and wrenching her back.

His arms afire with the effort and the rope searing his hands, Jones managed to keep Cat's descent steady. As she came abreast of the shelves, she grabbed the rails and brushed her feet lightly against the shelves. She was inches from the floor in seconds. Guiding one of the shelves from the rack, she flipped it upside down on the floor—giving her a clean surface to step on. She disconnected the rope.

"Clear!" she said into the radio.

Chapter 94

Pat and Adrian watched Cat drop through the window and then moved toward the three smaller buildings. They approached with caution. While they had seen no evidence of people on the grounds, someone might still be in the compound.

They were ten feet from the first door when Adrian stopped and frowned at the door in front of him. A two-by-four, painted the same color as the building, had been slipped into brackets bolted to each side of the doorway. The barricade effectively prevented the door from being opened from the inside. Looking up and down the row of barracks, he could now see that all the doors were barred. He felt a chill. The people living here had been imprisoned.

Moving closer, they saw the flies, buzzing around the doorway and finding access via a narrow gap between the bottom of the door and the landing.

"We are not going in there," Adrian said. "This is going to require a full-on forensics team. If anyone screws it up, it's not going to be us. We'll wait for SIPA."

"I agree," said Pat.

Heads down, their thoughts consumed by what they had discovered, they walked back to the bakery. As they neared the silo, they saw that Arnie was wrapped around the top of the ladder. Jones was examining his hands, rubbed raw and bleeding. Jones shouted at Adrian, "If I jump back over, I'm not sure I can hang on to the ladder. My hands are shot."

Adrian yelled up at Arnie, "Do you have a couple more carabiners?"

Arnie pointed at the equipment bag. "Two, maybe."

Rummaging through the bag, Adrian spotted another length of webbing, grabbed it, and stuffed the carabiners in his pocket. He scrambled up the ladder, and with the agility of a gazelle, leapt across to the roof. Before Jones could say a word, Adrian said, "I've done some climbing. Now let me figure out how to rig this."

Using the webbing and one end of the rope, Adrian devised a harness that he thought would hold Jones long enough to get him to the ground. Then he jumped back to the ladder. He looped the other end of the rope over one of the ladder rungs, did the same with the rung below, and again with a rung a little less than halfway down. Then he dropped the end of the rope to the ground. He and Arnie hurried to the bottom.

"You take the gloves," Arnie said.

Adrian looked him squarely in the eyes. "You manage the electronics for us. I don't need my hands the way you do."

Arnie gave a nod and slipped on the gloves. Adrian threaded the end of the rope under the bottom rung, played out a few feet, and stationed Arnie at the front. He grabbed the rope about two feet behind Arnie and shouted for Gabe and Pat to help. With everyone positioned, he yelled at Jones. "Go!"

Jones gave a silent prayer and eased off the roof, Arnie and Adrian feeding the slack. He was only three or four feet down when the bolts on the top rung gave way with a loud snap. The sudden drop jerked Arnie off his feet, and Adrian stumbled behind him. Both men tried desperately to hold onto the rope. Jones plunged halfway down before they regained control, straining mightily against the weight. They played out more of the slack, and he dropped closer and closer, He was five feet off the ground when the second rung collapsed. This time, there was no possibility of regaining the rope in time. He dropped to the ground, rolling onto his side as he fell.

Jones lay still for a moment, then waved his hand. "I'm okay. I may have cracked a rib. Give me a hand."

After they helped him to his feet, Jones said, "Let's not do that again."

Cat pulled her shoes out of the bag and slipped them on, the pain in her thighs and backside now sharply noticeable. Her pants were stained with blood, but not gushing, so not catastrophic. She ran her hand over her backside and came back with another smear of blood. Swallowing the pain, she made her way toward the front of the building.

The building was dark and eerily still—no lights, no sound of machinery. The familiar scent of freshly baked bread permeated the air, but was accompanied by an odor that was disturbingly pungent. Walking by the big machines, she found that some of the huge mixers still had raw dough in them—dough that had risen beyond the confines of the bowl and oozed over the sides. Conveyor belts were loaded with unbaked loaves ballooned beyond their baking receptacles, and ovens reeked of loaves baked far too long. Whatever had happened here had happened suddenly, the bread minders leaving their posts in the middle of production.

She found a set of wide, swinging doors, each with a see-through window. She examined the door frame for wires but found nothing. She pushed, gingerly, and stepped into a spartan reception area, devoid of any furniture except a single table and chair that faced the front door. After examining the door carefully, she turned the deadbolts and spoke into the microphone. "I'm opening the front door."

The metal door was big and heavy, and she struggled to push it fully open. She stepped out onto the small porch and found Gabe, Adrian, and Pat approaching.

"So far, just a bakery," she said.

She turned to reenter the building, stopped, looked around, and stepped back outside, nearly colliding with Adrian. "Wait," she said, studying the structure. She whistled softly, understanding what she had noticed from her perch on the windowsill. "When you go in, you'll see a wall to the left. I thought it was the outside wall, but it's not. Inside, the wall is only a few feet from the door, but outside, the door is a good fifteen or twenty feet away from the wall. There's some sort of concealed space. I'll wager that whatever is behind the wall has nothing to do with bread and cookies."

Pat came up behind her. "You're bleeding," she said. "How bad is it?"

"Hurts like hell, but I'll be fine. Another visit to the doctor, another tetanus shot, and I'll be good as new."

"Adrian and I went down to those buildings," Pat said. "I don't want to know what might have happened in there. The smell is there, and flies. We decided to let SIPA handle it, but we need to call them. Soon."

"Okay," said Cat. But that," she said, gesturing at the wall, "that comes first."

Chapter 95

They made their way to the other end of the building, where they found a large, fully equipped kitchen. Unlike the rest of the bakery, which had been left to rot, the kitchen was clean and tidy. A little farther on, they found a narrow doorway that led to a small reception area. Surprisingly, the door was ajar. Adrian and Jones checked the area carefully and found nothing suspicious. The room was well-appointed, with artwork on the walls and two upholstered chairs facing the receptionist's desk. The desk was sandwiched between the door leading into the bakery and the exterior steel door. No one could enter this office unnoticed.

Adrian began searching the desk. The sparse contents of the desk's drawers were neatly arranged—pens, pencils, sticky pads, and a stapler in the top drawer above the kneehole, a ream of plain paper and several small tablets in the top left, and tissues and a bottle of aspirin in the bottom drawer. The left middle drawer was empty.

Pat looked around the room and noticed the bar holders on each side of the doorway. Like those by the doors of the barracks, they were painted to blend in with the walls. It took her a minute to find the crossbar, which had been painted with a mountain scene and hung on the wall as art.

"What do you think?" she asked Adrian.

"I think these people have been up to some serious business. We just have to figure out what that business is."

Cat, hands on her hips, stared at the door. "Did they put up the barricade only at night? Or did they also use it during the day to keep people from popping in? Either way, it makes a strong demand for privacy. So, why was it not used last night? Why was I able to walk right in?"

Adrian hung his head and then looked up at her. "I don't think they were worried any longer. I think they have eliminated the workers and abandoned this place."

Cat nodded in agreement and said, "Did you notice that big kitchen? And that there are no tables? How did this work? The people living here took their food back to their quarters, and then ate there after being locked in for the night? These people were treated like slaves. How did Goran and Mirko get away with it for so long?"

Gabe, who had explored deeper into the suite, poked his head around the corner and said, "There are four other doors back here, all with numeric keypads. Arnie and I can work on them, but it will take some time."

Adrian opened his mouth as if to say something, then raised his index finger. "Hold on. I want to check something." He went back to the desk and opened the empty left drawer. *The middle drawer is easier to reach than the drawer below it, so why leave it empty?*

He pulled the drawer all the way out and turned it over, finding a clear plastic sleeve taped to the bottom with a sheet of paper inside. On the paper were written usernames, passwords, and four five-digit door codes. He wondered about the person who normally occupied that desk. A member of the family? An employee? *The weakest link,* he thought. He snapped a photo of the paper and put the drawer back in place. He and Cat moved to the doors in the hall, where each punched in a code.

Cat's door unlocked on the second try, opening to a sterile office devoid of personal touches. The room held a desk and straight-backed chair, two wooden chairs facing the desk, and a bookcase. There was a hardness to the room that spoke of someone who kept his personal life completely separate from his business life—no photographs, no mementos. The books reinforced her thinking, with topics ranging from the practical aspects of running a business to a tome about the former USSR's influence on the Balkan States. Her impression was that the office was not often used.

She stepped back into the hall as Adrian punched in another code. This time, the light turned green. He opened the door to a blast of cold air and spit out a startled, "Jesus!"

Goran Terzić lay reclined on a small settee, a blanket draped across his chest. Even in death, he had not found peace. His face was pinched in pain or perhaps anger, his lips forever frozen in an angry scowl.

The thermostat had been turned to its lowest level, but Goran's office still displayed more warmth than its mate across the hall. The furniture was upholstered in ivory muslin, with striped throw pillows of pale red, yellow, and blue, a Dali reproduction on the wall, and a photograph of his daughter in a gold frame on the desk.

Adrian checked the body, verifying that Goran was deceased, and found no obvious signs of foul play. The only disturbing factor was the expression on Goran's face—not what one would normally find in a natural death. He muttered, "Whoever did this is not leaving any loose ends. An autopsy will have to confirm, but my guess is poison. Not an easy way to die."

Cat stood in the doorway and eyed the room. "You know what's missing? We've found three desks and not one has a computer."

"No file cabinets, either," said Adrian. "Let's check the other doors."

The third keypad opened a small storage room with the usual office supplies—and a printer.

"Where there's a printer, there's a computer," observed Cat. "I'm waiting to hit the jackpot."

But there was no keypad for the fourth door. Adrian twisted the knob and stepped into a space that, in New England, would have been called a mudroom. There were trays on the floor for wet boots and pegs for coats and hats, and three doors. The first was an ordinary door, leading to a small bathroom. The second was another steel door, leading to the outside, and the other boasted the last keypad. This doorway, too, had holders for a crossbar.

"Once you go in, you can't get out," Cat said as she punched in the final code. She tried the knob, but the door was still locked. Gabe peered over her shoulder, looking at the sheet of codes and passwords.

"What's that?" he asked, pointing to the upper right corner of the sheet.

"Isn't that a date?" she asked, puzzled. She looked at the numbers: *11-31-16*.

"I don't think so," he said.

She punched the buttons. *Click.* She glanced up at Gabe with a look that said *How in the world did you know that?*

Gabe shrugged his shoulders and said, "That date is a long time ago. The paper doesn't look that old, and anyone with a mind for security would have changed the codes several times since then."

Cat pulled the door open. Her jaw dropped.

The room, running the length of the building, held multiple cubicles and workstations. Gabe's eyes were as big as saucers. "This is going to take some time."

Pat Desmond looked at her watch. "We have been here for an hour," she said. "I know we need the contents of those machines, but you're going to need help. I think it's time to get SIPA involved."

Cat and Adrian exchanged a look, with Adrian giving a slight nod. Turning to Pat, Cat said, "Make the call."

Chapter 96

Captain Rasim Graovac, of the State Investigation and Protection Agency, was poring over a communiqué from a colleague at MI5 when Pat Desmond's call came in. He was immediately on the alert, particularly since the call was coming on the heels of a CIA team arriving yesterday. He had worked with Pat on several occasions, and she had earned his respect, although trust was another matter. Trust and the CIA did not necessarily go hand in hand.

"Rasim," Pat said when he answered, "I hope you and your family are well. And I also hope that you might work with me on a situation that is just unfolding."

"What kind of situation?" he asked cautiously.

"Before I tell you that, I need your assurance that you will allow us to take the lead, just until we have a better handle on the scope of the problem. The situation is highly sensitive, and I cannot overemphasize its importance. And Rasim, we will give you full credit for uncovering this ... um ... issue, and we will express our gratitude that you invited us to help."

With a note of irritation in his voice, Rasim asked, "Why bother to call me at all?"

"That will become very clear when you get here."

Rasim looked down at the communiqué in his hand. "Would this have anything to do with Mirko Stefanović?"

Pat almost dropped the phone, then found her voice and said, "Rasim, I need your assurance."

He breathed a deep sigh and capitulated. "Where are you, and what do you need?"

"Very low-key, no more than eight people—in two cars only, no helicopters. I'm not kidding! Make something up—tell your people you're going for a picnic in the country—nothing about the operation until you get here and we've talked. Bring two or three superbly qualified computer techies, and three or four with hazmat suits and body bags."

Rasim felt his stomach drop. *Hazmat suits and body bags? My God*, he thought. Aloud, he asked, "Where?"

"The bakery that's run by Sretna Kafa—the one at the top of a hill east of town. And as long as you're coming this way, whatever it is that you have on Mirko Stefanović."

Pat disconnected the call and returned her sat phone to its cradle in the sedan. She stepped out of the car and turned to Cat. "He asked me if this had anything to do with Mirko."

Stunned, Cat bellowed, "He what?"

"He didn't say, but he will be here within forty-five minutes, so let's do whatever it is we need to do."

Cat ran back into the bakery, Pat following, and called the men over. "Get as much as you can, and do it fast," she said. "Gabe will tell you what to do. We have company coming in forty-five minutes … no, let's say thirty."

Then she turned back to Pat. "Let's get the ropes and other equipment back in the trunk, pronto."

"How are you going to explain your, uh, sore little tushy?" Pat asked.

"Door was unlocked; I went in. Slipped on some glass."

"And the broken window?"

"Didn't notice it until I slipped. Without electricity, the place was pretty dark."

Pat chuckled. "You always were a great storyteller."

Stuffing the gear into the cars, Pat asked about Mirko.

"The last I saw him," Cat said, "was when I was following them in the taxi. Goran was with him—I saw them leave the coffee shop and get into the car. But we lost them when we went up into the hills. I was on my way back when you sent me the news about Toni Swanson being killed."

"So, are we thinking Mirko killed Goran?"

"I don't know what to think. Did he kill all the workers, too? Why? What were they doing here? How is he connected?" She raised her hands and spread her fingers in frustration, as if she were making a desperate attempt to catch an invisible basketball. "Who the hell is he?"

Thirty minutes later, the team scurried out the back door of the bakery. Jones and Arnie took seats in the Jeep, while Gabe dropped into the passenger side of Pat's sedan. Cat, Adrian, and Pat leaned against the sedan, waiting. The team had agreed that only Cat, Adrian, and Pat would confess to having entered the building initially—and that upon discovering the computer room, they had asked Gabe to take a look. The others had waited outside.

A scant five minutes after they exited the building, two black Toyota Land Cruisers roared into the clearing. Cat and Pat leveled a gaze at each other. Cat gave her head the tiniest jerk, an unspoken message that said, *Go for it.*

Pat walked over to the lead SUV and extended her hand to the man emerging from the front passenger seat. Cat and Adrian followed closely behind. The members of the SIPA team unfolded themselves from the vehicles and stood back, respectful but watchful.

Rasim was in his late forties and bald, except for a wraparound fringe of dark hair. He was slightly shorter than Cat, with dark, hooded eyes and a worn, tired face that spoke of too many years chasing monsters. His smile, however, was megawatt-bright and revealed perfectly even teeth, an anomaly in the countries of Eastern Europe. Cat struggled to keep her face impassive, wondering if he had his dental work done in the States—perhaps tacked on to a training course at the FBI Academy in Quantico.

He beamed at Adrian, saying, "You were involved in preventing that bombing in Boston a few years back. I remember some of my friends at the FBI talking about it."

Cat wanted to melt into the dirt. If he associated her with the Boston operation, it could be a real problem. She had entered the country with a passport that showed her to be Marie-Françoise Bourget, not Catherine Powell. She got lucky. Rasim did not appear to recognize her.

Cat let Pat take the lead. Pat was Chief of Station, this was Pat's territory, and this was Pat's contact at SIPA. More important, Cat trusted her.

"Goran Terzić and his brother Daris were involved in the assassination of Maggie Marshfield—Ambassador Marshfield's wife—in Istanbul a few years ago," explained Pat. "There are other crimes that I'm not at liberty to discuss—at least not yet. Our evidence, unfortunately, is thin. We came to have a talk with them—to poke the hornet's nest, so to speak. We found the place abandoned."

She pointed at the barracks. "Over there, we think you will find the people who occupied those quarters. We did not go in, but there are flies buzzing around. Also, behind the buildings, there is evidence that the ground has been dug up recently. Being aware of the minefields in the region, we did not explore that further."

A shadow passed over Rasim's face as Pat spoke. He had seen his share of mass graves during the war. He listened intently, writing in a small, spiral-bound notebook. He looked over at Cat. "You seem to have hurt yourself."

Cat looked surprised, as if just discovering the rips and blood on her pants. "Nothing serious. It hurts like the dickens, but with a few butterfly bandages and a tetanus shot, I'll be as good as new. Can't say the same for the pants, though. I think they are beyond repair."

"What happened?" he asked.

"We were scouting the bakery. I took the front door and found it open, so I went in. I was looking for anyone who might be in the building. The electricity was off and it was dark. I slipped, apparently on some glass, and went down on my derriere." She noticed that he was staring at her undamaged hands—which one instinctively uses to break a fall—and decided to ignore his gaze. *Don't elaborate. Less is better.*

"How did the glass come to be on the floor?"

"There was a broken window."

"Someone entered the building before you?"

"I have no idea. All I know is that there was a broken window and I fell on the glass." She wanted to risk looking at his team, to see if they were buying her story, but kept her eyes fixed on Rasim.

"I see," he said. "And perhaps that same person unlocked the front door in order to exit the building."

Cat shrugged. "Perhaps. I wouldn't know."

He nodded and said, "Of course not. How could you?"

Pat stepped in and said, "We have left everything as we found it. There is an office area at the back end of the building. Go in the front door. The back doors are steel with fingerprint readers. In one of the offices, you will find the late Goran Terzić. We did not touch him, other than to confirm he was deceased. There are no signs of foul play, but your autopsy might want to check for poison."

Rasim's eyebrows shot up. "What else?" he asked.

Pat replied, "Our primary interest is a large computer room, hidden behind a false wall and with only a single door in and out. Computers are outside my area of expertise, so it would be best if you talked with our technology expert."

"Oh, yes," Rasim said. "That would be the legendary Gabriel Winters, who flew in yesterday on a private jet. He is apparently famous in the tech world, because my people all wanted to meet him at the airport and take him out for drinks and dinner. Where is he?"

Stepping out of the car, Gabe said, "Right here."

Chapter 97

The tech team—three men and one woman—followed Gabe to the back of the bakery and into the hidden room. Arnie trailed behind for support. After telling them that the wireless interface controllers had been removed on all the computers, thus disabling any wireless transmission, Gabe explained that the machines appeared to be grouped into three pods. "For simplicity," he said, "let's call them Pods 1, 2, and 3."

He led them into Pod 1, which had a dozen cubicles. He gathered them around the first cubicle. It had a sleek chrome desk with an executive chair, and behind the chair, an enlarged photograph of a window with a famous cityscape in the background. He moved behind the desk and sat.

"Stand in front of me and cup your hands around your face, as if you were the computer's camera. What do you see?" he asked.

The woman stepped into position and did as she was asked. "Oh!" she exclaimed. "I would see a very handsome man sitting in an office in Paris."

Gabe raised his eyebrows at the compliment, then said, "Yes, although I don't know about the handsome part. Now keep that thought for a minute."

He then told them that the computers in Pod 1 accessed the internet via cabling that ran out to the bakery's three satellite dishes. In most businesses, the computers would be tied together via a local area network—either wirelessly or with Ethernet. But each computer in Pod 1 was a stand-alone, having no connection to the other computers in the facility.

The same woman asked, "Did you say there are three satellite dishes?"

Gabe nodded. "Yes. Hold that thought, too."

One of the men said, "So, a cyber intruder could exploit one computer, but could not attack an entire network."

"Exactly," said Gabe. "And going a step further, each is connected to its own external drive that backs up all the activity on that computer. I believe that those external drives were collected on a schedule and given to someone in Pod 2."

He led them over to a second group of tables. "In Pod 2, each station has two computers: one is completely air-gapped—no connections to any other computer—while the other is connected to the internal network. The worker here would plug the backup from Pod 1 into the air-gapped machine, thus keeping anything harmful isolated. Then they would check it for malware and verify the data. Once cleared, the data could be transferred to the second computer—the one on the network.

"That brings us to Pod 3. Two desks, two people, three servers. Two of the servers can only be accessed by the people sitting here, so these machines are very isolated. The third server, however, is connected to Pod 2 and, I think, collects and stores all the data coming from Pod 2. I suspect that the people in Pod 3 reexamine the data and then store and categorize it on the other two servers."

One of the men frowned and said, "All this for a bakery? What is in the files?"

Gabe took a deep breath. "I did some quick checking before you got here. All the computers are password protected, but the backup drives are not. Most have been wiped clean, although I found two that had been set aside, maybe waiting for someone to look at them later. Perhaps they were just overlooked. I transferred the files to my testing laptop and this is what I found."

He opened his laptop and clicked on a file. The screen filled with a pretty young woman, late teens, blonde, blue-eyed, and with a cherubic, tear-streaked face. "I came home this afternoon and found my mother passed out in a chair. When I tried to wake her, she cursed at me and threw her drink in my face. I can't live here anymore. I want to be with you!"

A male voice said, "I wanted to wait until you could introduce me to your family, but now I do not want to meet them. The thought of you being abused is more than my heart can bear. I will send you a ticket to Athens. I have a beautiful summer home on one of the islands. You will love it, and we will be together."

Gabe turned off the video. "It goes on. She'll fly to Athens with a carry-on. He will buy her fabulous clothes. They will live lavishly on a Greek isle."

Rasim's team was horrified. "A trafficking ring, right under our noses," the woman said angrily. "A pretty girl like that can bring in tens of thousands of dollars."

Nodding, Gabe said, "I think that they put together a catalog of these girls, put the file on flash drives, and distribute them to their customers. That's why there are several boxes of flash drives in Pod 3."

"It makes me sick," the woman said.

"What do we need to do?" asked one of the men.

"Look for anything that might be evidence of everything that they were doing here. Is it only trafficking, or is there more? I'm particularly interested in Pod 3, so tear everything apart. Look for passwords or any other clue. I'm hoping that someone got sloppy with security.

"I also want to know which satellites those dishes are communicating with. Maybe that will tell us who is bankrolling this operation, because I don't believe for a minute that a guy who runs a bakery is doing this on his own."

Rasim cringed as he watched his men, with Adrian leading them, approach the staff living quarters. He was, he admitted to himself, glad that he had an excuse to stay behind. He turned to Pat and asked, "Now tell me, is Mirko Stefanović involved?"

"Yes," said Pat. "Now tell me how you know of him."

Still keeping his eyes on his men, Rasim said, "A note from a friend at MI5 landed on my desk this morning. It seems that Mr. Stefanović was spotted in Terminal 5 at Heathrow Airport yesterday."

Cat did a quick calculation. She had last seen Mirko at about ten in the morning, two days earlier, so he had a head start of over forty-eight hours. She wondered if the trip was previously planned. *If not*, she thought, *he left Sarajevo in a hurry. And people who are in a hurry make mistakes.*

"Where was he going?" asked Cat.

"Canada. Wait, I have it here," he said. He reached into the car and retrieved a sheet of paper from the SUV. "Toronto, evening departure out of Heathrow on BA," he said, using the letter abbreviation for British Airways.

Rasim explained that what drew the attention of the British authorities was not Mirko himself, but a facial recognition alert on another man. MI5 initially thought that the man was merely transiting London, but after watching the video footage again, determined that the man had been following someone. They wanted Rasim to be aware that one of Bosnia's citizens had been tailed in London by a man known to be a major player in the Russian GRU."

"And the name of this man?" asked Pat.

"Kornilov. Grigory Kornilov," Rasim answered.

Pat paled and turned to Cat, who turned her back and strode over to the Jeep. Reaching into the glove compartment, she retrieved the sat phone and dialed from memory.

When Paul Marshfield picked up the call, Cat said, "We have a big problem. We need someone in Toronto, now."

Chapter 98

Adrian strode toward Cat, his expression grim. "Twenty-six, so far. They're checking the units in the last barracks," he said. "It's bad—a lot of women and kids."

"Cause of death?" she asked.

"Poison. Cyanide, if I had to guess. We found plates with half-eaten food in each unit, some type of stew or goulash."

They both turned toward the sound of a commotion at the barracks. One of Rasim's men was running full tilt toward them.

"We have two alive—a mother and daughter!" he shouted. "Get some water and have an ambulance meet us at the bottom of the mountain. And hurry!"

Rasim bolted toward the Land Cruiser, pulled the handset from the console, and spoke to a dispatcher. Then he yelled, "Is she conscious? Is she able to talk?"

"The girl is unconscious," the runner said as he approached Rasim. "The woman is awake, but incoherent. The shed is in the sun, and it was stifling hot in there. I suspect they hid and then could not get out. Without water, it was a death trap."

Cat was already running back into the bakery, into the kitchen. She threw open the chest freezer, looking for ice. Finding none, she tossed a few bags of frozen meat and vegetables into a stockpot that was standing on the stove, then filled it with cold tap water. She filled a smaller pot with plain water and grabbed a stack of utility towels. Tucking the towels under her arm, she hefted both pots and hurried back outside.

They laid the little girl in the grass. One of the men knelt down and elevated the girl's feet, resting them against his thighs. Cat assessed her, finding a thready pulse, but the girl's breaths were shallow and ragged and her skin felt hot to the touch. Cat dunked the towels in the cold water and draped them over the girl's forehead and the back of her neck, then across her chest. When she dribbled a little water across the girl's lips, there was no response.

"Get her into the car," Cat yelled. "Turn on the air conditioner—as cold as you can get it. And keep putting wet towels on her. If she wakes up, give her sips of water. Put the mother in Pat's car and get some water in her. Go! Go!"

"What do you think of this?" one of the techs asked, as he shoved a narrow strip of paper in Gabe's face.

$$p+1/2pV2e+pgh=$$

Gabe studied the formula. "Where did you find it?"

"Third pod, in a slit in the seat cushion," the tech answered.

Arnie looked over Gabe's shoulder. "It's Bernoulli's equation," he said, puzzled. "Why would they need that?"

The tech squinted. "I'm lost. Who is Bernoulli?"

Spreading his hands, Arnie said, "It's a principle of fluid dynamics that establishes a relationship between pressure and speed. Airplanes use it in determining lift and air speed. Ships and submarines also make use of the formula in some fashion."

Gabe rolled his eyes and said, "Oh, everybody knows that. Let's see if they used it for security, too."

They walked over to the third pod, where the tech sat and typed the formula's characters into the password prompt. The screen blinked, and then opened to a clean desktop. The tech accessed the DOS prompt and entered a command to display the machine's file structure. "There," he said, pointing to a series of directories labeled Alexandria, Baku, Bangkok, Beirut, and nearly four dozen other cities around the globe. "Which first?"

"Minsk," Adrian replied.

The tech typed another command, and the screen rolled through dozens of files. He issued a command to open one, a video. Another young woman appeared on the screen, talking with an unseen man. As in the first video, the woman was being recruited to meet "the love of her life," this time in Warsaw.

"Minsk is just a half-day drive from Warsaw," the tech said.

The folders for Damascus and Karachi were much the same, except that the subjects were not young women. These were young men, marginalized and discontented, looking for a cause—and acceptance. There were hundreds of files.

The tech looked up at Adrian. "Should I continue?"

Gabe thought about the formula and its use as a password. It was easy enough to remember, particularly for a high-powered programmer, so why go to the trouble of writing it down and hiding it? Unless, he thought, someone had left it as a parting gift. "Yep. Keep going," he said.

After two hours of finding nothing more, Gabe pulled the plug. "We'll ship the files to the NSA, and I'll keep searching," he said. "If there is something there, we'll find it."

Chapter 99

August 18
Toronto, Canada

Mirko slept fitfully and woke early, ragged from three flights and nearly twenty hours of travel. The limited flight options out of Sarajevo had always been an irritation to him—even more so on this trip. His schedule was particularly tight: fly into Toronto, take care of business, and get out before evening.

He sipped his coffee and gazed out over Lake Ontario, the water beginning to glimmer with the day's first streaks of light. He had chosen the hotel primarily for its location, only a few blocks from the building where Noel Leblanc worked and, from there, a short walk to Union Station. He checked the clock again: eight minutes after seven. He wiped the cup with the washcloth, mentally reviewed everything he had touched in the hotel, and satisfied that he had wiped every surface, picked up his overnight bag and headed for the door.

He kept the cloth in his hand as he opened the door and left the room, pressed the buttons for the elevator, and exited the hotel. The bill would be duly paid from the account of a shell company registered in Delaware, with subsidiaries in loosely regulated Wyoming and Nevada, which had a few dozen additional layers of subsidiaries scattered around the Caribbean, Central America, and Africa. The arrangement ensured that money and ownership were virtually untraceable.

Twelve minutes later he was staring up at the thirty-plus stories of a shimmering glass tower overlooking the waterfront. He pushed through the revolving doors and presented himself at the lobby desk. "Peter Miller to see

Noel Leblanc," he said. "I have an appointment." His English was flawless, and the two aliases rolled off his tongue with ease.

Alert to any hint of suspicion, he watched carefully while his "Mr. Miller" identification was compared to the list of scheduled visitors for the day. Satisfied, the guard printed the visitor's pass and handed it over the counter.

Mirko clipped the visitor's pass to his lapel and rode the elevator to the twenty-eighth floor, where he was met by a confident-looking young man in his midtwenties.

"Good morning, Mr. Miller," the young man said. "I'm Avery Smith. Mr. Leblanc will be with you shortly. I'll show you to his office."

Avery led him through a trendy reception area and into the executive suite. The contemporary space was light and airy, with offices of ceiling-height glass panels mounted above cream-colored pony walls. The softly lit space in the center was occupied by a nest of sleek glassed-in worker cubicles. The open plan exposed a stunning panorama that stretched from the city skyline to the lake beyond.

Noel Leblanc's office was expansive and impossibly neat, with not so much as a paper clip out of place. Two white leather chairs faced a long glass desk, with four additional chairs positioned around a round table for working meetings. Two dove-gray settees sat on either side of a white marble coffee table between for more intimate gatherings.

Avery gestured toward the settee, and Mirko laid his briefcase on the coffee table. "What a view!" he exclaimed, taking a few steps toward the window.

"It is quite spectacular," Avery agreed. He pointed out a few landmarks and then said, "Mr. Leblanc should be here shortly." He again gestured toward the sofa.

"Thank you," Mirko said with a nod, before turning back to look out the window.

Avery shifted uncomfortably, torn between protecting his boss's privacy or offending his guest. The company he worked for, Parrish Holdings, derived much of its income from its lucrative government contracts. As such, they employed security measures to which each employee was required to adhere. His boss had already broken protocol by allowing someone without clearance into his office. He could not quite put his finger on it, but the man seemed out of place, and the circumstances of Mr. Miller's last-minute appointment were highly irregular. He finally capitulated and walked back to his cubicle. He returned to his work, but glanced up every few seconds to monitor the stranger.

Mirko could sense Avery's discomfort and watched disapprovingly as the young man settled into his cubby. He would have fired Avery on the spot for dereliction of duty. He let out a small sigh. Well-meaning Westerners could be incredibly sloppy.

He stayed by the window for another minute before turning around to study the office. Personal items were scarce—a few books, an award plaque from a local business organization, and a single framed photograph perched on his desk, an attractive woman embracing two young boys. Mirko recognized them as Noel Leblanc's wife and sons, although the boys were grown now—one a senior in college and the other a resident at Toronto General Hospital.

His back was toward the door, and he felt, rather than heard, the disturbance in the air as the door was pushed open.

"Mr. Miller, I apologize for being late," a voice said.

Mirko stood and turned to face the source of the greeting. "Hello, Noel," he said.

The color drained from Noel's face. To his credit, he managed to retain his composure. "Mr. Miller," he repeated, as he slowly shut the door.

"Call me Peter," Mirko said with a shrug.

Noel closed the space to the desk in two strides, picked up a remote, and pressed the button. Privacy shades dropped over the windows and the door. "What are you doing here? One of your Russian cronies came last week. He is supposed to be back here tomorrow," he hissed.

Mirko's heart jumped. He was the one who was supposed to pick up the product. His father had never mentioned anything about using someone else. *Why would he not tell me? Is he suspicious?* He managed to calm his anxiety and said, "We agreed that it would be better if I came personally. Daris told you that time was short."

"It was finalized yesterday. I have not had a chance to test it. And I don't keep the assembled code here. It's at home."

"Then you will need to inform your staff that we are stepping out for a breakfast meeting. And then we will take a quick trip to your home."

"I cannot just leave. I have meetings this morning."

Mirko's eyes narrowed. "This is not a request," he said. "We're going. Now."

Noel's stomach clenched. He knew what could happen to those who resisted—or to their families. He opened the door and waved to Avery, who dashed to his boss's side.

"Mr. Miller and I have decided to have our discussion over breakfast. Cancel my morning appointments. Extend my apologies and reschedule."

Avery's eyes widened. He had never known his boss to have a breakfast meeting. Never. "I'll take care of it," he said. "Shall I pull up a delivery menu?"

"Uh, no. We're going out."

The deviation from routine was so unusual that Avery could barely conceal his astonishment. He had never heard of Mr. Miller until scheduling this last-minute appointment. But his boss obviously knew the man, having confirmed the meeting and making his office available. And there seemed to be a stiff familiarity between the two, although his boss seemed distracted, even flustered. He could not dismiss the feeling of unease that had hung in the air ever since Mr. Miller had stepped into the office.

He watched his boss and Mr. Miller step into the elevator. As the doors closed, he sprang out of his seat and sprinted toward the bank of elevators. Two minutes later, he was in the lobby.

Avery craned his neck and twisted and turned in every direction, trying to spot his boss. His brow furrowed in puzzlement. Had he missed them? Or had they gone down to the PATH, the underground walkway that ran between many of the major downtown buildings? While PATH was also home to an extensive array of retail shops and eateries, Avery quickly dismissed the idea. His boss preferred spaces with sunlight. He would choose a restaurant that sat aboveground—a place with windows.

Wondering if perhaps their elevator had been a little faster, he fast-walked through the lobby and out the door, looking left and right. He told himself that he should just mind his own business and go back to his desk, but his feet took him in the direction of a nearby restaurant known for its hearty American-style breakfasts. He turned the corner and was nearly halfway down the side of the building when he saw the silver BMW nose out of the parking garage—his boss's car.

If Avery had been curious before, he was now in full-on detective mode. The BMW was turning toward him. He pivoted. Spotting a taxi pulling to the curb across the street, he sprinted toward it, arms waving. The driver acknowledged him with a come-hither gesture. He threw open the door, pointed at the Bimmer as it passed, and said, "Follow that car!"

His eyebrows lifting, the taxi driver turned in his seat and looked over his shoulder at Avery.

Avery met his stare. "I'll double the meter."

The man kept his gaze level.

"Triple," Avery said.

The man turned around, threw the taxi into gear, and pulled a one-eighty in the middle of the street. Horns blared, and several drivers demonstrated their displeasure with obscene gestures. The man ignored the fuss and kept his eyes on the target vehicle. "He's turning left on Jarvis. Any idea where he is going?"

"None whatsoever," Avery replied. But as they sped through the streets of Old Toronto and veered onto Mount Pleasant Road, he nodded his head. "You can slow down," he told the driver. "I think I know where they are going."

Rosedale, an affluent neighborhood about six kilometers north of downtown Toronto, was revered for its history, neatly manicured landscaping, parks, and lovely estate homes. It was one of Toronto's most sought-after areas. His boss's home—a sprawling Tudor with six bedrooms and seven baths—stood concealed behind a dense, three-meter hedge that kept nosy neighbors at bay. Avery had been there on a number of occasions—typically on holidays—for work-related gatherings.

The driver pulled to the curb just down the street, and they watched the BMW ease into the driveway and disappear behind the hedge.

"What do you want to do?" the taxi driver asked.

"I'm not sure," Avery replied. "Let's wait a few minutes."

Ten minutes later, a black SUV slid by and pulled into the driveway.

"Wow," the driver said. "Dip plates."

"Excuse me?" Avery said, confused.

"That SUV had red license plates. Diplomatic plates."

Avery was more puzzled than ever. Noel Leblanc did not run in diplomatic circles. He waited another five minutes and decided to check on his boss. He dialed the cell number but it went straight to voice mail. He could not decide what to do.

Noel Leblanc kept his secrets in a safe in his study—a safe accessible only with both a thumbprint and an eight-digit combination. Not even his wife could access the contents.

Taking nothing for granted, Mirko stood by the desk and turned on his phone's video to capture Noel's movements and the numeric sequence entered on the keypad.

In the safe, an aluminum box rested on a laptop. Noel lifted the box and placed it on the desk, prying open the lid. The box held an assortment of file folders and a handful of thumbnail-size metal flash drives, one gold and the rest silver. "It's all here," he said.

Mirko gestured toward the laptop. "Show me," he said.

Noel sat in the soft leather executive chair and pulled out the recessed shelf that held the keyboard. He turned on the desktop computer and pressed his right index finger onto the cable-connected fingerprint reader. He took one of the flash drives from the box and plugged it into the workstation.

Pointing to a file on the drive, Noel said, "This has the data for accessing the backdoor. And this," he said, pointing to a second file, "is the executable."

Mirko clapped Noel's back. "Great work!" he said. Then, pointing to the aluminum box, he asked, "And all those flash drives are copies of the code?"

"Yes," Noel nodded.

"Perfect," Mirko said. He palmed three of the flash drives while picking up the aluminum box. "And now we have to go."

Noel frowned. "Go where?"

Mirko slipped the drives into his pocket and said, "You cannot stay here. Eventually, the authorities will figure it out. You will end up in prison for the remainder of your life," Mirko replied. He did not add that Noel had now become a liability. There was no circumstance under which Noel could be allowed to maintain his current life. He knew too much.

Mirko ran his eyes across Noel's desk. Much like the glass desk in the office, this one had only a single photograph. It was a snapshot, old and faded, of a man and woman stiffly posed with their five children—four boys and a girl—two fair-haired and light-skinned, like their mother, the other three darker and moodier and resembling the father.

But it was not the children who drew his attention. Rather, it was the woman—the mother—who caused his stomach to plummet and his heart to stutter. Memories flooded back of a woman with a gentle touch and the scent of jasmine. *No,* he thought, *it cannot be.* And just as quickly, his mind raced to the inevitable conclusion. *Of course. It explains everything. How could I not have seen it before?*

Mirko snatched the photograph from the desk, a tsunami of anger building. He had endured years of indignities and abuse, while Noel had been raised by this woman. *My mother,* his mind screamed. Overcome with fury, he flew at Noel, pummeling him with his fists.

Noel tried to fend off the blows, and falling to his knees, crawled away. "What the hell is wrong with you?" he yelled.

Mirko turned and slammed the framed picture down on the desk, shattering the glass and cutting his hand. He pulled the photo loose and held it up for Noel to see. "This!"

His eyes wide with confusion, Noel yelled, "What are you talking about?"

Mirko could only shake his head. "We have to go. Right now." He roughly grabbed Noel by the collar and jerked him upright, pulling him toward the front of the house. He was halfway to the door when two hulking men, guns drawn, blocked his way. Mirko recognized them immediately as security officers attached to the Russian Consulate in Toronto.

"You are not needed here," Mirko said. "I did not call you."

One of the men shrugged and said, "We received orders to escort you to the airplane."

Noel staggered to his feet. "Airplane? I'm not getting on an airplane. I'm not going anywhere," he growled.

The man in front moved like lightning, putting Noel in a headlock and immobilizing him. The other stepped forward, pulled a syringe from the inner pocket of his jacket, and flipped off the cap. He was inches from Noel when the doorbell rang.

Mirko looked at the two behemoths and said, "He is not expecting anyone."

Leveling his gun at Noel, one of the men backed into the study while the other positioned himself behind the door and said, "Get rid of them."

Noel could only imagine what he must look like. His clothing and hair were certainly disheveled, and the left side of his face hurt like hell. He tried to straighten his shirt and smooth his hair, and then limped to the front of the house. He cracked the door and was startled to see Avery on the front steps, nervously shifting his weight from one foot to the other.

Noel thought fast. His eyes bored into Avery's. "Yes? May I help you?" he asked the young man.

Avery's jaw went slack. His boss was a wreck—blood seeping from a gash on his cheek and his shirt a wrinkled mess. In the blink of an eye, he recognized that he was in trouble, that he never should have followed the BMW. He had waited for some time in the taxi, wavering between going to the house and going back to the office. Finally, the driver had tapped his finger on his watch and complained. Avery had flipped open his wallet and passed several bills to the driver, telling him that he would be back in five minutes.

Now, his boss was pretending not to recognize him. Avery stepped back. "No, sir. I'm sorry to disturb you. I must have the wrong house. I was looking for Deborah Blake."

Noel nodded and said, "Next door. Number four." He started to close the door when an arm reached in front of him and threw the door fully open. As fast as a snake strike, the man clamped a towel over Avery's nose and mouth and dragged him into the house.

"Jesus!" Noel shouted. "What are you doing?"

The big man's eyes were hard. "Do you think that we do not know that this man works for you? He should never have come here."

"Oh, my God! He's just a kid! Let him go!"

The other man shoved Noel back against the wall and plunged the syringe into his neck. He looked back at his colleague and said, "Let's finish this and get out of here."

With Noel and Avery subdued, the men stormed through the house with the speed and destructive force of a tornado, grabbing laptops and desktops and tablets and phones and anything that looked even remotely electronic. They loaded the devices into the back of the SUV and dragged Noel to the rear seat, where they covered him with a floral comforter snatched from one of the bedrooms. Mirko did not know Avery's fate, but feared the worst.

As the two thugs wrestled with the equipment and Noel's limp body, Mirko backed away, surreptitiously lifting two of the drives from his pocket, pulling his pants leg up a few inches, and wedging the drives into the socket of his prosthetic leg. They would eventually search him, of that he was certain. He was equally certain that once they found the remaining drive in his pocket, they would be satisfied. They had not been hired for their brainpower.

Chapter 100

August 18
Washington, DC
Toronto, Canada

Jasmine Phillips—Jazz to her friends and colleagues—was at her desk in the Hoover Building when the call came in from Paul Marshfield. She had recently been in Miami, in response to a reported sighting of Husayn Muhammad Al-Umari, a member of the FBI's list of most wanted terrorists. A master bomb-maker, Al-Umari had been indicted for his role in architecting the 1982 bombing of a Pan Am plane en route from Tokyo to Honolulu. The source was credible, the photo spot-on, and the possibility of capturing the man had set the Bureau's counterterrorism unit afire with anticipation. But the Miami field office had been premature in declaring the terrorist found.

The suspect turned out to be an Egyptian who had immigrated to America at the age of two, attended school in Brooklyn and South Miami, graduated from the University of Florida, became a respected neurologist at Jackson Memorial, and now spent his retirement playing chess in a park in Coral Gables. He had the documents and, most important, the DNA to prove his identity. The Bureau's embarrassment was complete.

Jazz had spent the past three days completing a mountain of paperwork about the snafu. She was not happy. At the moment she heard Paul's voice, excitement kicked in. The rush, she thought, was almost as good as winning the lottery, because a call from Paul or Cat meant that big trouble was brewing. Big, verifiable trouble. And that meant big action.

"We need someone in Toronto, ASAP," Paul said. "Grab your go-bag and book the first available flight. I've cleared it with your director. Melodie is sending a file for you to read on the plane. Someone from the local authorities will meet you. Call me when you connect."

"On it," Jazz replied, already selecting her seat for the four o'clock on Air Canada. She sent a memo to her immediate boss, downloaded the file from Melodie to her laptop, closed out her workstation, and grabbed one of the two seasonal go-bags that she kept under her desk. Five minutes later, she was out the door and into an Uber.

Louise Leblanc drove into her driveway shortly after three o'clock, relieved to be home after a long meeting at the museum. For the third year in a row, she was heading the committee that organized and staged the museum's Winterfest fundraising event. Two days ago, their caterer had declared bankruptcy and closed its doors. The contractual obligations were beside the point—they had to find another caterer by the end of the week. All of yesterday and much of today had been spent making phone calls to assess availability, interest, and capability.

The garage door powered open, and she was surprised to see her husband's car. He was rarely home so early. She sighed, grabbed her briefcase, and made her way into the kitchen. She called out her husband's name and, receiving no response, assumed he was ensconced in his study. She poured a splash of vodka over two ice cubes and retrieved a folder from her briefcase. Flipping the folder open, she studied the list of potential candidates for the catering job. She absently picked up the glass, took a sip, and wandered into the great room.

Her foot hit something in the middle of the floor, causing her to stumble, and she knelt down to examine the object: a shard of glass. Puzzled, she wondered where it had come from. Then she saw the fallen ladder, lying tilted on its side, the remnants of an insanely expensive Baccarat table lamp smashed beneath it. She lifted her eyes, a half-second elapsing before the scene registered. Avery Smith dangled from one of the exposed ceiling beams, a rope around his neck, his pale face distorted in anguish. The glass slipped from her fingers, shattering on the floor. She let out an ear-piercing scream, ran toward the patio doors, fumbled with the lock, and stumbled into the backyard, where she was still screaming when the neighbors swarmed in two minutes later.

Jazz reached for her laptop at the moment she heard the chime signaling the aircraft's ascent through 10,000 feet. She had already toggled the privacy filter on and was opening Melodie's file by the time the flight attendant made the announcement.

She read the document three times, absorbing the enormity of what Cat and the team had learned. By the time she closed the laptop for landing, she was convinced that Mirko had flown to Toronto to either pick up or deliver something—and that his time in Canada would be short. Mirko was almost certainly a Russian operative; everything in the file seemed to confirm it. If they hoped to intercept him, it would have to be today.

The aircraft blocked in at the gate ten minutes early. With a seat toward the rear of the aircraft, Jazz was forced to wait as the seats in front of her cleared out. She tapped her foot impatiently as the minutes dragged by. When it became her turn to move, she stood and started to step into the aisle. An elderly couple from the next row nudged past her, then tortoise-stepped up the aisle. She grabbed her carry-on and backpack and trudged up the airbridge behind them. By the time they reached the mouth of the airbridge, she was seething with frustration. She stepped to the side and unlocked her phone.

"Ms. Phillips?" a voice queried.

Jazz raised her head to meet the alert brown eyes of a man in his late thirties. He was in uniform: gray shirt, navy pants with a yellow stripe down the side, and a navy all-weather jacket. The patch on his sleeve identified him as a member of the Royal Mounted Canadian Police, often called the RCMP or the Mounties. She noted the triple chevron on his epaulets and addressed him by rank.

"Good afternoon, Sergeant," she said. "Call me Jazz."

His smile was warm and friendly. "Catchy," he said with a chuckle. "I'm Nigel Briggs. Welcome to Canada." And then his smile faded. "There's been a development. My car is just outside. We'll talk on the way."

Nigel kept his eyes glued to the road as he brought Jazz up to speed. "We started looking for Mirko Stefanović after we got Ambassador Marshfield's call this afternoon. We know he arrived from London last night, but we had some trouble determining where he stayed. We grabbed a photo of him passing through Immigration at the airport, and we canvassed a number of hotels downtown. A desk clerk finally recognized him as one Peter Miller. She also said that Mr. Miller's English was impeccable, which was rather astonishing since we were told that he did not speak the language well."

Jazz digested the information. "He has been an asset for years. His English was documented as poor."

Nigel's eyebrows shot up. "Well, that tells us quite a bit, doesn't it?"

Jazz clicked her tongue. "That it does. This is going to give my friends quite a headache. Is he still at the hotel?"

"No," Nigel replied. "He checked out quite early. Camera footage has him walking to WaterPark Place—that's a complex down by the waterfront. Security tapes put him in one of the buildings at 7:43 this morning. He had an appointment with a man named Noel Leblanc, who is a big shot at a software development company. Twenty minutes later, the two of them took the elevator to the garage level and got into Mr. Leblanc's car. Traffic cams have the car leaving downtown and heading north. We know he must have left the main road near an area called Rosedale, because he disappeared between two traffic cameras. As it turns out, Mr. Leblanc lives in Rosedale."

"They went to Leblanc's house? That's almost twelve hours ago. Are they still there?" Jazz asked.

"No. We've run into a situation. At about three o'clock, Mrs. Leblanc came home to find a man hanging from a ceiling beam in her home. She is rather distressed."

"Not her husband, I assume?"

"No. The victim was Mr. Leblanc's assistant, a young man named Avery Smith. He did not leave the building with Mr. Leblanc, and we don't yet know how he got to Rosedale. There's no sign of Mr. Leblanc or your friend from Bosnia. We're working on it."

Chapter 101

August 18
Toronto, Canada

By the time Jazz and Nigel arrived at the scene, the sun had set, and darkness had settled in. The street and driveway in front of the Leblanc home were ablaze with red and blue flashing lights, and uniforms swarmed the property. Jazz took a deep breath, steeling herself for a jurisdictional dispute and possibly a hostile welcoming committee. She never knew how the locals would react to the FBI showing up.

Nigel gave her an appraising look and said, "Not to worry; they know you're coming. They might even be grateful. It will be a relief to have the public heap manure on an outsider for a change—particularly since Canada-US relations have been somewhat sour of late."

Jazz responded with a wry grin. "Thanks for the warning. Glad to be of assistance."

He burst out laughing. "They're going to like you."

She followed him up the driveway, where he introduced her to a team of investigators. One of the men stepped forward.

"I'm Sergeant Bromley," he said. "As to what we know so far, well, Mrs. Leblanc found the victim hanging from a joist in the great room, with a fallen ladder underneath. It could be a suicide. Thus far, we have not found anything indicating otherwise, but we are early in the investigation. The coroner's findings could tell a different tale. You should know that we found a flash drive in his pocket that is full of pornography, as well as videos that appear to be an organized effort at human trafficking. What do you know about any of that?"

Jazz tilted her head, her eyes narrowing. "We have just uncovered a significant human trafficking operation in Bosnia. This happened today, so information is somewhat spotty. I flew in because we just learned that one of the suspects flew into Toronto last night—after first eliminating any witnesses. About three dozen men, women, and children were murdered."

The revelation caught the group's attention as they suddenly realized that this investigation was about much more than the suspicious death of a single man.

Jazz ran her eyes across the gathering and spread her hands wide. "And then he came here, to Toronto. He came here to meet with Mr. Leblanc. Why? That's what we have to find out. He was here for a reason—something important enough to warrant being tailed at Heathrow Airport by a senior member of Russian intelligence. I am requesting permission to nose around a bit. Something here captured the interest of Russian intelligence. Let's figure out what that is."

Sergeant Bromley studied her for a minute and then nodded. "You will have to suit up."

"Fine by me," Jazz said. She started to leave and then turned back. "After we talk, I would like to have a conversation with Mrs. Leblanc. It would be easier if she could stay here until then."

"You think she's involved? She's a very prominent ..."

Jazz held up her hand to interrupt him. "Here's the problem," she said. "All we know right now is that the stench from Bosnia has made its way to this house. She may not know anything, but her husband, I promise you, is most assuredly involved. I will try to be kind."

At that, the sergeant grinned. "Better you than me," he said.

Nigel, standing beside her, tapped his shoe against hers. "Told you so," he whispered.

Jazz donned the requisite hooded jumpsuit, booties, and gloves and went inside. The house was considerably larger than it appeared from the outside, and if past experience held true, the investigators would be there for hours.

She trailed Nigel through the foyer, noticing the little evidence tags on the floor that marked droplets of what might be blood. They continued down the long hall, passing a study, large formal dining room, and two powder rooms. As she walked into the spacious living room, her gaze shifted toward the ceiling. She decided that a fit young man of average height could have climbed the ladder, looped the rope over the exposed joist, tied a slipknot around his neck, and then kicked the ladder away. *Too soon to know for sure,* she thought.

There was fingerprint powder everywhere—on the broken lamp, the ladder, the coffee tables—anywhere that Avery Smith might have touched before leaving this world. There seemed to be little to find in the room, so she walked up to Nigel and canted her head back toward the front door. "Did you notice the study?" she asked him. "Let's take a look."

The study's French doors were wide open, and additional evidence markers were scattered about the room. One of the techs was placing an item in an evidence bag.

"There was a struggle here," Jazz observed, walking over to the desk where the tech was working. "Could you just show me what you have there?"

The tech replied, "It's a picture frame. The glass was broken, and there's a blood smear."

"But no photo?"

"Not that we've found."

Jazz looked around the minimally furnished study and then turned back to the desk, modern and devoid of clutter. She turned to Nigel and said, "There is little of his personal life here, so whatever was in the frame was important to him."

She stepped behind the desk for a look, taking stock of the open—and empty—safe embedded in the wall. She let her gaze wander over the wall. Two plaques were displayed there, both from professional organizations in Toronto. Between them hung a framed newspaper article with a black-and-white photograph of Noel Leblanc. The article, touting the rising software whiz, was more than twenty years old. The photo showed a man with hair that brushed his chin, a mustache, and a short, boxed beard. His hair was neither light nor dark. Jazz judged it to be light-to-medium brown. His eye color was indeterminate. For a moment, something about him seemed familiar.

"Found anything?" asked Nigel.

Jazz stood motionless, studying the photo. When she turned around, she shook her head. "For a second, the man in this picture triggered something, but I've lost the thought. I wonder what he looks like beneath all that hair."

Nigel's phone buzzed. He looked at the caller ID on the screen and left the room to take the call. A few minutes later, he beckoned to Jazz, and she joined him in the hallway.

"They've been reviewing the street cameras," Nigel said. "About five minutes after Mr. Leblanc's car turned into this neighborhood, a black SUV—also coming from the south—turned onto the same street. About an hour and fifteen minutes later, the same SUV left the area, via a different street leading north. None of that would be unusual, except that the SUV had diplomatic plates."

"Diplomatic plates? Which mission?"

"The Russian Federation. They have a consulate about two and a half kilometers from here."

Jazz felt her mouth drop open. "Are you telling me the Russians had a car in this neighborhood at the same time that Mr. Stefanović was here with Mr. Leblanc?"

"It would appear so," Nigel nodded.

"Well, well. So now the million-dollar question is who they were after— Mr. Stefanović or Mr. Leblanc? Both? Is there any evidence that they came to the Leblanc house?"

"Not yet. We're canvassing the neighbors. Hopefully someone will have a security camera."

"I think it's time we had a chat with Mrs. Leblanc."

Jazz paused in the shadows of the hallway, taking a moment to observe Louise Leblanc. The woman was pale and haggard, continually shifting her position, twining and untwining her fingers, and shaking her right foot. Clearly she was upset, but Jazz could not discern whether she was simply fidgety, distraught about finding the body, or distressed about her missing husband. Jazz pursed her lips, wondering how much the woman knew and whether she should take a hard or soft approach when talking to her. She made a decision and walked into the room.

"Mrs. Leblanc, my name is Jasmine Phillips. I'm with the American FBI. I realize that this is a difficult time for you, but I have a number of questions to ask."

The woman looked up, wide-eyed, like an animal caught in a car's headlights. Jazz wondered if the reaction was merely surprise at the FBI's involvement or something more sinister.

"First," Jazz said, "I know you are very distressed that your husband is missing. The Toronto Police and the RCMP are doing everything they can to find him."

"Thank you," Louise mumbled.

"Do you know if there was anyone who might want to hurt your husband? Has he received any threats?"

Louise shook her head emphatically. "No. He is well-liked."

Jazz noticed Louise's use of the present tense when referring to her husband. Maybe Louise believed that he was still alive. "I saw the newspaper article in the study, when he was younger. He was quite a handsome guy. Was it love at first sight?"

Louise blinked, caught off guard, then recovered. She smiled wistfully. "It was magic."

Jazz smiled back. "Where did you meet?"

"Switzerland. He was on business; I was a tourist."

"That must have been romantic! Switzerland is such a lovely place. I've been to Geneva a few times, and tried skiing once in a place called Lenzerheide. I was awful."

Disarmed, Louise leaned back and relaxed. "We met in Zurich, but not at a ski resort. I, too, am a terrible skier. I think you have to learn when you are young."

"Exactly—before you are old enough to be scared," Jazz agreed. Then she asked, "There was a picture, on his desk, in a silver frame."

Louise was momentarily taken aback by the change in subject. "The one of his family? They are ... were ... very dear to him."

"Were? Oh, I'm sorry—have they passed away?"

Louise cast her eyes down to the floor and shifted uncomfortably. "Yes. All dead, I'm afraid."

"Mrs. Leblanc, I am asking because the photo is missing. Perhaps your husband took it, since it was special to him. Would you happen to have a copy?"

A deep crease appeared between the woman's eyebrows. Jazz could not tell if the woman was worried about the content of the photo or was simply trying to remember if there was a copy.

"Perhaps," Louise responded. "I would have to look. Why does it matter?"

Jazz tried to be reassuring, wanting to avoid putting too much emphasis on the photo. Louise's cooperation was crucial. "I've found that it's the little things that sometimes hold a clue. Perhaps the photo could help us find him."

The woman nodded. "I will look," she said.

Jazz sat up straighter, crossed her legs, and lifted her chin, adopting a sterner posture. "Mrs. Leblanc, a man went to your husband's office early this morning. This man and your husband got into your husband's car and drove here. Now both of those men seem to be missing." She held up a photo captured from the surveillance camera in the building's underground garage. "Do you recognize him?"

Louise stared at the photo, her eyelids fluttering briefly, before saying, "No. I do not know him."

"Did your husband discuss this meeting with you?"

"No, he rarely talks to me about his business."

"Do you have any idea who the man might have been?"

Louise shifted again. "I have no idea."

Jazz decided to turn up the heat and said, "The surveillance photo is not the best quality." She held the laptop so Louise could see the old photo of Mirko. "This is a better photo. This is the same man, twenty years ago, Mrs. Leblanc. Are you sure you do not recognize him?"

Louise appeared to be genuinely shocked. "Oh! He looked quite different then!"

"So, you do know him," Jazz said.

"I met him once, years ago. I was downtown, joining friends for lunch. I spotted my husband at a table, with this man. We were introduced but I never talked with him. I do not know him. I do not even remember his name."

"His name is Mirko Stefanović, Mrs. Leblanc."

Louise wore a blank expression and gave no reaction to the name. "I do not know. I met him only briefly I cannot tell you who he is."

"Mirko Stefanović. He is a Russian agent. Did you know that?"

Louise blinked in surprise and then showed a spark of irritation. "I have told you that I do not know the man," she growled. "How would I know anything about him? And my husband would never knowingly meet with a Russian agent. It could undermine the work that his company performs for the government."

"What type of work is that?" Jazz asked.

Louise's cheeks flamed red, and she threw up her hands in angry frustration. "I have no idea. I only know that his company has a number of important government contracts. I already told you that my husband does not discuss his business with me."

Nigel's phone buzzed again, and he withdrew to the hall to take the call. When he returned, he remained standing. "We know where your husband is."

Her interest piqued, Jazz sat up straight and lifted her eyes to Nigel. Nigel's announcement had the opposite effect on Louise, who slumped low into the couch and pulled a throw pillow tight to her chest.

"He boarded an airplane at Pearson," Nigel said.

Puzzlement erased the fear from Louise's expression. "I do not understand. He would never leave without telling me and he did not call. He never mentioned going anywhere."

Jazz lifted her hand to her forehead and squeezed her temples, thinking. *He boarded an airplane? How is that possible?*

"We have video," Nigel said. He placed his phone on the table, allowing Louise and Jazz to view it.

They watched as a black SUV drove up and parked next to an airplane parked on the tarmac. Four men exited the car. More accurately, three men exited the car under their own power. The fourth was pulled from the car and, supported by two muscled men, lifted up the steps and into the plane.

Louise was stunned. "What are they doing? Have they kidnapped my husband? Where are they taking him? You need to go after them!"

Jazz caught Nigel's eyes and mouthed, "Tell her."

Nigel swallowed and said, "We cannot intercept them. They are long gone. This footage was from eleven-thirty this morning. That aircraft is an extended-range Gulfstream. It will go nonstop and they are already more than halfway there."

"Halfway to where?" screamed Louise.

"Moscow," replied Nigel.

Chapter 102

Jazz and Nigel adjourned to the backyard, leaving Louise Leblanc in the company of two officers while she looked for a copy of the missing photo. The officers were under strict instructions to keep a close eye on Louise Leblanc, fearing that she might attempt to hide or destroy evidence. Nigel lit a cigarette, took three puffs, and stubbed it out.

"My first in a month," he said to Jazz's raised eyebrows.

"If I were a smoker, I would join you. But there is nothing that will stop me from having a couple of stiff drinks when I get to the hotel," Jazz said. "I don't get it. Why did they take Leblanc? And why kill the assistant? The Russians often operate with impunity, but this seems a little extreme—even for them."

"How much do you think Louise Leblanc knows?"

Jazz thought for a moment, then said, "I think she knows her husband was involved in something, but I doubt she knew many details. You may learn more when you interrogate her, including things she doesn't realize that she knows. I am sure there is more to this story than we know right now. Was he selling secrets to the Russians? Regardless, the kidnapping of a Canadian citizen is going to give Ottawa a major diplomatic headache. I'm assuming your government will file a formal protest with the Russians, but that's problematic. What will they say? Give us back your spy so we can throw him in jail?"

"Fortunately, that call will be above my pay grade. What will you do about Stefanović?"

"Good question," answered Jazz. "That will be up to the Bosnians. He's not Canadian, and he appears to have gone willingly. The only way they get him back is if the Bosnians press charges for the murders in Sarajevo. I just don't know how the evidence will stack up. And to second what you just said, that call will be above my pay grade."

Nigel nodded and said, "You need to call your people—before they hear it on CNN."

"Yes, to tell them that the man with all the answers has slipped through our fingers," she said bitterly.

She sat on a stone wall in the garden and patted the space beside her. "Join in," she said to Nigel. "They'll have questions."

Jazz waited for Paul to tie in the team in Bosnia, then introduced Nigel. "He's here to give you the Canadian perspective on what we've learned. I'm sure you'll have questions. But first, how are the mother and the little girl?"

Cat's expression turned grim, and she shook her head. "The girl died on the way to the hospital. The mother is in bad shape. The doctors are not optimistic. Simply horrible. And she is the only eyewitness. Without her ..." She left the thought unfinished. "What have you learned?"

"Stefanović had a meeting early this morning with one Noel Leblanc, a successful software executive. They met at Mr. Leblanc's office and then drove to the Leblanc home. Mr. Leblanc's car is parked in the garage, but the two men were missing. Mrs. Leblanc returned home this afternoon to find her husband's assistant hanging from a beam in the living room. Of note is that they found a flash drive on his person, with porno and a number of videos that appear to be part of a sex trafficking scheme. And there's more.

"The Canadians determined that an SUV with dip plates was in the neighborhood at the same time as Stefanović and Mr. Leblanc. The plates are assigned to the Russian Consulate, and the SUV was tracked leaving the neighborhood and entering the consulate grounds. They have footage of an identical SUV, also with plates, that left the consulate and drove to the General Aviation area of Pearson Airport. Four men boarded an extended-range Gulfstream, including Stefanović and Leblanc. Mr. Leblanc was, uh, assisted. Our assessment is that he was drugged. They should be landing in Moscow about now."

Cat clenched her fists, aching to punch the video monitor. She closed her eyes and silently counted to ten, letting the anger dissipate. "So, Stefanović is out of reach."

"For the moment, yes, although Mr. Leblanc might not be. The Canadians are digesting the incident and will probably issue a protest. The hiccup is that he was likely engaged in some sort of nefarious arrangement with the Russians, so they will be reluctant to give him back."

"Never mind his association with a mass murderer," Cat hissed. "Was Leblanc part of the trafficking ring?"

"The techs will go through his files—if they can find any. The kidnappers took all his electronics. We're hoping he has backups in the cloud."

"What else have you learned?"

Jazz winced. "Not much. I'm trying to figure out the connection between Stefanović and Leblanc. There was an old photograph of his family and a photo of him as a young up-and-comer here in Toronto. Something about that picture tickled my brain, but I can't quite put it together."

Cat drummed her fingers on the table. "Send the photos to Consuela Calderon. She is a magician with faces. We're headed to the airport. I'll call you when we are back in Washington. We've run out of leads here. Goran is dead, and the Bosnians tell me that his brother Daris is out of the country on some classified mission. They are being unnaturally tight-lipped about his activities, which makes me curious. We'll see if our people can dig up something more concrete. In the meantime, everyone here will have their hands full with those videos."

Pat leaned into the camera and said, "You should know that I had a brief conversation with Goran's daughter. Unless she is an Oscar-caliber actress, she knew nothing about her father's activities. We are going to hit her with more questions in the morning. There is always the possibility that she might know something that she doesn't consider important."

"Let's keep each other fully informed," said Cat. "There are just too many moving pieces here, and we don't want anything—or anyone—to fall through the cracks."

When the officers brought Louise back downstairs, she was pinned between them, each tightly gripping one of her arms. The two men were visibly agitated.

"What happened?" Nigel asked.

"She found the photo you were looking for, Agent Phillips, but then we caught her trying to slip another one inside her blouse." He handed two photos to Jazz.

Jazz peered at the first photo, a black-and-white snapshot of a family standing in front of a half-built barn. The mother was fair, the father more Mediterranean. The five children represented both sides of the gene pool: two fair-haired boys, two dark-haired boys, and a dark-haired girl.

She set the photo down and picked up the picture that Louise had tried to hide. Her eyes snapped open. "Is this Mirko Stefanović?" she asked Louise. "Were you involved with him?"

The blood drained from Louise's face. She opened her mouth, as if to speak, and then her expression dissolved into one of bewilderment. Jazz could not tell if she was trying to invent a response, or fitting pieces in a jigsaw. Finally, she looked at Nigel and said, "I wish to speak with my solicitor."

Nigel and Jazz exchanged a look, their thoughts coming to the same conclusion: *This woman knows much more than she is saying.*

Jazz used her phone to snap images of the three photos: the family with five children, Noel Leblanc as a young man, and the picture that Louise had tried to hide.

"I'll send these off to our people. Hopefully someone, somewhere, can shed some light on them," she said to Nigel. "In the meantime, I'd like to stick around for a day or two to see what else turns up and if Louise Leblanc has more to say. But for now, let's call it a night."

They rode back to the city in silence. Nigel pulled to the front of the hotel and turned to Jazz. "Why did they have to kill that poor young man? I don't see the sense of it."

"I think it was a warning to the people in the neighborhood," replied Jazz. "Russian messaging can be brutal, and it's effective. They let everyone know that they are willing to kill. I'll wager that several of the neighbors have already received threats. That's why no one will admit to having spotted the SUV."

Nigel blanched. "It's like we're back in the days of the cold war."

Jazz stepped out of the car and then leaned back in, saying, "The reality is that it never really went away."

Chapter 103

August 19
Sarajevo, Bosnia and Herzegovina

Pat Desmond stepped up to the door of the darkened Sretna Kafa and tried the handle. Locked. She tapped lightly on the door and waited. With no response, she pressed her forehead against the glass pane and peered into the gloom. A movement in the back of the shop caught her eye, and she gestured to the man just behind her.

SIPA Captain Rasim Graovac nudged Pat aside and rapped sharply on the door's wooden frame. He announced his credentials and added, "Open the door. If you do not comply, we will break it down and place you under arrest."

Goran's daughter stormed to the door and threw it open. Her face was mottled and puffy, and her eyes were swollen from weeping, but anger overwhelmed her grief. "What do you want?" she raged. "I have told you that I know nothing."

Pat locked eyes with the young woman and placed her hand on her shoulder. "We have nearly three dozen people who have been murdered, your father among them. We have to gather every detail to find out what really happened. I think you want the truth as well. Help us find out who did this terrible thing."

Nayla Terzić shrugged in resignation and led them to the back room, out of view of reporters and curiosity seekers who might peer in the front windows. The room served as both an office and—judging by the rumpled sofa and blanket—an occasional sleeping place as well. They huddled around a small table, with only a desk lamp to illuminate the space.

Nayla folded and unfolded her hands as she explained that she had been to the bakery only twice—that the bakery was solely the domain of her father and her Uncle Daris. She stated that since she had begun working at the café two years ago, when her father got sick, he had rarely gone to the bakery.

"He was very ill—lung cancer," Nayla said softly. "And he was suffering from dementia. It's why I started taking care of the shop. He would mix up orders, forget how to prepare the coffee, neglect to collect when taking the orders, and sometimes yell at customers. I tried to keep him busy with little things, like polishing the brass."

"Where is your Uncle Daris?" asked Captain Graovac.

She shook her head. "I do not know. I have not seen him since early summer. He works for army intelligence, and sometimes he will disappear for months. I have no knowledge of what he does or where he goes. He never reveals anything about his work."

Pat watched Nayla very carefully as she asked her next question. "What is the relationship between Mirko Stefanović and your father?"

Nayla shrugged. "They have been friends for many years. Daris knew him from the war. When my father brought our family here, we grew close to him as well."

Pat pulled out her phone and tapped to the family snapshot that Jazz had sent her the night before. "Do you recognize this photo?"

Touching the screen gently, Nayla offered a sad smile. "This is my father's family. Where did you find this photo?"

Ignoring the question, Jazz asked, "This is your father, here on the left, isn't it?"

"Yes," Nayla nodded.

"Who are the others?" Pat prodded.

"My Aunt Zora and Uncle Vedad—on the right—were killed by Serbs during the war. My grandmother, too. My grandfather died before that—a heart attack, I think."

"And the one standing next to your father? He looks a bit like Mirko."

"Oh no," said Nayla. "We did not know Mirko until after the war." She hesitated, then added, "I'm not supposed to talk about him."

Pat frowned in puzzlement. "What do you mean? You are not supposed to talk about Mirko?"

"No, my other uncle. We are forbidden to talk about him," Nayla replied.

Rasim and Pat glanced at each other. Rasim said, "Perhaps you should explain."

Nayla bowed her head and mumbled to herself, as if praying for guidance. Thirty seconds passed before she raised her head and spoke. "That is my Uncle Zlatan. From what I have overheard, I think he was a spy, recruited by the CIA. He was best friends with Mirko during the war, and he is the one who introduced Daris and my father to Mirko. All I know is that he moved to another country—years ago—and it was very secretive. We were never allowed to mention his name. If anyone inquired about him, we were instructed to say that he died in the war."

Pat's stomach tightened. She showed Nayla the photo that Louise Leblanc had tried to hide.

Nayla smiled. "That is my uncle. He was a very handsome man. My father had the same photo, hidden in a book. I think they were very close, because I would sometimes catch him looking at the picture and talking to it. I think they set up a meeting some years ago, but my father was upset afterward, because my uncle no longer looked the same."

Pat felt dizzy. "What do you mean?"

"I overheard my father talking with Uncle Daris. Uncle Zlatan had some surgery—you know—to change his appearance."

Pat held her breath as she showed the last photo to Nayla. "Is this your uncle?"

Nayla's eyebrows knitted together as she studied the photo. "It could be," she said. "He looks different, and his hair was lighter. I cannot say with certainty because I have not seen him since I was a child. I never saw what he looked like later. What color are his eyes?"

"I'm not sure," Pat said. "Why?"

"My uncle has gray eyes. Like my father's—and mine."

Chapter 104

August 19
Toronto, Canada

Jazz was waiting at the curb when Nigel picked her up at seven-thirty in the morning. As soon as she climbed into the car, he handed her a Starbucks cup. As he pulled into traffic, she sipped the hot coffee and told him about the latest events in Bosnia.

"The photo that Louise Leblanc was trying to hide was a picture of Zlatan Terzić, who is the brother of Goran Terzić and a close friend of Mirko Stefanović, who was with Noel Leblanc yesterday."

"And yet, she claims ignorance," Nigel said, rolling his eyes. "Her solicitor will be present today. Let's hope that he has persuaded her to be cooperative."

"We also learned that Zlatan Terzić left the country years ago, and had some surgery to alter his looks. I suspect that Zlatan Terzić and Noel Leblanc could be the same person. I would like to try and get her to confirm this."

Nigel glanced over at her, a look of surprise on his face. "Reach over and grab my satchel, would you? In the pocket there is an inventory of the contents of Noel Leblanc's bathroom—medications and such. I believe I saw something about hair dye."

Jazz pulled the papers from his satchel and scanned the list. She stabbed at the page and laughed wickedly. "Gotcha, Louise! This is perfect! Do you have any new information on the Russians?"

"Not yet. My understanding is the prime minister is poised to lodge a formal complaint with them today."

Jazz took another sip. "This could prove to be an interesting day."

They were about halfway to the Toronto Police headquarters when Jazz's phone buzzed. *Consuela.* She put the phone on speaker.

"Good morning, Consuela. You're on speaker. I have Nigel Briggs from the RCMP with me. We're in a car. If we're disconnected, I'll call you back. I assume you got the photos I sent. Any luck?"

Consuela's voice was tight. "There's no luck involved. I know that face like the back of my hand."

Jazz was nonplussed. "You recognize someone? Which photo?"

"All three, actually. They are the same person. Second from the left in the family photo, perfect likeness on the young man with the light hair, and surgical alteration on the young man with the dark hair."

"Ah! So Zlatan Terzić is Noel Leblanc," Jazz said with a satisfied smile.

Consuela said, "I don't know who Zlatan Terzić is, but the face in those photos is Michael Cantrell. I'd stake my life on it. Tell me you have him!"

Confusion spread over Jazz's face, followed by comprehension and then horror as she processed Consuela's words. She swiveled toward Nigel and shouted, "Pull over! Stop the car!" She blew out a long breath and lowered her voice, then asked Consuela, "Michael Cantrell? You're sure?"

"Like I said …"

"My God. We just missed him. He was on a plane to Moscow last night. Have you told Cat?"

"Not yet," Consuela said.

Nigel jerked the car to the shoulder and stood on the brakes. "Who is Michael Cantrell?"

Jazz held up an index finger. "Hang on," she commanded. "I'm adding Cat to the call."

The phone rang several times. "C'mon," she murmured. When Cat picked up, Jazz interrupted the greeting. "I'm with Sergeant Nigel Briggs of the RCMP. We're on our way to interview Louise Leblanc. I have Consuela on the line. She has just identified Noel Leblanc as Michael Cantrell. How do you want us to handle this?"

After a long moment of silence, Cat asked, "Are you sure, Consuela?"

"One hundred percent," came the reply.

"First and foremost," Cat said, "you cannot mention anything about Michael Cantrell to anyone, including Mrs. Leblanc. Early this morning, the Canadian prime minister instructed his ambassador in Moscow to lodge a formal protest with the Russian government. They are demanding the return of Mr. Leblanc. If they are successful, the US government will then seek to extradite him. But if we identify him as Michael Cantrell before he steps back on Canadian soil, any chance of Mr. Leblanc's return will go down the toilet—along with any chance of bringing him to justice."

"Sergeant Briggs, I cannot stress enough the importance of keeping this information to yourself. I will bring your government up to speed the moment Mr. Leblanc is safely within their grasp. I will leave it to Agent Phillips to provide more context for you. Keep me informed. I'm in the air, so phones are spotty. Leave a message, and I'll call you back."

Cat hung up, and Nigel looked over at Jazz. "Who in the world is Michael Cantrell?"

Jazz looked straight into his eyes. "The man who bombed Transoceanic 367."

Louise Leblanc and her lawyer took seats across the table from Nigel and Jazz. Nigel recognized him immediately: Keith Hardwick, one of the most successful barristers in the country. Nudging Jazz, he gestured under the table, pointing his thumb down. He had been hoping for someone more cooperative and was surprised when the lawyer requested that Louise be allowed to make an opening statement. The request was unusual, but Nigel nodded.

"Mrs. Leblanc would like to clarify her remarks from yesterday," Mr. Hardwick said. "She was under a great amount of stress, having found a dead man in her home and with her husband missing under suspicious circumstances. Please listen to her story, and I am sure you will understand that she was very much unaware of any shenanigans regarding her husband's business affairs."

Louise lowered her head, seemingly to gather her thoughts and the strength to tell her story. She looked up, and said, "I regret that I was not completely forthright with you yesterday. I was frightened and worried about my husband. I still am, but have decided that revealing the truth is the right thing to do."

She took a deep breath and said, "I actually met my husband in Germany, in Frankfurt, at the airport. I had just flown in to meet my boyfriend, but while I was over the Atlantic, he apparently decided to end the relationship.

He didn't even show up at the airport. I only found out after I called him. I was upset, as you might imagine.

"I found a little restaurant where I could sit down and figure out what to do next. Noel sat down beside me. He told me that he had managed to escape from Bosnia and fly to Germany. He told me that Serbians were trying to kill him. He was hiding until nightfall while he worked out a way of getting to Zurich. He suggested that perhaps we could help each other.

"He also told me that he had a lot of money at a bank in Zurich. I dressed him in some of my clothing, wrapped a scarf around his face, and bought train tickets to Zurich. We spent two nights there while he made arrangements with his bank. And then we flew to Thailand.

"In Bangkok, I reached out to some old friends. They facilitated an introduction to a plastic surgeon. After the surgery, we spent a couple of months at the beach in Phuket … um … recovering. The doctor recommended a friend who could obtain a Thai passport to match Noel's new face. We got married in Phuket, and then we flew to Canada. I was able to arrange a visa and job with a small software firm. He got his citizenship papers a couple of years later. Not long thereafter, he purchased the company. He has been there ever since.

"I was never involved in any of his business dealings, and I know nothing about the projects he was working on—only that the company had a number of government contracts and he was not free to discuss them. We held company parties at our home two or three times a year—that was the extent of my dealings with the employees there. That's all I really know."

Over the years, Jazz had interviewed all manner of criminals and their associates, family, and friends. She had lost count of the times when the people closest to the suspect were completely in the dark. While she was inclined to believe the woman, there were still questions to be answered.

"Where did he get the money to buy the company?" she asked.

"He said he used his investments. I believed him."

"So you did not, in any way, assist with the purchase?"

"I did not. He told me that he had made a killing investing in some of the new dot-coms."

"Tell us about any contact he may have had with the Russians or people associated with the Russian government."

"I am not aware of any contact with the Russians. And considering his secrecy about his government contracts, I cannot even imagine why he would deal with them."

"But you did see him previously in the company of Mirko Stefanović, correct?"

Louise nodded. "Yes, but I had no idea who he was."

Nigel hesitated for a moment, then said, "You have admitted that you were fully aware that your husband entered Canada under a false identity and that you facilitated that deception."

"Yes. I am guilty of that. I was young and in love. But it was years ago, and he has been a model citizen. Look at all he has contributed to this country! That should count for something."

"And yet, he continued to be afraid of the Serbians? Is that why he dyed his hair?"

Louise had the grace to blush. "He started doing that while we were in Phuket. And when he got the Thai passport, the photo had dark hair."

Jazz asked, "Mrs. Leblanc, what was your husband's name? Before you helped him establish a new one?"

Louise frowned. "I am not sure that I can recall the name he used."

"How about Zlatan Terzić?" Jazz asked.

Louise was still for a minute, and Jazz knew that she was trying to decide whether or not to confess that she knew the name.

"Yes, that was his birth name," she admitted. "I have not thought about it in years."

Jazz leaned forward, her elbows on the table. "Now is the time to be truthful. What else did you learn about your husband's past?"

Louise frowned and hesitated before saying, "There is only one thing I can think of. On our first night in Zurich, while he was in the shower, I looked through his things. He had his Bosnian passport, but there was also one from Canada."

Pressing the tips of her fingers to her eyes, Louise tried to recall the name. "Graham ... Graham Stadler. When I asked him about it, he became angry. But then he calmed down and told me that he had done some work for the CIA, and that they had arranged a Canadian passport for one of his assignments. He used that same passport for our flight to Thailand, but he burned it once we got to Phuket. We never spoke of it again."

Jazz almost choked when Louise mentioned the CIA, since Cat had admitted that they had manufactured the Michael Cantrell identity. Now she had to ask herself if they had also arranged a Canadian passport. *But why? Or did the Russians arrange it?*

After the interview, Jazz and Nigel sat by themselves in the small interview room. Nigel pushed back his chair and dropped his arms into his lap. "Do you think she is telling the truth?" he asked. "Do you think she knew about any of it?"

Jazz put her fingers to her lips and tapped lightly, then stood and walked over to the window. The chill of autumn was in the air, and there were splotches of red and yellow among the leaves. She had a brief fancy that the changing season foretold a turn in solving the Transoceanic crash and Maggie Marshfield's death—that anyone involved would soon wither and fall. She looked back to Nigel.

"I believe her," she said. "I think she was a naive young lady who was desperately craving a lasting relationship and was, instead, jilted by her lover. Along comes Zlatan Terzić—handsome, attentive, mysterious, a regular Prince Charming—to fulfill her dreams of romance. She was the perfect conduit for his metamorphosis into Noel Leblanc. She had her sons and her social status and a beautiful home. I doubt that she gave much thought to her husband's past or his business dealings. Ignorance is bliss."

He nodded thoughtfully. "I had the same feeling."

Jazz's phone buzzed: a video call from Cat. She joined the call and was surprised to see Cat speaking from a leather seat on an airplane.

"Where are you?" she asked.

"Over Nova Scotia, according to the pilot. We left in the middle of the night, after a long and intense debriefing with the Bosnians. How did it go with Mrs. Leblanc?"

Jazz said, "Nigel and I agree that she probably knows very little. But for the moment, I think it's best to keep the book open on her."

Melodie raised her hand and said, "I have news regarding the DNA tests. We already had results from Noel Leblanc's brother, Goran Terzić, and the RCMP sent samples from Mr. Leblanc and Mirko Stefanović. We shoved them all to the highest priority. As I was studying the photos of these men, I was struck by their similarities in appearance. When I learned that two of them had gray eyes, I suspected that they might be related. The DNA confirms they all had the same mother."

"Brothers!" Cat exclaimed. She pressed her fists into her temples, absorbing the ramifications of Mirko Stefanović having duped the American embassy in Sarajevo for years. She asked, "How does this tie in to the Russians?"

Melodie replied, "I did a deep dive into Grigory Kornilov's background. He has a reputation for brutality and is suspected to have planned a number of assassinations and other nasty business over the last two decades. Even so, he has largely flown under the radar. Suddenly he pops up in Sarajevo and London and is personally dealing with a minor player like Mr. Stefanović? It didn't make sense."

"Unless he has a relationship with them," said Cat.

"Exactly," Melodie agreed. "And Kornilov also has gray eyes, by the way, which confirms nothing but did heighten my curiosity. I found an old newspaper report. In 1960, Kornilov's wife and two young sons were reportedly killed in a car crash. Another son, a year older, was at school at the time of the accident. I'm postulating here, but I think his wife absconded with two of the boys."

Cat cradled her chin in her hand. Her eyes took on a faraway look as she thought about Melodie's conclusion. "That fits," she said. "But we don't have Kornilov's DNA as proof."

"That is correct," replied Melodie. "It's circumstantial at best, unless he claims them as his long-lost sons. Nor do we have any physical evidence that Michael Cantrell and Noel Leblanc are the same person. The airline did not take employee fingerprints, and it was years before DNA testing became available. All we have is a photo—and Consuela's certainty. I will say that the thing that cemented it for me was his wife's story of how the two met."

Paul joined the call. With fury in his voice, he said, "I just got off a call with our Canadian friends. Moscow has denied their protest. They are claiming that Noel Leblanc is a Russian citizen."

Cat, her face clouded by fury, slammed a fist onto a small table by her seat. She stared darkly at the screen. "He's going to get away with it," she fumed.

Chapter 105

August 19
Moscow, Russia

The aircraft door opened to the chilly Moscow dawn, the sky cloudy and dull. Hoping to make eye contact with his brother, Mirko Stefanović glanced over his shoulder. It was not to be. Zlatan—or Noel, as he was now known—was still hooded and restrained at the back of the plane. Mirko descended the stairs and was quickly encircled by three of his father's men, then shuttled to the waiting car. He endured the ride in silence and then followed the men up to the unfamiliar third-floor apartment where his father now lived. The space was larger, brighter, and more modern than the drab four-room apartment he had known as a child. He flopped into an overstuffed chair in the study, stretched his legs out, leaned his head back, and put his brain to work. Returning to Moscow with his father had not been part of his plan.

Grigory Kornilov was masterful at designing operations to undermine foreign governments—and revered by those he worked with—but he had been a brutal tyrant to his family. Mirko had terrifying memories of dark nights when his mother had begged for mercy—and of the bruises she had tried to conceal with makeup and layered clothing.

He and his brothers had seen their own share of their father's alcohol-fueled wrath. As the oldest—six years, compared to his brothers' three and four—he had tried to shield the younger boys from their father's fury, often absorbing the beatings himself. In bed at night, he had frequently fantasized about splitting his father's head with an axe.

On a bright and sunny spring morning, his mother had walked him to school and given him a long, tight hug before turning away. He could still see her looking back over her shoulder, her blonde hair peeking out from the embroidered green scarf that hid the mottled bruising on her neck. That afternoon, after waiting for his mother for what seemed an eternity, he had finally walked home alone. He had found their door unlocked, but the apartment was dark and quiet. He had nibbled at the remnants of the previous night's dinner before crawling into his bed, alone and afraid. His father, returning late and reeking of cigarettes and vodka-infused sweat, had awakened him in a rage and dragged him to the room where his mother should have been sleeping.

"Where is she?" his father had thundered before slapping him and shoving him against the wall. "I know that she told you. The two of you are always talking when you think I cannot hear you, always plotting behind my back. Where did she go? Tell me!"

Terrified, Mirko lost control of his bladder, a stream of urine trickling down his legs and pooling at his feet. He remembered his father's hand forming a fist and the lunge that followed, but nothing more of that night. When he had awakened, he was on the floor, and light was streaming through the windows. Soaked in his own urine, with pain shooting through his skull and his vision fuzzy, he had tried to sit up. He had vomited and collapsed back onto the floor. The next time he had awakened, the apartment was dark, and he found himself smeared with his own feces. He had managed to crawl to the bathroom, where he drank heavily from the tap and cleaned himself. On seeing his reflection in the mirror, he had turned quickly away, stunned by the sight. He scavenged the refrigerator for food and then cleaned up the mess.

The thought of his father returning had terrified him. The thought of running away—and the punishment that would follow—had terrified him even more. He had waited for his father to come home. Two days later, he had stood quaking as his father opened the door. His father had poured a large glass of vodka and told him that his mother and brothers had perished in an automobile crash.

"She was on her way to pick you up from school," his father had growled. "If you had not been such a coward about walking home alone, they would still be alive."

Four days later, his father had loaded him, along with an overstuffed suitcase, into their dusty-gray Volga and driven to School 57. Until recognizing his mother in the photo on Noel Leblanc's desk, it had never occurred to Mirko that the Volga was the very vehicle that his mother had supposedly crashed.

The boarding school had provided the benefit of distancing Mirko from his father's relentless abuse. Visits to his home had been infrequent and blessedly brief. While the school's culture was focused and strict, Mirko had flourished, developing a love for mathematics and the emerging science of computer technology. He had been an exceptional student, and for the first time, had formed close friendships. He and five of these friends had banded together and called themselves the Sochi Six, after the first group of Soviet cosmonauts. They had even entered university together.

His carefree days at the university had been interrupted two years later, when he was conscripted into the Soviet Army. The experience had been life-altering, teaching him how to contain his fear when facing danger, how to command, how to survive, and how to kill.

In the intervening years, his father had changed as well. He now limited his drinking and had never again raised a hand to his son. He had not, however, shed his taste for cruelty. No longer physically superior, he now relied on verbal assaults to belittle his son.

After Mirko's release from military duty, his father had secured a job for him as an entry-level analyst at the GRU. The work, tedious and unfulfilling, had made him long for his days at university, and he had begun fantasizing about leaving the country. Then, on a bitterly cold January afternoon, his father had summoned him to a meeting. Rising from behind the polished mahogany desk, his father had wrapped his arm around Mirko's shoulder in a tight embrace. The gesture had shocked Mirko. In his entire life, he had never been shown such affection.

"I am sending you to Yugoslavia on an important mission," his father had said. "You will go to Zagreb to learn the language. Then you will go to Sarajevo. The pretense of being from a different part of the country will explain your lack of familiarity with the dialect and local customs. When you are prepared, you will be given the details about the man who will be your target. You will ingratiate yourself with this man and learn everything about his life."

A week later, he had found himself in Zagreb, living with the family of a Soviet asset. After four months of immersion in the Serbo-Croatian language, he had received his instructions: travel to Sarajevo and initiate a relationship with a man named Zlatan Terzić.

Living in Sarajevo had been an eye-opener. It was hip, friendly, and fun. He had easily cemented a friendship with Zlatan, and they had spent many evenings together in search of drink, song, and women. He had enjoyed every minute of his newfound freedom—until the country had erupted in war.

For years, he had puzzled over his father's interest in Zlatan, asking himself how his father had even known of this young man—an ordinary man from a different country. He had eventually concluded that Zlatan's computer background, combined with his access to sensitive data, must have somehow come to the GRU's attention.

It was not until after he had accompanied his father to Turkey that he had gained some insight. His father had smuggled him out of war-torn Sarajevo, and a day later, they had driven into western Turkey. In a field not far from the border with Iraq, they had exchanged a bag full of German deutsche marks for a truckload of American weapons. His father's plan was that the American weapons would be distributed to the Serbians, who would use them against high-value Bosnian targets in Sarajevo.

Mirko had kept his ear to the ground, wondering about the targets in his father's sights, but heard little for almost a year. Finally, his father had notified him of the next intended target: Daris, Zlatan's brother—a known operative in Bosnian intelligence.

Mirko had balked when his father unveiled the details of the assassination plot. Mirko's role would be to goad Zlatan into holding a gathering at a preselected location—with Daris on the list of invitees. Once Daris was present, Mirko would step outside for a smoke, signaling the soldiers hidden in the hills. The soldiers would launch the mortars, obliterating Daris and anyone else at the party.

"What does this accomplish?" Mirko had asked his father. "How can you be sure that Daris will be there? If he does not appear and I do not go outside, the Serbs could easily rush to launch the mortars anyhow. This could kill dozens of innocent people—all for nothing."

When his father answered, his tone was harsh. "He will be there—you will see to it. The collateral damage to civilians is of no consequence, although it will serve our purpose well. Deaths of innocents will spark worldwide condemnation of America's actions, and Americans themselves will be horrified. It will sow disruption in their country."

Mirko was reminded of his father's words from that night in Turkey. "Death by a thousand cuts," his father had promised.

As Mirko had feared, the Serbian soldiers had been impatient. Instead of waiting for Mirko's signal, they had launched the mortars early, shortly after Daris had entered the crumbling building. Mirko, having planned to save Zlatan and Imela by coaxing them outside for a smoke, had still been inside the target zone when the bombs landed. As a result, Daris had survived, and Mirko had lost his leg.

Mirko closed his eyes and dozed off, fatigue from the long flight setting in. He awakened with a start upon hearing the sound of footsteps on the stairs and the heavy front door thudding shut. He took a deep breath, sat erect, and picked up a book that lay nearby.

His father stomped into the study, commanding, "Pour me a drink!"

Mirko stood and obediently walked over to the liquor trolley beneath the far window. He mixed the drinks and handed one to his father, who lowered himself into the chair that Mirko had just vacated. After taking a sip from his glass, Mirko mustered his calmest voice. "Why did you not tell me?" he asked.

His father arched his eyebrows, swirled the ice in his glass, and snorted. "So, when did you learn about Noel?"

Mirko's jaw clenched. "When did I learn that you have lied to me all these years?" He turned his back to his father and stared out the window. "In Toronto," he spat. "He kept an old photo on his desk. I recognized my mother's hair and the embroidery on the scarf—the same scarf she was wearing when I last saw her."

"You were always consumed with her, even after she deserted you. You should have hated her for it."

"Hated her? I was a child and she was my mother. For months I had nightmares about the terrible way she died. Instead of comforting me, you lied to me, beat me senseless, and sent me away."

Grigory waved his hand as if shooing away a fly and said, "Every time I looked at you, I saw her. It was for the best. For years, I looked for her. I followed every sighting of a blonde woman with two young, blond boys. I thought she might have gone back to her native Sweden, but never found a trace of her. And then one day, I happened by an analyst's desk. He was recruiting assets in Yugoslavia—people we were interested in, people with computer skills. I saw a face, and at first, I thought it was you. It did not take long to find her after that—living on a small farm near Goražde. A farm girl!" he snorted derisively.

Mirko's voice crackled with anger. "And then you set out to destroy them! Why? Revenge?"

Grigory looked at his son with disdain. "You were always soft. I wanted to see if Goran and Zlatan were like you. It was a matter of curiosity. But when I learned that his half brother Daris was working for Bosnian intelligence, I saw an opportunity to make use of the situation. Unfortunately, you were right. The Serbs had no discipline, and ..." He paused and glanced at Mirko's leg. "And you paid the price. When you later reported that Zlatan was in possession of an American passport, I was surprised. I asked myself, *How does a young Bosnian man acquire such a thing?* There was only one answer: he was supplying intelligence to the CIA. I took steps to ensure that the CIA man would fear for his own safety and evacuate from Sarajevo. Once he left, arranging a substitute to take his place was not difficult."

"How did Zlatan end up at Transoceanic? And why?"

"Why? Some of the Transoceanic employees were also working as couriers for the CIA. It was imperative to uncover them, and Zlatan was a perfect fit. He spoke flawless English, and he was very comfortable with women. How? It was a simple transaction. I offered one of their recruiters a briefcase full of cash. It was a fortuitous decision, because on his first trip to Paris, he took a photograph of a man that one of the stewardesses was meeting. This was a man we thought was dead, a man who could have done a great deal of damage to our operations. He needed to be eliminated."

"Eliminated by bombing an airplane?" Mirko hissed. "I cannot begin to comprehend why anyone would go to that extreme ... even you."

Grigory shrugged. "We did not know where to find him—he had no paper trail. We knew only that he was booked on that flight, along with the stewardess. If the plane had not been delayed for a day, the crash would have eliminated them both. As a bonus, it would also have eliminated a crazy Cuban who had been a thorn in our side for years. Three targets with a single stroke! It was genius!"

Mirko felt sick but managed to ask, "Are they still alive?"

Grigory canted his head slightly, a cruel smile curling his lips. "Two lived to see another day; the Cuban did not. Much later, we learned that the man had been living in Paris and had severe memory loss. If we had known, we might have elected a different course of action. But at the time, our information was limited. It seemed best to finish what you had started."

Mirko frowned, puzzled. "Me? What do you mean? What had I started?"

Grigory gave his son a withering look. "You are the one who fired a bullet into his skull," he said.

As the realization clicked, Mirko's eyes flew open. "The man I shot in Turkey? He is alive? Where is he now?"

"In America, we believe, although his precise location is unknown."

"And the woman?"

"She appeared at Sretna Kafa a few years ago. We don't know why, but she was taking pictures of Goran. Something had aroused her curiosity. We could not afford to have her asking questions."

"Why have you never told me any of this?"

"Because you would have put the mission in jeopardy. I could sense your remorse about forcing Zlatan and Goran to cooperate, and your fear that harm would come to them if they did not. But fear has its limits. What would you have done if you had known they were your brothers? You would have ruined everything."

"It is blown anyhow, isn't it?" Mirko countered.

Grigory set his glass down with a loud clunk and stared stonily at his son. "You were never good at the long game."

Mirko paused a beat, contemplating the meaning of those words, then asked, "You are going ahead?"

His father shrugged dismissively and signaled for another vodka.

Mirko refilled his father's glass. He wanted to ask when and how the software would be deployed but decided against taking the risk. There was simply too much at stake. Antoniya was waiting for him in Vietnam. All he had to do was find a way to quickly get out of the country with the flash drives. While he had not learned all the details of his father's project, he had every reason to believe that the software was worth a fortune. He had known enough to negotiate a price. A buyer was waiting.

Chapter 106

August 22
Langley, Virginia

Cat turned off Chain Bridge Road and pulled into the drive-through at Starbucks. It was still dark, sunrise more than an hour away. Since returning from Bosnia two days ago, she had slept little. She was dog-tired, fed up with the endless diplomatic jockeying, and in dire need of caffeine. *Weekend,* she fumed to herself, *and instead of enjoying a quiet day at home, here I am, headed for the office. Maybe tomorrow. Hah!*

Russia had refuted all charges by the United States and Canada in what had come to be known as the "Leblanc Affair." And while a fire had been lit and Western allies were united in their intent to bring Noel Leblanc and Mirko Stefanović to justice, discussion was at a standstill.

Cat wanted to slap everyone who was participating in this game of "Who Blinks First." She had no time for diplomatic seesawing. Leblanc and Stefanović were merely pawns. She needed resources, and lots of them, to thwart whatever Grigory Kornilov was planning.

She had just turned her head to give her order when she was startled by a tap on the passenger-side window.

"Open the door, Cat."

The face peering through the tinted glass belonged to Nate Carr. She had not seen the DIA operative since their standoff in Istanbul, when he had been so eager to label Maggie's death as an accident.

"Let me in," he said. "We need to talk."

Reluctantly, Cat unlocked the door and Nate slid in to the passenger seat. "Mocha latte with hemlock?" she asked.

"Very funny. Blond roast. Thanks."

She placed the order and gave him a sideways glance. He was dressed casually: khakis, navy Henley shirt, and a pale-yellow windbreaker. Deck shoes completed his nautical ensemble.

"Going sailing? Or still just muddying the waters at every opportunity?" she asked.

He rolled his eyes and said, "You're as sweet as ever. And here I am, about to do you a huge favor."

"And what would that be? Notice of your resignation?"

His eyes narrowed. "Cut the crap. This is important."

She thanked the young woman at the window, handed her the money, and said, "Keep the change."

The girl looked up, her eyes wide, and offered an effusive thank-you.

Nate snorted. "How much did you give her? Ten?"

"A C-note. I wanted to have one bright moment in my day before having to deal with you."

Nate's cheeks bloomed with anger as she drove to an open spot away from other cars.

She parked and took a sip of her coffee, then said, "To what do I owe this little surprise?"

"Mirko Stefanović," he said. "You need to back off."

The name came like a punch to her chest, but her poker face held steady. *How could he possibly know about Mirko? God—is Mirko on the DIA's payroll?* In a steely voice, she asked, "Now why would I do that?"

"His real name is Andres Kornilov. We've known about him for months. He's the son of one of the top dogs in the GRU. He did not kill the Canadian—a couple of Russian goons did that. Nor was he a party to the killings in Bosnia. He is extremely valuable to us. If you continue with your pursuit, you are jeopardizing an ongoing operation."

Cat kept her face impassive, but Nate had given her a piece of information they did not have: Mirko's real first name. She tucked it away and said, "How do you know he did not murder that young man?" Her lips parted as the realization struck. "Ah, you wired the Leblanc house. You have video."

"Can't say," Nate said.

Cat asked, "So Stefanović is a DIA asset? Is that what you're telling me?"

"I can't confirm that either way," he said.

Cat raised her eyebrows, expecting more, but Nate shook his head. "All I can tell you is that Stefanović had a plan to sell Leblanc's product to the highest bidder. Now they are both in Russia, unreachable, and we still have no idea what the product is."

Cat stroked her lips with her right index finger, debating how much to tell him. He was a weasel and a cowboy, and possibly corrupt. Trust was out of the question. "How do you know that Stefanović wanted to sell the product?"

"Can't say."

Cat canted her head and stared at him.

Nate's eyes hardened. "Don't cross me, Cat." He opened the door, stepped out of the car, and walked away, leaving the passenger door open.

"Prick," she muttered.

She drove to another area of the parking lot and stopped to inspect the car—the passenger seat, under the seat, the floor, the door pockets, and anything else that Nate might have touched, or any place where he might have dropped a bug or a tracker. Satisfied that the car was secure, she called Melodie and Jones.

She told them about her encounter with Nate. "So how would he know that Stefanović wanted to sell the product?"

"They have an informant. Someone who is close to Stefanović," Jones said.

Chapter 107

August 23
Northern Virginia

For the umpteenth time, Cat checked her secure email for news, wondering what was taking so long. Nothing. She had sent the copies of the ledger from Bosnia; the translation should be done by now.

She heard a rumble of agitated conversation and looked up from her desk. Between the slats of the plantation blinds, she could make out a sliver of the porch swing, the hunter green of her husband's sweater, and a slice of one of the Tuscan columns. A massive black arm rested against the column, the hand balled up in a fist, seemingly ready to pound her husband into pulp. *Jones.*

The front door flew open, throwing a blaze of sunlight into the foyer, and heavy footsteps thundered down the hall toward the study. Jones's shoulders nearly brushed both sides of the doorway. He was clearly agitated. Behind him, Tom shrugged helplessly, mouthing, "Coffee?"

She gave Tom a nod, then shook her finger at Jones in mock reprimand and said, "I took the day off. You're intruding on the first day I've had to myself in a month."

"We need to talk."

Jones gently lowered himself onto the settee across from her desk, having learned the hard way that his bulk and antique furniture were not always a good mix.

"Remember the DIA guy in the coffee shop in Sarajevo? Black hair—across from the Russian woman?"

She nodded, "I do."

"Guess who just showed up at the morgue."

"He's dead? How?"

"Gunshot wound. Police are operating under the assumption that it's a robbery gone bad—house torn apart and valuables missing. I'm inclined to disagree. I think the shooter was looking for something."

"How did you find out?" Cat asked.

"I've had a couple of guys looking into him since you told us about him. Something about that meet at the coffee shop had a foul smell. What was he doing there? Was he working that Russian woman, or was the woman working him? My guys watched him tuck in last night, lights out, and then they left. There was no activity at the house when they returned this morning. They got suspicious and decided to take a closer look. His body was visible from the window," Jones explained.

Cat leaned back in her chair and squinted at him. "If not a robbery, then why? And who would kill him?"

"Still working on that. But I think it's tied into our case. And in another interesting item, there are five US senators scheduled for a military transport out of Andrews this evening—destination Moscow. The purported topic of discussion is a tweaking of our trade agreement. Falling on the heels of the Noel Leblanc debacle, I'm guessing that there might be something else at play here. And here's the clincher: accompanying them is none other than your old friend from the DIA, that scumbag Nate Carr."

Cat let out a slow, deliberate breath. It didn't help—she was seething. *Nate Carr. For the second time in as many days,* she thought. "That asshole! He's in this up to his neck, and has been all this time. What the hell is he up to?"

"Good question. Do we have anyone in Moscow?"

Cat's eyes flew open. "Of course! The woman! The one at the bakery that night! She was sitting across from your dead DIA guy. It had to have been a meet! She was passing information to him, and he was passing it on to Nate."

Jones went through it in his head. "It makes sense. Stefanović lived alone. He was probably vulnerable to the attention of a woman. And she was pretty."

"Icing on the cake," Cat agreed.

Chapter 108

August 24
Istanbul, Turkey

Antoniya Davydova stood at the window, looking down at the people and parked cars below. The guest house was on a cobblestone street in Sultanahmet, the oldest part of Istanbul. The rooms were cramped but clean and cheap.

She had already been here for a week and was becoming increasingly nervous about what to do next. *Will they look for me here?* she wondered. *Can they even imagine that I would choose such a place? How long until they track me down? Should I stay here? Move to another place?*

She left the room only when necessary, having told the clerk that she was a writer and needed to be left alone. When she ventured out, she draped a scarf over her head. Twice, she had ventured into an internet café and accessed the encrypted messaging service the American had told her to use. There had been no response. She had then placed a call to the American's phone, a number to be used only in an emergency. The call had gone straight to voice mail. He would be out of the office for four more days. Once again, she counted her remaining money. It was enough to last for several months, but carrying so much cash was dangerous. She chewed on a fingernail and considered her situation.

Antoniya Davydova had not set out to be a spy. Tall and big-breasted, with alluring brown eyes and wavy dark hair that framed her high cheekbones, she was not only extremely attractive, she was well-connected among Moscow's elite. Her father had made a fortune in oil and gas, and she had grown up as a child of privilege. It was only later that she learned that most of his success was due to kickbacks and corruption.

Antoniya liked to travel, and she had expensive tastes. Her comings and goings were followed on social media, where she was generally referred to as a wealthy socialite. She had a reputation for being spoiled, sharp-tongued, and contemptuous of those she perceived to be of a lower economic or social status. Thus, people were continually trying to impress her, often sharing tidbits about their business shenanigans.

When her father had passed away, his empire had collapsed. The money had vanished. An acquaintance had approached her with an offer. She could continue to enjoy her lifestyle, under the premise that her own finances had been invested quite profitably. All she would have to do in return was pass the gossip along to her new American friends.

Antoniya had no training in tradecraft, and it was never intended that she would do anything other than keep her eyes and ears open. But there had been an occasion, on a sunless and frigid Thursday morning, when there was no one else to call upon. To everyone's surprise, she had performed brilliantly. From that moment on, she became a valuable resource.

Eight months ago, she had accepted an assignment to ensnare Mirko Stefanović. She had agreed, but only because she had never been to Sarajevo and wanted to be able to add another destination on her list of cities visited.

Mirko had invited her into his bed on the second night after they met. He was an accomplished lover, although his premature ejaculation made it evident that he had not been with a woman for some time. His face flushed with shame, he had apologized and then gone for another round. While she had expected to be disgusted at having sex with him—she had assumed she would be repulsed by his age and by the stub that was once his leg—she had been surprised to find herself attracted to the man. He was handsome, fit, and he doted on her. She was soon taking regular flights between Moscow and Sarajevo. They had been in a relationship ever since, and she had grown quite fond of him.

Although he had shared little about his business, he had made the occasional slip. She had paid attention. The bakery, she had learned, was financing a second enterprise—something involving software. She was savvy enough to realize that a low-margin business like a bakery would not generate enough profit to fund software development. And after one too many beers one night, he had told her that Russians were involved.

Antoniya had not fully appreciated the perils of her assignment until spotting Grigory Kornilov at the coffee shop one evening. She had already been there for an hour, waiting for Mirko, when Grigory had taken a seat at one of the outdoor tables. She had shivered at the sight of him. Her father had pointed him out years ago, later telling her that, "He is a man who enjoys killing people. For him, it is a sport." She had noticed Grigory's reaction when a woman, with a festival badge slung around her neck, had entered the shop with her camera. A shift in posture and a sharp blink of his eyes had told of his unease. He had left the shop just a few seconds after the woman.

When Mirko had rushed into the apartment and told her that they had to leave, her survival instincts had kicked into full gear. She had tried to conceal her dismay, kissing him and telling him that she would go with him.

That night, she had lain in bed and watched Mirko sleep. She had run a finger lightly over his chest and quizzed herself. *Do I love him? Maybe. But what is love? Living with someone forever? Could I be that loyal?* She had felt a twinge of guilt, but her instincts for self-preservation had won the day.

She had realized that she would need to find another place to live—but not in Vietnam. She had considered hiding out in Sarajevo, but it was a small city, and she was already somewhat well-known. Paris had come to mind, but France was one of many countries that required visas for Russian citizens. Waiting for a visa was not an option. Turkey, on the other hand, offered instant visas right at the airport. With a population of over fifteen million people, Istanbul seemed like a good place to hide.

With luck, Kornilov would not find her.

Chapter 109

August 24
Moscow, Russia

The tumblers produced a dull *thunk* as the key was turned in the lock. The heavy steel door swung open and Grigory Kornilov stood in the doorway, a black silhouette against the well-lit hallway.

"Not feeling well today?" he asked the man curled up on the floor. Without waiting for a reply, he said, "I hear that you are not being cooperative. If you cooperate, we will give you more food, and perhaps offer you better sleeping accommodations. Or maybe you would enjoy some time outside. Do you miss the sunshine and the sight of a blue sky?"

"Fuck you, asshole," the man on the floor said quietly. "I'm not giving you anything. You cannot keep me here forever."

"Sadly, Mr. Leblanc, you are mistaken."

With his right wrist and ankle chained to the wall, movement was a struggle, but Noel Leblanc managed to rise to his feet. He stood erect and said, "I demand to see a representative from the Canadian Embassy."

"Mr. Leblanc, you are being charged with espionage. Why else would the software architect of the Canadian electrical grid come to Russia?"

Noel's face was flush with hatred. "That is a lie, you son of a bitch!"

Kornilov chuckled and said, "Well, the Canadian government certainly believes it, because you have been lying all along. Once they discovered that you are actually a Russian citizen, they lost interest."

"What the hell are you talking about?"

"Surely you remember some of it. Leaving with your mother, leaving your father and brother behind, stealing away and starting over in a new country?"

Noel stared blankly at Kornilov. "Who are you?"

"Oh," said Kornilov, "I am your only hope."

Looking away, Noel said, "I don't think so."

"I see that you are finally showing some spine. Perhaps I should let you speak with someone you know better." He went back to the door and waved.

Nate Carr strode into the small cell. "Hello, Noel," he said.

Noel gasped. "What are you doing here?"

"I'm here because of you, Noel. You failed to follow my instructions. One more day, and I would have picked up the package. We would be done."

"But ... but ..."

"But what? You thought that giving it to Mirko was acceptable? That was not in our instructions. Nor did we ask you to include an encryption lock in the software. That addition is causing us to delay our operation. We need the key, Noel."

"I have already told your goons. I don't have it. I don't know where it is."

"Of course you do. Think hard."

"It was in the aluminum box. Your thugs took it when they kidnapped me. I want a lawyer."

"Noel, Noel. This is not Canada. This is not anywhere close to Canada. Unless you cooperate, this is hell."

"The one going to hell is you."

As Noel started to turn his back, Kornilov grabbed his other wrist, clamped a cuff around it, and clipped it to a bolt in the floor.

"What are you doing?" yelled Noel.

Kornilov waved at one of the guards, who held out a set of bolt cutters, waiting for Nate to take them.

He's testing me, Nate realized. He clenched his jaw and willed himself to move. He accepted the cutters and yanked Noel's pinkie finger into position between the blades. "Are you ready to tell me, Noel?"

"I don't know," Noel screamed. "Please! I don't know!"

Nate steeled himself and squeezed the tool's handles together. Noel's ear-splitting scream echoed through the building as his finger dropped to the floor.

"Tell me, Noel. Or shall we do another?"

"No, God, no! I don't know where it is! I have told you!"

Nate took two more fingers before Noel passed out. He handed the cutters back to Kornilov and said, "I believe he's telling the truth."

Chapter 110

August 24
CIA Headquarters
Langley, Virginia

The translation hit Cat's mailbox just before ten o'clock. She read the translator's summary page and let out a low whistle. When Jones and Marc had recovered the ledger in Istanbul, Marc had been enthusiastic, but he had only translated a dozen or so pages. The full translation had yielded far more than anyone could have anticipated. She rubbed her temples, massaging away a headache that was certain to come. The report was a keg of dynamite.

Analysts had determined that the ledger's entries were inked by three separate men. The third, presumably the Syrian driver named Abdul, had penned his last entry on the day before he slammed his fuel truck into Maggie's car. His handwriting in the ledger went back about a year and a half.

Starting in early 2005, the accountants provided an accounting of income derived from human trafficking. There were hundreds of names, initials, locations, prices, and buyers. In a little over a decade, what had started as a trickle of money had swelled to a multimillion-dollar income stream.

The ledger also held an unexpected treasure: an item that had nothing to do with accounting. The entry was an oddity: two numbers, a comma, two numbers, a comma, three numbers, a dot, and three more numbers. An analyst with a sharp eye noticed that the anomaly resembled an IP address. After conducting a quick *WHOIS* search at a domain registrar, he found the website. The name of the itemized entry, *Insurance*, was the password. The result was a scanned document—twenty-three pages of handwritten notes, almost like a journal, in the handwriting of an unidentified fourth man. The document spelled out the details of a number of criminal enterprises, leaving little doubt that Grigory Kornilov had been conducting an ongoing campaign to subvert US interests around the globe.

The document revealed that Kornilov had paid 1.3 million deutsche marks, the equivalent of about $750,000, to a group of rogue US Army soldiers in April 1991. In exchange, the buyers had secured dozens of crates packed with assault rifles, sniper rifles, ammunition, mortars, and mortar shells. The arms had been delivered to Russians who had volunteered in the Serbian Army, with instructions to use the weapons against the citizens of Sarajevo.

The author also specified payments to a number of persons with American-sounding names, including Michael Cantrell. Michael had received payments for hotel stays in Manhattan, rent, utilities, clothing, and cameras. In shocking detail, it told how Michael had been duped into believing that he was working for the CIA. Following what he believed to be CIA orders, he had purchased most of the components for the bomb that took down Transoceanic Flight 367. He had been told that the explosive itself was fake, and that they were testing security. Unbeknownst to him, a real high explosive had been supplied by Russian operatives. He had become suspicious and, out of concern for his personal safety, had fled.

"Coward!" Cat shouted.

There was a light tap on the door, followed by Oscar's voice. "Everything alright in there?"

"Get Jones on the phone," she called. "Please."

Her phone buzzed seconds later. "I got the report," she hissed. "Michael Cantrell thought he was working for the CIA. He thought his instructions to put a bomb on an American airplane came from the CIA!"

"That's a hell of a story. How did you learn this?"

"A website address was embedded in the ledger. It's a tell-all."

"Who wrote it? And why?"

"Both unknown, but I'm sure a whole lot of people will be trying to find out. What I find most reprehensible is that, when Michael Cantrell was faced with a moral choice, he ran. He could have reported the bomb—and didn't."

Jones was quiet for a long minute, then said, "To be realistic, who would have believed him?"

"Regardless, through his actions that day, he condemned four hundred twenty-nine people to death. He should be in prison, or dead," she fumed.

"What else?"

"The narrative validates Marc's story about the arms deal and Russian involvement in bombing the citizens of Sarajevo. It also states that a large cash infusion from a Russian official—Grigory Kornilov—financed the construction of the bakery. There are two code names mentioned—Khartoum and Blue—who were the architects of the bakery computer systems. The FBI and Interpol are going to be busy. The ledger itself lists hundreds of clients, most by their initials but some by their full names. The ledger's accounting puts that business in the multimillions."

"That's a lot of bread," Jones said. "Jail is too good for these people. But why? Insurance? Blackmail? Or revenge?"

"The password was *Insurance*. I think that tells the story," Cat suggested.

He let out a sigh. "I hope they changed the password."

Cat's phone buzzed. *Pat Desmond*. She pressed the answer button. "Pat. What's up?"

"I found the Russian woman. She had a ticket to Vietnam, then exchanged it for a ticket to Moscow. She never boarded the plane. She went to Istanbul."

Cat tapped her pen on the desk, thinking, and then said, "Chances are that she figured out what was going on, or Mirko told her. Either way, she rabbited. That means she's scared, and she should be. Once word gets out, Grigory Kornilov is going to dispose of anything—and anyone—tying him to this. If we found her, he can find her too. Thanks, Pat. I owe you."

Laughing, Pat said, "Oh yeah. A fine scotch would be most welcome!"

Jones said, "Istanbul has a big community of Russian expats, so she might have friends. What do you want to do?"

"Get the jet ready to leave tonight. All operational hands on deck," she said. "Paul, too, if he can. The in-person clout will help."

Jones did not hesitate. "I'm on it," he said.

Chapter 111

August 25
Moscow, Russia

Grigory Kornilov threw open the door to his apartment and stormed into the study. "You were screwing Antoniya Davydova! Where is she?" he shouted at his son.

Mirko looked up, startled. *How could he know?* "What do you mean?" Mirko replied innocently. "Isn't she in Sarajevo?"

"She had a ticket to Ho Chi Minh City. She exchanged it for a ticket to Moscow but did not board the flight. Where is she?"

Genuinely confused, Mirko said, "I don't know."

"You're a fool," Grigory said, drawing back his arm.

Mirko grabbed his father's arm, wrenching it backward. His eyes burning with anger, he said in a low, rumbling voice, "You don't get to do that anymore. If you try to hit me again, I'll fucking kill you."

His father dropped his arm, unfazed. "She works for the Americans," his father spat. "She's going to screw us all."

Mirko felt as if he had been body-slammed. *Working for the Americans? How is that possible?* But even as he asked himself the question, the answer became clear. Why else would such a beautiful young woman spend time with him? No other woman had given him a second look in years, and he had fallen for her, hard. He was not sure which was worse: having been betrayed by the love of his life, or that his father knew about it.

"I want to see my brother," Mirko said. "Where are you keeping him?"

Grigory turned, his nostrils flaring, and said with a scowl, "He is undergoing interrogation."

Stunned, Mirko cried out, "Why? He gave you what you wanted!"

"He has sabotaged the program. We ran tests on two small towns in Utah and California. It worked perfectly. The American news media even reported that the electrical outages were caused by a solar flare," he said with a snort. "But we had a problem on the third test. So far, he has resisted giving us the solution. He is braver than I thought."

Grigory's phone rang. He turned his back to Mirko and listened to the voice on the other end. Finally, he spoke into the phone. "Arrange a jet," he said. "We'll leave within the hour."

He disconnected the call and said to Mirko, "Get your things."

"Where are we going?"

"Istanbul."

Mirko and his father stepped aboard the small jet. Six people were already on board: three men and three women.

Kornilov handed each of them a folder. "Here is her photograph and a copy of the warrant we have issued for her arrest. I have sent the picture to our comrades in the area," he told them. "If you spot her, contact me immediately."

One of the men asked, "Should we include the Turks?"

"No," said Kornilov. "That would add complications. We go in, we find her, we take her, we get out. Done."

A woman asked, "Where should we look first?"

"She is spoiled, rich, and has no training," he snorted. "The money she withdrew from the ATM will not last much longer. Her accounts are frozen, so she has no access to additional funds. She often stays at five-star hotels, but they are expensive. Mirko and I will check them, just in case. You should concentrate on the four-stars."

Mirko caught a glimpse of the photograph, and his heart skipped a beat. *Antoniya.* He thought about the credit card and suppressed a smile, thinking, *They are seriously underestimating her.* He leaned back in his seat, thinking. He had become convinced that getting out of Russia might be impossible. Now his father had handed him an opportunity. *If I can just get away, if I can find the right moment. If, if, if,* he thought. And then he reconsidered. *I can't wait for the best time. The first chance I have, I have to take it.*

Chapter 112

August 25
Istanbul, Turkey

Shortly before noon, the US Ambassador to Turkey looked squarely at Paul and said, "It's good to see you. It has been a long time. Now, what is so urgent that it brings you and your friends to our corner of the world?"

Paul, Cat, and the team were seated in the conference room at the American Consulate in Istanbul, along with the ambassador, the consul general, and the consulate's chief of security. The ambassador, whose residence was at the embassy in Ankara, had made the five-hour drive that morning.

Paul leaned forward. "I'm going to give the floor to Cat, whose persistence helped bring us to this moment."

"I realize that our visit is not exactly protocol," Cat said. "But time is of the essence." She laid out the series of events in which Grigory Kornilov had been involved and the incriminating evidence her team had gathered. When she brought up the impending cyberattack, the ambassador held up his hand.

"Why is this different?" he asked. "There are dozens of ransomware attacks every day."

Cat nodded and said, "But we believe that this attack will be of a greater breadth than anything seen previously. It has been in the works for months and is financed by a human trafficking network that rakes in millions. Kornilov has pulled out all the stops with this one, to the point that he financed the purchase of a software company in Canada. That company has contracts with dozens of private corporations, as well as with the US and Canadian governments."

The ambassador, a distinguished man with salt-and-pepper hair, serious blue eyes, and a permanent worry crease on his forehead, was known for his ability to assess people and for his calm demeanor in the face of adversity. He tilted his head slightly and stared intently at Cat. "You're very concerned about this," he said.

She nodded again, impressed. "Yes, very. We have only a few snippets of code from what appears to be a highly complex program. We're still very much in the dark. But we believe that Kornilov is close to launching his attack. This man has repeatedly proven his capacity for monstrous acts. And this operation has been in the works for a long time. I'm not merely concerned, I'm terrified of what he might unleash.

"There are several parties with intimate knowledge of this operation. One is Mirko Stefanović, who is wanted in Canada and who is presently in Russia. Another is Noel Leblanc, an illegal Canadian citizen, also now in Russia. Both happen to be Kornilov's sons, using assumed identities.

"We are looking for a Russian woman who has been in an intimate relationship with Stefanović for several months. It's our assessment that she has some knowledge of their plan because, when we were closing in on the operation in Sarajevo, she fled. But instead of flying to Moscow, she came here."

"And you want to do what? Offer her asylum? Does she even want it? Or are you just guessing?"

Paul interjected, "She is a DIA asset."

The ambassador raised his eyebrows and peered over his bifocals. "Why are they not involved here?"

"She may have tried to contact them, but her handler flew to Moscow two days ago," Paul replied.

The ambassador studied Paul and then turned to Cat. "So, no safety net. Are you intending to bring her here?"

"Only if there's a problem," she answered. "We have a jet standing by. Our objective is to offer safe haven. Location will be determined by the quality and quantity of her information."

"I'll authorize it, but this is a big ask. Try not to provoke an international incident or do anything that will make me regret the decision. And you had better be right about this, or we could all be handing in our resignations."

After the meeting, the team got to work. Cat leaned over Gabe's shoulder and stared at the gibberish on the screen. "What have you learned?" she asked.

"She has another credit card, from a bank in Sarajevo. It's new, so the Russians probably don't know about it—at least, not yet. She took out a sizable cash advance on the day she left, so she has enough money for at least a couple of months—assuming that she lives frugally."

"But you've been digging through her social media, right? Living frugally is out of character for her, correct?"

"True, but she may not have much choice. My instincts tell me that, despite playing the mindless socialite, she's just acting the part. Some of her posts tell me that she is one sharp cookie. Not always the nicest person, but definitely shrewd."

Turning to the security chief, she asked, "Where do you think we should look for her?"

The man rubbed his chin. "Safety will be first on her mind, so eliminate the more questionable neighborhoods. Second, affordable. If she's smart, and I agree with Gabe that she seems to be, she would not risk another withdrawal. Thus, she needs to stretch what she has. Third, cleanliness and comfort. Fourth, anonymity. She has to blend in. The dark hair helps, but many neighborhoods, particularly those farther out of the city center, take notice of strangers. I would start with Sultanahmet—lots of tourists and it checks all the boxes."

"What else?" Cat asked.

"What about clothes? Do we know what she might be wearing?" asked Lindsey.

Gabe snapped his fingers. "She didn't check any baggage. That means that whatever she has was in a carry-on. And she made a stop before the airport. Clothing store. Bought some shoes, too."

Lindsey blinked. "You hacked her credit card account?"

"Let's just say I peeked," Gabe replied. "But why buy more clothes? She must already have plenty of stuff to wear."

"Because she left everything behind!" Cat exclaimed. She pulled out her phone and dialed Pat Desmond. "We need to find out what clothes Antoniya Davydova purchased before she left town. I'm sending you her photo." She gave Pat the names of the shops and added, "Hurry. We think she's in danger."

The security chief pulled up Google's map of Istanbul on the wall monitor in the conference room. "Let's try to divide this up in a logical fashion."

Jazz glanced at the screen and said, "That's a lot of ground to cover. There are dozens of hotels."

The security chief nodded. "Sure. It's a big tourist center. Topkapi, Blue Mosque, Hagia Sophia—they are all within a half mile of one another. She can wander around without attracting attention. But let's start by eliminating the four-stars. Even three-stars might be too pricey for an extended stay. Look for decent two-stars and go from there."

"I count three dozen, give or take," said Jazz.

"We'll do a sweep," Adrian said. "Make a list of the hotels and divvy them up. Hit the hotel check-in desks, and housekeeping staff, if you can. Here are two photos, one snapped last week in Sarajevo, the other from social media. The hotel people may resist giving you information, but all of you can recognize someone who is holding back. We expect her to be frightened so, if you find her, don't give her a chance to think. Get her under your wing and into the vehicle and take her to the airport. Don't stop for anyone."

"Adrian's advice is spot-on," Cat said. "Take it to heart, because the Russians are likely to be looking for her, too. Antoniya is the girlfriend of Mirko Stefanović, who is the son of Grigory Kornilov, a major player in the GRU." She held up two photos. "Memorize their faces.

"There is every possibility that they have already gone to the police with a trumped-up arrest warrant or terrorist threat. We may be on Turkish soil, but the Russians wield some power here. She is a Russian citizen, and the Turks may prefer to look the other way. Kornilov and his thugs will think nothing of killing anyone who stands in their way. Stay alert."

The phone vibrated in Cat's pocket—a message from Pat Desmond. The store owner had duplicated the outfits that Antoniya had purchased. Two pairs of pants, two jackets, two lightweight sweaters, a tote bag, and two scarves, all in hues of navy blue and charcoal gray. There was nothing about the clothing that one might notice in a crowd. The conservative outfits were as bland as oatmeal. The tote bag, however, had a wide streak of fuchsia, as if someone had tired of the blah palette and swiped it with a paintbrush.

"Hopefully she's carrying the tote, because she's going to be very hard to spot. These pictures are all we have."

As they piled into the two white vans that they had rented at the airport, Adrian said, "Code names will be Karen for Kornilov, Maria for Mirko, and Gary for the girlfriend. Check your comms and let's get moving."

Cat looked back at Paul. "Thank you for coming. We'll see you at the airport," she said before pulling the door closed.

Chapter 113

Grigory Kornilov stood in front of the Istanbul Shangri-La Hotel and began to second-guess himself. He had been sure that Antoniya would have chosen a major hotel, a hotel with security and cameras and abundant staff—staff who were trained to notice everything about the men and women who walked through their doors. *Is it possible that she went elsewhere?* he wondered.

He and Mirko had visited two hotels thus far. Despite the documents ordering Antoniya's arrest, the hotel personnel had been polite but uncooperative. They did not discuss their clientele except under the direction of the Turkish police.

Mirko asked, "Which hotel is next on the list?"

Grigory looked at his son and realized that he had it all wrong. The woman had been staying with Mirko, whose living accommodations were far from princely.

With a jerk of his head, he said, "We are altering our search. We will look at other places—two-star hotels, even hostels. The area of Sultanahmet is a good place to start."

Mirko shrugged his shoulders nonchalantly, but his stomach flipped. Antoniya had visited Istanbul often and knew the city well. She had told him about exploring Sultanahmet and how much she liked it.

After having no luck at six previous stops, Lindsey and Adrian approached the seventh hotel of the afternoon with resignation.

"This is like looking for a needle in a haystack. What if we're wrong?" Lindsey asked. "What if she's staying with friends? Or is in one of the big hotels?"

He looked sideways at her and squinted in thought. "We'll just keep looking until we find her—or until the Russians do," he answered. "I just hope we're right."

"Yeah, me too," she said.

Their next target was just up the street, on the other side: a cheery-looking three-story hostel with sunny light-yellow paint and ornamental wrought iron grills on the windows. Adrian was about to cross the street when he stopped suddenly and pulled out his phone.

He thumbed the device, tapped the microphone on his chest to activate the sound, and speaking quietly, said, "Go with me on this, Lindsey. Look at me and pretend you have morning sickness." Raising his voice, he said, "Are you sure we're on the right street? Karen and Maria say that they are already at the Blue Mosque."

Momentarily confused by the question, she wrinkled her forehead and then remembered. *Karl. Maria. Oh, God.* She had almost blown it.

"I don't know, but, honey, I'm not feeling well," she managed to answer, hoping that was enough. Having no experience with morning sickness, she would have to wing it.

Adrian, with worry in his voice, asked her, "Would you like to sit down? Would you like some water? Will that help?"

Lindsey nodded. She wanted to risk a look, but kept her head tilted down and clutched her belly. Out of the corner of her eye, she spotted them. The younger man was tall and muscular, with the hint of a limp. *Mirko.* The other was fleshier and at least two decades older, with high cheekbones, a nose like a hawk, and a scowl on his face. *Kornilov.*

A wave of anxiety washed over her as she flashed back to an encounter with another Russian—one who had almost killed her. She gripped Adrian's arm.

Adrian recognized her distress. Lindsey was brave but not immune to fear. The attack had left her with scars—both physical and mental—that were still healing. He pivoted around, as if looking for a sidewalk café. He had already noticed the sign in front of the yellow building—a sign advertising a restaurant. With his heart pounding at the risk he was taking, he took Lindsey's hand and said, "It looks like there is a restaurant in that hostel. Should we try there?"

Nodding, Lindsey squeezed his hand. He put a sheltering arm around her and led her across the street and up the two steps to the hotel door. A few steps ahead of them, the younger man paused and held the door open. Adrian glanced down at Lindsey and thought, *Right into the lion's den. God forgive me if this doesn't work.*

"Thank you," Adrian said, stepping inside. He put his arm around Lindsey's waist and hurried her over to the woman standing at the check-in desk.

"My wife is pregnant," he told her. "Would you have a glass of water and a place for her to sit for a few minutes? I don't know why they call it morning sickness when it goes on all day."

The woman reached into a cabinet behind her and pulled out a bottle of water. Handing it to Adrian, she pointed to a wicker chair by the window. Lindsey clutched her abdomen and gently lowered herself into the chair.

"Breathe, honey," Adrian said. "You'll feel better in a few minutes."

Grigory Kornilov watched the unfolding drama with contempt. *Another whining American*, he thought, and then stepped up to the desk.

"We are looking for a fugitive," he told the woman. "Here are the papers authorizing her arrest." He showed the woman a long sheet of paper and then a photograph. The woman seemed surprised.

"She is very pretty," she said. "But she is not here. Here we have college students and teenagers traveling with chaperones. But even if she were here, I could only give that information to the police."

Kornilov appraised the woman and said, "She is a dangerous woman who is wanted for treason and murder. It will be best to tell me where she is."

The woman's jaw clenched, but otherwise she seemed unfazed. "As I said, she is not here."

Kornilov faced her for another few seconds, then turned away, steering Mirko out the door and into the street.

As the door closed, Adrian watched the woman behind the desk. Her shoulders slumped in relief, and she collapsed into her chair. From the moment she had stated that Antoniya was not there and that she would only give that information to the police, Adrian had known she was lying. Antoniya was either staying there or had done so recently. He was sure that

Kornilov knew it, too. He decided to question her now. It was a risk, but delaying would only give Kornilov more time to mobilize his people.

"Ma'am," he said, moving toward her, "my name is Adrian Santori. I am with the United States Federal Bureau of Investigation. We need to talk."

If the woman felt intimidated, she gave no sign. She looked coldly at him and replied, "You lied about your wife."

"I did. But those men are going to hurt that woman if they find her. I want to find her before that happens."

"She is not here," she sighed.

He shook his head. "Maybe not now, but I think she was. Did she go to another hotel, or did she just step out?"

Her eyes bored into his. "Why should I trust you?"

"I can't think of any reason why you should. You don't know me. I can assure you that we mean her no harm. But the men who just left? The Russians? They definitely do."

The woman took a very deep breath, closed her eyes in silent prayer, and blurted out, "She went out about fifteen minutes before you came. She is quiet and keeps to herself, but I noticed her leaving."

"Any idea where she went?"

"Sometimes she brings back pastry and fruit. There is a market a few streets away. She also goes to an internet café."

He pulled out his phone and clicked on the map. "Show me where," he said.

Parking in Istanbul always presented a problem. They had ultimately opted to park the two vans on Torun Street—in a big lot abutting the grounds of the Blue Mosque—backed in against the stone wall to expedite a fast getaway. The biggest issue was that the street was one-way, as were many streets in the area. Adding to the challenge was the array of pedestrian-only streets, which were closed to vehicular traffic from ten in the morning until six at night. While the parking spot they chose was far from ideal, it was the best they were going to find.

Sitting in the driver's seat with his laptop perched on the center console, Gabe leaned tensely over the keyboard and cursed the small screen. They always packed a slew of electronic gear when traveling, but 47-inch ultrawide monitors were not portable. Tracking all the team members on the laptop was a genuine pain in the ass.

The team showed up as bright pink pinpoints on the map, labeled with their first names. When Adrian had activated his mic, Gabe had heard the entire conversation and set the team in motion. They were moving fast, everyone on a different path, converging in the area around the hostel and hoping to spot Antoniya. Arnie and Marc, assigned to drive the vans, veered away from their partners and would be at the parking lot in less than two minutes.

The voice of Jones exploded in Gabe's ear. "I've got her. She's just left the market on Mehmet Aga, headed up the hill. Bag with a pink streak. Blue and gray clothes."

Gabe looked at the map. "Damn. If she's going back to the hostel, she's going to use the pedestrian streets. You've got to block her. Make her turn left, toward the mosque. Otherwise, I'll have to drive all the way around to intercept."

"Too late. She made the turn," Jones said.

Running full tilt, Cat panted. "Maybe I can catch her. I'm on Utangak, a block and a half away. Jazz might be closer—she's paralleling me."

"I'm on Dalbasti." Jazz huffed. "Meet you at the corner. We'll herd her toward the vans."

The banging on the door nearly caused Gabe to jump out of his skin. He unlocked the door and then wriggled over to the passenger seat. Marc jumped in and started the vehicle, then gunned the motor and pulled to the edge of Torun Street. Fifty feet away, Arnie did the same. If Antoniya slipped by Marc, they would have her boxed in.

Marc's breathy voice came over the comms, "Come on, baby. Daddy's waiting. Come to Daddy."

The anomaly caught Antoniya's eye: among all the walkers, a woman was running. Running toward her. Not in running clothes. Not a young woman, but athletic, and fast. Light-skinned. It was curious, but not alarming—until a second woman, black-skinned, younger, also running, joined the first. They were less than half a block away. Antoniya stopped walking. In that moment, she locked eyes with the older woman and knew that they wanted her. She dropped the bag, spun around, and ran as if her life depended on it.

At the intersection, she started to make a left, toward the market, when she spotted a big man running toward her, and behind him, a couple, also running. She kept going straight, accelerating her pace until a white van pulled across the road, effectively blocking it. She jogged right, trying to go around it, when the vehicle's door flew open."

"Antoniya!" a man called. "We're American! Get in!"

She looked back. The older woman had opened her jacket. Pinned to the lining was a small American flag. She stopped, unsure of what to do. *Should I believe them? How would the Americans know where I am?*

She made one step toward the vehicle and suddenly, another woman ran up behind the American woman and pushed her from behind. The American slammed into the cobblestones and lay there, unmoving. The black woman's reactions were lightning-quick—she was on the assailant's heels in a flash.

"Get in!" the man in the van screamed at Antoniya. "Now, for God's sake!"

English. Native English. American, not Russian. She sprinted toward him and dove into the vehicle, her left foot dangling outside as she tried to hoist herself all the way inside. She felt a hand grab her ankle, then pull. She clawed at the seat, trying to find something to grab onto, when a man in the front passenger seat reached around with a gun. *Not a gun,* she realized. *A Taser.* She heard a scream and the grip on her ankle released.

Turning at Cat's cry when she fell, Jones's peripheral vision caught the man and woman who had been running behind him. He pivoted to face them, cocked his head, and wondered if they were really stupid enough to take him on. The man lifted his sweater to reveal the bulge of his gun. The couple were so focused on Jones that they were oblivious to Adrian and Lindsey closing in behind them.

Both sides of the street were lined with small shops, their doors open and a selection of wares displayed on tables outside. Adrian stepped over to a shop on his right—a jewelry and craft store—and picked up two round alabaster paperweights. He hefted one of them, then wound his arm back and fired it at the man's head. The man dropped like a stone.

Ignoring the shop's owner, who flew out of the shop like a mad dog, Adrian focused his attention on the woman. He could read the inner debate on her face: fight or flight. A moment later, she shrugged and went to her partner's aid.

Jones looked at Adrian in wide-eyed wonder. "How did you do that?"

Adrian shook his head. "Later," he said. "Let's move."

"Take care of Cat—she's hurt," Jones shouted. "I'll check on Marc and the others."

Lindsey took off as Adrian pulled some euros from his wallet. He shoved them at the shop owner, and then hurried after her. He found Cat on the ground in the middle of the road, her head propped on a bystander's lap and a noisy crowd milling around her. Her injuries appeared minor. She had a knot on her forehead, and her hands and forearms were scraped from trying to break the fall.

"How are you doing, Cat?" he asked her.

She ignored the question and asked, "Did you get them?"

"I think so. Jones is checking on everyone. But back to you. Are you okay to travel?"

"I never saw the person who shoved me. I was hit from behind, and I fell, pretty hard. My foot got tangled in that street barrier as I was going down. My foot went one way, and I went another. I think my left ankle is broken."

Adrian pulled up Cat's pant leg to expose the injury. Her ankle was misshapen, with an odd, angular bulge on the inside of the anklebone. "Oh, it's definitely broken. We'll stabilize it and get you to the van." He looked up at Lindsey. "We need towels, or fabric, something heavy that we can roll up to create a splint. And find something long to wrap around it."

One of the onlookers, a middle-aged woman, said in English, "There is a textiles shop right around the corner, in the bazaar. Come, I'll show you."

Lindsey and the woman rushed around the corner and emerged just three minutes later with a stack of heavy towels, two wooden dowels, and two robes. Adrian hurriedly fashioned a splint, wrapping the towels around the dowels, placing them on each side of Cat's ankle, and winding the sashes from the robe around her leg and foot to hold the splints in place.

Jones ran up to them. "Go, go! I've got Cat!" he shouted. He pulled her up and draped her over his shoulders in a fireman's carry. The first van was rolling toward them, the door open.

"In here!" shouted Marc.

Cat clenched her teeth and stifled a scream as Jones heaved her into the vehicle. Jones shouted that he would ride with Arnie and slammed the door. Marc hit the accelerator, taking the corner fast. Jones ran for the other van, jumping in just as the first police car appeared a hundred feet behind them.

"I'm in! Go, go, go!" Jones shouted.

The melee had spawned a swarm of curious onlookers, clogging the two intersecting streets and hindering the progress of the two vans. Marc's vehicle was in the fringe of the crowd, with a clear roadway ahead, when a man appeared a few feet away. He held a submachine gun aimed at the windshield.

Marc recognized him immediately: Kornilov, the man who had bought the truckload of weapons from the soldiers and who had ordered his assassination. He recognized the gun, too: a Bizon, a Russian-designed weapon with a folding stock that used a 64-round helical magazine. It could fire almost 700 rounds per minute. He stepped on the brake.

Kornilov moved around to the side of the van, gesturing with the weapon, and shouted, "Give me Antoniya Davydova, and I will allow you to leave. Give her to me, now!"

Marc glared at him and said under his breath, "No chance, asshole!" He was ready to stomp on the gas pedal when there was a blur of motion in front of the windshield. A man leapt onto Kornilov, and they tumbled onto the cobblestones.

Antoniya cried out, "Mirko!"

Marc was stunned. *Mirko? Here?* He tried to back up, but the van was hemmed in. The crowd had shifted to watch the struggle in the street. Mirko was bigger than his father, and stronger, but disadvantaged by a prosthetic leg that was not made for hand-to-hand combat. Mirko finally got the upper hand, wresting the gun from his father's grip. He struck his father's head twice with the butt of the gun, dragged him out of the vehicle's path, and banged on the van's door.

He pointed the gun at the bystanders, who fled in terror, then lifted the gun above his head. He shouted at Marc, "Help me! Take me with you, please," he begged.

With disgust in her voice Cat said, "Bring him along, but zip-tie him."

Adrian grabbed the Bizon and hauled Mirko into the vehicle. "Get us out of here," he said to Marc.

Gabe fished a few zip ties from his gear and helped Adrian bind Mirko's wrists. Then they tied his real leg to the seat frame.

"Airport or consulate?" Marc asked.

"Neither," Cat said as she began tapping on her phone. "We can't go anywhere until we iron out the status of our newest guest. I have to find out where to go. Just drive in the direction of the airport while I make arrangements, and don't lose Arnie."

Chapter 114

Shortly after escaping the chaos in Sultanahmet, Gabe offered Cat a pain pill. She shook her head, insisting that she needed to be clearheaded, and then ordered that Antoniya and Mirko be hooded. Adrian and Gabe rigged jackets, fleeces, and shoelaces into some semblance of hoods and slipped them over the heads of the Russians. They lay on the floor of the van, out of sight of passing vehicles. Antoniya whispered something to Mirko, in Russian.

"No talking," said Adrian. "You can have your reunion later." He looked at Cat, who knew a smattering of Russian, and raised his eyebrows in question.

Cat's brow furrowed. She jiggled her hand in a "more-or-less" gesture, and mouthed "I love you?" and then shrugged.

She had received instructions that guided them to a safe house located in the Bayrampaşa district, just to the west of the old city. The area was a haphazard mix of small factories, offices, shops, downscale housing, and a minimum of greenspace. They pulled up to an unassuming two-story office building of gray brick. Cat whispered to Jones, who got out of the van and approached the entry. With the shrubbery offering scanty concealment, he felt exposed. He looked around, twice, and then twisted the sconce to the left of the door. The key fell into his hand. He went into the building and stopped at the last door on the right.

Yazar Sons Ltd.
Drafting and Design
By Appointment

An acrylic frame on the wall held a flyer advertising the business, complete with phone number. Callers, however, were greeted by an answering device stating that appointments were fully booked for seven months hence.

Jones turned the key in the knob and entered the suite. The furnishings were modern and simple, with architectural drawings adorning the walls. The drafting equipment lent credence to the office's announced purpose. He checked each room, then wheeled an office chair out to the van. He lifted Cat onto the chair, and pushed it back to the office. The rest of the group followed, with Adrian and Marc escorting the two Russians. Once inside, they moved Mirko and Antoniya into separate rooms.

Marc asked, "Now what?"

Jones walked up to Cat and said, "We need to take care of that ankle. That's what."

"First we talk to them," Cat said. "Then we worry about my ankle."

Jones rolled his eyes. "Who first?"

"Antoniya," she replied.

Jones leaned against the wall and pressed the record button on the camera as Adrian pulled the hood from Antoniya's head.

"Where am I?" she asked.

Cat eyed her from across the room and said, "That's not important. What is important is your involvement with Mirko Stefanović and his father, Grigory Kornilov."

Antoniya's mouth fell open. "His father? I don't believe it!"

"Tell us what you know," Adrian said. "How did you and Mirko get together?"

"I was asked to get close to him."

"By whom?"

"Timothy. I do not know his surname. I know only that he works for the American government. I would give him information, and he took care of my, um, expenses."

"Did you have a relationship with this man?"

Antoniya was horrified. "Oh, never. I did not like him."

"Why is that?"

"He is not a nice person."

"Does he live in Moscow?"

"I do not think so. Most of our communications were by a special message service he told me to use. I saw him in Moscow only twice, at parties."

"Did you ever talk with him on the phone?"

"He gave me a number to call in an emergency, but I never used it until I came to Istanbul. I tried calling him to find out what to do, but it only goes to voice mail."

"And what did he ask you to do in regard to Mr. Stefanović?"

Shrugging, Antoniya said, "Get close to him. Learn everything I could about what he was working on and who he was communicating with."

"And you used the messaging service to communicate this information?"

"Yes, always."

"We'll need to access that account," Adrian said.

"I am not sure that is possible," Antoniya said. "I downloaded the program from a link he gave me at our first meeting. You would need my phone to access it."

"Where is your phone now?"

"At the shoe store."

Confused, Adrian asked, "The shoe store?"

"I thought if there was a tracker on my phone, they would think I was still in the store," she explained.

Adrian gave his head a little shake. People did the strangest things when they were scared.

"Okay, we'll try to find it. Can you explain why Mirko decided to go to Toronto?"

"To pick up a software program. I think he intended to sell it. He wanted me to go to Vietnam with him. He said we could not be extradited. But I had seen Grigory Kornilov at Sretna Kafa and became afraid, so I came here instead."

"And what was this software supposed to do?"

She shook her head. "I do not know. I know only that it took a long time to program and was very valuable."

"I'm going to have you talk with a sketch artist. We need to find out the American you talked to."

"You do not know him? He said he worked for you."

"For me?" asked Adrian.

"For the CIA," she said firmly.
"We'll find him, Antoniya. I promise you that."

Cat called Pat Desmond in Sarajevo and told her about the interview with Antoniya. "See if you can find that phone," she told her. "And secure it at the embassy. I want Gabe to have a look at it. It may be our only way of determining who her handler was."

She disconnected and Adrian wheeled her into the room where Mirko sat at a drafting table, scribbling.

"Mirko Stefanović," Cat said. "Or should I call you Andres Kornilov?"

Mirko blinked at the realization that she knew his real name. He stared at Cat and said, "And should I call you Ellie Lamberton?"

"Your English has improved considerably since we met in Sarajevo," she countered.

"It is easier when people think that my English is limited," he said. "They think I cannot understand what they are saying." He grinned at Jones. "You are recording this, yes? Well, I am speaking voluntarily."

Cat arched an eyebrow, wondering whether to trust this man who had deceived so many. She shrugged it off and got down to business. "Mr. Stefanović, you are wanted in Bosnia for the crimes of human trafficking and the murder of twenty-eight people, including your brother Goran Terzić. You are wanted in Canada for the murder of Avery Smith and suspicion of computer crimes against the government of Canada. You are wanted in the United States for suspicion of computer crimes against the government of the United States, conspiracy to bomb Transoceanic Flight 367, the murders of Rosalie Marchesani and Maggie Marshfield, and the attempted murder of Marc Bishop. I'm sure there are other crimes, probably too numerous to mention. You may wish that you had stayed in Moscow."

Mirko shook his head vehemently. "No, no, no," he said. "These things you accuse me of? These are the acts of my father. Some of these things I learned of later. But I did not have any part in the murder of all those people."

Cat asked, "Not even your brother?"

He winced. "I did not know he was my brother—not until Toronto. But I already thought of him as my brother. We were close friends, and he was dying. He was in pain; he asked me to end it. I could not refuse his request."

"Perhaps you'd like to tell me all about it."

Mirko did, spending more than an hour relating what he knew and presenting himself as a hapless puppet whose strings were pulled by his father. Cat was not sure how much to believe, but as much as she wanted to strap him in a chair and pull the switch, his story felt credible.

"We have more questions," Adrian said. "But, first, I would like you to provide us with a handwriting sample." He accessed a Wikipedia page on his phone and handed Mirko a pen and a sheet of paper. Start copying this page. I'll tell you when to stop."

Spreading his hands wide, Mirko said, "What is this?"

"Just do what we ask," Adrian said.

Shaking his head in disbelief, Mirko took a deep breath and started to write. When he had copied most of the paragraph, Adrian stopped him.

"That's good enough," Adrian said. "We'll be right back." He handed the paper, pen, and phone to Cat and wheeled her out of the room.

They found Gabe sitting on the floor, leaning against a drafting table, his eyes closed.

"Gabe," Cat said in a loud whisper.

Without opening his eyes, he moaned, and said, "What?"

"The ledger. You scanned it before we sent it to Langley, right?"

"Guilty. Can I go back to sleep now?"

"In a minute. Can you access it for us?"

"Now?"

"Yes, Gabe, then you can go back to sleep."

Gabe staggered to his feet and placed his laptop on one of the drafting tables. His fingers flew over the keyboard as he logged in and pulled up the document. "Here," he announced.

Adrian stepped up and held Mirko's handwritten page next to the screen.

From her position in the chair, Cat could not see the screen. "Is it a match?" she asked.

"Not even close. There's no way Mirko wrote those pages. We're back to square one."

Cat's shoulders slumped. "Who's left?" Then she raised her index finger, squinted, and sat erect. "Or perhaps the better question is, who have we not seen at all throughout the course of this investigation?"

Adrian banged his fist lightly on a desk. "Of course. Daris! All this time, he has been conveniently out of sight."

"Would Mirko recognize Daris's handwriting?"

"Let's go find out."

"What was that about?" Mirko asked as Cat and Adrian reentered the room. This time, Cat was holding a laptop.

"It's called an investigation," she said. "I have something I would like you to look at."

Adrian took the laptop from Cat and walked it over to Mirko. "Do you recognize this handwriting?"

Mirko focused on the document. His slouch morphed into a soldier at attention. "You found it!"

Cat could not hide her surprise. "What do you know about this?"

He looked at the screen again, and a wave of sadness washed over his face. He turned his attention to Cat. "Goran told me about this. He thought it had been destroyed."

"Did Goran write it?"

"No. Daris wrote it. Before the bombing of the airplane, my father arranged to have Daris taken prisoner by the Serbs. They tortured him. Then he sent photographs of Daris and Goran—and Goran's daughter—to Zlatan. He threatened to kill them all if Zlatan did not cooperate.

"Then, after the bombing, my father had ... um ... what do you Americans say? Um ... a noose around Zlatan's neck. My father threatened to expose Zlatan and to kill Goran's family if Daris and Goran did not cooperate. There was no choice; my father does not make idle threats. They had to protect their family. That is when they built the big bakery.

"From then on, my father controlled the entire operation. But Zlatan told Daris everything that had happened, and Daris wrote it down. He was so angry, but so afraid. I think he thought it might be useful someday."

"Today is that day, Mirko. Can you confirm that what is written here is all true?"

"I have not read it, but I have no reason to doubt it. Daris is smart. He is not someone who exaggerates. He pays attention to details and is a careful planner."

"Particularly murder," said Cat evenly.

Mirko dropped his head. "It is easy to be judgmental. He did bad things, but he is not evil. He is angry ... angry at the Serbs for what they did to his family and his country during the war, for killing all those innocent people, angry at the Russians—my father especially—for their role. And so very angry that they duped Zlatan into performing their dirty work. He has immense hatred for everyone involved, including the Americans who recruited Zlatan into the CIA to begin with. If not for that ..."

His voice trailed off and Cat could not help but wonder what other people would have done in the same circumstance. Anything, she realized. Moral and ethical boundaries could become very blurred when it came to those you love. She looked up at Adrian, who gave her a penetrating stare. He, too, had suffered great loss, but had chosen a different path.

She turned back to Mirko. "You did not tell your father about the document."

"No, of course not. I hid many things from him because I was trying to protect my friends. I hated what my father was doing, but I could not find a path to free them from his grip."

"And you betrayed your brother," Cat said.

Lowering his eyes, Mirko said, "Before I knew he was my brother, he was my best friend. He will never forgive me for what I did; I will never forgive myself."

Cat considered his statement. "Were you hoping that someone would read the document and punish your father?"

Mirko wrinkled his nose. "Maybe. I do not know. My relationship with my father is complicated. He is not a good man, but he is very powerful. To him, family is expendable."

Wanting to catch Mirko off guard, Cat abruptly changed the subject. "Let's discuss the software you were developing—software that targets vital American infrastructure. What does it do?"

Mirko blinked and gave his chin a small shake, then said, "I am not sure. My father has only said to me that the way to destroy the Americans is through a thousand cuts. He will do anything to destroy you, with no remorse."

"So, you have no specifics?"

"No. The software's functionality was never shared with me. Goran and Daris did not know either, although Daris imagined it would target transportation, food and water, banking, and electricity. As I said, he was a planner. He thought about it a lot."

Adrian stepped closer to Mirko and asked, "Who were you selling it to? North Korea? China?"

Bewilderment furrowed Mirko's face. "What? No! You have it all wrong! I do not know anyone from North Korea or China. The buyer is American! He works for your government! He approached me a long time ago, saying he knew the bakery was trafficking people and that we were using the money to finance a software project. I do not know how he discovered this, but I have been reporting progress to him ever since. When the coding was complete. I was to get a copy and give it to him. For this, he told me that the US government would pay me two million dollars."

Cat and Adrian exchanged a look, and Cat's stomach roiled.

"What is this person's name? And how did you communicate with him?"

He told the same story as Antoniya, except the man had told Mirko his name was Jeffrey. As with Antoniya, they had communicated via a private messaging service and an emergency phone contact.

"When was your last communication?"

"The night before I left Sarajevo. I told him I was flying to Toronto to pick up the package."

Fearing the answer, Cat asked, "Did you make the exchange?"

"No," Mirko said. "My father's men showed up at the house. They killed that young man and took the flash drives and all the equipment with them."

"Do you have your phone with you?" asked Adrian.

"No, my father's men took my phone in Toronto."

"So, we have nothing," Cat sighed.

"You have everything," Mirko said. "I have copies of the software."

Cat gaped at him in disbelief. "You what?"

He pulled up the leg of his pants, wriggled the two tiny flash drives out of the socket in his prosthesis, and then asked, "Do I still get the money?"

Cat examined the tablet in her palm and wrinkled her nose. "I hate painkillers. They make me fuzzy."

"Too bad. Take it," said Jones. "Gabe talked to our pilot. We're planning on a midnight departure. When we land, you're going straight to the hospital. Gabe will run the disc up to Fort Meade. Melodie and Trent are already assembling a team to work on it."

She swallowed the pill and downed a large glass of water. "It's Nate Carr," she said. "It has to be."

"We don't know that. Not yet," Jones replied. "I know he's an asshole, but treason?"

"Well, there's no way this could have been a legitimate op. Can you imagine how the American public would feel about one of our agencies effectively supporting a human trafficking ring? A lynching would be too kind."

"It would be helpful if the damn sketch artist had not picked today to be on an airplane. Maybe we should do a photo lineup, instead."

"No. I want a drawing first. If we give them photos, Antoniya and Mirko might simply pick someone. But if the drawing is a match for someone we already know, well ..."

Cat glanced down at her phone when it buzzed. *Paul. Video call. This should be fun.* "Paul. My apologies for not calling you sooner. We have been a little busy."

"I'm in the ambassador's office. He's pissed. Here he comes now ..."

"What in the hell?" the ambassador roared, his face red with anger. "This was supposed to be a quiet pick-and-run operation. Instead, you engaged in a street fight at the Blue Mosque and terrorized the crowd with submachine guns? What the hell were you thinking?"

Cat remained quiet, allowing him to vent. When she finally spoke, she did so without rancor. "I regret the attention that the altercation caused, sir. We were unarmed, except for a couple of Tasers. The Russians assaulted our team. They had the machine guns. Bizons, to be exact."

"I don't care if they had a damn tank. According to the Turkish police, you kidnapped two Russian citizens who were in Russian custody."

"They are misinformed, sir. The woman was out shopping. She got into our vehicle voluntarily to escape the Russians. One of them attempted to pull her from our vehicle. She has asked for asylum."

"The Russians have a warrant on her. You aided a criminal in evading arrest."

"An unlawful warrant, sir. The Turkish police were not present. The Russians did not want them involved because the warrant is total bullshit."

"Well, they're involved now. What about the man?"

"He's Grigory Kronilov's son, sir. He has asked for asylum as well. I will send you the video of our interviews with them."

"Do that. Maybe it will help smooth over this clusterfuck."

"We need to depart tonight, sir," Adrian interjected. "Cat was injured. We need to get her to a hospital."

The ambassador was taken aback, concern clouding his face as he now took in her appearance. She was doing an admirable job of holding herself together, but she looked like hell. The woman was obviously in significant pain. "Send me the video," he said with a sigh. "I'll do my best."

"Thank you, sir," Cat said. "I promise you this: you won't be sorry. We may have saved the country today."

Chapter 115

August 31
CIA Headquarters
Langley, Virginia

Navigating on crutches, Cat led Marc to a door at the end of the hall. "You have ten minutes. No more. Is that understood?" She looked first at Marc and then at the guard, who both nodded. Looking back at Marc, she squinted and said, "You made me a promise. If you harm him, in any way, you will spend the rest of your days on an uninhabited island in the Aleutians. I mean it."

Marc held up his right hand and said, "I swear."

Wondering if this was a bad idea, she instructed the guard to unlock the door and stepped inside the room.

"I've brought a visitor," she said. "This is Marc."

Mirko looked up, his eyes inquisitive. "Hello," he said.

Cat glanced at the handcuffs and said, "I'll be back in fifteen or twenty minutes to get you. They are going to hit you with a million questions, and they will ask the same questions again and again. Are you ready?"

Mirko nodded. "I can only tell the truth."

"Good. Ten minutes," she said again to Marc, then turned and left the room.

Marc stared at Mirko for a few seconds and then asked, "Do you know who I am?"

Puzzled, Mirko said, "You were driving the van. For a minute I thought you wanted to run over me."

Marc stared at him for a few moments, debating how to begin. He wanted to handle this professionally. He opened his mouth to speak, intending to say the words he had rehearsed. Instead, he blurted out, "You shot me."

Mirko's jaw dropped. He studied Marc's face intently until the realization struck. His eyes flew open in amazement. "You are really alive! My father told me last week that you were still alive. I could not believe it. All this time, I thought I had killed you. I am very sorry."

Sorry? Somehow it was the last thing he had expected Mirko to say. Marc leaned against the wall and took a deep breath. "Why?" he asked. "Why did you do it?"

Mirko pressed the heels of his hands against his temples. "Because my father ordered me to do it," he said quietly. "I know how that sounds, and you must think I was a coward for not standing up to him. You would be right. But when you have been under someone's control for so long, it is hard to break free. He gave me the order because he sensed something. He said that you were more than just a translator. It seems he was right."

Acid in his voice, Marc said, "So you just did what he told you to do. Hitler's men used the same excuse."

Mirko took the anger in stride. "He is an evil man and I am glad to be free of him. I want no part of that life. I can only ask you to forgive me for what I did."

The admission was unexpected. *Forgive him? When hell freezes over.* With his voice barely above than a whisper, Marc said, "I'm not ready to do that. Maybe someday, but not today. I will never fully recover from the bullet you fired into my brain. My life will never be whole."

Mirko sat still as a stone and finally said, "And I will never forgive myself. I am sorry."

Marc turned and knocked on the door. When the door opened, he walked out without looking back.

Cat hobbled into the conference room and took a seat at the far side of the table, along with Paul, Adrian, Melodie, and the CIA's deputy director of operations, Ken Zanuck. Facing them were four people from the DIA, including the assistant director, Caroline Buckner.

Ken Zanuck flipped through a few notes, tapping his pen on the table, and asked, "Any progress on Noel Leblanc?"

Cat replied, "None. He is still in Russia. They have denied any access under the claim that he is a Russian citizen."

Ken shook his head and sighed in frustration. "Let's talk about the software. Melodie, why don't you go first."

Surprised but razor-sharp, Melodie made the unexpected transition from bystander to participant without missing a beat. She looked over at Caroline and said, "First, thank you for the extra manpower." Caroline had loaned Melodie two dozen of her most prolific coders.

"The code in the program has several components," Melodie continued, "and each targets a specific segment of our infrastructure. It appears that different programmers worked on these components separately, so the style of programming varies. That makes it more difficult to unpack. We have a team working to identify those who actually did the coding. We believe that most of them are from Russia and Eastern Europe.

"Gabe Winters discovered that the Bernoulli formula they found in Sarajevo was embedded in several commented sections of code as a way of identifying critical routines. With millions of lines of code, it was a huge win because it took us directly to the functions that do the damage. We believe this programmer to be American, or educated in America."

"Someone feeling guilty, but not enough to report the crime," Ken observed. "Go ahead, Melodie."

Melodie nodded eagerly. "At the moment, we are heavily focused on the electrical grid component. If the grid is crippled, the country comes to an instant standstill and people die. We believe that malware was preloaded onto many systems as part of a scheduled update months ago and is simply waiting for a command to activate. We are using every tool in our arsenal to stop that from happening. Fortunately, it's also the component that the Sarajevo programmer worked on. That's enabled us to work faster on that. We're about eighty-five percent complete."

"And the other components?"

"We have teams working on each. It's tedious and slow work. We are only five to ten percent through them. Once the electrical component is secure, then we will redirect resources to the remaining components."

"Timeframe?" asked Ken. "Any idea when this attack will start or when you'll have the solution to stop it?"

"Negative," Melodie replied. "We know the clock is ticking. There were two small, very short power interruptions last week out west. They might have been anomalies, or perhaps tests. Our assumption is that an attack is imminent. But here's the enigma: it's been two weeks since this software landed in Russia. Why are they waiting?"

Cat canted her head. *Good question*, she thought.

Ken steepled his index fingers together and focused on Caroline. "Nate Carr. Have you found him?"

"No. He left Andrews with a group of senators on a visit to Moscow. He got off the plane at Sheremetyevo and checked into the hotel. He missed dinner, but no one thought much about it until he missed the meeting the next morning. We have initiated an inquiry with the Russians and asked to see security footage. Their video shows that he left the hotel at four o'clock. They claim that all they have is the inside of the hotel, which, of course, we know is not true."

"And it is still our prevailing theory that he was working for the Russians and is in Moscow voluntarily, rather than the scenario that has him in a hospital or a morgue … or prison?"

"Everything we know points to him working for the Russians. The drawings by the sketch artist are spot-on. Miss Davydova and Mr. Stefanović both picked him out of a photo lineup. We put photos of forty people on the table, and they didn't hesitate. We're sure he's the one who recruited them."

"Alright. What about your other agent? The one who was killed? Drew, was it?"

"Yes, short for Andrew. We think he may have become aware of Nate Carr's activities. His computer and phone were taken, but we were able to access some of his files on the cloud. He had a few cryptic notes about Nate—again, nothing that could be considered evidential. But he took some personal time earlier this month and traveled to Sarajevo. Cat has a photo of him at that coffee shop, presumably watching Miss Davydova."

"So, Nate Carr is not only a traitor, we're thinking he's also a murderer?"

Caroline shrugged her shoulders. "He's the last person I would have expected, but yes."

"He's probably living the high life at a dacha on the Black Sea," Cat said bitterly. "We may never find him."

"Perhaps not. But we will keep looking," Caroline said.

"Yes, we will," Cat agreed. "There is a point I need to have clarified."

Caroline looked at her quizzically. "Sure," she said.

"Antoniya stated that before Mirko Stefanović, she had worked other assignments for the US government. Was she your asset?"

After taking a breath, Caroline nodded. "Yes. We had an agreement with her. She was actually quite productive."

"And Nate Carr was her handler, wasn't he?"

"Yes."

"Anything recent?"

Brow furrowed, Caroline leaned forward, crossed her arms on the table, and turned her head toward the people with her. "When was her last assignment?" she asked them.

"Eight months ago," came the reply. "A report in her file says that she has been ill."

"And Nate Carr wrote the report."

The man beside Caroline sighed and said, "Yes."

Cat pursed her lips and let out a puff of air. "He made up a story and took her off the grid for the Stefanović assignment," she said.

"It would appear so," Caroline said.

"And he got away with it," said Cat, "at least until now, but it's sloppy. He knew we would look at her file. I know he is arrogant, but ..."

Caroline shook her head in frustration. "I agree. We just did not recognize that he had gone so far around the bend. We're already making changes to some of our procedures."

Ken folded his hands and fixed his gaze on Cat. "Let's talk about Mr. Stefanović. The Bosnians are in a tizzy about this. Are we certain that Mr. Stefanović played no part in the massacre?"

Cat looked at him steadily. "We cannot say that with certainty without a confession from Daris, but he, too, has disappeared. We know that he left Bosnia by automobile and crossed the border into Turkey. His whereabouts after that are unknown. SIPA believes that he is in Iran, but the Iranians are not cooperating. Mirko's prints were not found on the bottle of cyanide, nor were they found on the gun. The only prints belonged to Daris. Mirko claims that he had no foreknowledge that Daris would kill any of the staff.

"Does Mirko look out for himself? Yes," she continued. "Does he show occasional poor judgment? Yes, however, he believed all along that he was working for the Americans and that we knew what we were doing. According to him, Nate Carr was fully aware that they were conducting an operation involving human trafficking and the development of software for malicious intent. The only crimes that we can fully attribute to him are the illegal purchase of US arms and the shooting of Marc Bishop in Turkey—all at the behest of his father."

"You believe him?" Ken asked.

"Actually, yes," Cat replied. "And lest we forget, he actually did deliver the software to us."

"I think I've heard enough. Let's have our people go ahead and conduct an interview with him here—get it all on the official record. If their findings agree with yours, I think we can convince the Bosnians to ease up, and I would be inclined to recommend that his request for asylum be approved."

Ken leaned forward, picked up a file folder, and flipped it open. "The Russians are refusing to extradite Noel Leblanc, or whatever he is calling himself today. Justice has determined that our only recourse is to try him in absentia. The Transoceanic bombing case, however, is largely circumstantial, and they are reluctant to bring it to trial at this time. The case will remain open, and we'll hope for a break at some point.

"They are also considering charges under the Federal Computer Fraud and Abuse Statute and other related federal laws. At this moment, however, most of the chargeable offenses relate only to conspiracy because, so far, no harm has actually occurred. He could be charged with computer trespassing, but they want something that will put him away for a long time. There is no provision in the law for just scaring the shit out of everyone. Again, we have to wait."

He pulled off his glasses and set them on the table. "Last subject. Cat, bring us up to date on Grigory Kornilov."

"I'm giving the Bosnians everything we have," she said. "The tribunal that convicted all those men for war crimes committed during the Yugoslav war closed in 2017. Residual work is being handled by the leaner International Residual Mechanism for Criminal Tribunals. The most compelling evidence against Kornilov would come from the direct testimony of his sons Noel Leblanc and Mirko Stefanović. Marc Bishop would testify, with pictures, about the weapons transaction itself. The problem, as I see it, is that there is no evidence directly connecting those weapons to the actual killing of Bosnian civilians. It's all anecdotal. As for the witnesses to the purchase, Marc Bishop's testimony would be viewed with skepticism due to his medical issues.

"They may have better luck with the human trafficking aspect, although they would have to prove that he sponsored the effort. It will be difficult, because his hand is in everything, yet in nothing. Stefanović would bring great insight into how it worked and who was in charge. The ledger will help. It may not be enough to convict, but it will certainly bring unwanted attention to his role."

"He should be in prison," remarked Adrian. "I'd like to take him there myself."

"Maybe someday you'll get the chance," said Cat.

Chapter 116

The lie detector came first, with Mirko wired and doing his best to remain calm, knowing that one mistake could jeopardize his request for asylum. Then came the interview—a nonstop battery of questions and probing that could unveil almost any fabrication. They had been at it for over two hours. Cat sat at the end of the table, observing the interrogators as they went about the business of learning everything there was to know about the man sitting in front of them. Finally, the team stacked their papers and left the room.

"Is that it?" Mirko asked.

"That's it. They'll get together, discuss their findings, and issue a verdict when they are satisfied. It could be tomorrow, it could be two weeks, it could be a month. We just have to wait and see."

"That means that I am still in confinement, yes?"

"For the time being, yes. Be grateful for your accommodations. There were some who wanted to send you to Rikers Island."

"But I gave you the software and the antidote, so that counts for something, yes?"

Cat started to grin, and then frowned in puzzlement. "What did you say?"

Mirko squinted in confusion. "What? That I gave you the software?"

"No," Cat said, rising from her seat. "What antidote?"

Still confused, he said, "The one on the flash drive. The program that neutralizes the malware."

Cat took a sharp breath and said, "What are you saying? Are you telling me that there is another program that will take care of the malware? It is not on that drive!"

As soon as the words came out of her mouth, Cat knew. "Oh, my God!" she said, rushing to the door. "Stay here. I'll be back." She flew out of the room and down the hall, her phone at her cheek.

Melodie picked up on the third ring. "Cat, what's up?"

"Please get back here, ASAP. Gabe is in town; I'll bring him in, too."

"Okay, but what's going on?"

"There's something we missed."

Cat hurried to her office and opened the safe. The little gold flash drive was still there. When Mirko had handed over the drives, the team had assumed that they were identical. They had given the silver drive to the team of programmers and held on to the gold drive as a backup. It had never occurred to any of them to check whether they held the same data.

Melodie commandeered an air-gapped computer that was reserved for testing purposes, then plugged in the gold flash drive. "Let's take a look at this," she said, as she accessed one of the files.

"That one looks like a private security key, but let's check this," Melodie said, clicking on a folder, then opening one of the files inside.

Gabe hunched over her shoulder, focused on the lines of code that appeared on the screen. "This is interesting," he said. "The malware effectively replaced a number of good files with infected ones bearing the same name. This is doing the same thing. But if this is an antidote, as Mirko called it, we need to compare it with the infected files." An hour later, they were convinced that the program on the drive could disable the infection on servers all over the country. They also knew that they would have to test it extensively before they released the fix.

"What do you think that private security key is for?" Melodie asked.

Gabe wrinkled his nose in thought. "My guess? One or more of those files is encrypted and will only run when authenticated. I'll take a look. Give me a few hours."

It was approaching midnight when Gabe found the answer. He studied the lines of code on the screen and let out a low whistle. He picked up the phone and called Cat.

Noel Leblanc had equipped his doomsday program with the equivalent of an automated kill switch. One short routine in the code counted the number of times that the program had been run. After the second run, the program demanded a private security key to fit with the public key installed in the software. Without the private key, the program simply stopped.

Gabe was impressed by the routine's simple elegance and reliance on human nature. Of course, someone would test the software—at least once, probably twice. When the tests were successful, the observers would be convinced that subsequent activations would also work.

"What do you think his plan was?" he asked Cat. "If Mirko hadn't paid a surprise visit to Toronto, would Leblanc have been able to just disappear?"

"I don't know," Cat said thoughtfully. "What I do know is that for all his faults, Noel Leblanc did a very courageous thing. I wonder what convinced him to take that step, because he has never taken the high road before. Regardless, with two tests having been done, by now the Russians have certainly discovered that it no longer works without the key. I don't think they have a copy of it. That explains why we haven't seen any further probes or destructive actions. They must be livid. And I think that Noel Leblanc, if he is still alive, is paying the price."

EPILOGUE

Epilogue

October
CIA Headquarters
Langley, Virginia

Cat greeted Caroline Buckner as she approached the security checkpoint and escorted her to the seventh floor. They deposited their phones in the lockers and stepped into the SCIF, where Ken Zanuck waited.

"Have a seat," he told her. "We're just going to have a quiet conversation among friends. Nothing said here will leave this room."

The SCIF, short for Sensitive Compartmented Information Facility, was a heavily shielded chamber where—as the name implied—extremely sensitive information could be displayed and discussed without concern about being seen or overheard.

Cat took a seat across from Carolyn and looked her in the eyes. Then she said, "How long?"

Carolyn's eyes flickered in surprise. She tilted her chin and said, "I beg your pardon?"

"How long has Nate Carr been playing the part of Russian asset? Since before Maggie Marshfield's death or after?"

Composed and cool, Caroline replied, "I don't know what you're talking about."

"Sure you do," Cat snapped. "How long?"

"Before."

Cat sat back, digesting the fact that Nate Carr had known about the Terzić brothers all along.

"The Russians approached him?"

Nodding, Caroline said, "Yes. I suppose they considered him a good candidate, considering his ego and his need for money. His mother had been sick for several years. Her medical bills were through the roof."

"And he came to you?"

"He did. I don't think there is any circumstance in which he would actually betray his country. He's very ... um ... shall we say, adept. We've fed the Russians a lot of misinformation since then."

"And his obnoxious behavior made the lie easier for the rest of us to swallow. Personally, I despised him."

"That did work well, I will say. How did you figure it out?"

Cat thought about that for a moment. "He tried to warn me off investigating Noel Leblanc. I thought it was because he wanted all the credit; I thought he wanted the glory. But it wasn't that, was it? It was because he knew about the antidote and the kill switch, and he was afraid that the secret would get out. But when he hooked up with that congressional delegation, abandoning all protocols, that's when I felt a twitch. Sure, he wanted to be a hero, but he would have been censured, and that would have been a blow to his ego."

Caroline raised an eyebrow. "You're pretty good at this. You should consider a career with the CIA."

"How did he know about the antidote?" Cat asked. Caroline stared back, and Cat made a guess. "Did he convince Leblanc to write it?"

"In a roundabout way. Nate has been playing a very dangerous game for quite a long time. To Antoniya and Mirko, Nate is an American spying *on* the Russians. To Kornilov and Leblanc, he is an American who is spying *for* the Russians. In the latter persona, Nate reported to Kornilov and was tasked with keeping Leblanc reined in. In the former persona, he hinted to Mirko that an antidote, as you call it, would make the software more valuable. Mirko ultimately convinced Noel to write the code."

"Nate really did save the world, didn't he? Or at least our part of it. But he's in big trouble if Kornilov ever finds out about Nate's connections to Mirko and Antoniya."

"All true," Caroline sighed. "That's the primary reason why I supported asylum for them."

Cat frowned. "But if Mirko did not murder your agent Drew, who did?"

"Drew was not read in on Nate's status. He, like you, thought Nate was a traitor. We discovered evidence to that effect during our investigation. My instincts tell me it was a Russian hit. Witnesses claimed that two men were nosing around his neighborhood that day. Their descriptions match a pair of contract workers that have been on our radar for quite a long time. We used them once or twice, years ago, which is somewhat embarrassing."

Cat put her hand on her forehead and let out a puff of air. "I'll be right back." She left the SCIF and returned a few minutes later. She handed two photographs to Caroline. "These guys?" she asked.

Caroline's eyes grew wide. "How did you know?"

"I think they murdered an Army colonel in Memphis a while back. I talked to the detective who was, shall we say, less than pleased when someone from the DIA put out the word to back off."

"I remember that! The colonel was making a lot of noise about a couple of soldiers selling a truckload of arms. When he turned up dead, the top brass thought it best to avoid digging up more dirt, so to speak."

Tilting her head, Cat stared at Caroline. "I will share with you, Caroline, that the colonel was right. It happened, and one of our people witnessed it. That single event has led to an unimaginable trail of death and destruction." She sighed in frustration. "What happens to Nate now?"

Caroline's expression turned grim and she took a deep breath. "He went to Russia to try to recover the antidote, as you call it. Nobody knew that Mirko had grabbed the only copy. With the threat of a cyberattack looming, we were desperate to take whatever measures were necessary. Nate volunteered. Since then, he's been completely out of contact, although he has been spotted twice—both times with Kornilov. Our assessment is that he is in the process of proving himself, and that it will be a difficult period for him. They will test him in ways I can't even imagine. Will he pass muster? Eventually, they will either embrace him, in which case he might be in a position to send us intel, or they will shun him, perhaps offering him up for a trade someday. Either way, it's not ideal. If you have any ideas ..."

Cat nodded her head. "I'll keep that in mind. Thank you for being honest with us."

Ken Zanuck looked over at Cat and asked, "Anything else?"

"One more thing," she responded, leveling her gaze at Carolyn. "The DIA appears to know the Terzić brothers well. Does that include Daris?"

Carolyn remained composed and did not even blink. "You have a vivid imagination," she said with a shrug.

"It doesn't matter," countered Cat. "He murdered Maggie Marshfield and Rosalie Marchesani. He does not get to walk away. If it takes the rest of my life, I will find him."

Cat escorted Caroline downstairs and toward the front of the building, where they paused at the CIA's Memorial Wall. They faced the white marble wall with its dozens of carved black stars, each star a monument to someone who had given their life in service to their country. Maggie had not been a member of the CIA; she would never receive this tribute.

Carolyn bit her lower lip and said, "Your Memorial Wall and our Patriots Memorial—both honor our dead. What do we do for those who might as well be?"

Cat turned her head toward Caroline, understanding that Nate's secret could never be revealed and that he would probably never be honored by his country. As far as the nation was concerned, the man was a traitor. "We try to bring them home," she said.

★ ★

Acknowledgments

One Deliberate Act is a work of fiction. In the mideighties, I had the good fortune to travel to Dubrovnik, Sarajevo, and Zagreb, and became acquainted with a number of young Yugoslavians. Just a few years later, news accounts of the growing conflict in Yugoslavia caught my attention. In an era before widespread internet, I followed the events as closely as possible and worried for the safety of the young men and women I had met. While I did not know them well, and to this day, do not know whether they escaped the savagery of that war, I can only hope that they did. The events of that period provided inspiration for the novel's Sarajevo setting, although the characters, their circumstances, and their interactions are a product of my imagination. Any errors or inaccuracies in the narrative are solely mine.

I am extremely fortunate to have family and a circle of close friends who provide ongoing encouragement and support. Brian, your quiet confidence and enthusiasm keeps me going when my creativity hits a wall. Scott, I am eternally grateful for your patience. You are always available to listen, offer an honest assessment, and consider the plausibility of the random situations I throw at you. MM, you contribute in invaluable ways. Sallie Pecora-Saipe lends her critical eye and attention to detail, particularly with regard to the scenes from Istanbul—where we once enjoyed a spur-of-the-moment adventure.

My editor, Cheri Madison, has an amazing eye for detail and verification. This novel required a great deal of research. Thank you once again, Cheri, for your diligence and guidance.

Dr. Kerry Reynolds from Massachusetts General Hospital reviews terminology and procedures and offers advice when my characters are in need of medical assistance. Software architect Aram Hovhannisyan's programming expertise and broad understanding of the complexities of Eastern Europe contribute authenticity to the narrative and always keep me entertained.

Retired Pan Am captains Joe Anding and Stu Archer, and retired Delta captain Dave Cowley, provided invaluable input for the technical aspects of aviation, navigating the North Atlantic, and aircraft accident investigations.

I am indebted to those readers from book clubs and Friends of the Library groups who have invited me to join them for an hour or two. I appreciate—and enjoy—their interest and probing questions. When these groups gather, they often contribute to deserving causes by donating to library funds or charities that I support. I give back by offering to include a member in an upcoming novel. To Louise Burke, Rosalie Marchesani, Linda Clendaniel, Marianne Riel, Pat Desmond, and Toni Swanson, I hope that you enjoy the portrayals of the characters bearing your names. Robert Bailey, a good sport and true gentleman who always makes me laugh, joked about playing the part of a worldly playboy. I hope he feels appropriately honored.

I am grateful, as well, for the many readers who have continued to push me forward. Your support means everything.

And to all who have chosen to read this novel, thank you. I hope you enjoy it.

CPSIA information can be obtained
at www.ICGtesting.com
Printed in the USA
LVHW042052230523
747603LV00010BA/1170/J

9 798985 169218